THE FOLLOWER:

An accident of birth results in an indestructible hero

John Durbin Husher

The Follower: An Indestructible Hero Fights for His Country

ISBN:
Paperback   979-8-88615-053-7
E-Book   979-8-88615-054-4

Inks and Bindings
888-290-5218
www.inksandbindings.com
orders@inksandbindings.com

Contents

Preface

November 11, 2008

This was the story of Axel Tressler and how an accident led to his becoming an indestructible hero. Axel took this fate of birth and extended it to a usable force. Eventually, the U.S. Science Agency took his good fortune and provided him with a means of indestructibility. Read about our new hero and his exploits against the bad.

An Emergency in the Indian Ocean

The phone rang, and Axel knew it was a call from the U.S. Scienc Agency (USSA). *What now?* he thought, as he picked up the phone. It was Edward Kim calling about an emergency that required Axel's special talents. "Axel, we have a major problem that we think you might be able to solve for the country. It would take your unique capabilities to resolve an issue that the U.S. government is stuck with," said Kim.

"Tell me more about it," Axel responded." You know I would do anything to help, and you are the only one besides my brother that knows my capabilities."

Kim continued the conversation by explaining that there had been many ships pirated out of the area around Somalia over the past year and related that none had involved American ships to date. He described how things have changed over the past few days and how an American tanker carrying valuable cargo was attacked by a small pirate ship out of Somalia. The American crew was able to thwart the pirating of the ship by immobilizing the engine and taking some of the pirates as prisoners. Seeing that they were not going to be successful, several of the pirates grabbed the captain and another member of the ship's crew and abandoned their plan. They grabbed one of the ship's rafts and took off from the disabled ship. Kim explained that the U.S. Navy had sent ships to try and capture these remaining pirates and free the two hostages.

"But, I don't know where I come into this picture," commented Axel. "Can't the navy handle this situation?"

Kim explained that it wasn't as easy as it sounded. "With them holding hostages, the navy is in a stalemate. They were concerned that if they take any offensive action, that the pirates might kill the two hostages. We at the agency have discussed this sensitive situation and feel that you might be the best answer. We believe we could fly you to an airfield in Nazret, Ethiopia, in a fast long-range fighter jet, while having a military helicopter fly from Iraq to this field in Ethiopia, awaiting the fighter's arrival. We have already cleared this route through the Pentagon and Ethiopia. The helicopter would fly you to the Indian Ocean where this action is occurring. We would drop you about two miles from where the raft is located. When you are in full energy and with your special head gear, you can swim at about thirty miles an hour and be at the raft in a couple of minutes. Once there, we believe you would know how to handle the situation."

Axel thought for a few minutes about this possible plan. "How fast can you get me to Ethiopia and then to the primary location?" he asked.

Kim continued, "We have a fast jet flying from Travis Air Force Base, and it could arrive in the San Francisco airport in an hour. By flying you over the northern route, we could have you into Ethiopia by tomorrow morning. If everything goes as we have planned, you would be dropped two miles from the hostage raft by tomorrow afternoon." He then explained that, "A navy ship would be in the area to pick you up after the action."

"Sounds like a plan to me," said Axel. "I will be at the San Francisco airport within the hour. However, you are going to have to make some special arrangements for me, so I don't have to spend a lot of time passing through security."

Kim explained that he would provide Axel with a special six-digit code that would help him when he checked in to the international check-in counter. "All you would need was your passport, your driver's license, and this six-digit code, and you would be passed through on an emergency basis." They discussed a few other things, and, a few minutes later, Axel was with his girlfriend, Tori, in her car, speeding to the airport.

The airport was no problem as Kim had explained, and, before long, Axel was on a high-speed fighter jet flying faster than he had ever flown in his life. His heart was pumping as he thought about the task before him, but he was confident that he had all the tools it would take to make this a successful venture. He had ventured into tougher situations for the agency before and had been successful. At least, this one has a known target, and all it will take is for them to get him there in time. He knew he would have to energize his head cover to allow him to use his full capabilities. *I can do that just before dropping from the helicopter,* he thought to himself. He knew the Indian Ocean was warm, and there wouldn't be any problems with the water temperature. Now that he had thought through his personal actions, he closed his eyes and rested. Soon, he was asleep.

Axel had a good rest, and soon the pilot was taking the jet down toward an airfield that was foreign to him, but the plane was not foreign to the waiting committee. Axel hardly had time to get out of the jet before there was a car arriving. He gave the pilot a salute and thanked him for an exciting ride, and he was whisked away to a helicopter awaiting his arrival. Soon, he was on a rather slow, noisy helicopter flying toward the Indian Ocean. He was conscious of how slow this flight was compared to the jet plane he had just spent time on. But, it was daylight, and he could see all the terrain below and found it quite exciting.

The pilot introduced himself as Philip Mazer and his crewman as Donald Chevez. They talked about the mission for a few minutes to make sure they all understood what was to be done. The pilot and his partner had food aboard for Axel, and he chomped away at it. Chevez handed him a few candy bars and said, "They said you should eat some of these to bring your nourishment up."

Axel thought to himself, *I bet that was Kim from the agency. He knows my needs.* The copter flight took several hours, and soon the ocean was below them. Axel mentally sent a message to his inner computer, *Axelvation three, hood down,* and the invisible hood immediately deployed over his face and head and sealed with the special covering he had on his body. Mazer and Chevez were not aware of this transaction, since it was completely silent and unnoticeable. He was now ready for the expected action.

Off in the distance, the pilot saw the U.S. naval vessel and knew that the pirate raft must be close by. He knew he had to let Axel down about two miles from the raft and on the other side of the raft away from the naval ships. This would leave Axel about two miles from the raft and three miles or so from the naval ships. The pilot signaled to Chevez and Axel that he was going to take the copter down and for Axel to prepare for the drop. He took the copter down to about one hundred feet above the water. Axel helped the crew member swing the side hatch open, and they began to drop the fifty-foot rope ladder down. Axel started his climb down, and when he was near the bottom, the pilot dropped the copter down to be closer to the water. In a couple of minutes, the rope ladder was just above the water, and Axel leapt from the ladder rung to the warm water below. He then began his rapid swim toward the raft off in the distance.

The pilot watched Axel's progress and then looked around and shouted to his partner, "Look at that guy go. I have never seen anyone swim that fast. It's no wonder they decided to bring him here. He is a human speed boat. I don't know what he is going to do when he gets to the raft, but I believe our guys know what he will be doing." With that closing comment, the pilot took the copter up to flying height and began his journey back to Nazret to refuel and complete his journey back to Iraq. "Hopefully that guy will get our people from the raft without any harm to any of them," he said. With that passing comment, he turned the copter north and headed away.

The pirates in the raft had seen the copter in the distance, but they felt good now once they saw it disappear. They figured that the copter knew the same thing that the naval ships knew. "If they tried to take the two hostages off the tanker by force, we would kill them," one of them shouted. So, they were rather comfortable with their position there in the ocean, and they were feeling euphoric at the turn of events that had occurred over the last several days. They felt that some of their Somalian comrades would make it to the raft with a small boat and take all of them back to Somalia where they could sneer at the Americans and ask for a ransom for these two hostages. What they didn't know was the man swimming toward them at a speed faster than most ships was the guy few knew as "The Follower." If they had known this, then they wouldn't be so happy and would have had their guns ready.

Axel speedily swam in the direction of the raft and was there in a few minutes. As he approached, he slowed down to a speed that was normal for any other person. He didn't want to seem different to the pirates in the raft. "Help!" he shouted in an Indian language. The pirates saw this man in the ocean and figured he must be another member of the ship that got off and had been in the ocean for over a day.

"Hey," the leader of the pirates shouted to his cohorts, "Here is another one for us to take as a hostage." With that comment, two of the members reached over the edge of the raft and grabbed Axel's hand.

As Axel was lifted out of the water, he surveyed the raft to see where the two hostages were as well as the other members of the raft. He soon sized things up. One of the pirates was sitting next to the hostages with a gun in his hand. *Looks like a AK-47*, he thought to himself. The hostages were tied and unable to do anything. Axel talked to the pirates in a language that was of Indian origin to see if they were able to understand this language. They seemed surprised to hear a language they were used to hearing but not used to speaking. They understood one of the words was "thanks," as Axel smiled and moved toward where the hostages were seated.

Then, Axel tried to speak French to them, and they began to look at each other trying to figure out whether this was a crew member off the tanker. Then, Axel made one very swift move and shot his body toward the member next to the hostages. As he hit the pirate's body, the pirate flew out of the raft about twenty feet, and then Axel turned and started smashing his fists against the heads and bodies of the other pirates. They get a couple of gun shots off that hit Axel and have no effect. Axel made sure his body was between the pirates and the hostages, so they had no bullets flying at them. One shot hit Axel directly in the chest, and it ricocheted right back to where it came from. That pirate wished he hadn't shot that bullet, as it penetrated his head and he fell to the deck. Axel jammed his fist into the chest of one of the two remaining pirates, and his ribs were crushed to his backbone and he fell back into the ocean. The one remaining pirate tried to smash his rifle on the head of this intruder, but Axel grabbed the arm of this ugly kidnapper and threw the man hammer throw into the ocean some thirty feet away. Suddenly, it was quiet, and he turned toward the two hostages.

Axel had disposed of the pirate crew and began to untie the two hostages. They both had sat during this brief encounter with their mouths open, disbelieving what they had witnessed. They didn't know if this beast of a man was a friend or foe. Axel relaxed them by saying, "Hi there. The U.S. agency sent me."

"That sure made us feel better," said the one freed hostage that he found was the captain of the tanker. Axel directed each of them to take a position with one on the left side of the raft and the other on the right side of the raft. He jumped into the water and began to direct the raft toward the nearest naval vessel. With his powerful legs kicking like an engine, they were soon moving quite fast toward the U.S. Naval vessel. Axel had to hold back on his propelling of the raft, since it was not made for speed.

Meanwhile, the captain of the U.S. vessel had been notified as to what to expect and told to keep any actions as confidential. The captain of the vessel had been observing the actions with his binoculars and realized the person sent by the agency had taken charge of the raft and was heading in his direction. He had his radioman notify the proper authorities to tell them that the raft was now under control of the good guys and was headed toward his ship. The two hostages aboard seemed to be unharmed, and he would keep them appraised of any issues that came up. As the raft approached the naval vessel, Axel shouted to the two hostages and commented, "You are not to tell them what you observed. This is a U.S. secret, and we do not want anyone to know any details. Tell them I was lucky and got hold of one of the rifles and used it as a club to beat the pirates off the raft. Promise me now." The ex-hostage captain shouted back that he promised and knew his crew member knew how to keep a U.S. secret. Axel believed they didn't see the bullets flying off his body, since he was in their field of vision, but he knew they saw some things they had never seen before.

As the raft approached the naval vessel, the crew was all standing on the decks and shouting, "Three cheers for our men, three cheers for our men." Cheering was what they did for about fifteen minutes. This cheering gave Axel goose bumps, and his hair stood on end. Once aboard the ship, the captain of the U.S. vessel told his officer on deck to take the two members of the tanker down to the shower and then to the mess hall for some food. "Bring the other man to me," he directed.

When Axel was in the captain's quarters, the captain introduced himself as Victor Swartz and told him that he had talked to Edward Kim of the agency and knew that he was something special. "I am to take every step I can to keep your actions under wraps. The media will want to know what happened here, and we will just say we were able to talk the pirates out of their hostages. You probably need some food and rest. I will have food brought to my quarters and you can eat and rest in my quarters. This will keep you away from my crew, so they won't be asking all kinds of questions."

Axel told the captain that he had told the two men from the raft that they were to keep all the actions seen as secret and to say that he had taken one of the pirate's rifles and kept swinging it till they were all out of the raft. "They promised, but I am concerned that your crew was excited about this whole affair and will be bugging them for information about the actions that took place on the raft." The captain assured him that his officers had been told to keep it down and to make sure the crew was kept under control on the details. The captain made Axel aware of the fact that he had been making arrangements to meet one of the navy aircraft carriers by tomorrow. "They will have a plane fly you to Iraq. From there, they probably will fly you to Germany and then back home."

"Sounds good to me," replied Axel.

Just like the captain had indicated, Axel was put aboard a carrier the next day. After downing some food in the carrier mess hall, Axel was put aboard one of the fighter planes and enjoyed another great flight to Iraq. When they landed in the airfield outside of Baghdad, they were met with a fairly large group of soldiers who wanted to meet the American that freed the pirates' hostages. It seemed that no matter what you tried to keep as a secret, it didn't happen among the soldiers of our country. They seemed to find out no matter what. They didn't know the details, but they did know the person responsible was flying in on this plane. Fortunately, the commanding officer of the base was able to control the questions, and Axel acknowledged their cheers without spending much time on the details either.

Later that evening, he was told he would be flown to Germany early in the morning, and, from there, he would be flown back to the States. That evening, as he lay in his bed, he thought about the cheers of the soldiers and sailors he had heard today. It made him feel good. It made him feel proud. He had wondered whether his powers were a blessing or a curse, and, on this day, he knew the answer. Axel knew his mother and twin brother would be proud of today's actions.

Axel left Iraq the next morning on a military jet that took him to an air base just outside of Berlin. Here, he again was met by a group of U.S. soldiers that cheered for him when he left the plane and entered the main building for the U.S. military. He waved at his admirers and again felt the goose bumps. He didn't have long to receive the cheers, as a flight had been scheduled to leave about two hours after his arrival. It was to fly up over the northern route and then down into the California area at Travis Air Force Base. Axel just had time to go to the bathroom and to eat a couple sandwiches. It didn't take them long to prepare him for the flight, and, in short order, he was introduced to Commander John Russel of the Naval Air Force who would pilot the two-man fighter plane. This was another exciting affair for Axel who had never flown in a fighter plane before, and here he had flown on a few in just a couple of days. Axel had settled down for the long flight and began to think about the series of events that had brought him to this point in his life. It had been an exciting twenty-nine years. He closed his eyes and thought about it all and how he became "The Follower."

An Accident and Axel Tressler Was Born

Virginia Tressler was pregnant and had less than a month to go before giving birth, but she decided to take a commercial airplane flight to see her husband, Ted, who was on a business trip to the Boston and Worcester areas of Massachusetts. Ted had been gone for a couple of weeks when he phoned her and mentioned he would have a few free days from business, and maybe she could come up and they could tour the Boston area. She had always wanted to visit that area since she was a little girl. All those neat stories about the revolution and other events that happened in the area had always appealed to her imagination. So, it didn't take much for Ted to convince her to make the trip. Virginia quickly took the steps to set up the reservations with the airlines, and she would be leaving in a few days.

She called Ted and told him the details of the trip, so he could pick her up at the airport. The flight would be from Pittsburgh, Pennsylvania, directly to Logan Airport in Boston and would arrive at 7:30 PM on Friday. She could tell he was excited by the tone of his voice, and, after hanging up the phone, she hurriedly completed picking out her outfits to wear in Boston this time of the year. It was early spring, and the weather could be warm or cold. It could be sunny or windy with snow flurries. It didn't matter to her. She knew they would have fun doing something no matter the weather. She felt strong and in no way was bothered by the forthcoming flight or any travel involved for the next week she would be there before returning home for her last cleaning up of the house and the birth of her child.

The days went by rapidly, and she soon found herself going through security at the Pittsburgh International airport. Soon, she was on the flight and looking out the portal window hoping to make out some landmark in the terrain, but she could only see white clouds below. She knew the plane had been in the air about an hour and a half and was probably in the eastern part of Pennsylvania. She had hoped she would be able to see the land of the Quakers below, but it wasn't forthcoming. As she looked out again, she was interrupted by a surge of the plane as though it was having problems. *Maybe it's just bucking the wind*, she thought to herself. But then, it jolted sideways and back and forth, and she knew there was trouble. She glanced toward the aisle seat and the lady passenger sitting next to her. She was obviously having problems with the flight and now was looking very frightened, with her eyes wide open and gripping the arms of her seat.

Then, just as the plane began another dramatic surge, they were interrupted by the loud speaker and the pilot's voice calmly directing everyone to make sure their safety belts were fastened tight. He stated that they were experiencing rough wind, and he probably would be taking the plane up higher to get above an obvious storm. But soon, it became apparent that there were other issues causing the plane to buck back and forth. The pilot's voice continued to give directions, and they seemed more urgent.

Then, his voice sent chills through her body as he was directing the air stewardesses to take certain positions and precautions as though preparing them for a rough landing, a landing somewhere in the Poccono Mountain area in the eastern part of the state.

The pilot stated, "We are having problems with the control of the aircraft, and I have signaled the major airports in the area. We are not going to make it to any of the airports. I will try to land as best I can, and someone should be coming for us shortly. Please lean forward in your seats with your hands against the seat in front of you. All seats should be upright now. Do you understand? All seats are to be upright now."

Virginia took the position directed and held her breath. *Surely this is a dream, and this thing will come out all right*, she thought. She thought of her husband, Red, as he was called because of his red hair, and she hoped that she would live through this and deliver the child he so much wanted. The pilot was trying to resolve the problem and to correct the path of the plane. People were screaming, and some were crying and some praying. It wasn't quiet, and Virginia closed her eyes and prayed that she would live through this and deliver a child to Red. Every so often, Virginia would think the pilot had won the battle, since the plane seemed to right itself, but it was not long before another jerk of the plane occurred. It seemed like he was only flying on one engine and that one would spit and cause another rough period.

As she pushed against the back of the seat in front of her, she could hear people screaming, crying, and many were praying. *It is odd*, she thought, *that I can hear this above the sound of the plane as it erratically moves toward the earth below. We are in the clouds now*, she thought as she glanced toward her left. *It shouldn't be long now, and I hope the pilot has found a clearing to hit with his landing gear.* She knew his gear was down having heard and felt it a moment before. She had always listened for this sign that a plane she was on was about to land. Now, she prayed that this was a good sign, and it would end like all the other flights had ended.

Suddenly, there was an abrupt ending to her thoughts, and it only seemed like a second had passed before her eyes flickered amidst what appeared as a short dream. *Surely this mess is not real*, she thought. *The plane is upside down, and I am upside down and my seat is on my back.* She could see the ceiling, and it was actually below her. She shook her head back and forth to make sure she wasn't dreaming, but that pull on her stomach was no dream. It was her big stomach pushing down against the seat belt as she hung there in the air. She then began to try to move, but the belt was still holding her in an upside down position and her hair was flopping down in her face and toward the ceiling. *I don't think I am hurt*, she thought, *but maybe this is the way it feels when you die or when you are hurt. Maybe the brain shuts off the pain and allows you the freedom of life to still go on.*

She hurriedly continued her thoughts to try to make sense of her situation. *The belt is pushing against the upper portion of my body, and maybe the child is still safe.* She tried to feel her stomach, but her hands dangled downward and were pulled by gravity, making it difficult to do anything. Her extended fingers almost touched the ceiling below. *I must find a way to release this belt*, she thought. *The plane might catch on fire or explode. I must get out of here. How difficult to do anything when your body is upside down and hanging.* Fortunately, the seat had caught on another part of the plane and jammed, keeping her up in the air or she would have smashed against the ceiling, which now was below. *If only I can find a way to push the lever on the belt to release it,* she thought, as she tried to grab the release. *Maybe I can do it with my right elbow, which is closer to my waist than my hands and closer to where the buckle should be. I can pull my right arm up and push my elbow toward the left side of my body and keep pushing my elbow against my body, hoping to dislodge the seat belt.* She moved her right arm up, so her elbow was by her right hip, and she started to pull it against her body to move it toward the left.

How odd I feel now with the blood rushing toward my forehead, she thought. But then, she put that out of her mind and began pushing her elbow across her body, but it didn't catch anything. She thought that maybe the buckle was higher (or lower when you were upside down), and she pushed her arm downward and tried to swipe it across her body again. *No luck,* she thought, *but maybe I can raise my left hand up to my left hip and move it over and grab my right elbow; then, as it swipes past the buckle, I can grab it.* Virginia moved her left hand up till it was on her left hip, and, as she moved it toward the right, she could feel her right elbow. Then, she began to pull her elbow along with her left hand back across her body. *It sure is hard,* she thought, *but I can tell my hand and elbow are being rubbed against what feels like the belt.*

A further move and she felt the smooth buckle as her left hand touched the buckle and the release. She believed that if she could move a little farther to the left side, then she should be able to grab the buckle release. *There it is,* she thought. She had hold of the buckle release, but she was scared to pull it, since she knew this would cause her to fall, or it won't work at all. She knew that now she had to take her right arm and allow it to fall downward toward the ceiling to break the fall if the buckle worked. Down went the right arm toward the ceiling. She pulled the buckle release with her left hand and nothing happened. *Maybe I didn't pull it far enough,* she thought, *but I at least still have it in my grip.* She pulled harder, but the release didn't happen.

Now, she was scared and began to feel claustrophobic. She thought, *Something is wrong.* She slowly returned the buckle release back to its original position while maintaining her grip on it along with the rest of the buckle. *This arm feels the best because the hand is not dangling;*

it's holding onto the belt buckle and taking the pressure off my arm, she thought. She held the buckle and slid her thumb along the edge toward the left, trying to feel what was causing the buckle to not release. Her thumb felt part of her dress caught between her body and the buckle, and she began to scratch at her dress and the buckle with her thumb. Her hand was numb, almost like it was some free part of her body that wasn't under control of her brain, and, yet, her thumb's fingernail scratched away at the material caught in the buckle. She continued scratching and trying to grab the dress material.

Finally, she felt her thumbnail free the material from under the buckle, and the thumbnail pulled the material out of the way. Then, she slid her hand back to the buckle release and pulled hard. Suddenly, she fell, but not far, since her right hand cushioned the fall, which was only about a foot off the ceiling surface of the wreckage. She laid there panting and trying to catch her breath and to stop the hyperventilating that had begun when she feared she wouldn't be able to release herself. All of this took about a little over a minute, but, to Virginia, it seemed like half an hour.

Establishing Safety

Virginia was aware of many sounds: metal against metal, a seat falling, a moan, a crying, and someone screaming, "Help, help!"

Thank goodness, she thought, *I don't appear to be hurt, but I must make my way out of this wreck and save my child if nothing else.* Virginia was lucky in many ways, but now the main luck was that the plane was more or less upside down. This allowed her to crawl along the ceiling that was once above the middle aisle, and now it was below and more or less free of impediments except those that had fallen or had been flung in that direction during the crash. The ceiling was crushed down along with the side storage areas that were always above the passengers seating. Virginia got to where there was an exit on the right side of the plane, and it was now on the left side of this upside down plane. She found it was crunched, so that there was no way to open the hatch to the world.

What now? She thought, as she moved farther along the ceiling toward the captain's cabin. On her right (which used to be the left side of the plane), there was a window smashed open, and the sidewall beneath the window was ripped outward away from the middle of the plane. She now could see that this was where the left wing had been, and, during the crash, it ripped the wing off and pulled much of that bulkhead away from the plane. The other side also had the wing ripped, but it had crunched the right wing against the bulkhead and blocked any escape. There were people on that side that were crushed by this folding. This right side, where the left wing had been, she hoped would provide her enough room to squeeze through, baby belly and all.

Virginia crawled toward this opening, and, as she got to this area thatlooked like it had been opened with a can opener, she realized she was crawling over bloodied bodies that had various parts of their bodies missing. She tried to keep her eyes focused on the opening to avoid seeing these gruesome sights. As she moved through the hole, she could see other bodies lying outside, and some were impelled against trees. There was a man sitting against a tree with his left arm dangling and a bloody face, but he was alive, she surmised. There were a couple inches of snow on the ground, and she thought she should be cold, but she had no feeling whatsoever. *Odd*, she thought, *that the body seems to be protected against feeling to a great extent after an accident like this. It must be the brain that cuts off many of these functions, so the rest of the body can live for a certain length of time.*

Meanwhile, she crawled to a tree next to the injured man and asked him how he felt. "Not the best of days," he replied, "but I am glad I am out of there. We need to move away from this area, since a good bit of gasoline has spilled out of the wings. Fortunately, the left wing is back there some several hundred yards, and the gasoline is spilling out of the wing on the other side of the plane. It won't explode," he said, "but a big fire can start any time now."

Virginia addressed the man, saying, "Before we move away, we should check to see if there is anyone else that has survived and needs help. Also, there is considerable baggage scattered about from the bottom of the aircraft, and we should gather what we can to stay warm. We don't know how long we will be here." She told him her name was Virginia, and he said his was Larry.

Larry asked her if she knew that she had a hole in her forehead above her left eye. She reached up, brought her hand down, and was amazed to see the blood from the wound. "I didn't know I had that," she said, "but I guess we are lucky that we don't feel some things at times."

"It doesn't appear to be bleeding now," Larry commented. "So, it probably will be all right. Hopefully, it isn't severe." With that said, they started to move by walking at times and crawling at times to search the wreckage for other survivors.

"Hello," they cried out. "Is there anyone inside?" They could hear some moaning from the rear of the plane and decided to venture in that direction, remaining scared that the plane's gas leakage might burst into flames at any minute. Larry told Virginia to watch that she didn't cause any sparks as they moved along. Near the rear of the plane, the sounds became louder, and they crawled across some wreckage to where there was a hole in the side of the plane and knelt down and yelled inside. "Is there anyone there?" Then, they listened for any sounds, and they heard several moans. They each peered through a window above the hole and saw two men hanging by their seat belts. They soon came to the realization that the hole was too small to gain entrance, and Virginia's big belly didn't help the situation.

Since the window was just hanging above the hole, they decided to grab a piece of the wreckage and tried to bust the window free from the window mounts that partially surrounded the hanging window. Each of them grabbed hold of a piece of metal that looked like it used to be the side of a door. Virginia got on her knees and shouted instructions to the two men inside, telling them to close their eyes while they were banging away at the glass. It took about eight bangs with the metal piece for the glass to be dislodged. This left a hole that was now about two to three feet high and about a foot and a half wide.

Before crawling in, Larry reached in his pocket and pulled out a small Leatherman knife that had several small blades, one of which turned out to be a small pair of scissors. While crawling in, he said, "Looks like these little scissors will come in handy again. They missed the little knife at the check-in place," he said with a big smile on his face. He crawled in, only to find a body of a woman he had to crawl over to get to the first man. He felt her neck at the carotid artery to see if she had a pulse and felt nothing, and he almost vomited from the sight of the dead woman.

He now had to turn on his back to reach up to the first hanging man. "I am going to try to release the buckle," he shouted to the man. "You will only fall about a foot. Hold your breath." With that, he reached up and over his head and extended his hands upward toward the belt buckle and tried to pry the belt lock loose. He tried several times without success and decided to use the scissors, which now were lying on the dead woman's body. He slid his left hand between the belt and the side of the person, and, with his right hand, he began to try and cut the belt. He had little success, since the belt was too tough and too thick for the little scissors.

He withdrew his hands and opened another section of the little knife, which contained a small, sharp blade about two inches long. "Hopefully, this sharp little knife will do the job," he mumbled to himself. With that, he extended his arms again and began to cut across the belt, and, slowly, it gave way to his sawing action. It was amazing that he had cut the belt until there were only a couple of threads holding it, and it still held the weight of the gentleman. "I guess they knew what they were doing when they chose the material for these safety belts," he again mumbled to himself. "One more cut, and it will come," he shouted to the man. With another scrape of the knife, down the fella crumbled, breaking his fall with his arms. He laid there exhausted. "Are you able to crawl?" Larry asked. The man nodded his head and then noticed the woman lying face down.

"Was she gone?" he asked.

"Yes," Larry nodded, and the man began to crawl toward the opening where Virginia was peering in. As he crawled by Larry, Larry began to move on his back by lifting his knees and pushing with his feet to move his head; his back and butt end were facing the other man hanging upside down. It wasn't far to go, and this man appeared more lucid than the first as he struggled to free himself from the seat belt. Larry reached over his head and up to grab the buckle. This time, he had success, as he pulled on the buckle release, and the second man fell down.

"God bless you," the man said. With no more words passing between them, he helped Larry to turn his body over, so the two of them were able to crawl toward the waiting hole.

"Keep moving," Virginia cried out. "We don't know how long we have before something gives." As the two of them make it to the hole, they were helped out by Virginia and the other man. "We don't know how much time we have before a fire might start, so we should grab some baggage and move away from the plane," Virginia instructed. With those instructions, they began picking through the luggage. Some had burst open and provided obvious help in their selection of things they felt they might need; there were some things to keep them warm and maybe other things that would come in handy. Larry found a first aid kit among the scattered wreckage and gave out a shout about his catch. Within a few minutes they had what they could drag along and grabbed a large open piece of luggage and placed the findings in the double opening.

Larry and Virginia began to drag this large open beast toward the side where the snow laid on the ground; they were hoping to be able to slide it along the snow toward the front of the wreckage. The other two men were obviously still recovering from their bondage and were not as work worthy as Virginia and Larry, but they soon realized what the intent was and found themselves another big leather suitcase that was burst open. They threw away most of what was in it and began to select other pieces of what looked like more meaningful material to them. Soon, they began dragging their capture along the snow only about fifty feet behind the other two.

As the four moved forward, they continued to cry out, "Hello, can anyone hear us?" They were hoping to hear an echo back of someone's voice, but the only noise was that of the wreckage as it continued to spew out different noises of collapsing material. Virginia noticed that the one man could not use his left hand, and his left foot just dragged along, but they kept making progress. The one man had hold of the baggage handle and pulled it, while the one with the problems pushed from behind the baggage. The snow was a help and a hindrance—a help to allow the baggage to be dragged or pushed, but a hindrance in that their footing was not the best and would give way with a slide every so often. However, they continued to move forward past the nose of the plane and toward some trees in the distance. As night began to fall, they reached a group of trees that were about one hundred yards away from the wreckage, and there wasn't any snow under them. They were puffing as they reached this sort of oasis and believed this was far enough away.

They settled down on the dry ground and began to introduce themselves to each other. The man with the foot and hand problems was Michael, and the other was Sam. In return, Virginia and Larry introduced themselves. With very little instruction, each of them began to gather pieces of material they each had garnered from the wreck to make a place to sleep, while all of them kept hoping for a helicopter or some form of humanity to acknowledge their existence. "Hopefully, help will come before it gets dark," Virginia said. "You know, it would actually be good if the plane caught on fire now, so that it would provide a signal to others looking for us." With that, Larry indicated that someone ought to go back and get something soaked in gasoline, so they could start a little fire under the trees there and would have something to keep them warm during the night and provide a signal.

"Does anyone have a cigarette lighter, so we can light a fire?" Larry asked.

"Yes, I have a lighter," Sam said. "I better check to see if it works." With that comment, he pulled out the lighter and flicked it, and a warm light appeared from its entrails. "Thank God for that. I am in pretty good shape and will go back for a wick for our evening toast," he said. Larry indicated that he would go along with him to find something, acknowledging that Virginia was in no condition to be expending more energy while carrying a large tummy.

Sam and Larry made their way to the wreckage and decided that first they would locate another suitcase that was open and had some clothes inside. "We need to find one with no metal on it," said Sam. "That's all we need to do is cause a spark and start a fire where we don't want to."

"Makes sense," Larry remarked. They made their way to the side where the baggage was strewn about and soon found one. They filled it with shirts and other clothes lying around and began tugging it back toward the front of the wreckage and around to the other side. The smell of gasoline was powerful on that side, and they soon found a pool of it around where the wing had folded.

"It's a wonder this didn't cause a spark and ignite this when it crashed," Sam commented. "Let's dunk a few of the clothes in this and get out of here as fast as we can." They doused a few of the sweaters they had found, since they soaked up gas like a sponge. They placed these in the soft suitcase very gently and began their trip back toward the trees and the others; always being careful to not cause any sparks.

Upon arriving on the scene, they were surprised to find that Virginia was in pain and holding her stomach. "Oh no!" shouted Larry. "She's going to have her baby. Does anyone know how to do that?" A look around showed no hands. It was obvious that they were in trouble unless a helicopter showed up in the next half hour—it didn't. Larry took some of the material they had originally brought from the wreckage and placed it under her head and neck to make her as comfortable as possible. Then, he turned and took one of the bags and made a pile of clothes for their fire. There were many leaves lying under the trees that weren't covered with snow, and they looked dry and would likely make a good fire. "We don't want to use any more of the material until we have to," Larry said. Sam and Larry found some good dry branches, and, soon, they had a fire.

Meanwhile, there were some straight pieces of metal that had blown off the plane when it crashed, and Sam had picked those up and started to make a splint to put around Michael's ankle. Sam needed to remove the shoe, but he could leave the sock on as he went about the business of making a splint as best he could. After wrapping a T-shirt around the ankle and metal splint, he tore some strips from another piece of material and tied those around the amateur-like bandage. It hurt Michael while it was being done, but he said it felt a little better, since the job was completed. At least, this kept the ankle in place and immobilized, and he shouldn't have the pain that came with movement. It was in place, and now he didn't have the pain that came with movement.

Virginia tried to keep her composure as best she could with the pains coming fairly frequently now. As it grew dark, the flames from the fire kept her warm, but it didn't seem to help the pains that were coming more frequently now. This went on for half the night, and, even with the coolness of night, Virginia was sweating. *Will this night never end?* She wondered. *I know I will feel a lot better when the sun starts shining, and maybe some lookout planes will see us.* But when the sun began to rise and daylight began, the pain only got worse and more and more frequent, and she knew she was about to have the baby. She looked up at Michael who stayed with her most of the night and said that the time was almost there. Sam woke with the sun and took over. "I wish I had a drink of water," Virginia moaned.

With that outward moan, Larry took off for the wreckage to see what he could find. *The wreck is a danger and an oasis all at the same time,* he thought as he ran toward the oasis. *Thank goodness it is here, and we can scavenge from it. If only it can remain dormant till we get out of here.* With those thoughts, he approached the safe side of the wreckage and began to look in the windows to see if he could locate anything. "If anything is in there, it should be up by the pilot's cabin," he commented to himself. He peered in the window of the smashed-up cabin and saw two dead bodies literally squashed against the equipment and wall behind their pilots' seats.

When the plane got flipped around, it squashed the metal roof down on the cabin and made a mess of it. As he continued his search along the windows, he saw bottles of drinks lying on the ceiling that was now substituting for a floor. He kept mumbling to himself various things as he viewed the tortured plane. "Those must have come from the carts that the flight attendants pushed around on the plane carrying drinks of all sorts. Wow! There are places where the floor has been pushed upward and is touching the ceiling." Larry continued his mumbling. "That must have happened when the plane first hit. If I could smash a few more of the windows, I might be able to reach something with a piece of metal in my hand." *It's amazing,* he thought to himself, *how the ceiling of the plane now contains almost everything like a big trash barrel. There are shoes, parts of people, dead people, seats, clothes, baggage, pocketbooks, bottles of water, bottles of soft drinks, bottles of whiskey, cigarettes, money, newspapers, magazines, and a whole bunch of other things, all collected on the new floor.*

He soon found himself by the big opening where the left wing used to be. He got down on his knees, began to crawl in, and made his way in the direction he just came from. He intended to crawl along the ceiling to the bottles of fluid that he believed he could collect and carry back to the little camp they had set up. There were dead people all along the length as he traversed the length of the plane looking for booty. "This is like a horrible dream, a nightmare, worst than a nightmare, and it stinks to blue heaven," he continued to mumble. He could hardly keep from choking and throwing up, but he didn't have anything in his stomach to throw up, so he gagged and gagged some more. "There are more bottles than I can carry of soft drinks and water," he mumbled. "What should I do?"

He looked around and saw a dead man sprawled across his path with his shoes torn off his feet. "If I can pull his pants off, I could use those to carry the bottles." He tugged at the pants and was surprised that they came off easier than he expected. *No wonder,* he thought, *because his belt is unbuckled from the force of the crash, which probably threw him around like a sack of potatoes.* He tied the bottoms of the legs in knots and began to stuff bottles down the pant legs. "It's amazing how many bottles you can fit down two pant legs of a man's pants," he mumbled. Soon, he had more pant legs than bottles to stuff in them. He wished he could find more, but he didn't want to go any farther in the plane and wanted to get out as fast as he could. He tied the belt buckle tight to close the top of the pants as best he could and began to drag the pants out of the plane while holding onto the buckle. Once out, he was able to make fairly good time by dragging the pants in the crispy morning snow, and he was rapidly on his way to the group. *Hope Virginia is doing okay*, he thought to himself.

As Larry approached the group, he could see they were working vigorously to help Virginia who was now about to have a baby, he thought. "How's it going?" he asked.

"She was really having a hard time, and we don't know what to do to help," was the response. Larry took out two bottles of water and gave Virginia one and told her to drink as much as she could. Then, he took a T-shirt out of one of the bags and soaked it with the other bottle of water. He put it on the end of a stick and held it over the fire until he saw steam coming from the shirt. He pulled it in and wrung it out while almost burning his hand from the steamy shirt. Then, he put it out over the fire again and left it there to heat and evaporates what water was left in the T-shirt. He took the hot, damp shirt and rubbed it along Virginia's brow in hopes of making her feel more comfortable. Then, he reached down and pulled Virginia's dress up and pulled her panties down over her legs. He then took the cloth and wiped her whole bottom part of her body.

As he was doing this, she had a bowel movement, and he caught it with the T-shirt and threw the T-shirt away as far as he could. Then, he took another T-shirt and began the same procedure. "At least, she can be clean when this baby is born," he said. "I wish I could boil the water to make it cleaner, but this is the best I can do with what we have."

Virginia looked up at Larry and said, "Thanks, I think I needed that," and, with one large final grunt, out popped a baby's head. Larry cushioned it with the T-shirt and asked Michael to get another T-shirt and do the same treatment to it, so he could wrap the baby in something warm and as clean as he could get it. Virginia reached down and pushed on her belly, and out came the placenta as if to give finality to the situation. Larry reached in his pocket and pulled out the little knife he had used before. He handed it to Sam and told him to open the scissor part and heat it directly in the fire.

Meanwhile, Larry told Michael to rip a thin strip of the steamy T-shirt, so he could tie the umbilical cord of this young man with it. Soon, this was completed, and he took the strip of the steamy T-shirt cloth and tied a tight knot around the baby boy's umbilical cord about an inch away from his body. After that, he took the little knife and snipped the umbilical cord on the other side of the knot away from the baby. "There you are little lad," he said. "A little white ribbon and you are free of that long cord." He then handed the baby to Michael to wrap the boy in a clean steamed T-shirt. He then took another steamed T-shirt and wrapped the placenta in it and told Sam to bury it in the dirt somewhere. "We don't want any animals smelling that and coming during the night for their dinner."

Michael then laid the wrapped baby on Virginia's bosom for her perusal of her son. "And what will your son's name be?" he asked.

"I don't know," said Virginia. "I only know I still hurt, and it feels like there is another baby in there."

"That's probably how all women feel just after the birth," Michael tuned in. "We shall see."

As the day proceeded, they only saw one plane off in the distance, and it didn't see them. "They must be looking in the wrong place," they all said.

The Rescue

"This place is sort of hidden with the trees and rolling hills, and it doesn't help that the wreckage didn't give off much smoke or a night fire," commented Sam. So, their second day was spent looking for help and praying, but not for Virginia. She continued having pains as if giving birth to another child. She was not only having pains, but she was breathing very hard, as if to catch more of the atmosphere's oxygen. It seemed to be a very long day for Virginia and the rest of this crew, and, soon, night had come again.

They had made a couple of trips back to the wreckage to bring back some more clothes to keep the fire burning. Sam said, "Perhaps, we should make a bigger fire as it gets dark, so that any planes will see it clearly. Maybe we should wait till it's very dark and set fire to the wreckage. That plane we saw today would have seen a bigger fire, and one at night would really show our location. I am sure they are looking for us," Sam continued to comment.

Larry questioned, "If we do that, it eliminates our chances of gathering anything else from the wreckage. Do we want to take that chance?"

"Yes, said Larry, "I think we should take that chance. But to play it safe, we probably should make a few trips to the wreckage and collect anything that we think we might need in the next few days. We can keep the fire here going for days if they don't see the large flames from the wreckage. I think it's a good bet. Michael can stay here and watch over Virginia, while Sam and I make a couple of trips to the wreckage and bring back whatever we can before setting fire to the wreckage." They agreed that it was a gamble, but it seemed to be a good one. They knew that soon they wouldn't gather much more from the wreck. So, why not take it now and set the plane afire?

Off went Sam and Larry. Eventually, they made three trips and piled up the wonderful scraps they had retrieved from the wreckage. Meanwhile, Virginia found that she could breast-feed the baby. "It's a miracle that we can give birth to our kind, and then the Lord provides us a way of feeding them," Virginia commented. "This little guy doesn't even know we are in trouble. He only t how to suck a breast. At least, he is getting his nourishment. I wish I had a hamburger myself. The soda drinks are a big help, but it sure would be nice to be munching on a big, juicy cheeseburger," she said, as she rolled her head and eyes backward and looked up at the dark starlit sky. "I am having a hard time with these pains and my heavy breathing; plus, this little guy is riding my stomach."

With that comment Sam and Larry began their final trip back toward the airplane to see if they were able to ignite a large flame safely. Michael had been preparing something for them to use. He felt the gasoline should be ignited as far away from the plane wreckage as possible, and he retrieved two rocks about the size of a baseball and wrapped each with a soft cloth. Then, he tore a strip from a T-shirt and tied the wrapping as tight as he could make it around each of the rocks, while leaving a little tail of the knot hanging free. He handed one to both Sam and Larry and said that they should light the tail and throw the rocks from as far away from the wreckage as possible. "I don't want you guys going up with the flame. So, stay as far away as you can throw these, and run as fast as you can. I wish I could help you, but the leg won't give me the chance. Good luck."

With that send-off message, Sam and Larry took off with Sam holding a rock and Larry holding a rock and his lighter to put the flame to each. As they approached the wreckage from the left side, they paid close attention to any gasoline that might be passed up by mistake. Finally, Larry said, "I think this is as close as we can get." They were standing about sixty feet from the nose of the plane, and there was a puddle of gasoline about thirty feet in front of the nose of the crunched plane. Larry said to Sam, "Do you think you can throw that ball from here? It's a toss of about thirty feet."

Sam shouted, "No problem, this is about the distance of a softball pitcher to the catcher, and I have played a lot of softball. But if my arm is weaker now, then it will bounce or roll that far." He reached back with his right hand in a throwing position, widened his stance, and looked at Larry and shouted, "Ignite yours and then ignite mine, and then we both can throw our bombs and run."

Larry lit his and stationed himself just behind Sam's ball and flicked the lighter. Out sprouted a flame, and he reached forward and placed the flame on the dangling piece of cloth on Sam's ball. It lit up almost instantly, and he backed a step away. "Run Larry!" he shouted, as they flung the balls as far as they could toward the pool of danger.

Then, they turned and began running toward the safety of their camp. They hadn't taken five steps when they saw the world light up, and it was like it gave them extra energy because Sam soon caught up with Larry. They kept running toward their improvised shelter, hoping the flame would not advance toward them. About the time they got to Virginia and Michael, they heard a roar, and they dove to the ground. Lying there, they ventured a look backward toward their target to see where the roar had come from. It turned out the flame had not only ignited the main wreckage, but it had sprung a channel like fire all the way back to the left wing of the plane that sat back about a half mile beyond the main wreckage.

"I bet from the air this must look like a lit-up landing field," shouted Michael. They all laid back and enjoyed the brightness it provided, and it was already making it more comfortable as the flame took the nip off the cool night air. It was close to midnight, and they hoped there were planes out looking for some kind of signal. Within an hour, they heard the engines of an airplane, and, within a few minutes, it flew over their little fire. They saw its lights blinking, and the plane banked and proceeded back over their position, acknowledging that the pilot had seen their little fire as well as the big one, and then he was gone. There was about a second of silence, and then all four of them began shouting and dancing. This continued for about ten minutes, and then it was silent again except for the noise from the wreckage as it burned. Every once in a while, it popped like popcorn, and there were flares sent out in the air. They sat there quietly hoping for the best.

They waited excitingly, but Virginia's problems were so painful that she could hardly wait for anything. Her pains had been ongoing for almost two days since her baby was born. Michael, who had inherited the responsibility for watching over Virginia, spoke up. "Virginia has been hyperventilating for several hours now, and I don't know what to do to ease the situation."

"Try giving her a drink of the colored soda water. It has sugar in it, and that might help," said Sam. Michael opened a bottle and lifted Virginia's head while making sure the little baby wasn't disturbed, and then he had Virginia take a few gulps of the brown colored soda water. She had difficulty taking in the fluid as her rapid breathing made it difficult. But in between gulps of air, she took in a couple gulps of the drink. Maybe it was the soda water or maybe just the physical act of gulping the drink between gulping for air, but Virginia seemed somewhat relieved. After that, Michael gave her a drink about every fifteen minutes.

Only a half hour had passed when they heard the loud noise of a helicopter approaching. Sam and Larry stood up and stared into the dark night. Sure enough, off to the left, they could make out the lights of the helicopter. Soon, it was right above them and creating a lot of wind. Michael placed some of the remaining sheets of clothing over Virginia's face and over the baby to keep the wind and dust from causing any problems. A loud voice was emitted from a loudspeaker in the copter. "You down below; we are going to drop a line with a cellular phone attached to it. Take the phone, and, when it rings, push the talk button, and we can communicate with you."

With that, they were able to see the reflections of the flame from the wreckage shining against an object being lowered down toward them. "It's a phone," shouted Sam.

Larry grabbed the phone and released the line attached. In a few seconds, the phone rang, and Larry began a conversation with the helicopter. "There are four of us—no, make that five. There is a woman who had a baby since the wreck and three men. The woman has a small hole above her left eye, and she has been in pain since having the baby almost two days ago. She has been breathing hard for a couple of days, almost like hyperventilating. The baby seems to be well." There was a pause as Larry listened to what they were saying up in the copter, while the rest of them waited anxiously for Larry to tell them what was being said. Larry continued, "Yes, one of us looks like he has a broken bone in the hand and the ankle. The other two of us are just shook up but no major physical damage. Yes, I understand, and I believe that will work."

There was another pause, and then Larry said, "You are damned right we are hungry. We haven't eaten since the wreck. We have been lucky enough to have gathered some liquids from the wreckage." There was another pause, as the people in the helicopter were talking to Larry, and then Larry was commenting. "Go ahead; we will be watching for it."

With that, Larry put down the phone and looked up while saying, "They are going to lower a box with food and water in it." Soon, they saw the box come into view, and it was like Christmas with a present arriving. Sam helped Larry grab the box as it came within reach. After freeing the box from the line, Larry picked up the phone again. "We got it and look forward to your return. We will keep the phone, and you can keep us appraised of your progress every fifteen minutes or so." With that comment, Larry switched the phone off, and the helicopter rose up to a higher position and took off to the left.

Larry began bringing the others up to speed on what was happening. "They said they will return in a couple of hours at daybreak when they are able to see well. They will lower a hospital-type stretcher, and we are to put Virginia on it with the baby, and they will lift them to the copter. Meanwhile, another copter will come and land about a mile away, and four rescue crew members and a medic will come for the rest of us. They will have a stretcher for Michael to cart him back to the helicopter. Sam and I will proceed with Michael to the helicopter. I would guess we have about a four-hour wait, and, meanwhile, we can have our first meal in a few days."

In the box of goodies was a can opener, a loaf of bread, three cans of baked beans, three cans of spam, and two large bottles of Gatorade, along with a package of plastic knives, forks, and spoons. It might not sound like much, but, to them, it was a meal fit for kings. While eating, they received a call from the helicopter saying they had arrived at their base, and they already had everything ready to return. The copter pilot felt they could probably take off in about two and a half hours and be there just shortly after that. "Oh, by the way," said the pilot, "Red said to tell Virginia that he is so glad to hear he is a father and that she is all right." This was great news to hear while eating and drinking merrily within the glow of the burning wreckage.

It seemed like a long wait, and the night seemed colder than it had been, but soon they heard the sound of approaching helicopters. Then, the phone rang. Larry picked it up, switched it on, and listened. He nodded to Michael and Sam, "They are going to lower the medical stretcher for Virginia, so you should get her ready. They said they would lower some blankets for her, and there is an extra-large coat for each of us. I'm glad they thought of that. There is a medic on this copter and one on the other also."

As the stretcher was being lowered, the other copter soared off to the left. As they looked up, they were able to see a spotlight aimed at the stretcher as it slowly made its way down. Sam pulled the three coats from the stretcher and folded the blankets back. Virginia was lifted by Sam and Larry and placed gently on the stretcher, while Michael held the baby. Soon, the baby was resting in the folded arm of his mother, and Larry took the phone and told them to lift away. As the stretcher was lifted, they kept their eyes focused on this disappearing bed of mercy. As it reached the opening on the side of the copter, they were able to see it disappear within its confines, and they each yelled, "Yeah! Yeah! Yeah for Virginia and the boy," and then they turned and looked at each other for a minute. "Wow, it's like one of the family just left us," said Michael.

Before long, they could hear the men from the other helicopter making their way to their little camp. The medic looked at Michael's bindings and decided to leave them as they were, since anything he would do would just cause some pain. They would be able to handle this better back at the base. They soon were on their way through the woods with Michael being toted on a stretcher with two big soldiers bearing the weight. It took about half an hour for them to make it to the waiting helicopter where the pilot and another soldier were waiting. Within a few minutes, they had the stretcher, Michael, Larry, and Sam aboard the copter and everything ready to take off. As the helicopter rose from the ground, the flames from the wreckage became more obvious. "No wonder they could find us," shouted Michael. "The place is lit up like a football field." In short order, they were arriving at the base and wanting to know what was happening with Virginia.

"Oh, I forgot to tell you," said the pilot, as they walked toward the nearest building. "She had another baby boy just after we got her here. Twins born a little over two days apart and this one also seemed to be in good shape."

"Fantastic," the three guys shouted. "Twins, no wonder she was in pain and breathing hard."

While Virginia was resting and recuperating in the hospital, she kept thinking about what to call these twin boys she had been gifted with. To help her in her decision, Red arrived, having been flown in by another helicopter from Boston. He was elated at the sight of his two sons. He reached down and squeezed and kissed Virginia and laughingly commented, "Looks like the trip was good for them. It must be that good airplane chow you got to eat before they were born."

"I don't think so," said Virginia. "Now I have another problem to discuss. We have to name them. I have been thinking of several names to call them, Mr. Tressler, and I want to bounce the names off you and see what you think."

"I'm listening," he said.

"I would like to name the first child Adam, since he was the first child, like in Adam and Eve. The second child is a little harder to come by. Since he took so long to follow Adam, I thought a good name for him would be Axel. A rear axle on a car follows the front axle, and he seems like he is the follower, and Axel would fit him. What do you think of those two names?"

"To tell you the truth, Red said, "I don't know what reasoning you used to come up with those names, but I like both of them. I think Adam Tressler and Axel Tressler are two dignified names worthy of two fellows that came along on an airplane ride."

With that comment, Virginia's eyes lit up like two candles. "Oh, I am so glad you like those names. You don't know how hard I kept thinking about what to name them. It does sound dignified when you call them out as Mr. Adam Tressler and Mr. Axel Tressler. I hope they live up to the excitement that brought them into this world."

The difference in the names of Adam and Axel had no impact on them in their early lives. They were fraternal twins and therefore did not look alike. Adam was thin, and Axel was stockier. Adam had blond hair, and Axel's hair was darker. They were both smart and did well in school. Adam was more social than Axel. Axel enjoyed making things and messing around with electronic things. When there were games to play, Adam would be the one playing, and, later, Axel might join in; he was always the follower. When they were young and fought each other, as twins do, Adam always got the best of Axel. Sometimes, Adam thought that Axel let him win because Axel thought so much of his brother.

The Twins grow up

They were both bright and were considered smarter than their schoolmates. When their mates wanted to play a game, they came to see Adam. When their school mates had something that was broken, they came to see Axel. Adam was the taller one since birth, and he protected Axel as they grew up. But then, when they turned twelve and started going into puberty, things changed. Axel became more muscular and more active. At times, when he got excited, he showed an elevated strength. Now, it was Axel that watched over Adam.

One day, when their dad was working under his car, the jack slipped and pinned him under the car. He yelled, and Adam and Axel ran into the garage and saw their dad pinned under the car. At first, they tried to get the jack out from under the car, so they could jack the car up and get their dad out from under. They didn't have any success at getting the jack out, and they knew their dad was hurting. Axel began to breath rapidly and taking in great breaths of air. He walked over to the side of the car, bent his legs, and gripped the edge of the car. His breathing increased, and he grunted and lifted the car up about a foot off the ground. He held it in that position, while Adam reached under and helped his dad to release from the pinned position. When he was out, Axel dropped the edge of the car and stood and continued breathing hard for a few minutes. After a few minutes, he was his normal self and hugged his dad.

Axel seemed to be going through a change that was something besides becoming an adult. By the time they were fourteen, Adam was only one inch taller than Axel, but Axel was bigger boned and seemed to be stronger. He weighed a few more pounds than Adam but didn't think of it too much. Life was fun for them both, and it seemed to become more fun as the days passed. As each year passed, Axel never had to defend Adam, since he was already quite strong for his age, but they all stopped bothering Axel. Every once in a while when he had a chore that required some extra strength, he began to breath hard and more rapidly. For whatever reason, this brought on more strength, and he was able to lift heavy items that he didn't realize he could, and, afterward, he would sit back and breathe hard as though to catch up the energy he had just consumed.

When they were fourteen, they were called from school on an emergency. Their father had had a heart attack, and they were rushed to the hospital to see him. They got there too late, and he had passed on. This took a terrible toll on Virginia and the twins. This left a horrible hole in their lives. Virginia had been well educated but never had to go out and earn a living, since Red had such good positions in big companies all their married lives. He had left them well supported, and Virginia wouldn't really have to go out and earn a living. However, she decided to that she wanted to keep busy and took a job as a paralegal. The boys took on odd jobs to make sure there was added support in the family.

By the time the boys reached eighteen, it became obvious to Virginia and Adam that Axel had some kind of physical condition that needed to be checked. He had fantastic strength when he got excited. Axel would be starting college, and she wanted to be sure he was in good condition, and she could be free of worry. Virginia made arrangements for Axel to have a three-day physical check at a hospital in Pittsburgh. She had explained the situation with several doctors, and they recommended Dr. Newcome who was a neurologist. So, an examination was scheduled for Dr. Newcome to begin the three-day check the following Thursday through Saturday.

The Doctor finds the real Axel

The first day of the examination included blood samples, urinesamples, some x-rays and an ultrasound of Axel's carotid arteries and stomach aorta. By the second day, they decided to have him do some heavy exercises and check his blood pressure, his electro cardiogram, and his urine during the exercises and after each of the heavy exercises. They had Axel run on the treadmill while monitoring several things, such as his blood pressure, during the exercise and afterward. Something they saw resulted in their doing a systiscope of his kidneys by placing a metal tube with a bend in it up his penis to bladder and beyond. That was one exercise Axel didn't want to go through again. As a last step in these exercises, they had Axel lift weights. He kept lifting heavier and heavier weights and was soon above twice the weight of his body, which was an outstanding achievement. At the time his weight was 181 pounds, and he stood at five feet eleven inches tall.

Finally, they asked Axel to try and lift five hundred pounds while lying on his back. Axel took a position with his back on a matt between the two forks that held the bar that had the weights of 250 pounds on each end. The bar was about ten or twelve inches above his shoulders. They had a man on each side of the weights in case Axel had problems; they were prepared to grab the bar and sit it back on the forks. When Axel was prepared to begin the lift, he reached up, grabbed the bar, and tried to push the weight of the side stands and into the air above his chest, but as hard as he tried, he was unable to move the bar. The doctors that were observing this action told Axel to stop and wait a few minutes.

As Axel rested, he began to take large breaths. He was hyperventilating. The doctors watched curiously at this young man taking on these gulps of air. Within ten seconds, Axel reached up with his hands and grabbed the bar holding the weights. He raised the weights to his arm's length and then set the bar and weights back on the side forks. "Outstanding," Dr. Newcome and the other doctors exclaimed, as Axel continued taking some deep breaths to gain back his composure; and then he relaxed. That ended his third day and had the doctors buzzing. Dr. Newcome told Virginia and Axel that he would review the test data and give her a call in two days.

Two days later, Dr. Newcome called and asked Virginia to bring Axel to the hospital the next day to discuss the results of the study. Axel had already missed three days of school and didn't want to miss any more, so Virginia asked if they could come in on Saturday. Dr. Newcome said that would be fine, and he would see them at one o'clock in the afternoon.

When they arrived, Dr. Newcome took them to his private office and asked them to have a seat across the desk from him. Then, he began a weird dissertation that sort of sounded like a science teacher or a biology teacher. He described how the human embryo is formed when the man's sperm mates with the woman's egg. He described how, when there are twins, they are formed in a single placenta that is the first thing that is formed, and those twins will have exactly the same DNA. Then, he described the case where the twins are fraternal.

"In this case, there are actually two embryos formed from two eggs of the woman being fertilized by separate male sperm. In this case, the embryos each form a placenta to start the growth of the twins. This would be the case for Adam and Axel, since they are fraternal twins. Human beings are fortunate enough to have a placenta formed that allows the brain to be protected and to allow the brain to reach a large size for the size of a human being compared to other creatures. It is believed that this is the main reason that human beings reach their high level of intelligence. The embryo then begins to generate cells that contain their DNA that is a composite of the male sperm and the female egg."

"Each human being has twenty-three pairs of chromosomes made up of two chromatids, each containing twenty-three chromosomes. When the mating occurs, a chromatid comes from the father and one from the mother, and they therefore have the twenty-three pairs, totaling forty-six chromosomes. In the case of twins, each has forty-six chromosomes. The twenty third chromosome pair on the woman has two x's, and the male has one x and one y. If, when they mate, the twenty third pair has a y in it, the baby will be a boy. If it has two x's in the twenty-third position, it will be a girl. The embryo grows by these chromosomes splitting along with their DNA and forming twice as many as it had before the split. This splitting continues during the nine-month gestation period within the mother. The DNA splits and forms a pair of DNA cells exactly like the originals, and this keeps happening while the baby is being formed in the mother's body."

"Thus, more and more cells are formed and begin to form parts of the body with cells that are identical even though eventually some cells will make up a muscle, and others will make up other parts of the body. Eventually, genetic studies show that the key to the new child's traits are determined by the DNA (deoxyribonucleic acid) that is found in the chromosomes and are contained in a hard shell in the nucleus of the human cell. The DNA provides the specific genetic code for that given person. Mark Twain once said, 'When you are born, you are done.' From the standpoint of the DNA, this is true. The DNA and the human genome, which is made up of the genes determined in the DNA, are like a book that has been written. The child will have exactly the characteristics established by this DNA and its genetic code resting in the chromosome abode. (Incidentally, in a previous book I had published, I included a poem I wrote, 'DNA and the Genetic Code')."

"This DNA is within a nucleus of every cell and never leaves the nucleus to provide the code, but studies over the years determined that it provides the DNA directions to the RNA (ribonucleic acid) that is both inside and outside the nucleus of the cell. The RNA can move in and out of the nucleus of the cell, and one of the functions it performs is that of a messenger. This messenger RNAm, upon leaving the nucleus with the code it received from the DNA then selects the amino acids that the DNA code directed it to do. These amino acids that are selected provide the chemicals that determine the proteins that are going to be formed in the human body. There are twenty-six amino acids, and they can form all the proteins required by the human body except one."

"Although the cells are the same throughout the body, there are signals given to each, depending on their location as to what each is supposed to provide in the way of proteins depending on whether it is a muscle or the heart or some other function within a human. The human genome is like a book contained in the forty-six chromosomes that determine the genes formed by the DNA and which location in the body the gene or genes will be servicing."

Dr. Newcome said that he was explaining this for a reason that was very important. He realized what he had just described was known by many people, since it was taught in the high schools. Dr. Newcome said, "More young people know these details than the older generation because of books that were written just recently over the last ten years or so. I believe that it is good that people now understand about DNA, but there are many things that aren't discussed that they should know about."

Dr. Newcome continued his discussion and began to describe the thing that made Axel different from most humans. "Between the outer shell of the cell and this inner nucleus shell that contains the DNA, there are organelles that provide other cellular functions for the body just like the organs of a human body, such as the heart, kidneys, and liver provide separate functions for the body. See the figure below of a human cell. (Reference #1)

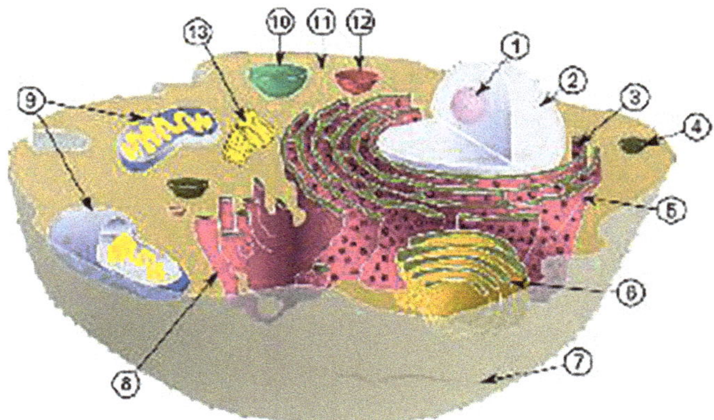

Diagram of a typical eukaryotic cell, showing subcellular components organelles

1. Nucleolus
2. Nucleus
3. Ribosome
4. Vesicle
5. Rough endoplasmic reticulum (ER)
6. Golgi apparatus
7. Cytoskeleton
8. Smooth ER
9. Mitochondria
10. Vacuole
11. Cytoplasm
12. Lysosome
13. Centrioles within centrosome

"One of these organelles is called the mitochondrion (see item 9 above), and, in humans, there are normally between two hundred and eight hundred mitochondria in each cell. Mitochondria provide the energy required for movement of the cell as well as providing the energy for many other functions. They are the *power centers* of the cell and the power centers of the human body; sort of like a microprocessor is the power center for a computer. Internally, the mitochondria are made up of a matrix of folds to provide a large surface area for its function. Its main function is to take food that has been converted to sugar and store the energy in this matrix using a chemical reaction to generate ATP. ATP is adenosine triphosphate, and it stores this energy and is considered the energy source of the cell and the body. When energy is needed, the ATP containing nutrients reacts with oxygen and generates this energy. After giving up the energy, the ATP is converted to ADP (adenosine diphospate), which is a low-energy molecule, and awaits the next sugar cycle.

When it takes on additional food energy, it is converted from ADP back to ATP and awaits the call for energy and its next reaction with oxygen. The oxygen is very important in determining the amount of power that will come from the ATP. If the mitochondrion has no oxygen, there will only be four energy packets of ATP released for each glucose (sugar) molecule. If there is oxygen present, there will be a loop present that is called the 'citric acid cycle,' and, from this cycle, one can obtain twenty-four to twenty-eight ATP energy packets for oneglucose molecule."

"So, you can see how important the oxygen is in raising the level of energy and how important it is for a person to take in glucose for energy. To give you an example of how effective the ATP is, let's look at a hummingbird. The hummingbird has approximately ten thousand mitochondria in every cell of its wing muscles, and each has many matrix folds inside the mitochondria to provide an enormous amount of ATP energy to provide this small bird his hard-to-believe ability to move his wings so rapidly. If a person has a hummingbird feeder hanging outside their house to attract the hummingbirds, they will soon realize how much sugar water this bird consumes a day. From this sugar water, his large amounts of ATP and the ability to take in large amounts of oxygen, the hummingbird is a focus of energy. This bird can fly all the way to South America during parts of the year and fly back from whence he came."

"The reason I am explaining this to you," said Dr. Newcome, "is because of Axel's particular case. Axel has the most mitochondria I have ever seen in a human being in his cells. Axel has approximately five thousand mitochondria per cell. This provides Axel with a unique situation where he has the potential of having more than three to four times the energy capability of a normal person. In fact, he can probably achieve an energy level that is up to ten times that of a normal person. All he needs is the required oxygen to supply these mitochondria and their ATP. That's why the tests showed that he couldn't move more than two hundred pounds of weight until he hyperventilated. You remember after failing to move the five hundred pounds that Axel subconsciously started to breathe rapidly, and then he was able to move the weight. Axel was supplying extra oxygen to those extra ATP energy sources. It is important for all of us to know how he came about this extra source of mitochondria. Mitochondria are inherited from the female egg and have nothing to do with the male sperm. In fact, scientists can trace the female mitochondria back to the original woman on earth. We cannot do that with the male. I believe the extra two days Virginia was carrying Axel in her womb caused her body to take emergency steps to protect her. I was told that she was hyperventilating during the two days after Adam was born as she lay close to the wreck waiting to be found. I believe that, during that extra time, Axel's body cells were being bombarded by something in your mother's placenta that provided this extra means of energy. I have no other explanation for this large deviation from the norm. Axel is an energy powerhouse waiting to be released."

"There are several other abnormalities that we found while doing the examinations. Axel has three complete kidney systems. They all seem to be normal with urethras from each all leading down to the bladder. I have seen this before. It happens in about one out of several hundred new births. I thought it might be due to his being a twin, but I have seen fraternal twins before with one of them having three kidneys and the other having the normal two. I have never seen twins where both of them had three kidneys. Although the three kidneys are not uncommon, what is uncommon is that you have three adrenal glands, one on top of each kidney. There are usually two in any other person. The adrenal glands determine a body's fight or flight actions. When a person gets excited by some uncommon occurrence, the adrenal glands release hormones that cause the person to take unusual actions. He has a sudden burst of energy. These actions are described in general by the fight or flight syndrome. The person involved either gains energy for fighting or for fleeing. The one hormone that is critical is cortisol. The cortisol increases blood sugar levels by converting fats and proteins into energy. Cortisol works in tandem with the insulin from the pancreas to provide adequate glucose to the cells where it is burned for energy. Cortisol ensures adequate levels of glucose in the blood, while insulin from the pancreas unlocks membranes to let glucose into the cells for the mitochondria to generate more or less ATP."

"Axel's system in some way has a harmony working between the extra mitochondria, the extra adrenal glands, the extra kidneys, and the action of the pancreas and the pituitary glands. His system allows more sugar to be released to satisfy the increased number of mitochondria, and this gives him more energy to perform a task, but the pancreas allows him to return to the normal amount of blood sugar after these actions and doesn't leave him tired, which is how most people would suffer after an unusual use of energy. There is one other abnormality; Axel's lungs are about 30 percent bigger than the average lung. This may be nature's way of providing for the higher ATP, since the ATP is released by oxygen. The oxygen also chemically handles the release of sugar from the nutrients stored in the cells. When a person gets excited, they sometimes start breathing harder to take in more oxygen. This is the body's way of providing the release of more energy through the combination of the oxygen, the ATP, and the body's stored nutrients. In Axel's case, he has more than enough oxygen capability to supply the needs dictated by the other organs of his body."

"We also noticed that Axel expelled a considerable amount of urine during the various tests he went through the other day. We believe this is due to the large amount of ATP actions occurring when you are in this high energy mode. The side effects of the large ATP action probably result in more water being generated or released during this time. The ATP action generates heat, and the body responds by providing water to cool you just like when you sweat. It's possible that this is why he has three kidneys, although this might just be a coincidence. However, the three kidneys probably prevent body overload by the large amount of water being generated, and it doesn't hurt to have three of them working for you instead of the normal two. I would suggest you drink more liquids after such an action to ensure you don't dehydrate your body. The liquids don't necessarily mean more water has to be consumed, although that would be fine. The other liquids, such as juice, beer, and the water that is within any food, would provide the extra water."

Virginia asked the doctor how Axel could use this extra energy and whether it could do him any harm Dr. Newcome said that he didn't know if Axel would be able to call on this extra energy any time he wanted; at least, he didn't know how.

"I would surmise that some external condition might cause Axel to start to take deep breaths, and this extra energy would come to the foreground. If he felt endangered, or if he believed that one of his family was being endangered, it might excite him and cause him to pump oxygen to the cells. I don't believe he is endangered by this extra burst of energy. The energy comes from food turned to sugar and then requires the added oxygen. I would assume if he hasn't eaten for some length of time that he might not be able to gain this energy even during an emergency. So, this automatically controls the rate at which he can provide this burst and doesn't allow extra energy burn off during normal conditions. He might eventually grow out of this; however, it is not likely because he didn't seem to have it till he went into puberty. So, it is a newfound capability and might even grow with age till he reached some limit. His mitochondria won't change. They are set for life. What might change is the way some phenomena cause him to be excited. He might grow calmer as he ages. Most people do. At this time, I don't know the limit of this power. We will want to test Axel every six months to determine if there are any changes or any danger. Eventually, assuming we find it is safe, we would like to really overload Axel to determine how much energy he can produce compared to the normal male."

With the above explanations and no further action required by the doctor, Axel and Virginia left the hospital feeling somewhat confused but happy that there didn't seem to be any finality about the findings. While driving home, Virginia asked Axel how he felt about the findings. "It was interesting to hear the doctor explain the workings of the cell, the DNA, and those mitochondria and made me think about the human body and its wondrous capabilities. I had wondered what my major should be in college this coming year, and I think I found out today. I want to study biology and how the body and its organs work. Maybe I can provide some answers some day to another person with issues that can't be explained, like Dr. Newcome did for us today. I can only thank you Mom for holding out for a couple of days after that plane wreck. It looks like it might have paid off for the pain you suffered. I always knew I had something different about me. Since I was sixteen, I never met another person I couldn't beat. I never took the initiative, but, when the time came, I always had the energy to outdo anyone who was aggressive toward me or toward Adam. I love Adam, and, when he was endangered, my body would begin breathing rapidly, and I would take on his aggressor and make short work of the problem. I guess I sort of made up for what he did for me when I was growing up."

Virginia smiled. She was happy to hear this mature rationale sent to her by her son. One outcome of this meeting with Dr. Newcome was Axel's better understanding of his body and its metabolism. He carried a pack of sugar chewing gum and some sugar mints in his pockets at all times. He thought it was like carrying a lethal weapon. If he needed energy, or thought he might, he could break out a stick of gum and chew away at it. Bread had the same effect, being loaded with carbohydrates that the body converts to sugar.

Axel Develops His Body Computer

When Adam and Axel completed the first semester of their senior year of college, each in separate colleges, they both had excelled with the highest of grades in their curriculums. Adam had majored in criminal justice and taken selected courses that prepared one for work in the Special Forces related to intelligence, securities, and the agencies that used these special talents. The graduates of this special course with the highest aptitude and showing the highest grades of this curriculum normally took on positions with the FBI, the Central Intelligence Agency or some unique position within the military intelligence. Adam had excelled in his studies and graduated number one in his class. It wasn't long before Adam accepted a position with a special agency located in the Pentagon and was very excited about the fact that they had considered him. Why not? He was first in his class. He was also fortunate that, while engaged in this new position, they paid for any advanced schooling he would take. He had been with them for over three years now, and things really looked good for his future. He was able to free up enough hours in a week to take some day and some night courses toward an advanced degree either in law or a Master's in political science. He had the brains and the energy for either. As far as Axel could see, his big brother (in age of a couple of days) was going to have a very successful career in whatever he chose to do.

As Axel had promised himself, he had majored in the biology of human genetics and had taken special courses on gene engineering and stem cell research. After completing his undergraduate degree, he went on to his Master's degree and was now completing his work on his doctorate. Beside this work on advanced courses to earn his doctorate, he had taken on the teaching of several courses to undergraduates. These were courses in biology to freshmen students and included several laboratory classes. Axel continued his investigation of mitochondrion, having several of his lab students volunteer their blood for him to examine versus his own blood. In two students whose blood he investigated, he found their mitochondria numbered about eight hundred. In his blood, the mitochondria looked not only more populated but slightly bigger in size. The number per cell was above five thousand.

Between his examinations using an electron microscope and papers that were available, he was able to understand the workings much better. The mitochondria had their own DNA, but they were in a single circle like bacteria instead of the double helix found in the nucleus of a human cell. In fact, it was believed it evolved from bacteria about two billion years ago, and, as Dr. Newcome had instructed his mother, it came from the egg of the female during the mating, and one could only track down the history back to Eve through the female line. It differed also in that it replicated by binary fission like bacteria and didn't necessarily divide at the same time as the nucleus. The mitochondria replicate their DNA in response to the energy requirements of the cell rather than as the cell divides. Just as in Axel's case, the mitochondria actions grow as the energy need arises and will remain dormant or be destroyed during times of low activity. They thrive on continuous use.

Everyday exercise routines carried out by the two students he was surveying showed a dramatic response by the mitochondria to this exercise routine. Each mitochondrion might contain up to ten copies of its DNA. The genome of the mitochondrion is contained in a circular DNA molecule with approximately sixteen kilobases, which are used to encode thirty-seven genes, thirteen for respiratory, twenty-two for tRNA, and two for rRNA (1), which is well below the number of the nucleus DNA. They do not encode for proteins like the nucleus, and even their own proteins are encoded by the nucleus and transported to the mitochondria."

Knowing this information for a standard human, Axel felt his mitochondria would perhaps differ, and he would be able to encode the DNA to do tasks that he wished them to do. His studies had shown that most mitochondria in plants, animals, and humans had originally been in a more powerful position in the early cellular structure, but they had lost much of this over the past two billion years. He thought, if they had lost some capability, then it should be possible to have them gain more capability back. Additional studies on ATP showed that, when they are in the citric acid cycle (sometimes called the Kreb's cycle), the cycle worked sort of like a hydrogen cell that he had been reading about that was being tried in the auto market to propel cars in place of gasoline.

In reading about the hydrogen cell, he learned that the hydrogen was split into protons and electrons on the anode side of the cell. There is a membrane between the anode and cathode of the cell. The protons are able to pass through it, but the electrons cannot. The electrons are taken out into a desired electrical circuit (in the case of a car, it provides the electricity for driving the car), and, after passing through the load, they end up on the cathode side and recombine with the protons and oxygen on that side of the cell to produce water, which is what the hydrogen was originally separated from.

Axel felt that the chemical reactions that provided the ATP in the citric acid cycle were similar to those in the automotive cell where there were many electrons generated from the oxidation of hydrogen. This left the hydrogen as a positive ion with a positive charge from the proton in its nucleus, which are pumped during the citric cycle. The cycle is meant to gain as many electrons from the food as possible to provide energy, and it is able to do this if there is enough oxygen present. Eventually, the hydrogen pumping within this cycle provides excess hydrogen protons that combine with the electrons and oxygen to produce water as the by-products of this action. Axel felt that this action and the forming of water were why he needed three kidneys and why he seemed to generate a lot of urine.

His objective was to determine how he would be able to use the electrical energy of these cycles in some way similar to the hydrogen cell used in cars. Axel felt there were other possible uses of the many mitochondria he had in his cells. It became obvious that there was electron transportation occurring during the citric cycle as well as proton pumping that occurred during this cycle. He was sure that eventually he would be able to use this electron/proton generation to provide a battery action for some of the things he intended to do. Like he did as a child,

Axel was always fooling around with electronics, and he hoped to one day tie this hobby into some use with the mitochondria.

Since Axel had become quite good at the use of the computer in his work, he began to look into the programming of the computer to solve some of his school problems as well as prepare himself for a special contribution he wanted to provide society. Each evening, when classes were over and he was free from teaching, he spent the time working on new programs for computer use. Eight to ten hours each evening were spent in this endeavor. As he neared the end of his first year in this mode, he set several objectives that were to act as goals he wanted to accomplish. This was based on his special condition with the mitochondria, the ATP energy, and his advanced understanding of the computer.

Axel Establishes computer objectives

By the end of his first year of teaching, he had made considerable progress on several of these objectives. They made up a strong list of objectives:

1. Find a way to be able to eliminate the use of the computer keyboard, and be able to address his computer by voice. When you think of eliminating the keyboard and if you don't want to see a screen, you can make a computer very small. That was his objective.

2. Having completed his first goal, he would be able to make a computer the size of a dime and have it do everything a normal computer does.

3. If he could make a computer the size of a dime, addressable by voice, then he should be able to find a way to have it implanted in his body.

4. If the computer could be placed in his body, he then would need to find a way to address it with voice and preferably by using his thoughts or with his voice. He believed he could have a fully functional computer in his body that he could control without anyone knowing it. This required that he develop several passwords to open the computer to his thoughts, as well as to what action he was seeking.

5. Assuming he completed the above step, he would then try to give signals directly to his mitochondria and his ATP to provide extra energy just by signaling. At the same time, signals would go to

the adrenal glands to ensure they were properly pulsed to support the energy release without any bodily complications. In this way, he wouldn't have to wait for something to excite him into action, since he would be able to direct the ATP into action for additional energy. His objective within this objective was to be able to signal for different levels of mitochondria action, preferably three levels.

6. Having completed the above levels, he would write a program that converted various languages to English by doing an analog-to-digital conversion for each language and enter a digitally controlled ROM for each language in the computer. Anyone talking to Axel in a language or by his reading their language would automatically be directed to the proper ROM code and result in the English decode. Once it was in English, it would be sent from the computer to his brain, so he could hear it in English, thereby allowing him to understand the languages of many foreign countries as he heard them. He felt that ten languages would be sufficient. Ten ROM codes would take up very little space in the computer and would be well worth it. Since the computer would be handling words in microseconds, a person speaking would have the English decoded rapidly since it would seem like the person was speaking in slow motion compared to the computer speed, thus giving the computer ample time for sampling and cross-checking the words in an unnoticeable time. There would be no apparent pause, as each word being spoken or read would be deciphered in real time within microseconds; in other words, as it was spoken. Later, he would find a way to send the interpreted English to the computer and have it decoded to the language in question and reverse feed it, so he could answer in the language of the person with whom he was conversing. This was a tougher problem to solve, and Axel thought he could do this when he had eliminated the other issues, but he was confident in the success of this, since words are spoken without any thought most of the time because the brain has learned and maintained that capability.

7. Perhaps, his toughest job would be to use the ATP as his battery. He didn't want to have to change the battery in the computer, which would require cutting it out of his body and then reimplanting it. Since there was no keyboard, no display and most of the time the

computer would be asleep, it wouldn't require much power. The key would be another special password to energize the ATP and use the flow of electrons across a membrane to provide the voltage needed.

8. Since there were times when Axel would want to transmit information via an Internet and this required more power, he had to find a way to do that. He would internally send the message to the computer, and there would be an analog-to-digital conversion, and it would then go through the same ROM used when doing translations. The message would then be transmitted digitally at low power to a transmitter that was on Axel's body and worked off a battery that had to be changed once a year. This could be a very small transmitter in one of his teeth that was powered by a very small lithium ion battery.

Axel thought, *If I could accomplish these objectives, I would be a walking data center with everything built in plus a person with unbelievable strength as I called upon the ATP cycles and their energy levels.*

By Axel's second year of teaching and working on the eight objectives set forth, he found success on several and frustration on others, but serendipity proved to be a big helper for him. It seems when you have the knowledge, the energy, the conviction and maybe something else, that serendipity pops up with some answers. One must be observant to recognize serendipity and its gifts.

Axel thought about the objectives and summarized them in his mind. *The first three of the objectives was fairly straightforward, as I found that using something similar to the approach used for closed captions on television screens pointed me in the right direction. I also could use a voice pickup like the one in the cellular phones. This was quite small. I also experimented with small MIS structures that were very small physical structures made by the same methods as integrated circuits to form a device with a cantilever beam or a diaphragm that is voice activated and vibrates like a very small speaker to pick up and transmit my voice.*

Step number six of developing ROM codes for different languages was fairly simple. Most of these ROM codes were available, having been designed and used on everyday computers in the countries concerned. Axel was able to install these on a hand-wired breadboard and see their functions operate. This gave him half of his desired capability. He could translate the other person's language into English and understand what they were saying. He couldn't answer in their language yet, but he could answer them in English. This would require more work to be able to speak in these other ten languages. Axel was now in a position to do objective four, but he felt he could put that off until he completed the other objectives. He had developed a method of using his thought patterns as an input rather than speaking. It required a voice password spoken, and then it was able to turn on and receive thoughts as though he was inputting them by speaking.

Axel then developed a stripped-down computer with considerable RAM memory and a flash memory for the main memory. With some software changes he had written, he was now able to input into the computer without a keyboard and a fairly large CCD memory for a display if needed. He thought, "*My first venture would not use a display, since I intend to run it on text alone. Perhaps, in the future, I can find a way of using the CCD array in place of my eyes, but that is for the future if everything else works.*"

Step five of being able to direct his signals to the mitochondria was one of the ones he was lucky enough to have serendipity give him the clues he needed. At the same time, the serendipity provided step number seven. While examining his blood under the electron microscope, Axel had an accident that proved to be a lucky one. He was looking at one of the mitochondrion in high enlargement, and he noticed that, every once in a while, it would twitch, and heat was being generated as though the ATP was being activated and then giving off heat. He was fortunate enough to have a thermocouple placed in the blob of blood and could see that the meter's dial hand moved every so often. He wondered why. He couldn't see the ATP, but he knew that when it was going through the citric acid cycle, that it gave off heat as a by-product. Axel went about finding what was generating this activity. He waited and watched, and nothing happened. Axel was confused because the activity had stopped, and he hadn't done anything to stop it, let alone know what started it.

Axel stopped doing anything and thought about it for a while. What he had seen as activity started when he had been working on the electron microscope. So, he decided to go back to that point and see if it would start again. As he began to move his hands around to work on the electron microscope, he saw the activity occur as it had before. He decided to stop doing anything and to sit still for fifteen minutes to see if the activity occurred while he was motionless, and, lo and behold, nothing happened. Then, he began the hand movements again, and there it happened again; the mitochondrion twitched. Something he was doing with his hands and movement was causing this action.

After about an hour of experimenting, he realized that he was building up enough static charge to cause this phenomenon to occur. So, a pulse of electricity was what was needed to activate the mitochondrion. *"But, how much of a pulse?"* he asked himself. Axel went to the equipment cabinet and pulled out the pulse generator. He set it up and started experimenting with short low-voltage pulses with a short duty cycle. It immediately worked, but that wasn't what he was looking for. He wanted to find the lowest pulse with the least energy that could activate the cell. He took the pulse to a shorter duty cycle with a pulse of one volt in height with a pulse width of one microsecond and a duty cycle such that the next pulse appeared a thousand microseconds (one millisecond) later. This still was enough energy to activate the cell. Then, he decreased the duty cycle, so he got a pulse every second. This also was enough energy to activate the cell. So, then he cut the width of the pulse to five hundred nanoseconds and one second between pulses, and this was also enough to activate the cell.

Axel's thoughts then told him that he should just use a single pulse of five hundred nanoseconds in width and half a volt in height and no repetition of pulses. When the pulse generator was set to this level and activated, this again proved to be a viable amount of energy to put the cell into this brief motion and to generate heat. The very interesting feature of this phenomenon was that the amount of heat being detected by the thermocouple was the same now as it was when he had been putting more energy into the pulse. This told him the cycle of the mitochondrion was almost independent of the energy being applied by the pulse. It must not take much to reach a threshold, and then the cell goes into action; when it completes its activation cycle, it is through and stops.

The key was to find the lowest threshold that would activate this cycle, and it was obvious from his experiments so far that it a very low energy was needed to activate one ATP episode. Axel set the pulse generator to the lowest level the pulse generator could achieve. This was a pulse with a width of one nanosecond (one billionth of a second) and only a millivolt (a thousandth of a volt) in height followed by an off time of one second before the next pulse occurred, so it had a very low duty cycle. Even with this low energy being applied, it was enough to cause the reaction. At that point, Axel decided to stop for the night and figure out how to come up with an even smaller and measurable pulse of energy. If he could find that, then he would be able to determine how much energy he would have to supply to his internal computer to activate the mitochondria and reach different energy levels for his body.

His big hope was to find how to activate about a third of the mitochondria, and two thirds and almost all of them. He should be able to find these energy levels if he could find a pulse generator that provided lower energy levels than this one he had. He also would be able to determine the amount of power needed to power up the internal power supply that was used to power his internal computer. He should be able to find one in the laboratory by the next day, and then he could make these measurements. It might take more than one evening, but, if he started tomorrow, then he would be able to determine how close he was to finding the answers. Little did he know that this wasn't about to happen in the next few evenings due to other circumstances. This turned out to be a very important evening in his life, and it would affect what was to happen the next day.

Determining how to power his body computer

The next evening after the classes and having a bite to eat, Axel settled down with the intent to work on finding the energy needed to activate the mitochondrion and then find out how many of them he would have to activate to provide his various energy needs. One thing he did decide was that without a battery to get the computer to start, he had no way to provide a pulse to the mitochondria when he wanted to.

Therefore, he would eventually have to provide the computer that was put inside him with enough power to begin with; therefore, he would have to have it installed in the "on" position by holding a charge on it while it was being installed. Once it was in his body and in the "on" position, he could then provide the pulse from it to activate the part of the mitochondria that would be needed. Therefore, the computer power would have to be in the "on" position at all times. This might not be a problem, since the computer chip was from a laptop computer that used very low power and could be put in the sleep mode without turning it off—ever.

Axel had found a lower-power pulse generator during the day, and he hooked it up in preparation for his experiments. As Axel prepared to do his experimenting, he noted the time and put it in his notebook: 6:58 PM. He hadn't set the pen back down when he heard some screaming coming from the floor below. He leaped up and ran to the stairwell and started down as his heart kept pounding away. He could tell the screaming was coming from more than one person. He got to the level below, and it was fairly dark in the hallway, but he could hear from what direction the screams were coming. He took the left hallway and ran to the next intersection, and, down on the right side, there were two guys that looked like they were beating up two girls. As he ran down the hall, he yelled for them to take off, and his heart was pumping and his breathing was coming rapidly.

As he reached the scene, he saw two big guys grabbing at two young women. He grabbed the one guy and tossed him onto the wall and turned to grab the other. He was a big fellow that could have played on the Steelers football team, and he leaped at Axel. Axel, more or less, caught him in the air and threw him about ten feet away. By this time, the other guy was back up and had pulled a knife. He surged toward Axel with the blade extended, and Axel made a rapid move to the right and grabbed his arm by the wrist and pulled him around in a circle, and he could feel the guy's shoulder blade being pulled out of its socket. The guy screamed, and, with a rapid motion, Axel reached down and grabbed him by the leg and lifted him over his head, swirled around, and threw him about ten feet against the railing of another stairwell. As the man's back hit the railing, he could hear it snap, and it sounded like a board cracking, and he slunk to the floor in utter pain.

As Axel turned to pick up the closest girl off the floor, he saw the "Steeler-type guy" coming at him again. Axel didn't turn away, but he rushed at him instead. This must have confused "the Steeler," since he could see Axel was about seventy-five to one hundred pounds lighter than he was, and he didn't expect him to fight back. Axel shifted to the side as the guy reached him, and he grabbed him by his left arm and left leg as he slipped by and Axel whirled and threw him against the same railing as his buddy. Again, he heard a big thump, and the guy dropped near his buddy. They were both collapsed on the floor next to the railing. By this time, Axel could hear other footsteps from the people a level below running up the stairwell, and one of them was a security guard. He immediately ran toward Axel, thinking he was one of the thugs.

At that point, the one girl ran to a position between the guard and Axel with her hands in the air like a quarterback who just threw a touchdown pass. "No," she screamed. "Not him; he is the one who helped. He is the good guy."

This brought the guard to a halt, and he shouted, "What's happening?"

The girl told him that those two guys jumped her girl friend, Ellen, and her as they were leaving to go home. They had worked late in the lab on some experiments and were shocked when this occurred. Both of the men had grabbed them by the blouses and were in the process of tearing them off of them when this guy ran down the hall and surprised them. The guard looked at the two that were moaning on the floor like two big rag dolls. Then, he looked at Axel and let out with, "And you did this, how?"

Axel sort of mumbled something out like, "I got excited when I heard them screaming, and my adrenaline must have been flowing from being scared, and I did something that I could not normally have done." Axel thought to himself, *Now I know some of the potential I have with the hyperventilating and the overactive mitochondria.* Axel immediately got a tired feeling, so he sat down on the floor and took some deep breaths. In a few seconds, he felt up to par and got up to take part in any conversation after that.

Meanwhile, the two girls were giving Axel hugs and thanking him, and they couldn't stop praising what had occurred. "I never saw anyone that strong," the one girl said. "He tossed them around like they were rag dolls."

Axel was feeling better and feeling a little embarrassed by the attention he was receiving and said he needed to go back to his work in the lab above. The security guard had called 911, and the police were arriving. Soon, Axel was answering their questions as they helped the medical people take the two assailants to the ambulance below. The dialogue with the police followed the same dialogue Axel previously had conveyed to the security guard. Likewise, the girls were answering the same questions. Several times they asked if Axel used any weapons, which was then followed by a search of Axel's clothing to see if he had anything in his pockets or under his pant legs. They did a complete scouring of not only the area on the floor but on the floor below and above.

Axel listened as the two girls provided their experience and kept pointing toward Axel and praising his heroism. Both girls were good looking, but the one girl was beautiful, and her name was Tori Madison. Axel watched and listened at the same time and found himself drawn to her in some way. She had dark hair and the bluest of eyes, a combination that one does not usually find together.

He listened to her description of the events of the night, wanting to know, as did the police, how all this came about. "We are both juniors in the school of biology and were doing a lab experiment that was part of our normal schooling. We come here three afternoons a week to work in the lab. We start at about 2:30 and usually finish about 6:30. We are required to complete three labs a week with a minimal amount of time of four hours for each lab. We usually are done in four hours, but sometimes we might go a half hour or so longer."

"After the lab, we normally go to Kathleen's coffee shop for coffee and a roll. If we are really hungry and want something more to eat, we go to Nardi's Italian restaurant and have spaghetti. Both of them are located about a half mile from the school, and, one week, I drive, and, the following week, Ellen drives. Tonight was my night to drive. I picked up Ellen at her dorm, and we probably arrived here at around two today. We finished our work at about 6:30 this evening and spent about a half hour cleaning up and gathering our belongings and paperwork. When we leave in the evening and no other students are using the lab, we are required to lock up. This only requires that, as we leave, one of us turns the latch just before closing the door, and, when it closes, it is automatically locked."

"We just had done this and were beginning to discuss some of our lab results when these two men came around the hall corner and grabbed us. We screamed, but there wasn't anyone around that could hear us. The man who grabbed me held his hand against my mouth and began to fondle my breasts as he held me close to him. I tried to kick and scratch, but he was too big and soon had me in a clutch hold. He took his hand away from my breasts and reached behind and pulled out a knife. While he was doing this, I screamed loudly again, but then the knife was next to my throat, and he half whispered, 'Scream again, and I cut your throat.' After that, I almost fainted and was in a kind of shock."

"Then, I heard some scrambling and a voice hollering out, 'Take off,' and, shortly after that, the man released me and began defending himself against this man who had come to our rescue. I looked and saw this young guy running toward this big man and didn't know what to expect. I didn't know what he could possibly do to relieve the situation. I soon found out. He was marvelous. He grabbed the man and threw him against the wall. As he was doing that, the other man let go of Ellen and started toward our savior."

"I thought the man holding me had been big, but this guy looked huge. He made the other guy look like a kid. As he leaped toward our savior, I was amazed that he was grabbed and thrown in the air about fifteen or twenty feet against the wall with his head hitting and sort of knocking him out. But then, the man who had grabbed me had got up off the floor, and, with his knife, he came at our savior. As he pierced the air with his knife, the man shifted rapidly out of his way and grabbed the arm that held the knife and jerked it, and I could hear him scream as the knife flew, and then the was being twirled around like a rag doll and then thrown against the railing where you found him."

"Our savior then turned as if he knew the bigger guy would soon be on him. Instead of backing off, he ran toward the other bigger guy and grabbed him by the arm and leg and lifted him up and whirled him around like another rag doll and threw him against the rail over there where you found the two of them. They were both unconscious, and the young guy came toward us and wanted to know if we were all right. We just stood there speechless. All of this had only taken a few minutes, but it seemed like hours. He asked me again, if I was all right. I nodded, and then Ellen said, 'Maybe.' We stood there and examined ourselves while looking at this obviously strong man who had come to our rescue. Who was this doll? Who are you? We had asked. He was just going to say when you (the security guard) arrived and stood a few feet away to analyze the situation. He was trying to find out who the good guys were and who the bad guys were. I don't blame him, since the big ones lying against the floor and railing looked like they were the ones in trouble."

Tori spoke out, "Those are the bad guys there, and this man is our savior."

The guard ran over to the two on the floor and took a handcuff and hooked a wrist from one and put the handcuff through a rail and hooked the other cuff to the other guy's wrist. There they lay with their two arms extended toward one another with cuff to cuff through one of the rails. They were ready for the freezer. The guard had called 911 earlier when he began to run up the stairs to survey the situation, and the police cars could be heard pulling up outside with their sirens wailing.

The police wanted Axel to go with them and the two girls to the station and have their depositions taken. Axel asked if he should drive, and they said that they would drive and then bring him back afterward. Before long, Axel was in the police station telling the same story to a woman who was typing this all down. After being there for about an hour and a half, they brought some paperwork for Axel to sign. It included the date, time, his full name, address, telephone number, and e-mail address. Below this personal information, there was a typed description of what had occurred as Axel saw it. Axel was sure the girls would each have to sign their impressions of the events of this evening. He hoped that their versions and his matched. After that, the deposition was signed by Axel.

One detective asked him a few personal questions about how he had developed his strength as he walked Axel to his car. Axel indicated that he was the smaller of fraternal twins and had to defend himself against his larger brother most of his life and then had participated in several sports in high school and continued to follow a weight and bodybuilding program while in college and since teaching college.

"You never know who is going to try to take a whack at the teacher," Axel commented.

The detective asked a few personal questions as they approached the place where Axel's car was parked in the instructor's parking spaces outside the main school building. He told Axel he would wait till he pulled the car out of the parking space while handing Axel his card. He looked at it, and it read, "Wilson Cooks, County Detective." He stuck it in his wallet, and the detective said if he ever needed anything to give him a call. With that, Axel was on his way. Soon, he was home. It was 10:30 at night. Axel thought, *"It sure is hard to believe that the last four hours were so dynamic, and now everything seems so quiet and still, but the stillness sure is nice."*

Axel and Tori

Axel had rented a couple of rooms above a garage that was only about five miles from the school, just far enough away to be out of the dorm area, local renting, and the school traffic. It cost a little more, but it was quiet, and the house was private and gave him the kind of environment he needed to further his education and work on his computer hobby. There were steps that went up the side of the garage that took him up to the higher level and gave him a private entrance. He rented his place from a nice couple in their early fifties. They had two children, a boy and a girl, and both had gone to college and graduated; they were married while going to school.

So, they were off on their own with the boy working for Motorola in Phoenix, Arizona, in the semiconductor industry, and the girl and her family was living in Colorado. *In some ways, I have been lucky*, he thought. *My bad luck related to my dad passing away of a heart attack when I was fourteen. Fortunately, he left an insurance policy for Adam and me to ensure both of us would go to a good school and advance in life. Fortune followed both of us, as both Adam and I received scholarships, and we ended up in the top five of our high school graduating class. With full scholarships, both of us were able to save the insurance money for the time we left college and began to earn an honest and worthy living. My teaching of labs and a freshman class in biology has provided me enough to live well, and the extra money I needed to live away from campus came from the dividends I was receiving on the equities I had purchased using the insurance money.*

He also received some interest from the money he had in the bank. Life had been good, and now he wanted to take advantage of his mother's couple of days living outside a wrecked airplane carrying him for a couple of days past Adam's birth and turning that into something positive. Axel thought, *I need to take the extra mitochondria she was able to provide me and make something very positive out of this accident of nature.* He now knew he was strong, and he wanted to use this strength to do something good in life.

Axel continued going over the previous chain of events in his mind as though they were just now happening. He thought to himself, *Today is Thursday, and I have taught my Thursday lab and one freshman class, so the rest of the day is mine, and I intend to spend it working on the objectives that got interrupted the night before.* Axel began working on the computer in the lab on the third floor that was right next to his office.

He had hardly begun when he actually smelled something pleasant. It smelled like nice perfume, and he knew there was a person nearby, a woman, before he saw her. Axel turned in his chair, and there was Tori standing in the doorway of the lab. "Hi there," she said in a quiet voice that was like music to his ears.

This is the good-looking one, he thought to himself. "Hello," Axel said, as he got up off the swirling leather chair and advanced to meet her. "How are you doing today?" he asked, as he looked into those big blue eyes.

"About as good as I felt before the episode last evening," she responded.

Then, they spent about half an hour talking about her schooling and how it was going. In a few months, she would be past her junior year and would have the summer off before the final year. She had done well in her studies. Axel knew that because he had gone to the main office upon arriving at school today and looked through the records that showed her age, her various grades, her major, and some other less important information. She had just turned twenty-one a month ago, and her GPA was at 3.35 for her first two and a half years at the university. In a month, she will have finished three years of her biology major. Axel had thought about this all day and wondered how a woman that good looking could be that intelligent.

He was awakened from his daydreams and looking at her by her voice interrupting this train of thought. "Are you with me?" she asked.

Axel nodded his head and told her he was thinking about some work he was doing when she arrived. "No, that's a lie," he said, "I was thinking how beautiful you are." She blushed at that comment, but Axel could tell she liked the comment. Axel thought to himself, *You dummy. Now she is going to think I am hitting on her rather than just surprised to see her, but I am hitting on her.*

After that initial outburst, the conversation settled down, and they passed the pleasantries of the day. She said that she was going to be taking off for her dorm and wanted to be sure she told him how much she had appreciated what he had done for her and Ellen the day before. "You know," she said, "when I looked up and saw you running toward us last night; I actually felt that we had placed you in an untenable position. There was no way you were going to survive the encounter, and Ellen and I would have been victims of these beasts. You completely surprised me, and I think you surprised those two guys also."

"Yes, I got a little lucky. I think they were so sure of themselves with you two girls that it carried over when they saw me and probably felt it was their night to win. So, I caught them off guard it would seem."

"That might be true to some extent," she said, "but you showed energy that was beyond normal. Have you been involved in this kind of thing before?"

He kept staring at her as she spoke. He was completely entranced. He had not paid that much attention to most of the girls here in school or women outside of school until this time. He was too busy working on his thesis and his computer hobby. This meeting with this woman was unique and was kind of weakening. Once again, she broke his train of thought as she reminded him that he was in deep thought and staring at her. "Sorry," he said, "that was not intended, and this time I can't lie. It wasn't about my work; it was about how adorable you are."

She smiled and blushed and sort of tried to wisp that embarrassing look away with a comment. "Is that one of your standard lines with women?"

"No, no, no, please don't take it that way. I am not used to being in this position and find it odd for me to be taken this way. I have never said that to another woman. I think it might be the contrast between last night and how you appeared then to now when you are relaxed and quite charming. You actually took me off guard more than I took you off guard."

She smiled and said she had to go. She had decided on her days when she would be in the lab and that she would be leaving with the rest of the students so as to be lost in the crowd. She didn't want what happened last night to happen again. Axel could understand that and walked with her to the stairwell. As they got to the top of the stairs, Axel asked her how Ellen and she were going to handle the three lab nights a week when they had to leave at a later time. "I don't know," she said. "I have been thinking about that all last night and all today and have a fear that it will be difficult at best to stay until 6:30 and walk out into the evening."

With that comment, Axel heard himself volunteering to meet her and Ellen each evening and walk them to their car. It just came out of his mouth without thinking. This was unusual, since he didn't give any of his evening time away from his objectives. She stood on the top stair and looked up at Axel and said, "I have been hoping you would say that. I believe Ellen and I would feel quite safe if you were around. We only have about six weeks left of this lab, so it won't be forever. Do you mind? Are you really sure?"

Axel told her it would be a pleasure, and he would look forward to seeing them on Monday, Wednesday, and Friday when their late lab class was completed. "It will only take fifteen minutes to walk you to your car, and I will be back to my work within a half hour. That is nothing. I can stay an extra half hour and catch up. I don't have anywhere to go. I'll see you tomorrow at 6:30. I will come down to the lab, so you can see me and know that everything is cool for you and Ellen. See you tomorrow."

After that, Axel turned and went back to his work. As he walked away, he thought about her. *She is pretty tall and well built for her height. I am six foot one, and she comes to my shoulders in flat shoes, so she must be five foot seven or eight inches tall. I bet she looks great in a dress and high-heeled shoes. It would make her about five foot ten or so.*

Then, he thought about what the doctor had said about his body and how his lungs were about 30 percent bigger than most people. *He was right. As thin as I am, I have a big chest for this body. I need a size 44 jacket. The doctor said my chest is shaped different from most guys. They have flat chests, and he called mine a "chicken breast" type. It doesn't go flat across, but it protrudes out more. I guess I need that for my lung capacity. Tori looks like she has a good lung capacity. She doesn't wear dresses to show off her cleavage, but I can tell she is healthy in that area. Most of the time, she is wearing dungarees and a sweater or blouse that hangs outside her dungarees. I guess there are a lot of things I like about her. I like her full head of hair and the color that is slightly blond and there are highlighted streaks of blonder hair that make her beautiful. She has great eyes that are blue like Lake Tahoe in Northern California. She is almost always smiling and her teeth are white and regular in shape. I guess I like the way she talks also. It always has a quiet reserve to it when she is serious and it raises up in tone when she is smiling while talking but not too high a tone. She is nice and tall for a woman. She must be five foot eight without heels and the other day she had high heels on and she came up to my nose. I guess she is just a great looking woman from head to toe. I think I am going to enjoy walking her to her car after their lab. Maybe I can get further than the car with her. I'll see,* he thought.

Establishing the computer energy

The following day, Axel was sitting next to his computer with thoughts of Tori in his head. It was hard to get back to this work of enjoyment. He didn't think that would ever happen. *This is my number one priority in life. I can't let a pretty woman disrupt that in any way. On the other hand, I believe she relaxes me when she is talking, and that should be conducive to thinking with a clearer head once I am back on my objectives, the thought of her seems to take my brain off of course. Like a ship with a broken sail.*

Axel had borrowed a pulse generator that was able to go to lower voltages and narrower pulses, and he always had the duty cycle to play with. The duty cycle is the time measured between the leading edge of one pulse to the leading edge of the following pulse. The longer the time, the lower the average power being consumed or generated. This pulse generator could go down to pulses of a nanosecond wide with heights varying from one thousandth of a volt (a millivolt) and a duty cycle anywhere from a microsecond to a second. He decided to work the opposite direction that night.

He would start with the lowest energy to see if he could succeed in activating the single mitochondrion at the lowest energy. If that worked, then he wouldn't have to do any further testing, since that was the lowest capability this pulse generator could generate. Axel set the pulse generator at a pulse width of one nanosecond (a billionth of a second), during which time, it would put out a pulse of one hundredth of a volt (0.01 volt or 10 millivolts) in pulse height, and he would try a duty cycle of one microsecond. This would mean the short pulse would only be on for one short pulse of one nanosecond and off for 999 nanoseconds, and the next pulse would hit. This would reduce the power to approximately one thousandth of the already low power of the pulse he tried the other night. He knew if this worked, then he could put out a pulse of this amount with the computer that would be installed, and he could control it. He also knew if this worked, then he would have enough power to activate a considerable number of the mitochondria.

Soon, he was set up and turned the pulse generator on, and the mitochondrion was immediately activated as Axel could tell by what he saw on the thermocouple meter that was measuring the heat. There was one major problem: it appeared to stay on. He immediately turned the generator off to ensure the mitochondrion didn't overheat. Then, he sat there and kept looking at the mitochondrion for minutes trying to determine what he was seeing. "Nuts," he shouted out. "You nut, Axel." It was no wonder it appeared to be on. With a duty cycle that was a pulse every millionth of a second, it was probably turning on and off, but it was such a small duty cycle that his eyes could not see the on and off, and the thermocouple meter was trying to pulse on and off, but it couldn't follow the duty cycle either. The response time of the thermocouple meter was too long and wasn't able to go to zero between pulses.

What I need to do is open up the time on the duty cycle to one second. This would give this short and low voltage pulse at a rate of one per second, and my eyes could follow the pulsing of the mitochondrion, and so could the thermocouple. This would be a really low power level, since there would be this one pulse that took a billionth of a second, and then it would be off for 999,999,999 billionths of a second, he thought.

Now, Axel was ready to go again. He doubted this would be enough power to pulse the organelle, but, as he turned the pulse generator on and held his hand behind his back so as not to generate any static electricity and get a false signal, the generator was now on. Axel peered at the display of the electron microscope, and, lo and behold, he saw a pulse and then another. He glanced aside to see what the thermocouple was doing. It looked like a referee counting out a fighter who just got knocked down: 1, 2, 3, and so forth. The pulses were coming, and the meter could not make it to zero. It would hit a high and flicker around the high, trying to drop lower, but, before it could drop very low, the next pulse would come and move it back up to its high. Axel's heart was beating like a drum. He believed he was almost turning his own body mitochondria on from pure excitement. He turned the pulse generator off, sat back, and let out a huge sigh of relief. He looked back at the display, and the mitochondrion was still and remained functional. *No pulses from the generator and no pulses from the mitochondrion. That's great,* he thought.

What he had witnessed blew his mind, and he sat back and wondered if this was right. If he could activate the individual mitochondrion with that small a pulse of power (energy times time), then he knew he could activate many with a pulse from a computer that might not even be able to put out that small a pulse of power. Then, he decided to figure it out another way. How could he mathematically determine approximately how much power a normal human being required to activate their body mitochondria?

The average person in the United States eats approximately two thousand table calories each day to replace the energy they used. These calories are converted to energy by the body, especially the sugars and carbohydrates. These two thousand calories per day equal so many joules of energy. Every joule per second equals a watt. A watt is one joule per second. One table calorie equals 4,184 joules. Two thousand calories per day equals 8,368,000 joules a day. To get the power in a second, he had to divide that by the number of seconds in a day to determine how much power this would be in a second. There are twenty-four hours in a day and three thousand six hundred seconds in an hour, which calculates to 86,400 seconds in a day. Divide the watts per day of 8,368,000 by this number of seconds in a day, and a person uses 96.85 watts a second. This energy consumption is about the energy of a one hundred-watt bulb in one second, and, if it burned for twenty-four hours in a day, then it would equal the energy that man burns up in a day. So, *"We are like a one hundred-watt light bulb walking around or sleeping for a day and burning the energy of a one hundred-watt bulb."*

Since there are a million microseconds in a second, this means we use 96.85 divided by a million, and we get 96.85 microwatts in a microsecond or 96.85 nanowatts in a billionth of a second from the food we eat each day. This would equate to about a billionth of a billionth of a watt in the time and duty cycle of the pulse generator. With the pulse in the generator being only one nanosecond wide over a very long duty cycle, the power from the pulse generator is approximately one billionth of a nanowatt or one billionth of a billionth of a watt. So, the pulse generator energy is in the same ballpark as the amount of energy of food calories one takes in a billionth of a billionth of a second each day while consuming two thousand calories. This checks out.

Axel shouted out, "It works!"

He was feeling that the response he was seeing from the mitochondrion to the pulse made sense, and, in fact, he believed he would have more than enough energy for a single activation of a mitochondrion. With this in mind, he worked on methods to activate one thousand five hundred mitochondria and two thousand five hundred mitochondria simultaneously, since that was half the mitochondria he had in each of his muscle cells. Axel thought about this, *If I could achieve that, I know that a pulse from the computer would be able to lift the energy level to a level that is close to the level that I must be achieving when I get excited and hyperventilate. There would be enough energy to activate the adrenal glands as well and ensure this system stays under control and provides the extra sugar for the mitochondria. Dr. Newcome said, after the pulse and the use of the energy, my body would be able to use this activation, and, afterward, my system would be able to return to standard operating procedure without being overly fatigued. I hope he was right. The day will come for me to check this out.*

In order to have this chip consolidated to one chip; Axel had a friend in the semiconductor business who had the capability of doing this. He called Jay Husher and told him of his custom chip. He didn't divulge its use to him, but his company took many jobs like this where they didn't know the end application. The chip and the process required to produce it was one similar to one of their standard foundry, and he had to add only the ROM codes and the pickup sensor, and then he had to place additional wires where he needed them. Jay said they could make those changes and have a chip ready in four weeks. It cost Axel a nice sum of money for the company to produce the chip, but it was well worth it if it produced the results Axel was looking for.

In five weeks, Axel received his chip and began to test it out on his test table in the laboratory. The first thing he checked was his ability to activate and use it with voice commands. This worked quite well, as he had presumed it would. Next, he had some ROMs with various languages on them. He checked out the French, Spanish, German, Russian, Portuguese, Chinese, Japanese, Iranian, and Iraqi, and he left one open for later. First, he played French and had the computer signal to a printer, and he saw it print the French in English. Next, it was Spanish and the same results.

Over the course of two nights, Axel had checked out each of these. During the evening, he made a composite CD that included each of these languages coming in various orders. In each of them, he copied a couple of sentences, so, when he was done, there were nine languages mixed with several sentences of each. Then, he turned the CD on while the computer listened and the printer printed out the mixed languages into English. The experiment was a success. This proved the computer had the capability of picking up several languages interspersed without a problem. Axel was excited. He felt this proved the capability of this objective.

Next, he turned off the printer and picked up a small tape recorder. He now wanted to turn on the CD and have the computer provide him the words, and Axel would speak them out in English for the tape recorder to tape. He pushed the button on the computer and turned on the CD. The various languages burst out, and the computer converted them to English that he was able to hear from the small voice and analog sensor, which he would then speak out in loud English for the tape recorder to pick up. Then, he compared the tape recorder to the printed version and found a few hiccups that he had to work on, but he knew he was well on his way to putting this objective to bed. Sometime in the next week, Axel would see if he was able to use the output pulse of the computer to raise his internal energy level via the mitochondria and adrenal glands. He needed to find this out before having the chip implanted in his body.

By the middle of the second year, Axel had completed every exercise he had intended for this computer and his body's system. He had developed code names for activation of the computer and various activation levels for three energy levels of his mitochondria. The computer would decode these inputs and be able to have three levels of energy, so he developed codes that would turn on one thousand six hundred, two thousand six hundred, and four thousand mitochondria of each muscle cell. On one weekend, he took the equipment needed, borrowed a cabin from a friend, and traveled up to Lake Tahoe to make the tests in secrecy. The chip was still not installed in his body, so these were safe tries to see if they even worked. The code for activation of the computer was Axelvation zero, and, for the three levels of energy, the codes were Axelvation one, Axelvation two, and Axelvation three. These were codes he knew he wouldn't forget. Axel got up early that Saturday morning and ate a good breakfast with good energy. The breakfast included cereal with milk, sugar, and bananas, along with a sweet roll, a V8 juice, and two slices of toast with margarine.

Testing the computer and Axel's body functions

Axel took the equipment outside and set it up on a picnic table beside the trees. This was an ideal place to try this, since it was remote from the world and had a few elements about the cabin that would provide him some physical things he wanted to try on the various energy levels. He had an ax and a fairly large piece of a trunk from a tree. He had tried to chop the large hunk of wood that was about ten inches thick but with no success. With the computer and everything hooked up on the table and wired into his system, he then said out loud, "Axelvation one," and he saw the red light go on beside the computer (which he wouldn't have when it was in his body). Then, he said "Axelvation two" and picked up the ax as he felt his body hyperventilating, and, with one swift loop of the ax, he cut the wood that had defied him in two pieces. So, he knew the system was working, and he would now try the next energy level.

This cabin had a walkout porch on the second level. It was ten feet above ground, and there was a three-foot wooden railing around the porch. So, he wanted to jump at least fourteen feet and land on the porch. Even if he could do it, he would need to have the skill to land properly. Would it be like jumping over a three-foot fence that he could normally navigate? In order to make sure he didn't kill himself, he put one of the mattresses from the bedroom on that level out on the porch and another on the ground below the porch in case he didn't make it and fell back to earth. When he was ready, he spoke out in an excited voice, "Axelvation two." With that, he could feel the hyperventilation go into effect, and he bent his knees and jumped. He leaped well over the porch rail and all and was actually about another three feet over when he descended onto the mattress. The landing felt like he had just jumped down from about six feet or so. It gave him a jolt, but it was bearable, as he flexed his legs as he landed on the soft and springy mattress. He was glad he had decided to put the mattress there for safety reasons. Axel was very excited about this accomplishment.

The key thing is that he leaped as if he was doing something normal like jumping over a two-foot fence. It wasn't a sharp jolt, and he was sent flying. The normalcy of the practice got him over his scared feelings. He had been wondering, if it did work, if it would it feel abnormal and jerky. He decided to try it again without the mattress and see if he could limit the jump height. He went through various means of changing the height and the landing and found that the control came from the amount of knee bending and effort he put forth as he sprang from that position. "This was quite a success," he said out loud. With these levels done, he became concerned about using the fourth password (Axelvation three). He knew it would give him tremendous energy, and he saw nothing that he wanted to accomplish at that cabin that would require that amount of energy. He would save it for a well-needed time, in an emergency, more or less. With this success today, he couldn't wait till the device was installed in his body. He knew that would be some time over the next few months.

The only one who knew of his adventure was Adam. Adam and Axel were so close since they were little kids that there wasn't anything that each of them would keep from the other. Every once in a while, Adam would give Axel a phone call and ask about the progress on the project. When Axel was about two months into this thing, he told Adam that he would need someone to implant the device in his body that he could trust with the operation and the target he wanted to achieve. Adam told Axel to leave that up to him. He worked for a secret agency out of the Pentagon, and they had doctors that did weird operations all the time on animals and people to check out new detection methods they had developed or something they found an alien to this country was doing.

At the end of Axel's stay at the cabin, he called Adam and told him about the results and reminded him that he would need the operation soon. Adam told him he would get back to him in the near future. He had a personal friend and confidant named Dr. Edward Kim that headed up the division that Adam worked in. On many occasions, Adam had kept Kim up to date about what might be needed to carry this to completion. They had discussed what was required, and he had pre-warned him recently that progress was occurring and would need his help in the near future about what was needed to be done. He did not tell him Axel's name and said this would be kept a secret, so that Axel wasn't personally attacked by any alien wanting to know any secrets or kidnapping him to try to determine how to copy this capability. One thing they couldn't copy was Axel's inborn ability to use his mitochondria of plenty.

Kim would have to figure out where the device would be located in the body to allow these commands to work without causing any side effects. Adam said that Kim was excited about the project and had done a computer model on using this "black box" to insert in the body and to determine the optimum location to perform the needed functions. Adam said that Kim had run the model only recently and only had to make a few minor adjustments to achieve the goal set forth. Axel asked Adam how his name was to be kept a secret. Adam said that the project would be given a code name that didn't relate at all to the function to be performed. It would be filed in the secret files of the agency with only Kim having knowledge of the function and Adam, alone, being privy to the function and the recipient. The code name of the project would be **"The Follower."** This made sense because Adam had always kidded Axel about his being the follower in their births and several other events in their lives.

As Axel worked on the computer to ensure the objectives were being met, he had several reservations about some objectives being met and some functions that needed modified to make sure they were easier to accomplish. For one, he would have all languages being spoken to him go directly to the ROM code sections of the computer, including English. The software was set up, so, when any language was being spoken to him, it was directed to the decode section of the computer, and it sampled it; if it was English, then it went through an automatic decode in the analog-to-digital converter and went directly to the CPU to be crunched and read into memory for storage in case Axel wanted an exact word-for-word printout later. The printout would be done external to Axel's body. In parallel, Axel's normal hearing and understanding of the message would be performed as it was normally done, and he needed the computer only used for storage in case he wanted to review any of it at a later time. All other languages would go to the decode section and would be sampled by the ten ROM codes, and, as soon as it found a match, the conversion to English would be done automatically, and that ROM would gate which language and where the CPU was to store it. In this way, there was a storage section of the main storage that only stored Italian and one for German and the same for the ten languages to be stored. In this way, these sections were not only receiving and decoding the language into English but storing it in a select memory bank for that language only. Since it was in a specific memory bank, if Axel wanted to retrieve it, he could do the retrieve in English or in the language that it was spoken in. He had checked this out, and everything was working as designed.

The thing that bothered Axel was how he could eventually speak the language as well as understand it when it was spoken. Making these special memory banks for each of the languages made this much easier to do, but Axel didn't know how to provide this to his brain functions to allow him to speak those languages. He had discussed this issue with Adam when he first got started on it. One day, he got a call from Adam, and he said that Kim had worked out how to provide these functions. He had analyzed this on a software program he had invented and knew how to give the proper signals to the specific locations in Axel's brain that would allow this speaking function to be carried out. Axel was really excited about that.

Even though he was close to his doctorate in biology, he didn't have the capability for trying this function without the software and equipment that Kim had access to. Kim wanted to know if he could borrow the breadboard of Axel's design, so he could hook it up through his software program to try out the function. If things worked properly, he would be able to have a CD or memory stick that had different languages on it. He would then have the CD turned on and have the various messages given in the various languages with a delay of two minutes between each foreign language.

If the system worked correctly, then Axel's computer would pick up the phrases, convert them digitally to English, and send them to their proper foreign language storage areas as Axel had described. They would stay there for ten seconds, and then the CPU would fetch them from the memory and decode them back through the ROM codes, and out would come the message in the foreign language, and it would be played back through the recorder's speaker. Kim would then hear the message in English followed by the foreign tongue as though he was speaking it. This would check out the system's ability to interpret properly and send the proper signals.

He had no way of checking it out with Axel's brain, so he had a software model of the brain to send the message to and hear its interpretation come back. Each two minutes, the next foreign message would follow in a different language and would be checked out. He got it working well after resolving a few problems. Kim felt he had worked out the problems on Axel's computer, and he told Adam to send that message to Axel.

In the actual case, all of the functions that Kim checked out on Axel's computer would work much faster on the chip that Axel had and would be installed in his body. Any foreign language message would go to the computer and would be deciphered in English and stored in the section that stored this foreign language only. The English version would go to his brain, and, when Axel answered, it would be answered in the language needed and out would come the voice in a normal level in the language that had been spoken. An example would be someone speaking in German asking Axel how to get to his home. The computer would receive the message, decode it in English, and then store the English in the German storage space of the computer while sending the message to Axel's brain in English. He would answer by thinking the answer in English. This answer would be sent from his brain in English directly to the decode section for German and would be retrieved in German and sent to Axel's brain, and the answer would be spoken by Axel in German as to how to get to his house.

When Axel eventually was able to perform this function the first time, he was startled to hear his voice speak this German tongue. He almost turned around to see who was behind him and answering. The computer time for any of these messages was in microseconds, so there was no delay in Axel speaking the answer to any foreign question or directive. It's amazing how fast a computer can do things. The message in any of nine foreign languages would be spoken and would be answering in real time.

The memory in the computer was several thousand gigabytes, so it could store more than Axel would ever need. In order to keep his computer memory fresh, each night all the messages received by the computer that day would queue up to be erased at midnight. If Axel wanted to keep one, he would say, "Keep this message" or "Keep all the Iranian," and it would store it back in its proper storage place. All others that were not directed elsewhere by eight o'clock the next morning would automatically be erased. This gave Axel eight hours to make that decision. If something came up that impeded his keeping any of the messages, then he would say "delay erasing," and it would delay for a day.

Tori

Soon, the laboratory sessions were completed by Tori and Ellen. This left Axel sort of empty feeling, since he enjoyed walking them to their cars three times a week. Sometimes, he would ask her if she was doing anything the next day or that evening, and they would always seem to find the time to see each other. By now, she knew Axel's feelings for her, and he was beginning to wonder when she would reciprocate. Time went by, and they were always having good times together, but it was like friends and never seemed to go any further than that.

Maybe that's where it's supposed to start, as friends. However, Axel was now interested in it becoming more than a friendship. He never felt this way before, and it was frustrating. She was bright, funny at times, and really good looking. Axel would see other young guys in her school class trying to make a hit, but it never worked, and it always made Axel jealous. He felt she must really like her schooling. Many times, she would sit and talk about biology and genetics as if she was trying to learn from Axel and get ahead in her class. Axel was more interested in getting ahead with her, but he didn't seem to get to first base; therefore, he was always playing the game as a friend. In some respects, this was okay, since he enjoyed her company, and time would go fast when she was around.

She didn't speak about her folks even when Axel opened the subject and told her about Adam and how he was born a couple of days after him. Axel described what he knew about Adam and his job with the Pentagon, and this really interested her. Several times, he asked her if she wanted to go to a movie or a ballgame, but she just changed the subject. Then, Axel asked her if she wanted to go to a dance, and she said that she loved to dance but didn't have the time. And so, Axel's days were made up of teaching, working on the computer, talking to Adam on the phone about the computer, or spending a little time with Tori covering some subject she wanted to talk about, but it seemed he never got to first base about what he wanted from her; maybe time would tell.

One day, Axel met Ellen in the cafeteria, and they discussed several things, and it wasn't long before they were talking about Tori. Ellen said she knew he had a crush on Tori, and she began to open up the dialogue on Tori. "Don't feel like you are not her cup of tea," she said. "She is that way with all the guys, but she at least is interested in you. However, don't look for love from her. Tori got burnt her first year in college by an older man named Dan. Not too old, but a student who had finished his undergraduate work and was in his final year of his Master's work."

"He was probably about six years older than her. It wasn't long before they were heavy into this love affair, and I could see she couldn't go a day without seeing him. After a while, her class work dropped off, since she was not studying in the evenings because she was with him. She used to talk to me about him and say how wonderful he was to her. I don't believe I ever saw a woman so crazy in love. I didn't know if this was going anywhere, since the guy seemed to be here, and then he was gone like the wind. She would sit around moping, and I would try to brighten her up, but she would be this way for a couple of days till Dan appeared on the scene again. He would take her out, and they would go to a movie or something, and I could tell when she came home that she was satisfied for the time being. Then, they would go somewhere, and I wouldn't see her for a couple of days. The weekends though were odd. Some weekends, they would go somewhere, and then, another weekend would come up, and he wouldn't be around, and she would be walking around in a daze. One Friday, she was all excited because Dan was coming after class, and they were going somewhere. I didn't see her all weekend. Then, on Monday afternoon, I got a call from the medical ward of the school hospital, and the nurse said that Tori was being held there, and she had asked the nurse to call me and tell me she was all right. I asked her what the problem was, and she asked if I would come and talk to her about Tori."

"Just ask for Jessie when you get to the hospital," she said. "I told her I would be there in fifteen minutes. I hurried to the hospital not knowing what I was about to find. It sounded so anonymous when I was talking to Jessie on the phone. I always thought of Tori as being strong and healthy and couldn't conceive of anything that would cause her to be ill. I got to the hospital and began talking to Jessie. Jessie told me that Tori had suffered a nervous breakdown. I asked her what would cause that, and she said she had tried to have Tori discuss what caused the problem, but she wouldn't let loose and would start crying. I was shocked and went in to see her. She was lying in a bed in the ward, and I pulled up a chair next to the bed and began talking to her and not trying to find the reason for her problem."

"I felt if she wanted to tell me what had happened, that she would; if not, then maybe I would try to pull it out of her. I kept talking to her and saying things that would open the door to something, but it seemed that I was getting nowhere. Then, out of the blue she said, 'He's married.' I asked her who she was talking about. 'Dan,' she said. He's married and has a three-year-old boy. I was startled and asked her how this came about. She said that Dan picked her up on Friday at about five, and they were going to go to a restaurant to have dinner. When they got there and had ordered, Dan began this long conversation with her. He told Tori that he hadn't been honest with her and continued on telling her that he had been married for over four years and had a son who was three. He was now finishing his schooling and had accepted a job in Baltimore. He, his wife, and their son would be leaving the following week. This was like a train wreck to Tori. 'How could he have deceived me for that long?' she cried."

"Now, I knew why there were times when he would be gone, and I wouldn't see him for days." Tori continued, "After that, he got up and left. She got in her car and drove around crying and didn't even know where she was. She drove all night and didn't eat. This continued through Sunday, and, finally, she was completely exhausted and pulled up along the road. Before she knew it, she had passed out; it was probably because she hadn't eaten for a couple of days and only had stopped driving when she was low on gas, and, then when she pulled over on Sunday evening, she blacked out. She didn't know who came along, but they called 911, and, soon, there was an ambulance, and they brought her to the hospital. They put a needle in her arm and began feeding her intravenously with sugar water. They wanted her to have food in her, and they were concerned about dehydration. When she felt a little stronger, she knew she needed to lean on someone's shoulder, and she had the nurse call me. She told me that she was glad that I could come."

"Tori spent one more day in the hospital, and she was released. She called me on her cell phone and asked if I would meet her at the coffee shop. While having coffee and donuts, the conversation began like we had never stopped talking the day before. She didn't know if she could complete school.

I told her to give it a try. Maybe the mind needs to shift onto something else. She finally got back into her studies, but she was very quiet and not the same person. The second year at school started well, but she was still this quiet and changed person. Then, we had the incident with the attack after the lab work that day that you saved us from harm. This was a stroke of luck. She immediately was in a different frame of mind. She enjoyed seeing you, and her studies took her to the top of the class. As good as she felt, I knew she wasn't at the top of the heap. She almost was, but it just wouldn't break."

"So, one day, I was having a sandwich with her, and I asked her how she felt about you. 'Oh, Axel is great,' she said. I waited about ten seconds and then said, 'Did you get laid yet?' She looked up startled and began nodding her head back and forth. I asked, 'What's the matter?'

"She said, 'Nothing, I just can't let myself be attached to anyone let alone have sex with him.' I told Tori that you are definitely mad about her, and she can't treat you like a bump on a log or you will go and find someone else to direct your attention."

"She said she didn't think so, because you're too good a person to just walk away. "I told her that you were too good a person to be led around on a string. A man can only go so long without being able to display his love and express himself. I told her she wasn't going to find anyone better. Tori said that she had thought about that at times, and then she said that she would get tense and couldn't let loose. She thinks she loves you, but she doesn't know, because she is scared. She is afraid if this gets to that point, then, after a while, you will get bored with her, and she wouldn't be able stand that. She said she feels like she is on a fence, and, if she goes one way or another, then she will end up being disappointed, and she can't take another one of those. She said she gives you all her free time and that you both have fun together, and, when you leave to teach class or work on your computer, she feels a sense of loneliness, but then, she sees you the next day, and everything is okay."

I asked her how long she thought that would last, and I said, one of these days, you are going to finish doing what doing what you are doing and will take off to complete your life's work. I told her that you have a strong will, and, you think this is not going anywhere and decide to continue your career elsewhere, then you will walk away. You are just here to finish certain things, and then you will be gone. You know—and she knows—that this is not your life's work. You are working on something that takes up your time, and, when it is finished, you will go. I told her that she had better wise up and encourage you, because she would not find anything better."

With that said, he sat there in amazement looking at Ellen. "It's too bad you aren't the one I am hooked on," Axel said to Ellen. "You have me pegged pretty well. I sure am glad you spent this time with me to give me the scoop on Tori. I wouldn't have believed it if I heard it from anyone else. You are a true friend to her. Now, I know a little more about what makes Tori tick, and I have to find a way for her to break loose from her past. Time has its way, and something will happen to make this click. I guarantee you one thing, Ellen. I am not married, and I love that girl. It took me months of enjoyment with her company to realize that was the feeling I had. I never forced the issue because I sensed there was a problem, and I didn't want to screw up our 'friendly relationship' with an awkward advance. Well, I have to go and teach some young freshmen what makes their biology tick. Meanwhile, I have to figure a way for Tori and me to tick. Take care and thanks again."

Axel remembered walking away from that conversation with a sense of satisfaction that it wasn't him that wasn't making the connection with Tori. It took some pressure off him and allowed him to spend more time with the computer and cleaning up some odds and ends. Axel felt that being himself and leaving Tori to be herself would someday come to a better relationship, not that it wasn't good now, it was, but it could be better. He believed he just has to give it more time.

The computer had been checked out on a breadboard, and Kim had finished his modeling and running the program to his satisfaction. Now, it was getting to be the time to have it inserted into his body. At times, he felt uptight about it, wondering if it would cause some problems. Like all technical gadgets, they have some unknowns about them or they have failures of parts and have a questionable reliability. But then, he would think of the many things our country has done like going to the moon or having landings on Mars, and those electronic masterpieces were really masterpieces. Most of them worked beyond their expected lives and gave out data when they were supposed to be dead.

Between Kim and Axel, they had worked out the bugs, and they had gained more confidence as time passed. *No use getting squeamish now*, he thought. Axel gave Adam a call and told him he was ready to have "The Follower" program come to fruition. He felt Adam would be the best judge of when this could be completed in complete privacy, and he was Axel's link between Kim and Axel.

Adam was excited and told Axel he was proud of the work he had done, and he had complete faith that this would work out and give Axel an enormous advantage over the best of individuals. "How many people on earth can understand and speak ten languages and have total control of filing any and all of the conversations they would have in their life if they wanted? How many would have the enormous energy that would come with this? The only thing I worry about is whether your body will be able to take it. I realize that Dr. Newcome said that you also have a balanced system with the extra kidneys, extra adrenal glands, and the balance with the pancreas and pituitary glands that should see you through these events without any harm and the ability to bring your body back to normal like a soft landing of an airplane. I worry about your arms and legs and whether they can take it. Kim thinks he has some answers for this," Adam said.

Axel told him he had been working on his body for years with lifting of weights, aerobic exercises, and running five miles at least three times a week, and he felt strong. "But I appreciate what you are saying, since there is a physical limit to what your limbs will take in any of these endeavors," Axel said.

With that said, Adam said he would call him back on his cell phone when he and Kim had a date set. He would handle the paperwork with the agency and be responsible for the file on "The Follower." He would give Axel two weeks advanced notice, so he could finish up any work he had to do for the university and any personal things.

Axel felt like he had put everything in place, and now he felt good about everything, and the next day he picked up Tori after she had completed some classes and took her to the sandwich shop. When they finished their snack, he asked her if she would like to go to a movie. This time, he didn't really ask her because she might turn him down, so, he just said, "After we finish, we will go to see a movie I have wanted to see." She looked up as if to say something to avoid this, but Axel didn't give her a chance. He looked down at his watch and said, "The seven o'clock show will be starting in a half hour, so we better get going."

With that comment, they up and left. It was a good movie, and, while watching it, he held her hand and squeezed it tight every so often as if he was giving her a kiss. When Axel drove her back to her dorm and walked her to the door, he reached over and gave her a kiss. This was like throwing a switch because every time they went out or met, he reached over and gave her a smooch. And now, she seemed to be looking for it.

A few weeks passed, and Axel got a call from Adam saying that he should fly to Washington two weeks from Wednesday. Adam had made arrangements for a hotel room and a rental car. That evening, Axel took Tori to dinner and told her he had to go away for a while. She looked stunned. He told her he was only going to be gone for about a week or two, so it was no big deal, but she took it as a big deal. *I guess she has become comfortable with our everyday schedule, and it was like someone has just thrown her off her schedule*, he thought. *Well, I guess I have. I have become used to our daily procedures, and I know that I will miss them too; turns out, these worked things up a bit. The kisses each day became a hug and kiss and lasted longer, but it was still only a kiss—but a great kiss.*

Wednesday soon arrived, and Tori drove Axel to the airport. When he was about to go through the section where they check your ticket and your carry–on luggage, he reached around and wrote Adam's phone number on a little business card he had from the school and handed it to her. "If you can't get me on my cell phone, then you get hold of Adam. He will know what I am doing, and he will give me any message you leave. If you want me to call back, just tell him. Adam's wife's name is Laura, and they have a son named Josh. I will be seeing them pretty often when I am not working. So, if you can't get me or Adam, you can leave a message with Laura. Meanwhile, I will try to call you each evening at around eight o'clock your time. Does that sound okay to you?" he asked.

She nodded and had tears in her eyes. He reached over and pulled her to him and gave her a big hug and kiss. "See you in a couple of weeks. I love you," he said. Then, he turned and went through the security entrance.

The Agency and the Making of the Indestructible Man

Axel's flights carried him to Houston, and, eventually, he arrived at the Washington airport. Adam was there to meet him, and he had another man along with him. Adam introduced the man as Dr. Edward Kim. This was his first meeting with this young genius who Adam had written to him about. He was a physicist and responsible for technical direction within the agency that Adam worked for. Kim didn't know Axel was Adam's brother, and Adam introduced him as Axel Sumpter. Axel thought Kim knew that this wasn't his real name, but he also knew it was for the best when working for or within the agency. Anyone working in their line of work was used to this anonymity.

They went to dinner and discussed the program for "The Follower." Things were going to start moving fast. Kim would pick Axel up at the hotel at seven in the morning, and he would be taking him to his laboratory. As Kim entered his car, he gave Axel a special pass that had his picture on it, as given to him by Adam. The name Axel Sumpter was printed below the picture, and it had a large twelve-digit number on it; Axel felt that was the numerical code number for "The Follower" and its twelve digits. He didn't bother to ask him, since he felt Kim and Adam knew what they were doing.

Kim said, "You will need this every time you want to come or go at the facility where I am taking you. You will not be returning to your hotel, but the room is still in your name, and the car remains in the parking space for you. You will be staying onsite till we decide you are in good shape and ready to leave on your own. Adam will visit every other day while you are here to check on your progress and provide you someone you can data dump on. You might have some personal problems you want to relay to him. Here is a cellular phone that you must use every time you call from this site. I want you to give me your phone, and I will return it to you when you are ready to go back home. Adam said you have a girlfriend that you might want to call. You make the first call, give her this number, and tell her she can reach you only on that number. Do you understand?"

Well that was like watching a spy thriller in the movie. Here Axel was, a normal college teacher, about to venture into a cloak-and-dagger-type theme. He couldn't believe it. Even though he had prepared for something like this for a couple of years, it was strange. He felt alone and in a strange new world, yet the people walking around were normal people—at least at first sight. But all of a sudden, there were no students around him, and he wasn't giving lectures, and he wasn't taking Tori somewhere; he was in a strange atmosphere. But if he thought that was strange, it was only the beginning. It was like child's play compared to what he was to be going through.

To relax Axel about what was going to happen starting the next day, Kim took him to his laboratory and showed him the equipment he used to generate his computer models and his simulation of Axel's body. This was big time and fascinating. He gave Axel a demonstration of the program, playing out on a computer model that represented his body. Then, he showed Axel a three-dimensional view of a person with no skin on. It was more than a skeleton, since it was a complete body with all the organs, and, in fact, it had three kidneys, three adrenal glands, and everything he knew about Axel. It was if he had taken a person and skinned him. You could see the blood vessels, the muscles, the organs, and the places where nerve endings collected, and, in some places, there was skin, such as the skin on the hands, feet, face, and ears, since they were to play a different role in this feat.

He showed Axel where the small computer chip would go and how the wires would be connected using nano wires to the various parts of the body that were to be the extensions of this computer. He didn't have the ability to provide the extra amount of mitochondria to the body, but he was able to synthesize this by providing extra working parts that simulated the ability to provide the extra energy this mock body would generate and use. First, he demonstrated the ability to talk to it in various languages and have the body speak back in those languages. Of course, in this case, it wasn't real. He had provided the software and programmed the answers back to the previously programmed questions. They always answered them the same way. He had no way of duplicating a brain that could choose from many answers to questions in various foreign tongues.

Next, he showed Axel, using a password he had installed in this structure, how the computer put a message into the computer and how it could read out the message. Then, he showed how the computer answered messages via the use of an Internet password that was part of the Pentagon code system. The substitute for a brain took the message and thought out an answer (preprogrammed just for this demonstration) that went to a large agency computer, and it was then relayed to the address designated. In real use, it would be a message Axel thought of that then was stored in the computer memory that was used for sending messages, and the message was sent to Agencyfollower@cent.com. On this given demonstration, the central agency was told to ignore any messages sent today. They knew that we were just debugging the system.

One very neat thing was the ability to look up the meaning of any word or synonym of the word and provide the meaning to the memory bank for Axel to call up. It also had the capability of querying the web for any subject and getting the meaning of which Axel was to choose from any of ten. When he reached one he considered adequate, he instructed the computer to store just by thinking of the word "store." Essentially, Axel had all the capability that he would possess, as if he were sitting at his desk and writing about a subject and wanted additional data or information. Once in his body, Axel would have the ability of using any browser, search engine, or any other means of searching the web for any answer. He would essentially walk around like a walking library—with unusual strength.

Kim demonstrated as best he could how the animated being would use Axel's three levels of energy using the three passwords. The energy levels that were reached were not linear. They went from about five times his usual energy to ten times his usual energy to twenty times his usual energy. Kim warned Axel that he didn't know if his body could stand the use of the third level. Even though it was available, he didn't need to use the full impact of it unless he wanted or needed to because of an emergency. Axel could limit the amount of energy at each of these levels by the effort he put forth within each. For example, Kim said, "You might use level two to jump up to a height that was twenty-five feet high or maybe only ten feet high, depending on the effort you put forth in this energy level."

Kim suggested that Axel use a few aids in his ventures. He gave him arm and leg equipment to place on if Axel knew in advance he was going to use the energy level three. These consisted of sleeves designed for his arms and legs. He could pull all of these on or on either of his arms or legs and, if needed, on both. The arm sleeves consisted of a material made up of nanowebs, which were made up of strong material from spider web material and titanium nano tubes. These were very light, in fact, almost weightless, but they were able to take fantastic tension and impacts and absorb them rather than Axel's arms absorbing them. The leg sleeves were made of the same strong and light material with hinges just below the knee caps and just above the knee caps on Axel's legs. These would absorb any dramatic push off of his legs and alleviate the strain on his leg muscles and the bones. A small patch like design of the same material would be on the inside and outside of each knee, so any thrust by the muscles of his legs would be transferred across the knee cap and back side of the knee from the muscles on the lower part of the legs to the upper level of his legs.

Likewise, if Axel were to lift something very heavy, then the energy would be transferred from the lower leg to the upper thighs in a smooth movement that transferred the energy without great stress on his muscles. The neat thing about these pieces of equipment was that they were thinner than a silk stocking, and Axel could wear them every day if he so chose. The agency designers had taken samples Axel had sent them of his skin in his legs and arms, and these "garments" were so thin and so matched to the color of his skin in these two locations that Axel could be in the nude, and one couldn't tell that he had anything on his arms or legs. Besides these strength-absorbing capabilities, the material was almost impervious to impact, whether it was by the force of something like a bat or to a forty-five caliber bullet shot from a pistol ten feet away.

In addition, the agency had made a special one of the same material and qualities that fit from Axel's neck to his waist. Its total weight was less than one ounce and provided not only a bulletproof back and chest but one that could take high impact and spring back to shape to essentially shed his body of the energy hitting it. Axel decided to try these on and was flabbergasted at the fact that he didn't feel like he had anything on. They were designed to breathe, so his body wouldn't take on any exertion without the ability to sweat while shedding any energy level that hit him. This was needed biologically. Axel had at least learned that while earning his biology degree. He mentioned to Kim that he was now both protected and energized over most of his body.

"What about my head?" Axel asked.

"This is a difficult subject to handle well without hindering other faculties required of your eyes, ears, nose, and brain," Kim said. "We are working on a sort of 'matched face' hood that would cover your face and head. The material is so thin, light weight, and flexible, and it matches your skin perfectly, so we believe we can make a hood that when folded is about as big as a grain of rice, and it will be attached to the middle of your skull below the hair line. When you make a verbal command that we will provide you, it will activate a nerve in your head skin and release this, and it will pop up and swing down over your head and face and meet your neck material and latch like Velcro. The eye portion is clear as glass, and you will be able to see through it, and it will be unnoticeable by others. It will cover your nose but leave holes open where your nose holes are located. It will cover your ears and slightly pin them back toward your head but leave a small transducer at small sections, so you can hear and have your ears protected. It will cover your lips, and, if you keep your mouth closed, you will be completely protected. In general, we feel that everything could be handled with the other garments, but, if you feel you are about to enter into some dangerous venture that might find you being shot at or incur some other possible danger to your head, you should shout out the password ,and your head and face will be covered. We feel that now that you are here, we can combine all the parts of the super cover into one piece and place it on your whole body except the headgear as mentioned. You will be able to wear the whole body suit without knowing it. When you want the hood back in place and hiding, we will give you a code word that will release and snap back the hood into the small shape on your head like a rubber band after it is stretched and released. This one has given us some trouble, but we will work it out. It weighs less than a half ounce and will overlap your neck."

"When it is in place, you will state a command we give you, and it will automatically seal to your neck, thereby making your body impervious to impact and most weaponry. Knives cannot cut any of it, and it has a total rebound capability, so you won't feel the impacts as they will be shed at the angles of impact. If someone hits you with a bullet that comes at a ninety-degree angle to your body, it will rebound at 180 degrees from the impact and fly straight back to the shooter and probably kill him. It is so accurate that it might fly back into the barrel of his gun and cause the gun to blow up in his face. If at any other angle to your body, they will leave at that angle away from the body. This total skin, except for the headpiece, has been checked out by a model of your body, and it has responded magnificently. There is another unique feature. It is waterproof, and, if you go into one of your three energy levels and decide to swim, you will swim faster than most speed boats, depending on which level of energy you choose."

This blew Axel away, and, at that time of questioning, he ran out of questions. If all of this worked as Kim had checked, it would be beyond the wildest dreams Axel had ever imagined about his special capabilities and how he could put them to use.

After a few hours of instruction on the equipment, the computer capability and other odds and ends, Kim said they should go eat a good meal. It would be the last till the day after tomorrow. He said that the next day Axel was to be taken to a special operating room where the transfer of equipment would begin. The first step would be to implant the chip and just connect it to the places needed for "mind work." He would then be awakened, and, while lying on the operating table, the team and Axel would go through the necessary exercises to determine that the computer, the Internet capability, the searching capability, and all related software were working as planned. They felt, if this worked, then they could take it to the next level, and, if it didn't work, then they needed to find out why. All this needed to be checked out before employing the other capabilities that required strength. If it didn't work, then the whole thing would be aborted.

At that point, Axel said, "Let's eat. I am starved."

Axel thought he was going to go to some fancy restaurant and have a feast, but he was disappointed when Kim said, "The meal will be brought in here. We know what you like, and we have boiled it down to about one third of what you normally eat. We need you to be sort of dormant relative to going to the bathroom other than urinating. You will be eating foods that are mostly proteins today." With that, he pushed a buzzer on his desk, and, a few minutes later, this bland-looking meal was brought forward. Axel wasn't impressed by the diet, but he was impressed by its small size.

After the meal, Kim took Axel down the hall to a room that was provided for him. He said that Axel would be awakened early in the morning, so he was to go to sleep early to get as much rest as he could. Kim said, "If possible, blank all of what's going to happen tomorrow out of your head." And with that statement, he left Axel alone.

It was now ten o'clock, and Axel was weary and ready for some good sleep. That was good because he didn't want to think about tomorrow and had taught himself a technique on how to go to sleep easily and rapidly. He had once read that a person could fall asleep better with his eyes open rather than closed. So, the technique consisted of his picking an object out of his almost-closed eyes as he lay in bed and staring at it without blinking and counting to himself. In about twenty-five seconds, his eyes would close, and he would keep on counting; before long, he was asleep. *It works; turns out you need to think of something that is rather boring and easy to do without thinking. Counting fits this bill,* he thought.

Before long, he was asleep, and it only seemed like a short time, and he was being awakened and led to a shower. After that came a smock like the ones they give you when you are going to get an x-ray in the hospital, and, before long, he was lying on the operating table with some needles in his body. Axel didn't know how long he was out, but it seemed like minutes, and he was being awakened by Kim. Kim told him to relax a bit, and then they were going to go through the routines they had discussed last night. Axel laid there wondering if this was a joke. He didn't feel any different. *What was the next step going to be?* He thought.

Kim said that the first thing to do is activate the computer. "You have your password 'Axelvation zero' to turn on the power of the computer. The computer is already in an on stage but at low power. This password will use the energy from your mitochondria to power it up and make it ready for full use if we have wired the system properly. If you repeat 'Axelvation zero,' it will turn off the mitochondria power. If the system turns on, you will hear an internal voice say 'system on.' This will not be heard by us, but you must tell us if it has worked. Ready?"

Axel nodded he was ready. With this, he stated the words, "Axelvation zero," and, immediately, he heard the internal voice, and he winked at Kim. "Now turn it off," Kim instructed. Axel mentioned the words again, and a voice to his brain said, "System off." He again winked at Kim.

"Now the harder part," said Kim. "I want you to think the password and see if it turns the system on just like it did when you spoke it." With that instruction, Axel thought the words "Axelvation zero," and the voice in his head came back "System on." He had a big grin on his face as he looked at Kim. "Now while the system is on, I want to check out the ability to interpret ten languages and see if you repeat them back in the same language," said Kim. With that comment, he began in German and ended up in Iranian, and, each time, Axel understood what they meant in English, showing that the interpreter was working and immediately voiced them back language by language, and he was astounded by the response.

"I knew it was me, but it didn't sound like me," said Axel. "I knew this would take time to get used to."

Kim then said to him, "Now, I am going to state something to you in each of the ten languages. Each will be a different question, and I want you to see if the interpretation to you in English allows you to think the answer in English and see if the voice answers in the foreign language. Are you ready? Here goes."

With this, a voice recorder/speaker asked Axel questions in the foreign tongues, and he answered them—having heard them in English and thinking the answers in English, but out of his mouth the answer in the foreign tongue would come. The answers were recorded and translated and would then repeat in English what his answers were.

Kim jumped up and shouted, "Yes! You did a good job of designing the ten ROM codes, and we did a good job of placing the interpretation book in your cells." Kim said that this alone made this a powerful tool and a jump into the next level of intelligence. He sat back and said that he thought they had better give Axel a drink of juice before proceeding with the more difficult work they had to do.

They sat around thinking about what they have accomplished while consuming their juice. The talking was in an excited nature for what they had done had been exciting so far. It wasn't long until Kim said it was time to install the other capabilities. With that, Axel was rolled back onto the operating table, and, before he knew it, he was on his next trip of unconsciousness. Again, he didn't know how long he was out, but he could imagine at least a few hours and didn't even ask, since it wasn't important. This time, they woke him and asked him to sit on the edge of the table.

Then, Kim asked, "How do you feel?" Axel told him he felt fine.

"Anything different about how you feel compared to normal?" he was asked. Axel told him he didn't think so.

"Good, you now have the body skin on your whole body except for the head and face hood. Are you sure you don't feel any different?" Kim asked. Axel told him that he felt great, and Kim told him to get down off the table and walk around. This was soon accomplished, and Axel still didn't feel any different. "This is great," shouted Kim. "This will stay on you all the time. No one will know it. I can't even tell, and I know that it is on you. I wanted to make sure you felt comfortable, since the one concern I had was that you might feel it and be uncomfortable or it might make you warm or something that we didn't take into account." Axel walked around some more and said he felt no different from how he normally did. Kim said, "With this skin on, you can jump or use your legs or arms or body to achieve something that your body or bones couldn't normally take. This material will provide your body structure extra strength to be able to take enormous impacts on your body. When you jump to heights that would normally affect your legs, this body suit will take up the impact, and your legs and their bones will be protected."

With all this prep work being done, Kim said it was time to determine if the energy levels worked and if they were compatible with the skin they had put on Axel's body. "We want to take this easy, since I don't want to overextend you. Sit back on the table, and give the command to the computer to put you in the first energy level. I want you to think the command, since we know that this silent communication is working."

Axel was excited and sat there contemplating not being able to do what they intended. He was actually scared of what would happen and if his body could take it. He looked at Kim, and he knew these guys were brilliant, but there might be a problem where the body skin wouldn't take the full impact of what he might do. But, now it was time to try. He started with the first level, which was the safest level. He didn't feel too bad doing the first level, since his body muscles and bone structure had already had this level of energy when he took care of the two guys that had tried to harm Tori and Ellen. As he thought of that venture and Tori, he wondered if she would be able to tell the difference in him. *That's scary*, he thought.

But now, while sitting on the table, he gave the command via his internal signal, "Axelvation one." He immediately felt a little twinge in his lungs as his breathing picked up. He knew that he was in action phase one. He smiled and winked at Kim. Kim said, "Walk over to the weights, and lie beneath the weight bar. Then, I want you to start lifting the weight bar and putting it back in place, and watch as my assistants put additional weight on the ends of the bar. I want to see what you are able to lift. I know that you normally can lift between seventy-five and one hundred and twenty-five pounds. Let's see what you can do with the same amount of strain that you would normally exert when lifting seventy-five to one hundred and twenty-five pounds."

Axel advanced to the bar and weights, got on the pad below them, and looked up at the weights. "Let's start with 125 pounds," he said. They put sixty pounds on each end of the bar and said to start there. Axel reached up with a little feeling of uncertainty in his mind and body, grabbed the bar, and lifted it above his chest as he lay there, and it was rather simple. He knew it felt like he was lifting something, but it wasn't a big chore. They added weights, and, each time, he was able to push them up in the air and return the bar to their resting places on each end. This continued, and Axel began to feel a little strain as he lifted twelve hundred pounds.

"Put another one hundred pounds on each end, and that is as far as I want to take this," Axel shouted. With that, the weight was added, and Axel strained to take the fourteen hundred pounds above his chest and return the bar and the seven hundred pounds on each end to the holder. With that, he had to rest for a few seconds and take several big breaths before rising up and facing Kim. "Not bad for a one hundred and eighty five pound weakling," he said.

Kim jumped for joy and again shouted, "Yes!"

Kim was excited but told Axel that was all they were going to do today. "This alone was remarkable," he said. "I want you, your brother, and me to go and get a good dinner, and you will return to your room and get some sleep for tomorrow."

Kim took them to a nice restaurant. After finishing the meal, Axel asked Kim if he would have any problems going to the bathroom and about any trouble he would now go through to have a good bowel movement. Axel looked at Kim and said, "How do I go to the bathroom with this skin over my body?"

Kim smiled and said, "Just like normal. Your body and the skin and your brain will allow it to work. The skin should allow the rectum to release the sphincter muscle as well as the penis to have a hole for dispensing any liquid and close when you are finished. You shouldn't feel any difference."

Axel smiled and said, "I hope you are right because I believe I might have a hard time getting this skin off to clean my butt." With that understood he went to the men's room and had a good session as Kim had said he would. *It was a great engineering feat they have done with my body*, thought Axel.

The Agency determines Axel's limits

When Axel got to his room, he took out the cell phone they told him to use. It was 8:15 PM, and it was 5:15 PM back in California. He wanted to see if he could get Tori on the phone. He tapped in the phone number, and, in no time, there was an answer. "Hello, this is Tori."

Axel waited till she said it twice just so he could listen to her beautiful voice, and then he said, "Hi there, sweetie."

"Axel!" she shouted. "Is that really you?"

And with that beginning, they had a great conversation, and he told her how much he missed her, and she said the same thing back. He could tell she was excited by the sound of his voice, and he wished he could reach through the phone and squeeze her. He told her he was having a great visit with Adam and going through all his work areas. He told her he would probably call her each evening about this time and would be home in about a week. He gave her the special phone number and told her not to try to call him on his normal cell phone because he was required to use this one. After talking for about fifteen minutes, they cut it off, and he took a shower, forgetting he was in his new skin. It wasn't until he had been in the shower for about five minutes that he thought about it and the fact that it didn't feel any different. He was happy that he felt like he was getting clean.

Before he knew it, he was being awakened the next morning. He had a good night's sleep, which was another good mark for his skin like covering. Before long, he was having breakfast with Kim and was surprised to see Adam there. Kim asked him about the covering and if it bothered him at all during the night and during the shower. He was relieved to hear Axel's responses. They discussed what would be tested today. They had to see further responses to Axel's first level of energy and then would check out the second level. All instructions were given to Axel in a couple of the foreign languages that Kim was fluent in, and the answers from Axel were very clear and fluent also. As Kim spoke and Axel thought about his response, it seemed the words came out of his mouth immediately. This turned out to be a good warm-up for what was to occur this day. Adam just sat there in amazement. He knew Chinese, and he therefore could understand when Kim spoke in that language, and Axel followed with an answer or question in Chinese.

When they arrived at the laboratory, Kim decided to do two tests before going forward with the second energy level. First, he had Axel activate energy one, and then he told him to lie on his back and lift the weight up in the air that he had finished with the day before. It was the weight he had done yesterday and was still sitting there on the bar waiting for him. They must have thought out this routine well. Axel then got down beneath the weight holding bar and lifted it with very little effort. It felt like fifty pounds. Then, they added one hundred pounds to each side, and Axel lifted the sixteen hundred pounds with a greater effort being required. But still, he was amazed at that lift, and Adam stood on the side and cheered this effort on.

The next step was scary. Kim wanted to shoot a twenty-two rifle bullet at Axel from about fifteen feet. He said he would shoot for the stomach. Axel stood there awaiting the killing as calm as he could, but he knew that his mitochondria were still up without his needing to do anything. He knew it was still up from lifting the weights, but he was nervous not saying the code words. He stood there, and Kim handed the gun to Adam and told him to, "Shoot now."

Axel really was concerned, not because Adam was a bad shot, but because it didn't seem right for a brother to be shooting his brother. But Adam moved to an angle, aimed, and fired away. Axel had his eyes closed and didn't feel it as the bullet ricocheted away at the angle. Then, Kim took out a thirty-eight-caliber pistol and said he was going to try this. He shot, and the bullet flew back in his direction. Since he knew it would do this, he made sure he aimed at an angle to Axel's body, and the bullet bounced off his body and pierced a target about fifty feet to his right. Kim said, "I wish I could try your head, but we will have to wait a day or so for the head gear to be checked out before trying it on you." Kim was quite happy with the results of the skin protection gear, but he had great confidence in it, since he had tested its ability on a dummy prior to this.

The next test was to check out Axel's second level of energy. Kim had him sit on the edge of the bed before activation and asked Axel to eat a few pieces of candy and drink a sweet soft drink. He wanted him to have enough glucose in his system to be able to handle the extra energy supply that might be needed. Axel thought of it as being like throwing more coal on the fire. He asked Kim if he had to turn off the first level that was on, and Kim shook his head back and forth in denial. "I want you to turn it on with your memory rather than speaking it out," he said.

With that, Axel thought out the command, *Axelvation two*. He could feel his body responding, and he winked at Kim and his brother. Kim then told him to go back over and lift the weights that he had previously lifted to see if the function was working. After lifting the sixteen hundred pounds, they added another two hundred pounds to each side, and Axel lifted the two thousand pounds with little effort. Energy level two was working, and he couldn't tell the difference other than he was activating more energy from his mitochondria.

Kim spoke some instructions to him in Iranian, and Axel replied in Iranian. "You want me to jump up to the second level balcony," Axel responded in Iranian.

"Si," Kim responded in Spanish. Axel had practiced this with his breadboard back in California before the computer was installed in his body. He knew about how much energy he had to give his legs. He bent his legs, and then off he went and only slightly overshot the height he wanted. He knew Kim didn't want him to jump down now, since this could impact his legs. Next, a challenge would come that Axel hadn't expected. Kim told him to jump down from the balcony but to do it differently than he would under normal circumstances. Kim wanted him to jump slightly to get over the banister, and, just before his feet hit the deck below, he was to holler "up."

"This will cause your legs to bend and will give a slight jumping-up position to offset the downward thrust," said Kim. "Then, as your body just touches the ground, within a microsecond, you will be leaping upward. This upward thrust is to cancel out most of the downward thrust, so there is no major impact on your body. Your body will be lifted about two feet in the air, and then, when you hit, it will have the same impact on your body as a two-foot drop. Keep your legs bent during the whole procedure," he said. "Also, don't be concerned. Even if the up signal doesn't work, your legs will be able to take this impact, since the body cover will absorb most of the impact."

Axel thought about this and then gave it a try. He might have been a little excited, and his body was lifted about three feet in the air as his feet touched the ground, and he got this bounce. Still, the three-foot drop was quite easy to take compared to the level he had jumped from. "That's wonderful," Kim remarked.

"I was always concerned about getting to high levels and not being able to come down," Axel said to Kim.

Then, Kim said, "Now I want you to extend your energy a little more and jump to the roof, which is about twenty-five feet above you."

Axel looked up and knew that he had not tried this before. He thought it out, and he knew if he didn't jump high enough, then he would begin falling back toward the ground, so kept that in his mind; if that happened, then he would need to say "up" just before hitting the ground. With that plan in mind, Axel bent his knees and gave it a little more humph than his first jump to the balcony. Before he knew it, he was standing on this flat roof looking down at his brother and Kim. His brother was in a trance. He hadn't ever seen Axel do this circus act before.

"Now," directed Kim, "I want you to leap to the roof of the adjacent building. To do this, you should take a position with your body and legs like you would if you normally were going to try to do this. Remember, you need enough energy to make it there. It is about thirty feet away, but it is at the same level, so you don't need any lift. Think of it as a broad jump; in fact, I should have checked you out on a broad jump on the ground before you got up there. The slant of your body will head you in the right direction, and then, as you approach the other roof, you must just bend your legs. If you do something wrong that causes you to not reach that roof, you must take proper measures to land safely by saying 'up' as your feet are about to hit the ground. If you overshoot, you can handle the landing the same way with the word 'up.' This includes you hitting to the far side of that roof or if you overshoot it to the point that you won't land on the roof; keep in mind the word 'up.'"

Axel wanted to make sure he made it, and he thought, *Thirty feet that way should be less energy than the twenty-four feet I had to use to make it to the roof. It should take about the same energy as the twelve-foot jump to the balcony.* Axel wanted to try it, but he had to build up the nerve, since this was the first time he had to try something that was really different from what he had done before. He hollered down to Kim, "Isn't there a signal I can use if I feel I am over jumping the target to cut the energy?"

Kim replied, "No, there isn't, since the energy comes from your body and the interaction with the floor or ground you are standing on. While in flight, you have made your bed, and must sleep in it. However, the overshooting will usually take you toward the ground, and you can use the word 'up' to help you there. You also can spread your arms to gain air resistance if your leap looks like it is going to be too long. The spreading will act just like it does with those skydivers that use that technique."

With that last information, Axel turned and gave it a reasonable push, and he landed almost in the middle of the next roof. He then looked down, and there was no place to land there, so he turned around and gave it the same leap he had previously used, and then he was back on the original roof. From there, he now knew how to get down.

When Axel was down on the ground, he was going to turn level two off, but Kim said, "Now, we are going to test the strength a different way. This one that is passive and gives us a good level of understanding of your level two energy without putting a chance of danger on you. But before we proceed, I wanted to tell you they have the hood completed, and they have done several tests on it for strength and even wrote an algorithm on the computer to simulate the nerve in your head that will be used to employ the hood. We will test it on you tomorrow. For now, I would like to see you tear this phone book in two. No one has been able to do that, and many have tried. This will give us an indication of your hand strength."

With that, he handed Axel the phone book for Los Angeles. It was quite thick, and he didn't know if he could get a good enough grip on it to try. He took the book and sat down with it on his lap. He held it upright on his lap and moved his left arm and hand around on the right side of the book. He took his right hand and gripped the book as best he could just below his left hand. With that, he torqued his hands in the ripping motion and was surprised by the ease with which he could rip the book in two. He turned to Adam and said, "Do you want to arm wrestle?" Adam smiled and said he couldn't believe it, and he guaranteed Axel that he didn't believe he could win that challenge.

Next, Kim handed Axel a javelin and said, "Let's go outside and see what you can do with this on the field." Axel previously had thrown a javelin a few times at his high school and at the college field, and he knew about what his capability was. Adam and Kim also knew his capabilities after having looked at his records at the two schools.

They went outside, and there was a race track around a soccer and football field. It was used by the school for races against other schools and other events. Axel looked down the field and knew, if the second level of energy could do anything, it could send this javelin to the end of the field. Instead, he looked at the scoreboard just above the seats at the end of the field. If he could hit that, it would mean the javelin went about twice the length of this football field. He hadn't thrown one for several years; therefore, it took a few practice throws to gain a rhythm. When he was satisfied he wasn't going to fall on his face and stick the javelin in his foot, he took a stance and indicated he was ready.

Axel knew that he could take several rather long and fast steps with the energy level two. This alone would give him the momentum needed to throw the javelin farther than he had ever thrown it before. With that in mind, he decided to lay the javelin down and take a run without the javelin. His stride was about twice what he had previously experienced back in the real world, and the speed with which he covered the normal distance was up, and he almost fell on his face as he planted his left foot and took a practice heave. He felt strong and balanced. With that achieved, Axel walked back to the javelin and took a position and strode those few steps he had just practiced and let the javelin fly. This was easier than doing it without the javelin, and he finished with his left foot dug into the turf, his right leg in a straight line parallel to mother earth, his left arm ninety degrees to Mother Earth, his right arm extended, and his face looking at the flight of the "weapon."

The javelin shot through the air and was headed straight toward the scoreboard. The javelin pierced the scoreboard and stuck like a dart on a dartboard. "Yes," Axel cried out and looked toward Adam and Kim.

They were jumping up and down in joy, and all he could think of was, *Who's going to pay for the damage to the scoreboard?* That was not what Kim was worried about. He said the school would ask too many questions of how a javelin could be sticking out of their scoreboard. Axel told him he would take care of the javelin if he could make up a story of what caused the damage, and his agency would pay for the damage.

With that decided, Axel took off and was soon at the scoreboard looking up. It was near the top of the board, and he measured his jump and leaped to the top of the board. Once there, he leaned over the edge, grabbed the javelin shaft, and tried to pull it out, but it was tougher than he had thought. Knowing his hand was protected by his new skin; he made a fist and punched holes around the javelin's entry. This was enough for him to then pull it out. After that was done, he leaped from the top to the field about a hundred feet away and about a forty-foot drop. He was quite happy with his ability to judge that jump, and, just before hitting the turf, he shouted out "up." As his foot hit the turf, his body went immediately to the jump position, and he was lifted about three feet from the ground. So, his impact from all that was only what a normal person would have experienced if they jumped from a two- or three-foot height. For Axel's second energy leg strength and the impact alleviating skin, it felt like a hop. He had normally felt more than this while jumping rope. Kim took care of the damage issue to the scoreboard.

Kim said that was enough for today, and they should go and have a nice dinner; tomorrow was going to be another day for new tests. After dinner and returning to his room, Axel decided to try Tori again. It was nice to hear her voice, since it mellowed him. After a day like today, he seemed tight as a stretched rubber band, and, with her voice, he felt like a string. *Unbelievable*, he thought, *how a woman's voice could soothe a man.* It was better than medicine. It was like lying in his bed after a tough day. "Hello," he continued. "What did you do today to keep yourself busy?" (He did not know a better line than that to start the conversation, even though he would have liked to have said that he wished that the two of them were now going to bed together.)

"It's still early here," she commented, "and Ellen and I just finished school and were on our way back to the dorm. We wanted to watch the football game on TV but needed some food in us before that."

"Gee, I thought you would be thinking of me and giving me a call on your cellular. Does it only receive calls and not send any?" he kidded her.

"No," she said as she laughed, "but I did think about calling you later on today. I enjoy hearing your voice. It comes across clear like you are in the next room. Since you have been away, I have realized how much I miss you. I find myself expecting to see you when I come out of school, and, when you aren't there, it's a lonely feeling. I hope you miss me that much."

Axel told her that each day he wished he could walk out the door and grab her. She laughed at that. They spent a few more minutes consoling each other, and then he was off to bed.

Kim said the next test was a double critical one. "We are to see if the hood performs as we had hoped, and then we have to find out how much protection it gives you, both when you are in an energy level and without being in an energy level. But first, we have to have a minor operation that requires a local anesthetic but no more than that. This should be painless and take little time, since we already prepared your body for this back on the day when we were providing your skin protection."

He was right, the work they did on Axel's head was painless, and they were done in less than fifteen minutes. Afterward, they sat down and had a coffee with Adam and discussed the events to date. Kim said they were quite pleased that the work had gone as well as it had. He had had his reservations about the energy levels Axel's body could reach with his extra mitochondria and other body differences. He had been totally surprised that the doctor's comments about the ability of Axel's body to reach energy levels beyond those of a normal person had proven to be correct. Axel guessed Kim's ego kept him from saying that the work the agency had done was beyond his wildest dreams. Axel made a comment that he had believed his doctor, since he had gone through several of these energy transactions before ever having any agency changes or additions. Kim also could have commented on the computer Axel designed to be able to provide the signals for all of this and all the other provisions it supplied.

As they continued their conversation, Kim asked Axel if he had tried to use the Internet capability that he had built into the computer. Axel had totally forgotten about it in the excitement he had been experiencing over the past few days. Kim said, "How about seeing if you can send a message to Adam and your girlfriend, Tori, while we are sitting here?"

Axel gave the signal mentally to his computer and called up his Internet. He then sent a text message to Adam while they were sitting there. Adam activated his small system and soon saw the message arrive. "Now," continued Kim, "how about activation of your cellular phone and talking to Adam?" With that instruction, Axel gave the signal that he had practiced back home many times on the breadboard system when designing and debugging it. He then mentally called in Adam's cellular phone number. In a few seconds, Adam's phone signaled. At first, Axel mentally discussed things with him while remaining silent at the table. Then, he tried it by speaking out. Then, to really give them a demonstration, and knowing that Adam understood Chinese and Spanish, he began speaking in each of these languages very quietly and could actually hear it nice and clear and loud on Adam's phone just about ten feet away. He smiled as he changed from one language to the other. They both were impressed; Axel could see this on their faces.

Now, Axel decided he was going to call Tori and see if she picked this up. With that, he mentally dialed Tori's cell phone number, and she answered. He asked her where she was, and she said that she was in the hall at school talking to a friend. Axel told her he was trying a new kind of phone and could only be on for a few minutes. She said she was excited to hear from him this early in the day. Axel looked at his watch, and it was almost noon there, and it was almost 9:00 AM back in California. They talked small talk for a few minutes, and then he was off. Adam and Kim just looked at Axel with a questionable look about them. They hadn't heard any of this. Axel stared at them for a few seconds, and then said, "Listen to this." Then, he instructed his computer memory to play back the conversation to Adam's cell phone number. His phone rang, and he listened and held the phone next to Kim's face, so he could hear.

Back played the total conversation that Tori and Axel had just finished. This surprised even Kim. "Unbelievable," he said and followed by saying that he didn't realize the capability of the computer design. After a few minutes, Kim said he wanted to see how the hood worked. He told Axel to use his normal password for energy activation and state, "hood on."

Before doing this, Axel reached up and felt the little sand grain in the middle of his head under his hair. "Do you really believe that a hood to cover my face will come out of this small grain of sand?" Axel asked.

"We have taken a great deal of research time and money to make it happen, and we expect it will," replied Kim. "We have completely outlined every feature of your face and head and placed it in the software of your internal computer. We know that part works. We have written the software in both the computer and last night in the hood. We now need to see if it works physically and fits your face's every crevice. Let's see if we have been successful," he said.

Axel stared at Kim and then at Adam, and then he gave the mental signal for the hood. All he noticed was a slight flash of light as though he had blinked. He continued looking at them and said, "I believe the hood is on. Can you tell the difference? Do my eyes look different?"

Without waiting for an answer, Kim reached up with his hand and tried to touch his eyes. He couldn't. Axel could see the hand, but he couldn't feel it in his eyes. Kim picked up a pen he had been writing with and threw it into Axel's face, and it bounced back toward him without Axel feeling anything. Kim told Axel to look to his right at the sun, which he did. Kim said, "When you look at the sun, I can see a reflection that is different from I would normally expect. In the future, when you have the hood on and don't want anyone to notice it, make sure you keep your head at an angle away from lights. Direct lighting will be okay, since it will not give that glare. You should practice blinking your eyes as you look down, so there will not be a transitional difference that is noticeable. I believe you will get used to doing this with a little practice at home."

Next would be the real test of the hood. Kim wanted to shoot at Axel's head with a twenty-two pistol, a twenty-five pistol, followed by a thirty-eight pistol, and finishing with a forty-five army pistol. This was scary. Kim realized this took some courage on Axel's part, and, because he expected this, he had brought a twelve-inch by twelve-inch piece of the material. He said that, when they went out on the field, that he would shoot at this with a forty-five pistol to show the strength of the material. As previously mentioned, the material was a compound made up of spider web threading and titanium nanotubes. Axel already was living evidence that it was light and strong, and now they would find its ability to withstand bullets.

The three of them went out, and Kim had arranged to have a pair of posts that would receive the piece of material between them. After attaching the material, he made comment that the force would be so much that he had to have a special holding mechanism that could withstand the impact of the bullet. He said that when the bullet hit the material, it would shoot the bullet back toward the shooter or off to an angle, depending on how the gun was aimed at the material.

He set up the material in two completely different modes; one was just to have the material between the two poles with screws holding the material at the four corners, and the second set up would have a double length of the material forming a circular band like many basketball players wear around their heads to ward off sweat. Some just called it a sweat band. This band would be placed over the two poles and pulled down at the same height as the other single layer material had been screwed on the other set of poles. He indicated that the force of the bullet would be so much that it might rip out the screws on the one that was screwed to its pair of poles. With the same type of shot on the other band of material, the force of the bullet would cause a force to be dissipated around the whole band, and this special material would take up the energy around the whole band and be relieved by its rebound strength, and there would be no tearing of the material. The bullet would return like it was shot from a slingshot. He pulled out the forty-five pistol, moved to within eight feet of the target, and kneeled down so as to have to shoot slightly upward. In this stance, he expected a great deal of the force to strike the material and the bullet flying back over his head. He aimed and shot, and the bullet ricocheted over his head, and two of the screws were ripped out of the wood.

Now, Kim said he wanted to show the others something that they didn't expect. He stood and aimed the gun directly at the material, and he would be shooting at ninety degrees to the target; they would expect the bullet to fly backward at the shooter. Both Adam and Axel yelled that he was going to get shot. With that, Kim shot, and the bullet dropped off the material as though it had no force or energy. "What was that?" both Adam and Axel shouted.

Kim said the study with the material showed that it had so much strength and resiliency that the total force and energy were absorbed by the material with only a minor amount of the material being deflected away from the bullet strike. Their studies showed that the material would only deflect about 0.1 mill or a tenth of a thousandth of an inch toward the force. "This is better than the best steel we can make. This spider web and titanium nanotube material is a wonder. You will be doing us a favor and a favor to your country just by testing out this material. This means with your hood you won't feel a twenty-two- or thirty-eight-caliber bullet and only a flicker with a forty-five," Kim said.

With that explanation, Kim said he was going to shoot a twenty-two pistol at Axel followed by the thirty-eight and then the forty-five. Axel was glad Kim was confident he would get that high in the count. Without any warning, Kim pulled out a twenty-two piston and shot Axel in the head from about ten feet away. Axel didn't even feel it, even though he knew it had hit him in the face. Kim couldn't miss from there, and a twenty-two pistol had very little recoil to spoil the aim. Now, Axel gained confidence, but, when Kim did the thirty-eight pistol deal, he closed his eyes with the same result as the twenty-two bullet had.

"How about that?" Axel yelled. "I feel like Superman in the comic books, only it's real." Then, Kim pulled out a forty-five pistol. This was the gun that was developed during a past war to knock down large human beings that would normally reach their enemy even if shot. The forty-five was designed to at least knock them down, so the shooter could then take more shots if he wanted. So, Axel was expecting to die or be knocked down or something that wasn't fun. In order to protect him a little, Kim took Axel to a place where he could stand on a mattress, and, if the shot knocked him down, then he would at least fall on something that was safe.

Now, Kim stood ten feet away from Axel and aimed, and Axel closed his eyes; then, he felt a sort of twitch on his right cheek bone from the impact of the forty-five shell. He opened his eyes, and everyone was just standing and waiting for his reaction. Then, he decided to make his day, and he fell down like he had been shot and laid on the mattress, while Adam rushed over and kept hollering, "Axel, Axel, Axel."

Then, Axel answered, "What Adam?"

He began to laugh, then Adam began to laugh, and finally Kim broke his stoic face into a big smile. "We have won," he said. Then, he looked at Axel and said, "Now release the hood by saying your password 'release the hood,' and it should happen immediately." Axel followed his suggestion, and life was back to real again.

Axel's new body experiences

A few days later, Axel was back on the plane anxious to see Tori. He thought about what had happened for the last week. Kim and Adam instructed him to not tell a soul about this experience. They didn't know how they would use Axel's talents, but now they could sit down and consider the options. Meanwhile, Axel was like on vacation. He thought about this first trip to Washington DC and the implications it brought into his world. He was going back to the sane world, to the world of teaching, to the world of academia, to taking jumps that were a few feet high, and to seeing Tori and hopefully a love affair. *Maybe being away has brought her to realizing my love for her*, he thought. *I wasn't just a friend, and I hope that she knew this and will return the feeling.* She was going to meet him at the airport, and Axel was ready to give her a big hug, a hug from someone that was more than a friend. Maybe he would have enough gumption to tell her he loved her. He didn't know how she would act. He knew how he wanted her to act, but, sometimes, the vanity of a person restricts their emotions. He would find out if his vanity was stronger than his intentions.

It seemed longer than normal for the flight that took between five and six hours depending on which direction you were going, east or west. This seemed to take half a day at least. However, eventually, Axel was walking toward the turnstiles that brought the luggage from the flight. As he arrived there, and didn't see her, he began to wonder if she got the time right or got delayed at school or whatever. *Seems like what you expect doesn't ever happen. Then, when you least expect it, it happens,* he thought. He started to watch the bags coming off the ramp and onto the turnstile. It was like counting sheep when you want to go to sleep. Then, someone tapped him on the shoulder and said, "Hello there, handsome." He turned around, and there she was. She was even more beautiful than he had remembered. She looked like she got older and prettier at the same time. Or was he just tired? He reached around and gave her a big hug, but no kisses, none from her and none from him. Maybe they both were too proud or had too much vanity or maybe those words both meant the same thing.

Anyhow, he thought they both had it, whatever it was, in spades. *Damn, why didn't I just give her a big kiss?* He asked himself. *I wanted to, and the time was right. What a ding-a-ling I am.* He collected his bags, and she drove him out to his apartment house above the garage. He asked her to come up, but she said she had some things she had to do. She said she was really happy to see him and gave him a little hug, like a sister gives her brother when he comes home from school or wherever.

However, Axel decided to grab her and he gave her a big hug and a kiss. He said, "That's what I wanted to do when I met you at the airport. I couldn't go in the house without giving you a big hug and kiss. I really missed you." She said she really missed him and thanked him for the big hug and kiss. Then, she was gone and on her way.

Axel went up the side steps to the house, and, when he went in, he was in a blank stupor. After all the exciting things that happened, this was a letdown. He thought, *I should be excited, happy, and, above all, content, but those are not the feelings I have.* He went to the phone and called his real girlfriend—his mother. He wished he could tell her what her two days of holding off having him after the plane wreck meant to him now. She would think of it as a miracle. She would be amazed if he could tell her the experience he had just gone through. It was a miracle. She would realize he was one of a kind; but he couldn't tell her.

With that, he called his mom and told her how much he loved her. Just before hanging up, he said to her, "Mom, I want to tell you that your two days of holding off having me were not in vain. While I was in the east, Adam's company tested some of my strengths, and they were like Dr. Newcome had told us a few years back. It looks like it is a positive and doesn't seem to cause me any problems." He felt that wasn't giving any secrets away, and he knew she was glad to hear this.

The next day, he went to the school and told them he would be ready to continue his classes after the weekend. This had been his promise to them when he had wanted the time off to go east. They were more than happy to see him back and told me him that he deserved some time off. He hadn't taken a day off for the almost three years he had been teaching. Before he knew it, he was back in the same groove, except he didn't have to meet Tori on the three evenings she used to take late lab. He missed that. He also didn't have much to do with his spare time now that the computer work was done.

Every couple of days, he would go out to a farm where a previous roommate (Rich) had a small farm that his folks had given him. He wasn't the farm type, and Axel probably visited it more than he did. When he was out there, he was free to try the various options that were now within his command. He would leap distances that were unreal and never ceased to be amazed. Axel would go out to the river that ran past the property, and, when he was sure there was no one around, he would leap across the river using energy level one or two, depending on the width of the river.

One day, while walking along where the river was the widest and there was a strong current, he decided to give swimming a try using energy level one. He got behind some bushes and took everything off except his shorts. He got in the river and said out loud, "Axelvation one." Axel immediately got the sense of energy and began to swim rapidly down the river. He was going as fast as many power boats that he had seen on the river. He had swum for about five miles up the river against the current and feeling no pain when he approached a fairly high concrete wall off in the distance. It was off to his left downstream from a dam that had been built a little farther up the river.

The dams were placed on this river for raising and lowering boats that went up and down the river. There were locks built alongside the dam that the boats would enter, and the water level raised or lowered depending on which direction the boat was going. They were like a small version of the Panama Canal that was built some sixty or seventy years ago. This was as far as Axel had expected to swim, and then he would turn around and swim back to where he had left his clothes. When Axel was a couple hundred yards from the concrete wall, he heard the kids on the wall yelling and jumping up and down and screaming, "Jim's drowning! Jim's drowning!" Now, he really swam fast. In seconds, Axel was at the spot and diving down into the water. He had a hard time seeing, so he surfaced and said to himself, *Hood on*, and, immediately, he could see, since the water really wasn't in his eyes.

Axel went down about twenty five feet or so, and there was a boy caught in metal webbing that must have been there since they built the dam. He swam to him, and he was already unconscious. Axel grabbed the metal, pulled it apart, grabbed the boy's body, and swam to the surface. At the surface, he did a kick that was normally done when treading water, but, with his energy, it threw him up in the air above the wall where the kids were screaming. Axel hollered "up" as he approached the surface, and he was now gently jumping to the surface.

Axel immediately started to give the boy artificial respiration by compressing his chest lightly (lightly for him or he would have damaged the boy) and began breathing in his mouth while holding his nose. Soon, the boy was breathing but in bad shape. Axel asked the kids where the closest hospital was, and they said two miles up the river at Brownsville. With only his shorts on, Axel began to run along the river and then up onto the road. Before long, he was passing cars that seemed to be going slow to him. In a minute, he saw a sign, "Brownsville hospital next right," and he made a right and went up to the emergency entrance. Axel ran in and told a nurse that the kid had been drowning, but he had got him breathing.

They immediately took the boy and put an oxygen mask over his face and whisked him away. Axel asked the nurse if she had a robe he could put on, and she went and got him one. Axel waited, and, after a half hour passed, someone came into the hospital and said they thought their boy was here. He had been drowning and brought here by someone. The receptionist pointed at Axel, and they rushed over and asked him what happened. Axel told them what he felt he could tell them. "Where's the doctor?" they asked, and Axel had no answer for them; however, almost at the same time, a young gentleman came down and told them that their boy was responding quite well to their efforts, and it looked like he would be okay. "Thanks to this man," she said while pointing at Axel. "He retrieved him from the water, gave him artificial respiration, and then carried him two miles to this hospital. Without that, your boy would be no more. I have never seen anything like it."

The parents couldn't thank Axel any more than they did, and, when the doctor asked Axel his name, he said, "Justin Spencer," for the lack of another name. This happened out of his mouth, since he didn't want them to know his true identity and had known Justin from years ago while living in Ohio. When the parents began to talk to the doctor, Axel slipped out the door and began running faster than he had ever run since he had gained this extra energy. He didn't even jump in the river when he got to the place where he had pulled the kid out of the water. Axel kept running until he was opposite the place where he had hidden his clothes. With a rather casual leap, he made it across the river to the other bank about eighty feet away.

Soon, he was clothed and on his way home. When he got there, he was still quite excited and wanted to find something to slow him down. He decided to call Tori who he hadn't seen for two days. She must have been sitting next to her cell phone because she answered with one ring. "Hi," Axel said. "What's happening?"

"Not much," she said and continued to talk about various things.

"How about a movie?" Axel asked. He was surprised when she said that would be nice. He didn't expect that since things had been kind of down with her lately. "Good," Axel said in an excited tone, "I'll be over in about fifteen minutes, and we can go for a snack before the movie. Meanwhile, pick out a movie you would like to see." As Axel hung up the phone he realized he should have said more to Tori about how he felt about her. He knew she would sooner or later decide to drop him or tell him about her past experience and move on from there. While on the phone he could have leveled with her or at least tried to make things easier for her to discuss things. It was kind of quirky to just ask her out to a movie but nothing came to his mind when she decided to talk to him. "*Well, that is done with.*" he said to himself. Let's see where it goes from here. Here is a beautiful girl and the only one he has really got attached to. He had always been too busy for girls. He is now, but she is so different that he has been putting off other things to spend more time with her. Now we will see where this goes.

Before long, Axel was at her place and gave her a big hug when she met him. It felt good and helped to cool Axel down, still being kind of up from the experiences of the day and kind of needing that hug. Soon, they were at the fast food place down the road and having a cheeseburger.

They talked small talk for most of the dinner, but, at the end, Axel said that he felt that she had changed since he had gone away and then came back. "Is there something I did or said?" Axel asked. She said no that it was her problem. Then, she set about telling Axel the same story that Ellen had told him about her being jilted by this man, Dave.

Axel pretended not to have known anything about it and just watched her pretty face as she went on about the past incident. Then, she surprised him with, "You know, I began to have those same strong feelings about you, and, when you went away for a couple of weeks, I gave it a lot of thought and came to the conclusion that maybe I was headed for the same disappointment. So, I decided to cool it and go about my business and not let this happen again."

Axel put his hands on his chin, rested his elbows on the countertop, and looked her straight in the face, eye to eye. "My name is Axel, not Dave," he said. "I have the highest regard for you. I didn't take as long as you did in finding that you were something special, and I fell in love. You might need some more time, and I am not going to push it. Let it happen if it will. You won't find me running away from your feelings toward me. You also won't find me pushing it. We are both young and have plenty of time while you are in school. Besides, I want you to be sure this is not a hit, but the real thing. I don't bounce around emotionally, and I don't have a wife and kids. When you are sure, we will both know it. This reminds me of a song that goes, 'You can't love me if you don't.' Now, let's go see the good movie you picked out."

Over the next few weeks, things were good with this affair, and, just about the time Axel thought it was going somewhere, he got a call from Adam. "Axel, we have an important assignment that we are having some problems with, and the agency, especially Kim, believes you are the right person to carry it out. It is in the country's best interest, and I don't know anyone more qualified to handle this. We need you to fly out here as soon as tomorrow, so we can brief you on the possible assignment. We have already contacted the airlines, and your ticket will be waiting at the airport when you arrive tomorrow. Whatever you are doing with school, have them find a substitute for you. Call them right after I hang up. Do you have any problems with this?" he asked.

"I know you wouldn't call me about this if you didn't think it was a number one priority issue. I really have to sit down and figure out all the things I need to do to make the flight tomorrow. So, there is no use talking about it anymore because it would be wasting time. Give me the airlines, the time, and the flight number, and I assume I am flying to Washington, DC."

"Yes," said Adam, "You have that right. I will meet you at the airport when you arrive. See you." With that said, he hung up.

Axel called his administrative head and told him he had personal problems that required him to leave immediately and didn't know when he would be back. Axel told him he would contact him some time in about a week to let him know the status. He was very appreciative of the fact that these things happen, and Axel wasn't to worry and to make sure he got everything done that he needed to do. He didn't know that Axel felt the same way, even though he didn't know what it was that he was about to venture out on.

After that call, Axel called Tori. This was a little harder, since they had just gone through the mutual feelings they had for each other and decided they were going to let time work it out. Here Axel was telling her, almost in the same breath that he was going to be gone to help Adam on a problem that required a biologist, and then he wouldn't explain any details about the problem. Axel finished the conversation by saying, "I know this might sound strange to you, and, one of these days, I will tell you about it, but I can't now. I just want you to know that I wish I were coming back tomorrow. I am not escaping. I am not fleeing. I love you and will see you soon." She accepted that since she had learned that Axel did not speak with a forked tongue. He said it as it is.

The next day, Axel drove to the airport and soon was on his way back to Washington, DC. He wondered what this trip would bring. *The last one was a dizzy one*, he thought to himself. With these thoughts in his mind about his history and what brought him to this second plane trip to Washington DC., Axel looked around the plane, and most of the passengers were watching the end of a movie or were stirring around waiting anxiously for the plane to land. It was only about ten minutes till the scheduled landing. *Those conversions that the agency made in my body are probably what they want from me now*, he thought. *It wasn't boring to me then, and I know what is waiting for me in Washington, DC. won't be boring this time.*

Then, he heard the pilot make another announcement, "We are about to land. Please make sure your safety belts are secure, and your seat is in the upright position. The stewardesses will be by and check as well as pick up anything you have to dispense. Thank you, and we hope you will choose this airline on your way back."

Axel and the terrorist cell

Adam and Kim were waiting to meet Axel at the baggage check out. They looked happy to see him, and Axel felt the same way about them. He got his baggage, which was only one bag, since he didn't know how long he was going to be here. Adam grabbed the bag and said, "I'll carry this weight. You will be doing all the weight carrying and hard work from here on in." Axel wasn't sure what he meant by that, but he took it for what it was worth. He knew when he got that phone call last night that from that time on, it wouldn't be a "cup of tea," as they say. He knew they wouldn't call him to compete in the jumping contests out there or the spear-chucking contest, and he knew it wasn't time for javelin throwing.

They bull shitted about things like the weather and other small talk on the way to where they were going—Axel knew not where. Soon, they were in a nice restaurant having a good meal. Axel hadn't eaten on the plane and was in need of some nourishment. Those mitochondria were waiting for their food and energy. He hadn't thought about it, but they weren't eating in the main dining room of the restaurant. They were in a room that was remote and private, and the only one they ever saw was the waiter when he took the order and when he was given cash for the meal. Then, it was quiet, almost like waiting for a professional golfer to make a putt. But this sure wasn't a golf course, and there weren't any other players around.

After a while, Adam began to discuss why the agency brought Axel here. "We are expecting a terrorist attack from the information we have been able to obtain so far, but we don't know where or how. We think it might be related to something in Washington, near the capital, but that is only a deduced thought. We have nothing to really say it is going to happen there. We do know that the terrorists that will be involved are in Baltimore at this time. It is a fairly big terrorist cell. The problem with Baltimore is that it is so close to several major cities, and the problem could end up at any of them. There is Baltimore itself, Washington, Philadelphia, New York City, and even as far away as Atlanta. Take your pick. We have a troubling situation that has worked out for us so far. We have our own 'mole' in the group in Baltimore. It's through him that we know so much but not enough to take any actions. We want this to play out as far as we can afford to, so we can determine the higher-up directing this scenario. We don't want to just grab some monkeys and not the big ape. This wouldn't serve the purpose of finding out what they have that could hurt the country. They could have something biological that could be used in the water systems. It could be related to germ warfare. It could be as dramatic as a nuclear-related system, but we don't think so."

"We know that the terrorists have not had the technical know-how or material to carry out an atomic bomb. In fact, it is hard to believe that they would have anything that is at the level of capability that we have in biological warfare either. However, there is always the danger of anthrax and these unsophisticated terrorists making connection with some pissed-off college professor or some chemistry college genius to help them over the threshold. Then, there is the flu that killed tens of millions of people back in the 1920s. Samples of this flu are held in places in Russia and the United States. If anyone got hold of this and put it in spray cans, there would be hell to pay. Therein lies part of the problem. They might find some money-seeking, high-level biologist from one of our universities that could take them to that level of capability. There are some great schools within the distance of those big cities I mentioned; schools with high-level capability in the use of biological methods that might provide a weapon of mass destruction. That's one reason for us picking you. Your degrees in biology and the advanced work you have done in that area would make you an ideal person to be involved and determine what is real and what is propaganda."

"The agency believes that terrorists are more likely to use biological weapons than a nuclear threat, although there are several nuclear sites within the areas mentioned. There might be a possible sabotage of one of those, but the failsafe systems built into these make them hard to sabotage and be successful. It might cause a scare, but you know what, a scare is almost as bad as an incident where there are casualties. People's minds are affected by either one. Here in a country where life has been safe for many years, there is no room for anything but safety. There are many facilities around the areas mentioned with potential issues. There are poisonous gases. There might be potentially plague-producing pathogens. All of these are easier to disseminate than nuclear potentials. They could produce a dirty bomb perhaps, but that would be difficult to produce and isn't really as deadly as some of the biological possibilities. One very good scientist, either from the United States or from a foreign country, with a vendetta against this country for whatever reason, might be very dangerous when supported by a bunch of anti-Americans terrorists—terrorists with money. It's for these reasons that we have agencies like ours that are constantly on the lookout for just the slightest hint of problems. That's why we have you here today. We know we need help." With that said, Kim waited for Axel's comments.

"Yes," Axel commented, "but how does this involve me? How do I pick up on this? This would be like a new world to me. What and who are my contacts? How do I contact them? This blows my mind."

"We understand that," said Adam, "but we might have lucked out on this. We have a mole in the Baltimore cell. He has been there and involved for two years, and this thing is coming to a head. He has convinced them he knows of a biologist who has a gripe with the U.S. government. He told them if they needed more help on anything to let him know, and he would contact this man and make him available. He told them that this person has more against the United States than any of them do. He didn't use your name, since we had instructed him to stay away from doing that. We told him, 'When the time comes, we will give you his name and credentials.' That's where we are now."

"We have developed a whole history for you with a new name, address, credentials, passport, pictures, and anything else you might need. You will be an Iranian who came to this country and went to school in this country, and you speak English very well with a slight accent. Of course, you will be able to speak and understand Iranian with your unique capabilities. You are so smart; you are just shy of a doctorate, only missing your doctorate thesis." Kim finished his comments and looked toward Axel.

"I understand where you are coming from," said Axel. "I just don't know if I can pull it off. What if they expect things of me with this education that I am not able to produce?"

"We understand, and it seems you fail to understand your own capabilities. Keep in mind that when they are asking you questions, we will be hearing them if you so choose, and we will address our computers and have the answers within minutes. All you have to do is to question their questions while we are pursuing the answers. Just delay them with bullshit for a minute or so, and then lean back and pretend you are thinking or challenge their immediate need for the information. While they are trying to satisfy your wishes, we will be looking for the answers. Remember, our systems are working in nanoseconds, while the humans you are talking to think in parts of seconds, at best. They don't know the capability you have within you. Your internal computer and Internet system are unreal. If you activate these with your mental thoughts, then we will be actually listening like if you were on TV. You are a walking, invisible source of information."

"Likewise, we are an invisible source of information and the answers you will need. In most of the subjects anyone would bring up, you are infallible due to the computers backing up your brain via the Internet. You will be able to delay answers by saying things like, 'Sorry, I have been away from home so long that I forgot some of the language. Would you repeat that?' While they are repeating this, we will have found the answer, and then you can nod your head that you understand them. Then, you can now answer if you want. There will be times when you could answer but decide on your own that you don't want to. We believe you have the smarts about you. There is another thing we know; they cannot harm you. You are wearing a suit of armor they cannot see. If the time comes when you want a hood of armor, it is there for the stating by you. You will be like a man playing with boys it would seem to us."

With that said, Axel nodded, indicating he would take this on. "Now, how do I get ready for this venture?" he asked.

"That's why we zoomed you out here. They want to meet you two days from now. You have two days to read through the material we have describing yourself and your past in case it comes up. With your brain and with your self-designed computer inside you, you can write it all down in the memory of the computer as you read it. By two days from now, we will have a hard time knowing you. In fact, you will have a hard time remembering who you were. Your new name is Michael Kasian. We have handkerchiefs with the initials M. K. on them. We have paperwork you received from the university addressed to you. Everything we could think of that a person has had in their past we have supplied you. If something comes up that isn't in there, make sure you are on your internal Internet, and we can hear it and provide it one way or another."

"If you need something sent to you by mail that would authenticate your being you, it will be sent by mail as though it came from Iran, so they can see it and do a paper chase, which we will make sure it provides them with what we want them to know. Our mole has mentioned your name, and they have checked it out and are satisfied with the information they received. We made sure of that. We won't tell you the name of the mole yet, but we will in two days. Meanwhile, we need to fly you up to New York, so when you fly to Baltimore, it will appear as we have made it appear, that you are arriving from Canada. You have been in Canada awaiting this assignment as far as they know. You arrived in Canada from Germany where you were working for a small chemical company named Afalin, having gone there three years ago from Teheran."

Now, Axel was on the flight to New York where he would be spending another day studying the things he was supposed to know before taking a flight from New York to Baltimore. In his mind, he thought of the mole and made sure his name was placed in his solid-state memory of his internal computer. Manny Judit evidently had been a junior engineer with one of the startup companies that work on synthesizing chemical solutions to diseases. He had been with them for four years. Axel did not know if he really worked there or this was also an agency made up to set him in a position to act as a counterintelligence source of information. He had been with this cell group for almost three years. The cell group evidently had a lot of confidence in him. This was either because they thought he was so sharp or they were so weak in their understanding of what they were doing. Axel thought about this and guessed that sometimes they could go with a weak cell made up of gophers if they had some genius like talent at the top of the ladder.

He knew that some way he must find out where the energy, money, planning, and upper muscle were coming from—probably a slick, unnoticed, and well-hidden top guy that no one would expect to be planning something against our country. Axel thought, *I sure hope I am able to perform with the little background I have in intelligence, criminal justice, and whatever else it takes to do this. I did take some special courses on criminal justice in the three years since I got my biology degree and was working on the computer design. I had started to think I wanted to be a policeman instead of a biologist. But, after a while, I liked the computer work so much I thought maybe I was made to be a biology software expert that would write programs on ways to cure disease.*

"*No matter,*" he thought. "*I am what I am now, and I hope I have the guts to carry it out.*" With that, Axel looked down at his hands and realized they weren't really his hands. They looked like they always did, but they were almost indestructible. The thing that amazed him was as indestructible as they were, he could feel with his hands like they were not covered. "*That's amazing,*" he kept repeating to himself, "*that they could make material that didn't feel a bullet, yet my hands, even with the material, could feel the slightest touch. The enemy better not know this or they could drive me nuts by torturing my hands. I wonder if that would work or if there's a limit to what they can feel and anything beyond that is blocked. I should have tried this out while I had the time a month ago. Oh well, I hope I don't have to find out. It's unreal what the agency has been able to do. Talk about great biologists and chemical scientists; this film on my body is a magnificent achievement. I am sure I am playing the guinea pig on this one. If it works out, they will be doing this on others. I understand it cost over one hundred million dollars to just make my covering. I guess I could be called the Many Million Dollar Man like that million dollar man that was on TV when I was a kid.*"

These thoughts, along with the reading through of the material that was on his internal computer about this cell or about his background, was being reviewed on the trip up to New York. Several days later, he was on a flight to Baltimore. Axel had called Manny Judit from New York and told him what flight he would be on. Manny said he would meet Axel at the baggage claim of the Friendship, Baltimore airport.

As the plane landed in Baltimore, Axel had flip-flops going on in his stomach. He knew that now he had to play a man he wasn't. He had to be an actor like Clint Eastwood for a short time. Then, his thoughts drifted rapidly to Tori. *I hope this doesn't take too long. I don't want Tori to have a lot of time to find someone better than me.* For a second, he became envious of anyone who would try to take his place with her like he was playing a role for someone here.

As he walked toward the baggage pickup turnstile, he saw the man called Manny. So, he had at least embedded that in his brain properly. Likewise, Manny saw Axel and waved, and Axel waved back like they had been friends for life. Here was a guy Axel knew nothing about. As far as he knew, he was the head of the cell—not likely. On the way to the hotel where Axel would be staying, Manny winked at him and indicated that he wasn't to speak about anything while in the car. "This is my car, and they might have it bugged," he wrote on a piece of paper. Then, he lit a cigarette, took the lighter, and burned the note.

Already, Axel was beginning to feel like he was in a movie. *Here I come, Clint; you are in trouble now. No more leading roles for you*, he thought as he smiled. It was a few minutes before 7:00 PM, and Manny asked if he would like something to eat. "Sure," Axel said, and Manny quietly whispered to him that he would be able to talk by pointing to his lips and making his hand go open and closed to indicate soft talking while saying out loud that he was starving. If the car was bugged, they wouldn't hear the soft whispers.

While they were eating, Manny told Axel that the group was expecting to meet him tomorrow in the evening and that he would pick him up. "Meantime, you can spend the day walking around or taking taxis around to various sights in Baltimore and out on the Chesapeake Bay. There will be six of them," Manny said.

He gave Axel their names and told him what each one represented in the group. "For one, there is a leader of the group named Mersha. He is the one that pulled us together over time. I don't know if he knew some of them from previous action or not. I do know that they respond to him quite well. I am sure there is at least one and maybe more in the background that are providing Mersha with the money and the directions. Until now though, he has not revealed what our action is going to be. However, it must be something that requires more intelligence in the group. That's where you come in. About two weeks ago in a meeting, Mersha asked if anyone of us knew any biologists or chemists that we could safely bring into the group. It had to be someone that one of us knew quite well and said we could trust. It had to be someone who has achieved some level of success in the fields of biology or chemistry and probably has no good feelings about the United States. I got back to the agency and told them of this request. I guess that's where you come into the act. I don't know what you have done in the past, but the group has checked this out through their upper contacts, and you came out looking like a rose. Then, three days ago, they contacted me and told me to get hold of you. I told them you were in Canada, and I would make contact with you. The rest was handled by the agency, and here you are. I hope you are prepared."

Axel told him he had boned up on the situation and asked him to observe what was going on during any of their meetings. "If you see me avoiding some questions, I want you to think about ways to get me out of the corner they might have me in. I believe the agency has done a thorough job of preparing me for this, but, since they didn't know any more than you just told me, there could be holes that need to be filled." Axel didn't tell him about his personal capabilities, since he felt it served no purpose, and, if the agency thought it did serve a purpose, then they would tell him or tell Manny to provide him with certain information.

Starting a laboratory for the terrorist cell

The first meeting was just to learn each other's names. The head man, Mersha, introduces Michael (Axel) to the other members and told them he had brought Michael on to add some biological skill and knowledge to the group. "We will be meeting for the next few nights to just get used to each other. So, each of you should spend some time with Michael, so he gets to know you."

There were meetings for the next three evenings; they were all at different places to ensure privacy and not alert anyone to seeing them together for more than one night in a row. Axel thought about that, *I guess that would only happen at bowling team get–togethers and this is not a bowling event. But, I have been expecting that we would get on to what it is that I am expected to do and what intelligence I am supposed to be providing.*

Then, on the fourth meeting, Mersha took out a piece of paper and began to ask Axel some questions. They were about biology and stem cells, and Axel immediately turned on his internal computer and Internet system. Mersha's first questions were rather freshman-type questions that Axel had learned early in his education. "Do you know anything about adult stem cells?" he asked.

"Yes, I do," Axel replied.

"Would you please describe the general method used to produce adult stem cells?" Mersha asked.

Axel described (in Iranian) the fact that there are adult stem cells in every part of the body, including the organs, muscles, and nerves.

"For example, adult stem cells can be derived from the umbilical cord and placenta or from blood, bone marrow, skin, and other tissues. The problem is finding them. One must search diligently for them. For a given part of the body, if you were able to sample the cells, there would be an unspecialized cell found among the normal cells. By this, I mean the cell is almost like an embryonic cell that is taken from a mother's embryo or from a fetus that is about eight weeks old. The cell would be like a virgin, not having begun to be specialized into a part of the human body. It has only been in the last couple of years that we have been able to realize that these unspecialized cells are present throughout the body. Experiments on mice have resulted in fantastic results. They have taken skin cells from the mice and placed them in Petri dishes under the proper conditions, and they multiplied quite rapidly. In a month's time, there were millions of them. They have been able to take fully developed parts out of mice and insert these stem cells in those areas, and they immediately began to repair and reform the parts that were eliminated."

Mersha seemed satisfied with these comments and then asked, "How do you go about generating the millions of unspecialized cells from the adult stem cells?"

"As I indicated, the adult unspecialized cells were placed in Petri dishes that had been coated with mice cells on the bottom of the Petri dishes or some other inert material. It was there to provide a rather rough base rather than the smooth one of the glass of the Petri dish. The adult stem cells were placed in these dishes with the proper soup like material, and, under the proper conditions and temperature, these stem cells began to replicate themselves. These replicates were also unspecialized, or they were called 'undifferentiated' by some biologists and chemists, since they retain their virginity. After a given amount of time, each Petri dish was full of these replicated and unspecialized cells, and one had to take care to transfer some into new dishes to continue the expansion of the lot. One can generate billions of cells in this manner. To date, scientists have done many tests and performed dramatic results, but, other than bone marrow transfers, which are done with adult stem cells to reduce rejection, there have not been any human experiments that have received adult stem cells to resolve a medical issue. All the dramatic results have been achieved on animals, mostly mice."

"Bone marrow transplants have been done for thirty years where the stem cells of matching individuals were used to fight leukemia. This has worked reasonably well, but the biggest problem was with rejection over time, since the cells were not from the individual but from a person who offered his matching cells. The recent advancement in bone marrow transplants have been achieved by taking adult stem cells from the person who has the leukemia and using a method similar to the Petri dish method I mentioned, and they have generated huge numbers of unspecialized stem cells of the person with the leukemia. When things have advanced to the point where they are ready to introduce these stem cells into the individual, he or she is radiated heavily to essentially kill the leukemia cells, but, at the same time, it will kill the healthy cells of the person, including his white cells."

"Keep in mind that the white cells of the body fight infection, and, without these cells, the body is prone to disease. Immediately after the radiation, the patient must be kept under very strict isolation techniques, so he will not contract any disease before the unspecialized stem cells are introduced into the patient. These unspecialized cells begin to be specialized into healthy bone marrow cells. The body doesn't reject them, since they were originally from that person's body. The results have been greatly improved over the old methods, and the person doesn't have to take medicine for the rest of his/her life to keep the body from rejecting these cells. The goal at this time is to be able to repeat this kind of scenario on other organs or other parts of the body to fight many deadly diseases. It is felt that Parkinson's disease, hepatitis, dementia, kidney diseases, and others will one day be cured via stem cells, either embryonic or adult stem cells. It is felt by some doctors and scientists at this time that cancer might be due to random adult stem cells within the body that somehow begin to replicate and become invasive. They tend to eventually metastasize and spread in the body until the person is overcome with this cancer. This may be nature's way of using random unspecialized stem cells. We think of cancer as being something out of control, but, if it is started by a rogue stem cell that begins to replicate itself, it is doing what is expected of it. Scientists believe they can eventually use adult stem cells or embryonic stem cells to overcome many organ failures and many diseases and maybe eventually cancer. Is that what you are asking about? Does this answer your needs?"

Mersha said, "This has been a good start. Would you be able to accomplish this generation of stem cells?"

Axel said to him, "I could if I had the right equipment and the right people to help me. It would require a class one clean room as well as the equipment."

Mersha sort of looked up in the air and finally said, "That might not be a real problem. There are a lot of semiconductor companies that have either gone out of business or transferred their processes overseas. In Silicon Valley, there are probably ten to twenty class one clean room buildings that are either up for sale or for lease."

Axel agreed, but he decided to push this a little farther to see where it was headed. "Why would you want to take on the task of generating huge numbers of stem cells? What good would that do, or what bad would that tend to do?"

Mersha looked at Axel and said, "We shall see, but, for now, let's not take this any farther. How about making out a list of equipment you would need, including the type of facility and utilities you would need? When could you have a list made?"

Axel thought about it for a few seconds and said, "Give me a week." Mersha felt this was reasonable and asked if any of the others had any questions for Michael. They all looked at each other like they didn't know what Michael was talking about.

Axel then asked if any of them had ever worked in a class one clean room on any kind of technology, and he didn't receive any positive answers to this question. He received a few minor questions from the rest of the crew, but it was obvious that he would be the one directing this, and all the questions would be coming from Mersha, if any. It was obvious that Axel was the one to be questioned and not the one asking the questions.

After a short while, Mersha said that he had to go and would like to meet a week from this Friday. He said that he felt this gave Axel a few extra days to make up the list. With that, they called it a night, and everyone went out to their cars and went on their way.

Axel drove to the hotel, and, while doing so, he asked from his internal system if they got the whole message back at the agency. "Right on," they replied. "You did a good job Axel in telling them just enough to wet their appetite without really telling them anything of value. We don't know where this is going, but we didn't expect anything about stem cells. We don't know what that implies. It's possible that they were just testing you, and they really don't want to know if you could handle a facility making stem cells. Knowing the players like Mersha and his gang, we will now see if we can track down any information on them and also what would be the connection of stem cells to anything. Let's call it a night."

With that, Axel turned off the Internet to the agency, thinking, *Maybe now I can use my system to call Tori and see what's cooking there. That sure would be a big shift, going from Mersha and his gang to Tori. My mind is so up high right now about the stem cells and other things that maybe I won't be able to have a normal conversation with Tori.* "Hey Tori, what's happening?" And with that, he started a sane conversation with a good-looking woman about three thousand miles away.

That evening, Axel got a call on his internal net from Adam to tell him they had received everything, and they were involved in hunting down data on Mersha and the other guys. Axel said, "I was befuddled at this time about what they had in mind. I guess they couldn't tell me too much, since they were just meeting me and feeling me out for what I could contribute."

Adam said he was amazed at how well Axel's internal system worked. "It's the only system I have ever been a party to where you have constant communication of what is going on without anyone knowing it's happening. You did a great job on the computer system you designed. You are like a walking 'bug' that we use in our business to pick up information, but we have to plant the bug. With you, the bug travels. That's marvelous, and I am very proud of you and your work. The internal computer and Internet provided the ideal spy system, and I hope the enemy of this country never gets hold of such a capability."

Later, when he went to bed, Axel thought about the system and knew that he needed to be aware that no one ever finds about this system or he would be a target. *Of course, to take me, they would have to overcome my strengths and the outward skin like guard system that protects me.* His thoughts continued, *This surely is not the same as the college scene for me, and now I know what Adam has to do every day of his career. Pretty tough and now I can play an important role in his life. I couldn't do it for any other person that I like more.*

After three weekly meetings with Mersha and his crew, there was no further information to be gained about their final objective. Axel was beginning to wonder if they were using him as a decoy. It was like they were just going through the motions. Then, on the fourth meeting, there was a new entry to the game. A rather tall and distinguished-looking man was introduced to him as Jamal Turkhogue. There was some small talk between the various guys, and then Jamal signaled for Axel to go in the next room to talk.

They sat down at a table, and he said that he would rather keep the discussions away from the rest of the party. He then told Axel that the group has leased a site on Scott Boulevard in Sunnyvale. The building was forty thousand square feet, and twenty thousand of it was a class one clean room. It had all the facility requirements Axel had specified, and they now were going about finding the other pieces of equipment that he would need to handle the growing and harvesting of stem cells. After some description of the building and what was in it, Axel asked him if he could be privy to what was actually going to be done with the stem cells.

Meanwhile, he had activated his internal system, so the agency could hear all the things he was hearing. Jamal sort of talked around the subject, and Axel decided to take a huge step forward. He raised his voice, and, in Iranian, he said, "I don't want to just be doing stem cell research. I want to do something for our mother country and want to be hurting the United States. I see no use for stem cells in doing something to hurt the United States."

Jamal listened but put Axel off with an assurance that eventually he would find out the big picture. He whispered, "Eventually you will be astounded at what we are going to do and the major part you will play in this attack on the United States. I can't tell you now, but it will be soon, probably when we get the Scott Boulevard facility in shape and the right equipment in place."

Axel asked if he could go and see the facility, and Jamal said he thought it wasn't a good idea at this time. "We don't want a lot of people around the place at this time that might attract someone's attention," Jamal said. Axel nodded and told him he was right about that, and he could wait, but he emphasized that he was anxious to get started. With that, they concluded the discussion, and Jamal was on his way.

The meetings for the next few weeks were fairly mundane with Jamal giving Axel an updated list of the equipment they had received. Axel asked Jamal to give him a schedule of when the equipment would be installed, hoping to flush out the timing, since that would give him an idea of how anxious they were and also whether they had competent people to install the equipment. Jamal said that he would provide that information.

The following week, in addition to the equipment received, Jamal provided Axel a list of equipment installed and the schedule on the installation of the other equipment on the list. Axel asked him if he had turned on the laminar flow stations that supplied clean air to the facility and whether they were checked out for their lack of turbulence. He didn't know what Axel was talking about, since he had no experience on a clean room or laminar flow stations. Axel described how the laminar flow stations worked and what a class one clean room meant. He told Axel that he would bring another person to the meeting next week who was going to be the manufacturing manager for the facility. "His name is Kirpal, and he knows all about that stuff," said Jamal.

"We will see," said Axel.

Sure enough, the following week, there was no one else except Jamal and Kirpal that came to the meeting. Kirpal gave Axel a rundown on his experience and what equipment they had already installed and which equipment had been checked out to their satisfaction. *He knows what he is doing*, Axel thought to himself.

Kirpal kidded about the fact that they were able to get the equipment for about a third of the normal price, since much of it was purchased from companies going out of business. Axel queried his comment about so many companies going out of business, and Jamal rephrased the statement. "They are either going out of business or they have sent the production overseas and closed the local plants."

Axel was sorry to hear that and thought, *Too many of the advanced technologies are going overseas, and, if we ever get in a war, we will be sitting high and dry because the needed capability will be in some other country and run by the people of that country instead of in the good old U.S.A. and our patriotic people. Who knows, they might be in the country of the enemy.*

The more the team of people progressed to completion of this part of whatever they intended to do, the more nervous Axel began to feel. Anyhow, as Kirpal talked, the people at the agency were listening and taking this all down. This allowed Axel to feel confident that they would be able to stop whatever they intended to accomplish in the future.

Axel learns of new powers

While Axel was working with Jamal and Kirpal, he had plenty of time to do other things during the week and weekend. They didn't want to have the facility work going on during the weekend so as not to arouse anyone's suspicions. During these times, Axel would take a ride down the roads between Baltimore and Washington or go just north of Baltimore and head out toward the Chesapeake Bay. These roads were fairly empty, especially during the week.

He would park the car in the woods and would run along the beach or on some lonely road. There, he could keep trying out his immense capabilities. He had purchased an electronic pedometer that allowed him to determine how fast he was running and the distance he was covering. It only went to twenty-five miles an hour, which he could do when he as in Axelvation two. He modified the equipment, so it could handle fifty miles an hour.

One Thursday, when lying on the beach and no one was around, he decided to check it out. He ate a candy bar before the event to ensure he had enough sugar in his system to feed the mitochondria. In addition, he had some high-level sugar pills and put one under his tongue, and away he intended to go. Axel gave the signal internally to the system for Axelvation two and began to run along the hard sand that was about one hundred feet from the water. He was soon going twenty miles an hour and slowly upped his rate, and then he was at twenty five miles an hour. As he approached thirty miles an hour, his body became tired, and he slowed down. Then, lied down on the sand and rested. It didn't take him long to recover, and now he knew what his second level speed was and his ability to carry it for a certain time. He knew his third level would enable him to go even faster, but he would only be able to handle the higher speed for a shorter time.

He thought, *Maybe the sugar level could be boosted, but my body would tire out. I probably could go forty miles an hour for about three or four minutes under level three. I have never tried to use level three for any major energy use. I have turned it on but only to check to see if it was working. Maybe I will have to use it one of these days for an emergency. I hope not, but I at least know it's available.*

It was fun being able to try these things out. Instead of going to weight lifting class, he would go out along the Chesapeake and either run at a thirty mile-an-hour speed for about fifteen minutes or he would go into the woods and practice his leaping skills, picking out a heavy branch that was sticking out and go to level two and leap to the branch.

At times, Axel would overshoot the branch, and, on his way down, he would signal "up" just before hitting the ground, and he would achieve a soft landing. *Now, I know how they felt when the astronauts landed on the moon*, he thought. He also realized more and more that the superior coating of his body gave him more than "bullet proof" protection. The outfit gave him structural strength. As he jumped down on a level below or jumped up to a higher level and landed the suit took up most of the impact rather than his arms or legs taking the impact. This was another major advantage of the special body coating. The same thing came into play when he took his fists and struck something harder than his own arm would normally not be able to withstand, the body armor took most of the impact and it only felt like a normal blow by Axel's arm.

One day, while running along the lonely beach, he decided to dive in the bay and swim, wanting to check out something with his level two and his hood down. He swam out about a half mile going at a terrific rate and then signaled for "hood down." It was down, and then he did a flip and began swimming down deeper under the water. He went down rapidly, and he could keep his eyes open and could see, and it was like he had super goggles on his eyes. He could out swim the fish, and his ability to hold his breath seemed to be about five times a normal level. *Part of this is because of my lungs being large*, he though. He could swim under water for almost five minutes, travel at a terrific speed, and see everything as clear as if he were running along the beach.

He continued doing various things in the depth of the water. Because he was able to swim fast and hold his breath for a long time and having the body protection, he could go to depths of approximately two hundred feet and return to the surface without getting the bends. The body skin acted like a pressure suit. When he got to the surface, he would leave the hood down for about ten minutes and then release it back to the little bead on his head. With his hair being wet, he needed to part his hair to make sure the hood would shoot back to the same small spot without being hindered by his hair. He didn't know if he needed to do this, but he took the precaution until he could gain more confidence in these unreal capabilities he possessed. When his hair was dry, there was no problem, and the hood shot right back to the little spot.

One day, while beginning his swim, he prepared the agency, so they could monitor the event and take readings. He had an underwater camera with him, so he could take camera shots while in the deep water to show them what he was seeing. He thought about the ability to take pictures and considered that one day he would have to set his internal computer, so it could take pictures of what his eyes were able to see. *This would give me another level of expertise above the normal human*, he thought. Then, he began to laugh at himself. *What am I talking about? With my computer on and connected to the agency, everything I see, they see, and they can make the best pictures in the world with their fantastic camera facility—better than I could ever take with a camera*, he thought.

He told the agency that he wanted to have them take motion pictures of everything he saw on this swim. "And later, I want you to make some still shots of the most beautiful of these pictures," he said.

"No sweat," commented the guy on the other end of the conversation. "You are on camera as of now. Go take your swim and your eye view of everything, and we will record it. Tell me when you want to stop recording."

On one of these excursions, Axel thought about his mother and how she would enjoy hearing about the capability she had given him at birth. He thought, *I was the follower and she provided this capability for me during those hurting hours she had.* He promised himself that he would tell his mother of his exploits when she was older and her days were limited. He knew he had to tell her. He owed her that. She would be so proud. She would also be happy to know that he helped Adam in his profession. He thought, *The two of us have always got along, and now I am paying him for being first and paying my mother for providing this unreal capability.*

As the weeks passed and the facility for the stem cell work began to shape up, Kirpal and Manny set Axel up to tour the plant. As he walked around and checked things out, he was impressed with the job they had done. *It is too bad they are on the wrong side in this equation*, he thought.

Fortunately, they don't know that they are on the wrong side, he thought, as they pointed out the progress with great pride during the tour. After the tour, they sat in one of the offices and had a cup of coffee and talked. Axel told them that he wanted several things.

"I want to be paid more money, since I am taking a huge risk. I want more information about what this is going to be used for or I won't carry out the biological part of this experiment. I want to meet the person responsible, and I want his word that I will receive positive answers to my two requests."

With that said they proceeded into the next office and talked among themselves. When they were finished, they agreed that they would contact the main man and give him the message. "Make sure you find out when I will have the information and when will we have the meeting that I have asked for," Axel said.

"We believe we can have what you ask for within a week. Just keep cool. We respect what you have done to date and want to keep you with this program. In the end, you will be amazed at what we will accomplish." With that said, they parted company, and Axel felt like he was now about to make some progress for himself and the agency.

Of course, my computer and Internet were on the whole time, so this whole conversation was now with the agency, he thought, and he would talk to the agency about it later.

They talked to Axel later and said they would have followed Manny and Kirpal, but they were concerned that maybe they would be scared off if they ever found they were being followed. "So far, this has gone quite well," was the message Axel received back from Adam and Kim.

After that vote of confidence, Axel cut off the computer to the agency and called Tori. The phone rang and rang, and there was no answer. That kind of concerned him, and he left a message that he had called. He let her know that he missed her more each day, and maybe, with luck, he would be home in a few weeks. Then, he called Adam and told him that he was telling Tori that he was out here to help him and to make sure if she ever got hold of him or Laura on the phone to not tell her the truth. "You will have to make up a story of the agency wanting some help on some biology work," he said.

Then, Axel went out and drove back to his pad. He thought about what he had just done and rationalized with his self, *I guess I was kind of lonely, a feeling I never seemed to have before meeting Tori. Damn, why didn't she answer my call?* He decided to mix a dry martini with a few olives in it and partially drown his loneliness.

He just got the martini mixed, and his internal phone alerted him. It was Tori, and now he felt a little better even without the martini. "Where were you?" he asked.

"I was in the school pool taking a swim," she said.

"Wow, I would like to see you in a bathing suit about now. I miss you a lot, and seeing you in a bathing suit would probably be too much for me to handle."

"Oh, I didn't realize you hadn't seen me in a bathing suit until now. Do you want me to send you a picture?"

"That would be the next best thing to having you here," Axel commented. "If you send a picture, send it to Adam and Laura's address, and they will get it to me."

They talked for about fifteen minutes, and then she had to go to some class with Ellen. *That ended my long-distance love life,* he thought. *I guess I have never really told her I love her in a dramatic way, and she has never said the same to me. Perhaps she thought it was just a rouse to get her to go to bed with me. That wasn't my intention then nor is it now. I have to find a way to convey this simple act of showing love so she knows it is for real.* Axel promised himself, when he got back, he would tell her, and maybe they could finally go to bed together. He thought about that a lot but didn't know how she stood on the subject. *I guess I will find out for myself someday. I just know my gonads hurt after that phone conversation, and I have to do something to relieve that, but, first the martini.*

As he downed the martini, he thought about the good work he had done on the computer and the phone and Internet capabilities. *If the terrorists were trying to bug my room or follow me around to see if I have made phone calls, they will be confused. They would probably report to their bosses that I never make phone calls and never talk to anyone."* With that, he smiled. They can't hear a smile either.

It was only a few days later when Axel got a call from Kirpal on his hotel room phone. He told Axel to meet him at the fishing wharf at 2:00 AM, and they would meet the person controlling the strings. This got Axel's heart pumping. He had wondered who this would be and what level of person he was in the scheme of things. He called the agency on his internal phone and told them what was happening. He thought, *One of the things they told me was to try and have the phone calls from these guys last at least three minutes, so they could get a location on the phone call, and, perhaps, if we were lucky, it would be from the main center or another lab.* "Every time you get a phone call on the hotel phone, turn on your internal phone, so we can get the drift of the call and possibly the location." Axel told them he would keep the internal line running the whole time he was with "Mr. Big," whoever he was, and he would take care of the monitoring of the hotel phone calls as they had asked.

The wharf was about fifteen miles away, so Axel got ready and took off. He arrived at the wharf at twenty till two, so he was there in plenty of time for the meeting. He took a walk out on the wharf and sat on one of the wooden benches. It was a nice day for a change, and he enjoyed the birds flying around and some walking along picking up scrapes of food. As always, at places like this, next to the water, there were sea gulls and white shit all over the place. *It's a wonder more people don't get hit with that stuff,* he thought. *But it is just statistics, and, sooner or later, if I sit here long enough, some bird shit will hit me.*

Then, as he was smiling to himself, he was suddenly awakened from his thoughts with a voice announcing their presence. "Hi Michael; how's it going?" Axel looked up, and there was Kirpal with a well-dressed man in a charcoal pin-striped suit, light blue dress shirt, and a neat blue and gold tie. He looked like he was going to a stock meeting or something special.

Axel didn't think he dressed that way just for him. It sort of surprised him, since he had been expecting someone from the Middle East, but this man and his name didn't match that picture. He definitely looked like he was from Europe. He was a tall, trim fella with graying hair. *My guess, he is fifty*, he thought.

"Hi," Axel replied, as he stood up from the bench and faced the two of them.

"This is Dr. Lewis Ishler," Kirpal indicated, as he lifted his hand to address the man.

Axel extended his hand and met his with a shake. "Nice to meet you, sir," he said.

Ishler responded with, "The same for me. I have wanted to meet you, but wanted Manny and Kirpal to be sure of a few things before I entered the picture. Do you mind if we walk along the wharf as we talk?"

Axel found no problem with that, and, as they strolled along the wharf, Ishler talked in a low voice, and Axel had to be particularly alert to catch each word he spoke. As they walked, Ishler said that he had authorized Kirpal to double his pay for the job he would be doing. He was quite satisfied with the efforts made to date. He believed that the equipment being installed was the right equipment for development of stem cells for particular applications.

Axel asked him what the application would be. He said that he would tell him that information in time, but he wanted to be sure of his capabilities before he took that next step. He promised Axel that it would not be boring, that he would be excited by the opportunity, and that it would take his level of academics to a new level. "You will be learning as you are teaching," Ishler commented. Axel tried to gain more information, but it wasn't coming. Then, Ishler asked, "Do you know the difference between a bacterium and a virus?"

"Certainly," Axel answered, being sort of shocked that he would ask him about something so basic and juvenile while talking to a person of Axel's level of experience in biology. "Bacteria are much bigger than a virus and are easily seen with a microscope, but some of them need dye stains to show them up. Viruses are much smaller, and an electron microscope or something of that level of magnification is needed to see the virus. The bacteria do not need a host to live and multiply. They divide by a power of two and quite rapidly when they go into their expansion mode. They can take extreme temperatures both cold and hot and can live hundreds of years in a remote location without a host.

This doesn't mean they can't live on a host. They obviously can. There are many different types of bacteria, and they are both good and bad. Some of them we couldn't live without. In our stomachs, there are all kinds of good bacteria, as well as bad. There are many kinds of food that are aided by bacteria for their chemical reactions. There have been many antibiotics that have been developed to set up defenses against the bad bacteria. However, such good medicines, such as the sulfa drugs, penicillin, and derivatives of these super antibiotics are no longer capable of defending the body against the mutations some of the bacteria have established."

"One of the biggest infectious diseases that were once conquered by sulfa drugs and later by penicillin was the staphylococcus. This used to kill people until the early 1930s, and the sulfa drugs came along and were able to nail this baby. But mutations soon made the sulfa drugs ineffective probably because of overuse of this drug during World War II. Then, along came penicillin, and it handled the staff infections till penicillin was overused, and the staff infection then had to be treated using derivatives of penicillin. Now, there is a more potent staph infection in the hospitals that can't be treated except by very powerful medicines. The staff infection that infects people outside of the hospital is a weaker strain and can be handled by prescription drugs. Relative to viruses, they need a host to live. They cannot lie around on a door knob and wait to be picked up. Someone once called them hitch hikers because they hitch a ride on the person who is sick from the virus and are passed on to others by coughing, shaking hands, or rubbing against others, and they are passed on in every conceivable way imaginable. The virus will enter a cell and multiply quite rapidly and then burst out of the cell in large numbers and spread through a person's system. They mutate rapidly and a good example is the flu virus. This virus changes every year."

"Here in the United States, we are fortunate that the flu virus seems to occur in mid-Asia and eventually makes its way to the United States and the Western world some time later. Since it takes time, the U.S. medical society is able to determine the mutation and make a serum to protect against it. This is done after determining the mutation and deciding on the countering serum needed to set one's body up against that strain. Hundreds of millions of chicken eggs are dosed with the proper counter mutation early each year, and, months later, the serum is extracted from these eggs to provide the flu vaccine. However, this is a statistical game. The vaccine may be established for what was thought to be the strain that would make it to the States, but, sometimes, it is the wrong one they have chosen. When this happens, the flu will strike more severely than most years."

"A couple of years ago, they picked the wrong version but were fortunate enough that the problem version never made it here or if it did it was only in sporadic sections of the country. The flu vaccine was originally discovered by two doctors at the University of Michigan using a dead virus, one of which was Jonas Salk who later went to the University of Pittsburgh and used a dead virus to cure Polio. The HIV virus that results in AIDS is a retro virus. This virus actually enters the body in an unrecognizable form. It works in the opposite direction than the genetics of a human work. In the genetics of a human, the DNA (deoxyribonucleic acid) that contains the genetic code is in the nucleus of the chromosome and cannot leave the nucleus. It is in the form of a double helix, which makes it physically impossible for it to move through the nucleus shell. However, the RNA (ribonucleic acid) can go in and out of the nucleus shell. The DNA writes the code on the RNA, and it leaves the nucleus in a linear form called mRNA (messenger RNA). This is called a codon, which goes to an area in the cell called a ribosome. The complement from the double helix leaves the nucleus as tRNA (transfer RNA) called an anticodon, and it picks up the proper amino acid or acids. It then goes to the ribosome and meets with the Codon, and they form a protein that was called out by the DNA. This is how all the proteins are formed in the body."

"If you think about this cycle and now think about the HIV virus or any other retrovirus, it does the opposite. It actually goes into the nucleus and writes its code into the DNA, and the DNA is now completely different from what it originally was, and the body now is controlled by this virus-infected DNA. This is why it was so hard to find the HIV virus when people originally started to get AIDS. When checking the body for a virus, the HIV virus didn't show up. It took time for it to show up. When the American doctor and the French doctors finally came up with the HIV virus, they then could monitor the blood banks and rid them of blood that was tainted. This helped tremendously, since it allowed people to get transfusions without getting HIV and the eventual AIDS. Does that give you enough information Dr. Lewis?"

"Yes," Dr. Ishler responded. "How long does it take for the person to get AIDS?" Ishler asked.

"It varies. Some people get AIDS in weeks, and others might take twenty years. With the new concoction of medicines the people with HIV get, it can be put off indefinitely—maybe till a cure is found," Axel responded.

"Do you believe there will be a cure found?" Ishler asked.

"Yes I believe they will find a cure. I believe they will be able to find a way using stem cells to reprogram the DNA back to its original state. This will take years. Having the human genome available, we will find how the various genetic pairs affect various parts of the body and eventually will determine which pairs could be modified to eliminate the HIV codes. When that has been done, we will provide stem cells with those pairs available and will be able to replicate the embryonic or adult stem cells having these genetic pairs. These will be injected, and they will offset the HIV. The sooner this can take place after a person acquires the HIV, the better the chance of the cure. Eventually, we will probably develop a vaccine that will inhibit the ability of the HIV to infect the human cell."

This amount of detail seemed to satisfy Dr. Ishler, and the rest of the time they were just discussing things in general about the lab that was being set up. Altogether, they walked and talked for about two hours, after which Ishler was on his way. Axel thought and allowed the agency to hear his thoughts, *I think I just met the guy who is going to either be the leader or lead me to the leader of this terrorist cell. Now, I am going to find out what they want to do.*

On his way back to the hotel room, Axel talked to the agency. They were all excited about the contact with Ishler and the discussion that Axel had provided them in real time. They said they had files on him showing he had done some great work in Germany about fifteen years before and was well respected in the scientific field. Most of his work had been on the development of the genetic code when he first started out of the university. He had done some work on finding improved vaccines for the flu virus about twenty years ago and then spent some time teaching and investigating the science of viruses in Iran. "Since he went to Iran about fifteen years ago, there hasn't been much heard about him. It's like he dropped in a hole, and nobody knows what he has been doing. He is on a visa now from Iran and hasn't caused any commotion among the U.S. scientists."

They could see why he might be involved in something to do with stem cells, since his background indicated he would be proficient in that area if he had spent any time with it in Iran. The agency had been trying to find out if he has or ever had any emotional issues with the United States for anything in the past. They still were working the problem and trying to find out what it would be that would interest him in stem cells. Most stem cell work was proactive work, and they were concerned he might be involved in something not so proactive. They were going to get back to Axel as soon as they found out what he had been working on in Iran. They did have some indications that he had continued his work on viruses; the question was whether it was for the good of man or the bad of man.

Axel develops a terrorist stem cell laboratory

Eventually, most of the equipment was in place at the stem cell lab, and Axel was told he could now start spending his time there on a 100 percent basis. He hoped this would bring a focus on what they were to be doing. The first day there, while checking out the various equipment, he was surprised by Manny and Kirpal who came to the lab and made the rounds with him. During the trip around the lab, Axel mentioned that he needed a technical assistant he could trust to help him with his work. "There will be times when I won't be here, and I need someone I can trust to be here backing me up and helping to direct the operators we will be hiring."

They said they would take care of this, and he should write a description of the qualifications needed. At this point in the discussion, Axel spoke out, "I want to see Lewis Ishler again. I don't want to do anything with the stem cell research without knowing what the end product is going to be." They assured him that they would contact Ishler, but, in the meantime, they wanted to send some operators they had screened and have Axel check them out to see which ones he wanted for the various jobs. "I won't do anything about the selection of operators until Ishler talked to me about what we will be doing with the stem cells. I don't want an open loop, and I want to know if the work on the stem cells is compatible with the end product. It's not that I am concerned about what Ishler's main objective is for the end product, but whether I believe it's a feasible project. I don't want to spend my time on a losing proposition. I am serious about dropping out of the program unless I can be trusted to know the end product and its use."

Manny indicated that his last conversation with Ishler was a positive one. "He seemed to be impressed with your credentials and felt good about the project's direction. I believe he is now at the stage of the program where he believes its best chance for success is to tell you what the whole picture is."

Kirpal said he would contact Isler that evening and set up an appointment. "I will get back to you as soon as I contact Ishler and have a date for us to meet," he said.

With that, the two of them took off, and Axel continued his review of the equipment. *I have to admit I was interested in working on the stem cells and this new lab*, he thought to himself. *It's too bad that it probably is not for a good cause, but it won't be a waste of my time. This is a chance to do exciting work on the front edge of technology. Whatever I learn as I proceed will pay off in dividends somewhere, sometime. I want to get married and have a family, and, for that to be successful, it helps to have a professional position nailed down with a good salary.* These thoughts rambled through his mind as he fiddled with the equipment. He thought of Tori and wondered if she ever thought of him and the long-term possibilities of a family.

Early the next day, Axel was back in the lab and checking out the air flow of the laminar flow hoods. He wished he had an assistant to carry out this rather mundane task. As he reached up to correct one of the blowers, his phone rang, and it was Ishler on the phone. "Axel, I want to set up a time to meet with you," he said.

"Certainly," replied Axel, "your time is my time. I only have my work here to take up my time, and I really can't move on this much farther without a discussion with you."

"How about my coming over to the lab in about an hour?" Ishler asked. "Would that be a good time?"

"Sure thing," responded Axel, "I will be here for a few more hours getting things set up."

Ishler arrived in less than an hour and began talking to Axel in generalities. "The key thing is to be able to produce unspecified stem cells and have them proliferate into large quantities of unspecified cells with the end goal of eventually being able to program them into large quantities of specified (differentiated) cells for our needs. We could use embryonic cells or adult stem cells. I can obtain both. Which would you prefer?"

Axel thought about the question for a few seconds and then responded. "Both types can be used for what you ask. The question I have relates to what is the final cell type that you want to be specified from this large amount of unspecified stem cells that will be produced?"

Ishler replied that he couldn't discuss the final specified cells until he was sure that Axel could keep his end of the bargain to be able to provide large quantities of unspecified cells. "Too many good scientists have tried to produce large amounts of unspecified cells from stem cells, but they have failed. Many times, as the unspecified cells proliferate, something happens, and they become specific cells and therefore cannot be used for our end means. Why, Michael, do you think you will be successful in producing millions of unspecified cells, cells that are like virgins, pristine, and in their original state? It is of the utmost importance that you are able to have these unspecified stem cells multiply into the millions with each remaining unspecified and exact duplicates of the original stem cell. They must remain in this condition until we want to specify them to meet our objectives."

Axel thought about his answer and knew that Ishler probably wouldn't detail his end goal until he was able to show that he could produce large quantities of unspecified stem cells. So, Axel decided to continue the discussion to see where he was going with this, so he asked. "Are you sure you can obtain good embryonic cells and adult stem cells for me to work with in some good quantities? It might take several shots at this before we are successful."

Ishler walked around the lab as if he were thinking about an answer. Then, he turned and said, "I can get one or the other in good quantities. Which would you prefer?"

Axel thought a second and said, "I believe it would be easier to work with embryonic stem cells. They are definitely less likely to become accidentally specified, and you only have to go through one phase to have them proliferate. With adult stem cells, you have to sometimes make them specified and then reprogram them to be unspecified. How would you come about these embryonic cells?"

Ishler said they would come from another country where it wasn't so difficult to obtain embryonic cells. "We have ways to transport them and keep them viable. We have two methods of generating embryonic cells. One is from the actual mother, and the other way is in vitro. We have even taken this one step further. In the mother, fertilization occurs in the oviduct and then normally travels down the oviduct and into the uterus. These cells can be removed prior to the actual implantation. The inner cell mass of cells has the potential to generate any type of cell used by the body. Once they are set in specially prepared Petri dishes and division begins, we can take one of the first eight cells produced, use it, and return the other seven cells to the mother, and she will have a normal birth. The method of using the in vitro cells is somewhat different. These come from married couples that have problems in producing a fertilized egg. In this case, there are many left over after insertion, and these would normally be thrown away. However, we get permission from the donors to use these, and, therefore, no one is deprived in this case."

Axel asked, "At what point would you consider telling me what the end use would be? There are several points in the process where it is obvious we are capable of generating large quantities of unspecified cells. From that point, the only other thing that remains a question is how long they will remain unspecified with no problems."

Ishler walked around the lab quietly and seemed to be thinking about the subject. At one point, he stopped his prancing around and said, "When you prove you can take stem cell blastomeres (single embryonic cell) and have them replicate and proliferate in large numbers, and they prove to be unspecialized, when you can reach this level of proof of your capability, then I will then tell you what we intend to use them for. To show you that I am not trying to trick you and wait till you have generated millions of unspecialized cells over a six-month period, you can prove your capability when you generate one month of unspecialized cells and show that they can remain unspecialized for another month. At that point, we can destroy those cells, and we will then be ready to begin the actual function we want to produce. I believe this is a fair point for both of us. You prove you can do the job, and I will then allow you to begin the large job and will tell you its intention. What do you say about that?"

Axel thought about it a while and realized that Ishler had a point. There was no reason for him to tell him anything until he proved he had the capability of generating millions of unspecialized cells. "I agree," Axel said, as he nodded his approval of that approach. "When will you deliver the embryonic cells to me?" he asked Ishler.

Ishler didn't expect acceptance of the plan so quickly from Axel, and he strolled around the lab in deep thought, and then he turned to Axel and said, "We should be able to deliver cells in the specially prepared dishes you have provided us in three weeks. You now have a good working crew that has been practicing on dummy cells. Keep the practicing going, and I will call you in two weeks to let you know whether we are going to be on schedule or not. If we are, the cells will be delivered in the following week. They will be brought to your lab, and only you will be allowed to accept them." At that point, Axel (Michael Kasian) mentioned that they had promised him a technician or technical assistant for the rough work he saw in the next few months. "Yes, you are right about that. Things have been moving so fast that I forgot about that," replied Ishler. "Do you have someone in mind?"

Axel walked around a little and played the game that Ishler had been playing. He turned and said, "I think Manny Judit is sharp enough to handle the technical aspects we will be facing. Besides, I know him a little better than I know anyone else I have met."

"Yes," commented Ishler, "Manny is pretty sharp. He has been with us a few years and has proven his capability and his support for our work." Ishler sat down and thought about it for a minute and then gave it the okay. They discussed several details for a while, and then Ishler completed what he had come for and went on his way.

No sooner had Ishler left than Axel commented on his internal Internet, "What do you think about that?"

"Well, it sounds like this thing is getting closer to jellying," said Kim. Adam was there also and gave Axel the "hi" over the net. "We are really going to do some searching for the place they obtain their cells. This would possibly give us the first clue as to who is involved and what they intend. We now know it isn't a dirty bomb, but we need to find how they would use the large number of stem cells to provide their dirty work. We sure would like to find more concrete info before you have to carry this any further. What we don't need is for you to carry this to the point of their intended use, and they skip away with the intended weapon before we can apprehend them. However, we are confident in your skills and capabilities and believe you probably could handle this on your own if everything went in the shitter at the last moment. We think you are handling this well, and the whole program is working under control. We just hope it stays that way. If you need to have any information other than what you already know, let us know. We are impressed that you have been able to handle the technical complexity of this so far without our needing to support you with much." Kim continued, "Since Ishler is going to be gone for two weeks before you hear from him, we believe you should take a week off and travel back to the university and the girl you told us about. Adam thinks you are probably getting 'hot nuts' about now."

And with that, they laughed. Axel responded with, "I don't believe going back there will cure that. The woman I see doesn't even know if she accepts me as a lover yet, just a friend. Maybe I could make some progress on that if I had a week. I will call her when I disconnect and see what her status is. I haven't talked to her or sent an e-mail for a few days. She probably thinks I am having a ball. I'll let you know what arrangements I make in the next few days," he said. And with that, Axel disconnected.

Axel went to his car and could hardly wait to call Tori. He turned on his internal system and mentally dialed her cell phone. It bussed a few times, and then there was the great sound of her voice. "Hello, this is Tori."

"What are you doing for the next few days?" Axel chimed in.

"Axel, is that you?"

"It sure is and happy to hear your sweet voice," he said and then laughed. "Listen, I have a chance to leave this job for a week or so and wanted to know if you are going to be free any of the time."

There were a few seconds of silence, and she said, "I have made other plans, but I can change them. Are you sure you will be here?"

"Yep, with bells on," Axel chimed.

Tori remarked, "Tomorrow is Friday, and I have classes, but I will be off for the weekend, and I can probably miss a couple of days of school. That would be exciting."

"Great," Axel shouted. "Maybe we can go up to the North Country and stay at Lake Tahoe for a few days. Would that be okay?"

Again, there was that pause of indecision that didn't sit well with Axel. "I would like to go away with you for a few days, but I must say right now that we must have separate beds. There will not be any of that kind of stay in the North Country. Are you up to that?" she asked.

"Yeah, I guess so. I just want to be near you and enjoy you (knowing inside that this was not true, but it was the best he could hope for at this time) and show you a good time. I miss you," Axel spouted out.

"Yes, I miss you too. I keep hoping you will call me and the days keep going by, but I know you have your work to do. Sometimes, I wonder if that is what you are away doing, but I have no right to think that way. We are more than close friends, and, one day, I might get over this paranoid feeling. So, what time will you get here?"

Axel's heart began to beat, and he gave a sign of relief as he said, "I will be in there tomorrow about eight in the evening and will be at the luggage pickup about eight twenty or so. Maybe if you arrive around eight thirty, I will have my bag out front, and you can pull over. How does that sound?"

"Okay, I will be there around eight thirty or a little after, and maybe we can go and have something to eat," replied Tori.

With that and some small talk, they were off the phones, and Axel was happily driving toward his place. He thought about tonight's meeting and felt he had made a major step by getting Manny assigned to be his assistant. Here, he would have someone close to him who he could trust; plus, he was a pretty sharp guy and could actually add something to the program. *What he doesn't know, I could teach him*, thought Axel. *Plus, it will be nice to have someone around to talk to just to pass the time of day. It gets rather lonesome on this grind twenty-four hours a day. Here's someone I can go out and have a coffee with and shoot the shit. Guys need other guys to talk to. There is guy talk, which is bull shitting, but it's different from bull shitting with a woman. Sometimes, it is just a relief to talk about the ball games and the scores and who is playing great ball and who is screwing up. That sort of gets a lot of heat off a guy.* "Seems like you can bust the balls of any ballplayer when all you are doing is talking about him, and he isn't around to defend himself. I think all guys do that to a certain extent," he thought out loud.

Axel's action saves kids lives

The plane was landing in San Francisco, and Axel could hardly wait to jump out of his seat and go and meet Tori. *God sure did the trick right when he made a woman for man. There is nothing like it*, he thought. *Only yesterday, I was thinking about how a guy needs a guy to bullshit with, but it is different with a woman that gives you a heart pain or a gut pain just by looking at her, and Tori sure does that for me.*

He hurried to the baggage pickup, but, once there, he only had to wait for the bags to arrive, as it seems is always the case. He saw his bag, grabbed it, and hurried outside. Axel looked right and left and back again and didn't see Tori's car, but just before disappointment set in, she pulled up in her car. The heart pain and gut pain hit again. *Never fails*, he thought to himself. She jumped out of the car and opened the back lift of the three-door vehicle. He looked at her, and there wasn't anything he had seen that beautiful since he had left San Francisco. Axel looked around for a second to make sure he was right. *Yep, not a girl around as good looking as Tori*, he thought. Then, he grabbed her and gave her a big hug and a kiss, which he was surprised when it was returned in kind. That made the trip worthwhile right then and there.

"Hi good looking," he cried out.

She sort of blushed as she hollered back, "Get in the car before the police patrol gives us a hard time about double parking."

Before he knew it, they were on their way on Route 380 and then onto 280 toward Stanford where his garage home was located. When they arrived at the house and he had unpacked his bag, Tori told him she had made reservations at a motel in South Shore Tahoe for the next day and five days after that. "That's fantastic," Axel shouted. "I completely forgot to make any reservations and didn't know for sure when you would be available. It should be a great time for skiing. February is a great month. It has the snow pack, and, at the same time, the weather is not that cold. Sometimes, you find women skiing with only bathing suits on when it is sunny and about thirty-two degrees out. They get a better sunburn than they do during the summer. Besides, it is nice scenery for the guys."

Tori smiled at that comment and said she hadn't planned on bringing her bathing suit with her. *Too bad*, Axel thought. He would have liked to have seen her in a bathing suit about now—or nothing. They went to a nice restaurant and had a light meal, and Tori drove Axel back to this house.

"I will pick you up tomorrow at about 8:30 AM It's about a three-hour drive, so we will get there close to noon and be able to catch the first afternoon of skiing. I can hardly wait. I haven't been skiing for two years and really miss it." With that final, comment she was on her way as if this was nothing more than a "pickup service." Axel gritted his teeth.

Sure enough, at around 8:30 AM, the horn blew the message that she was out there waiting. Axel ventured down to meet her and told her they would go in his car. He already has the skis on the roof of his car and his bags in the trunk, and he had tire chains in case they hit snowy weather on the road. Axel took her skis off the top of her car while she was putting her bags in the trunk. Like all women, she had two big bags, like she was going to be away for a longer time than a few days.

As they traveled along the highways to Tahoe, they chitchatted about her schooling, and Axel told her some tall stories about what he was doing for Adam in Washington. He didn't want to tell her the truth, mainly because he didn't think she would believe it. Actually, Axel found it hard to believe. It was like some spy story he had read in a book or saw in a movie. So, he didn't have a hard time making up a simple story about a biological problem he was working on for Adam.

During the first three days at the Tahoe skiing areas, they skied at three different courses, ate at three different restaurants, and had fun dancing at three different places. They enjoyed the north shore for its natural beauty and wilderness feeling. They enjoyed the south shore for its business and many places to go. In between those two places for skiing and having fun they enjoyed crossing the border between California and Nevada. In Nevada they could gamble a little and enjoy the closeness of the crowds in the many nightclubs. It was quite a bit different than the atmosphere of the ski slopes. There was friendliness at both areas, but of a different type. At the South shore and in Nevada they found some great places to dance and wonderful music to listen to. He loved dancing with her, especially the close-up ones. *"Tori is built like a "brick shit house,"* he thought to himself. *"With all the bricks in place, and the smell coming out of the smoke stack was a wonderful smell. I wonder what kind of perfume she wears,"* he thought to himself. *Whatever it is, I wish I could bottle it and take it back to Baltimore with me. She acclimated to wherever she was at the time. When in the snow she was full of energy and brightness; seemingly always laughing and smiling. When in the nightclubs or the warmth of the ski cabins she melted into the background and became a part of it. Here she seemed a few years older than in the snow and sexier to me. I don't know where she gets her nice clothes but they sure suit her and make her even more attractive and more appealing to me. It was wonderful being around her and I know she is happy to be with me. It was nice being like a brother in some contents, but there were times to drop the brother feeling and be more emotional with me. Being in Tahoe sure brings all the venues one would want for feeling love and a healthy feeling of being alive.*

Every once in a while, he would give her a soft kiss on the neck and whisper in her ear that he missed her something awful. She would give him a little hug in return, but he was looking for more. But even the hugs felt great and gave him a chill up his spine. *I sure am glad that the outside agency coating I have for protection doesn't dampen my sense of internal feel, and it's a wonder that it does give me the thrill of a cold chill or whatever it is that you get when the girl you adore gives you a little hug,* he thought.

As they danced, Axel wondered if Tori would ever open up and return his obvious love he had for her. *She must have really been hurt by that other guy. She isn't actually cold, but she is pretty stoic in some ways. It's like her sex emotions got cut off. All the other emotions are there but not this final one, the one that provides the "Croix de guerre" one gets when the love is consummated in a sexual act and the man is warm inside the woman— the one a woman must receive when she is filling the release of her total love.* She's majoring in biology; she surely knows what the man can go through if he is almost there but not quite. He gets "hard balls".

Oh well, he continued thinking, *if I can't get that, at least this is the next-best thing. Maybe someday she will have a release, or maybe I'll be surprised and she doesn't love me. That would really be a downer.* They danced on and had a great time together like the best of friends, which they probably were.

The next day's events turned out to be not as mundane. Tori and Axel had just finished their morning skiing and were at the bottom of the hill taking off their skis intending to go in and have a cup of coffee and a roll. As Axel released his second ski, he happened to look up the hill, and, without thinking, he thought the phrase "Axelvation two" and leapt toward the bottom of the slope some thirty feet away where there was a group of young kids playing. As he was landing, he stated "up" and landed with a soft hop onto the packed snow, and, at the same time he stated, "Down hood," and the hood completely covered his face. Axel threw his body across the bodies of as many kids as his could cover and told them with a loud shout, "Lie still."

What had triggered this action was a snowmobile that had evidently flipped over on the high upper slopes and threw its occupant. Meanwhile, it gathered speed as it headed out of control down the hill toward the group of playing kids. Axel had only been across them for a second when the snowmobile collided with his body and threw it into the air. The snowmobile continued in the air and hit the base of the lodge with a loud crash. Meanwhile, Axel also flew in this direction but landed well short of the lodge. He lay there, aware of what had happened and having been protected by his suit of armor, but something was wrong. It had knocked the wind out of him, and he felt faint and passed out for a few seconds.

He was in a state of shock from the impact of the fast-flying snowmobile. He had never tested the body armor for impact like this. He lay there sort of feeling stupid for a while. He knew he had to do something before anyone arrived at his body and found him not to be hurt. So he muttered the words "Hood up," and, immediately, the hood was gone from view. His ski jacket had been torn from his body, and his shoes had been thrust off his feet. The ski pants were ripped from the thigh of his leg to his waist. It would be obvious to any observer that this man would be hurt very badly. However, as Axel lay there, he realized that this would be the case. This impact hurt him more than the bullets that had been shot at him, but he knew they were superficial and he would be feeling fine as soon as he rested his body for a few minutes. He thought to himself, *"Now I know what this armor can take and my body can be protected by."* Other than the shock and knocking the wind out of him, he wasn't hurt at all, but he knew he had to play that role as the people were running to the kids and him. So, he closed his eyes and lay motionless as if unconscious.

Within seconds, there were people surrounding him, and he heard more than one person yell, "Leave him alone till a medic gets here." Like a good skiing area, there were medics and doctors in the immediate vicinity. Before two minutes had passed by, he heard two voices, one of Tori yelling, "Oh no, someone help him." She placed her lips close to Axel's ears and shouted, "Axel, Axel, please be alive."

Almost at the same time, he heard another voice. "Move away lady. I am a doctor, and I must look at him." Axel felt the doctor listen to his pulse on his neck, and he put his head next to his heart and listened. "He seems to be all right, but we can't tell. Let's get the stretcher and get him to the hospital."

Before long, he was being carried on a stretcher to an ambulance. The next thing Axel heard was the sirens, and, just after that, he heard that wonderful voice again as Tori whispered in his ear, "Be okay Axel, be okay; please be okay. We will be at the hospital soon."

Upon arriving at the hospital, Axel was taken immediately to the operation room. Evidently, they felt he should be in a position to be operated on if the need came about. He was placed on the operating table, and Axel decided that this had now gone far enough. He opened his eyes and asked, "What happened?"

The doctor told him he had been involved in an accident, and he was now in the hospital, and they were checking out his body for injuries. They were baffled that he looked like he was untouched beneath the rags that were left of his clothes. Axel then sat up and said he was okay. "How could that be?" the doctor exclaimed.

"I don't know," said Axel. "I guess I was knocked out for a while, but I am alert now." The doctors made him move his legs and arms and asked him if he had any pain. They had him move his head from side to side to see if any problems existed. Next, they told him to urinate in a cup for them. They wanted to check for blood or other possible clues to any damage done inside of him. They had him read a chart on the wall to check out if his eyesight might give an indication of some damage to his body. Axel read the chart down to the smallest line.

They even wanted to take a blood sample, but Axel refused. He said he was scared of needles. He didn't want them to be trying to stick a needle in a body that wouldn't accept a needle. (This was his thinking and he didn't even know if they could put a needle in him. He would have to ask Kim about that the next time he talks to him. Maybe a needle is possible to penetrate between the threads of the material.) Finally, they had him get up from the table and walk. He did this and then did some deep knee bends to show he had no problems. They gave him two aspirins, had him drink some kind of solution, and told him he would have to stay the night, so they would be able to monitor any effects of the accident. "Sometimes, the person is under shock and doesn't feel pain for hours. We want to monitor you for any signs of lingering problems."

A nurse brought a wheelchair in, had him sit in it, and began to wheel him to one of the rooms. He was rolled to an elevator and taken to the third floor. He was only there for a few minutes when Tori appeared in the doorway. She just stood there in astonishment. She approached the bed and began to cry while kneeling and holding his hand. "Oh Axel, I am so glad you are alive. I don't know when you left my side out there today, but, the next thing I knew, your body was flying in the air. I recognized the red ski jacket and ran toward the accident as soon as the snowmobile stopped with a crash. How did you get there so fast? The parents are downstairs waiting to thank you for saving their kid's lives. You prevented four kids from getting killed. They cannot believe what you did and want to thank you as soon as they are allowed to visit the room. The press is down there also. They want a story of what possessed you to take that gamble with your life to save those kids. Are you sure you are okay and are not avoiding the doctors? They cannot believe you don't have a scratch on you. The snowmobile must have hit you at sixty miles an hour and smashed against the lodge stone wall and was demolished."

She kept rattling off things as fast as her voice would allow. It was obvious to Axel that she was the one in shock. As she spattered on with words that were meant to convey to him her amazement, excitement and joy of his body being in one piece, Axel rubbed her hair on top of her head and said, "Don't worry. I was lucky, and the thing must have just missed my body."

"I can't believe this," Tori exclaimed. "When I went over and saw your motionless body, I was sure you were dead. That crash would have ripped open the kids that you covered. I am so proud of you Axel. That was a brave thing you did. There are not many people that would do that in this world. You saved several lives and the parents are downstairs wanting to talk to you. You must talk to the parents. They so want to thank you. Do you believe you are in good enough shape to allow them to come up to the room? They will only allow two at a time to come up, and I will be allowed to stay. The nurse already told me this. Can I bring up two of them now?" Axel gave her permission and was sort of embarrassed; knowing that there was no way the snowmobile could have hurt him with his suit of armor. He had to admit to himself that the snowmobile hitting him knocked the wind out of him and caused him to lose consciousness. It was much worse than getting shot by a forty-five, but still he felt good and was happy for the kids.

Soon, a man and lady in their late twenties or early thirties came up to the room along with Tori. They both extended their heartfelt thanks to Axel. "I don't believe that anyone could have done that without any respect for their own life. That is the bravest thing I have ever witnessed, and I am so happy for you that you made it through that traumatic experience. I still cannot believe my son is alive, and you made that happen. I know there are three other sets of parents waiting to give you a hug."

Axel answered back, "I believe there are many men in this world that would have done that if they had the chance. A man, if he is raised right, respects the lives of young people and will not think twice if given the opportunity to save a child." The woman broke down in tears and asked if she could hug and give Axel a kiss. He nodded, and she reached down and put her arms under his back and pulled him up and kissed him on the forehead, with tears running down her face the whole time.

Axel was so embarrassed and so moved that tears came to his eyes. "Thank you, madam. That is more than I deserve."

They wanted to know his address, so they could send him a card every so often. Tori offered to give them Axel's address. She also gave them his e-mail address. With that, she said, "Many times, it is easier to send an e-mail than send a card or make a phone call." They thanked her and were on their way.

During the next hour, Tori brought, one by one, the parents of the four children up to Axel's room. The story was the same in each case, with the parents praising Axel and giving him a hug and kiss with some kind words. Tori told Axel she was so proud of him. They talked a while, and, soon, it was time for her to leave, since they didn't allow unrelated visitors after 9:00 PM. Before leaving, she leaned down next to Axel's face and said something he was proud to hear and would remember the rest of his life. Tori said, "Axel, you are not only handsome and intelligent, but you are brave and caring. I am so happy to know you and enjoy being around you." With that, she gave him a kiss on the lips and was soon on her way.

Axel lay there for many minutes after she left, stunned at what had occurred during that day. He closed his eyes and thanked the Lord for his mother's gifts and for Adam having him go out to the East Coast. Without that body armor, there was no way he would be alive today, and he knew that he would have tried what he did even without the safety of that armor. He thanked the Lord for that upbringing his parents had given him. Then, without much thought, he realized he was very tired, and he closed his eyes and had a restful and peaceful sleep; happy with himself.

The next day, Tori arrived early to see if Axel was still in good condition and ready to head home. Sure enough, there he was with his nightgown on and reading the local paper. It had headlines in it that stood out, "Brave young man saves the lives of four." He read it and felt a little guilty, knowing that he was well protected during the incident. He had wondered to himself if he should tell Tori about his capability. It was sort of unfair to keep this from her. Then, he realized that it might eventually compromise the position of the agency if the Baltimore terrorist group ever heard about it. So, he chose discretion above valor in this case. Maybe one day when the Baltimore situation was handled and if Tori and he were still friends, or lovers, or married, then he would tell her the whole story. He looked up and saw Tori entering the room. "Ready to go?" she asked.

"I guess I would be if I had some clothes to wear," replied Axel.

"I think I took care of that problem," she said as she held up a set of sweat pants and a sweat jersey. "I hope you wear a large," she said. Before long, they were on the road back home. She asked him how he felt, and, although he felt great, he said, "I am a little sore from the experience but ready to roll."

"I am amazed," she said, while glancing in his direction. "What you went through is an act of God to have done that and not suffered major damage to your body. I was and am very proud of you. I will miss you while you are gone. I will miss feeling so comfortable and safe around you. I think you know that now. I hate driving you to the airplane but I love the fact it is me driving you and not someone else." With that said, she winked at Axel and gave him a big smile.

Stem Cells work on pigs

The next day was sort of uneventful, and, before he knew it, he was on the airplane and on his way back to Baltimore. He was thankful that Tori was free to drive him to the airport. He sent an internal phone call to Kim and Adam telling them he was on his way back to the lab. He didn't mention the experience he had at Tahoe and hoped this would go unnoticed, both by them and anyone in the Baltimore cell. Then, he gave Manny Judit a call and told him he was on his way and would appreciate him meeting him at the airport. He asked Manny if anything of note had occurred at the lab and was assured that everything was in good shape. "Did you get a call from Ishler?" he asked.

"No," Manny replied, "I didn't receive a call from anyone of importance. We did get some additional equipment that you had ordered before you left, but that's about it."

After a few days back at the lab, Axel got a call from Ishler. "The Petri dishes with the embryonic blastomere cells are ready and will be hand carried to the lab tomorrow," he said.

"That's great," replied Axel "We have things lined up here and are ready to begin the proliferation step in the experiment. We'll look forward to receiving the material."

After that, Axel had Manny come into his office, and he explained the steps again that he must have told him ten times already. "We must make sure we have the timing down and the temperatures controlled at all times. It is also important that the air quality of the lab is being controlled to better than one micron per cubic meter. We can't afford any contamination from the air environment in the lab. The blastomeres will keep dividing, and this represents the proliferation. As each Petri dish reaches a certain level, another Petri dish must be ready to accept cells. The dishes and the cells within them must be handled quite gingerly as cells are moved from a full Petri dish to the next and allow the new dish to continue the proliferation."

"During this time, the temperature must remain in the controlled desired temperature range. If the cells touch one another, they will become specialized, and they are worthless. No two cells can touch each other. One Petri dish full will accommodate approximately fifteen new Petri dishes that have been properly prepared with the rough organic material we have been using. These Petri dishes must be prepared approximately ten hours prior to use with only plus or minus twenty minutes of error allowed. Then, they must be moved into position as we have practiced. When the blastomeres have expanded to the proper area of the main Petri dish, they are then not touching, and they are to be moved within ten minutes to the new dishes and done without causing any damage to each of them."

"Done properly and with the controlled temperature, you should see the blastomeres regain their proliferation almost immediately. The main dish will continue to generate additional cells, as will all the other dishes. You need to have a trained operator on each of the new dishes and watching their proliferation. If, at any time, one of them sees the cells in their dishes take specialization, they are to take that dish and dispose of it as we have trained each of them. When they see the proliferation proceeding as planned, they are to inform their partners to begin to prepare the new Petri dishes for taking on the larger number of dishes that are providing new cell generation. Now, repeat that back to me."

With that instruction, Manny began his repeat of the instructions. He then went and had all his operators rein formed of their procedures. So the operators would not forget the instructions, a CD was played over the loud speaker and kept repeating the steps in the process.

The next day arrived, and Axel, Manny, and the operators were awaiting the beginning of the massive growth. There would be some failures in this task, but the main objective was to keep this proliferation going for one month. Axel said, "At the end of that time, when we have a considerable number of cells, we can stop and then place them in incubators with a constant temperature control. The objective is to continue looking at these dishes for which we have stopped the proliferation and see that they remain unspecialized. This is the key."

At ten o'clock, the blastomeres arrived in their dishes that were in controlled temperature chambers. Immediately, Axel and Manny began their part of the procedure, and now the process would continue day and night for the next thirty days.

During the thirty-day period, the dishes were reviewed under a large number of microscopes that were placed above the dishes as new dishes were generated. These were electronically tied to a television monitor that constantly displayed one of the dishes, and, after a set time, the next dish was displayed on the monitors. In thirty days, the lab was about half full of dishes in controlled temperature areas. This part of the experiment went on without a hitch. Now, the proliferation was halted by an action taken by Axel and Manny. Now, the procedure was to see that the cells in these dishes all remained unspecialized for thirty days. This would prove their capability of being used when the specialization was desired.

As before, the dishes were in a controlled temperature and being monitored by a microscope above each dish, and the vision was transferred to the monitor. Manny and Axel reviewed the monitor scans on their first go-around. Everything looked good on the first go-around, and now the procedure of watching the TV monitor was taken on by a different operator for one hour and then another for the next hour and so on. This procedure continued for thirty days.

Meanwhile, Ishler and some new faces appeared at the site to view what was happening. Ishler talked to Axel about the progress and the possible next steps. Ishler remarked to Axel, "Things appear to be proceeding quite well, and it looks like you are going to meet your end of the bargain. I will probably drop in every five days or so while this step is proving out. However, if you see a problem, I want you to call me immediately. You have my cell phone number."

"No problem," said Axel. Then, Ishler and his compatriots left the building.

Ishler came again in five days and then didn't come for another ten days. Then, he followed that with a visit in five days. At the end of this twenty-five-day period, only one of the dishes had failed, and it was discarded accordingly. As Ishler was getting ready to leave, Axel stopped him with a comment, "We should talk." Ishler turned and asked Axel what he wanted. Axel looked at Ishler and said, "I think it's time to talk about where we are and what you are going to do next. In five days, we will have met the objective and will be in a position to specialize these cells. Isn't this what you have been waiting for? Shouldn't I be prepared to carry this to the next intermediate step? And what is the next intermediate step?"

Ishler pointed to Axel's office and said, "Let's go in here and talk."

When they were in the office, Ishler began a long discussion about what the next step should achieve. It's important to realize that Ishler always spoke in English when he was talking out among the operators and others, but, when Ishler and Axel were alone, they spoke in Iranian. Ishler continued this discussion in Iranian, and then, all of a sudden, he stopped and looked at Axel and said, "Do you speak or understand Russian?" Axel felt a trap coming and decided to answer in the negative. He felt that some time in the future it might pay off if no one knew he could speak and understand Russian. "That's unfortunate," Ishler continued, "because I will be bringing someone with me in the near future that speaks Russian but no Iranian. He can speak and understand a little English." With that, Ishler continued his discussion, but, in the end, it boiled down to a few sentences. "I would now like to see if you can take a harmless virus and cause it to be accepted by each of the cells without their being specialized (or differentiated). A harmless virus or any virus should be able to enter an unspecialized cell and the cell retains its pristine nature; in other words, the virus enters without a resultant specialization of the cell. The virus is a parasite and needs a host to live on."

"The host range of the virus will depend upon the presence of certain receptors. Thus, if a host lacks the receptor for a virus or if the host cells lack some component necessary for the replication of a virus, the host will inherently be resistant to that virus. For example, mice lack receptors for polio viruses and thus are resistant to the polio virus. Similarly, humans are inherently resistant to plant and many animal viruses. We need to find if each of these unspecialized cells will be ideal lodging places for a virus without the cell itself being affected," Ishler said.

"Yes, but suppose they are; what then?"

Ishler looked directly into the eyes of Axel and said rather abruptly, "Then, this experiment is a failure, and the total project is a failure and we can stop immediately." After a pause and a period of silence in the room, Ishler's temperament changed, and he smiled and continued his dissertation. "If, however, we retain the unspecialized cells with a virus in them, 'we have a ballgame,' as the Americans say. If we provide a virus that is not a harmful virus, the virus should be able to play an active part in having the unspecialized cell accepted by some part of the body where we want it to act. The virus acts as a pointer to point toward the area one wants the cells to proceed to. Let's assume we have a defective lung, and we pick a virus that normally goes into a lung. We can now use the unspecialized cells with this virus to point to the lung and enter it. Once in location, such as in a lung that is defective, these stem cells will become specialized and will begin to generate healthy cells like the ones in the nondefective part of the lung."

"Have you seen this happen?" asked Axel.

"Yes," replied Ishler. Axel thought a while and then said, "The one problem that could exist is that the virus needs a host it can live off of. If the virus is left for any length of time, it will become inactive and cease to exist as a virus."

"Yes," replied Ishler. "The studies I made in Iran indicate a virus can remain in a cell for approximately three days without a form of nourishment; any longer than three days, and it becomes ineffective."

"Where do you propose we try these ones we have nurtured along?" asked Axel.

Ishler replied, "I believe we should bring in five young hogs this weekend. We can remove part of a lung from each of the five hogs, and then we can try the experiment on them."

"Why hogs?" asked Axel.

"Because the virus we will bring will come from the lungs of hogs. They live in hogs from their day of birth till the day of the hog's death and cause no problems."

Axel was stunned by this answer and thought, *If this is true, then this doesn't sound like these people are terrorists. It sounds like they are true biologists that want to take stem cells to this level.* Then, Axel asked, "What happens if it works? Where do we go from there? What's the next step? I know you don't want to cure hogs' lungs for a living. I know this is not the end target. Where are you going with this?"

Ishler brought back that sneaky smile of his and said, "If this step works, we are in business; however, what business is the question. I will not answer that question at this time. I will answer it when we see if we can provide five hogs with new sections of their lungs."

Axel looked at Ishler and commented, "Stonewalled again. It seems that I take this project one step further along the axis to success, but I don't know what that success is. Why not give me the big picture? Perhaps, if I knew the direction you wanted to go, then maybe I could provide answers where you have none. You are not using the power of my brain to its fullest. Do you realize this truncation of my understanding of the final goal might be the thing that keeps this project from reaching the final goal?" With that comment, Axel vented some Iranian cuss words and pounded on the table. "This is not fair," shouted Axel.

"I realize this is frustrating for you," said Ishler, "but I want to make sure of success before I provide any information on the final goal. It is like working on a patent, and I don't want anyone to know what my patent goals are. This is not meant to be a discrimination against you, Axel. It is just the way it is."

Axel looked at Ishler and said, "Now, it's your turn to do something worthwhile for a change. Since you have been able to experience the successful transfer of a virus to an unspecialized cell without the cell being specialized, you must tell me step by step how you did this."

Ishler looked back at Axel and said, "You know, I forgot about that. I just took it for granted you would know how to do that step. You are right, and I will give you the complete directions on the key steps in doing this. You have the equipment I used, so I know you will be in position to be successful on this. I will send you an e-mail on exactly how to do it, step by step. You will receive this by tomorrow morning."

With that, Ishler changed from his Iranian speaking to English. He opened the door, walked out into the lab, and bid everyone farewell. "Good work, so far," he exclaimed. Axel stood there in silence, frustrated, and unable to satisfy his need for an answer. Everyone in the lab was of a different feeling, feeling they had made major accomplishments over the past couple of months.

Axel thought about the day as he drove home. He had achieved various goals and received several surprises during this day. He kept wondering where the virus was taking him. He decided to contact the agency and discuss this with Kim and Adam. He had been sending all of today's comments to them via his internal Internet and phone system and hadn't heard from them. He continued his thoughts as he traveled along and dialed in the agency. Kim answered, "I figured you would be getting hold of me after today's surprises.

How do you feel about that Axel?"

"I guess I am a little confused. I thought Ishler was going in a different direction than today's surprise. What do you and Adam make of this?" asked Axel.

"We have been thinking about several things. The first thing is that he mentioned your ability to understand Russian. I am glad you gave him a negative on that one. The next surprise, of course, was the one about the virus and its end use. We are a little confused about that one."

"Same here," commented Axel. "That took me by surprise, but, the more I thought about it, the more I became enchanted with it. Whether this is Ishler's end goal or just an intermediary step, it is a powerful step. If we can do this, it would be a major step in the direction of good—no matter what the following steps are. It intrigues me. I thought about the acceptance by the cells of a virus, since he mentioned it. We know a virus must have a receptor within the host for the virus to take hold and infect the human cell. Without a receptor, the virus can exist in a human cell, but it won't infect it. At the same time, a human cell normally has defenses it sets up to combat the virus. Many of these defenses are based on the history of the host and the defenses it built up in the past."

"Cells have a memory when it comes to defenses against an antigen. In our case, the cells are pristine. They have never acted as cells. They have no receptors or no built-in defenses. They are basically inert until they become specialized. In our case, we have several hundred thousand cells that are unspecialized. They have no history, and they might be ideal for providing an intermediary host for the virus. If this is the case, an injection into the lungs of a hog with these pristine stem cells might find that the virus indeed helps to direct the stem cells to the proper section of the hog's lungs to begin to specialize and build active lung cells. This being the case, we might find that, a month from now, we have hogs with healthy lungs and living alongside of other healthy hogs that have not gone through this cycle. That would be a wonderful achievement. If we can attain that and keep Ishler from using anything we learn from this to cause harm, we will have indeed accomplished something remarkable, something that could be used to benefit society. In this case, Ishler will be giving us information on how to transfer the virus to the unspecialized cells without their becoming specialized. It took him years to learn this, and we will have it on one long e-mail by tomorrow. If nothing else, we have learned a valuable and significant piece of information. I am going to work on preparing a procedure for transferring these viruses to the stem cells we have generated. It will be interesting to see what I come up with and compare it against his findings."

With those comments, Axel cut the communication and proceeded home, while his mind kept thinking about a solution. He wondered, *Now, maybe I have three problems, one with how to have the virus placed in the cells without the cells being specialized or ruined, another on how to transfer the cells and their virus to the hogs in the proper condition to function as we want, and the last is to determine if Ishler and his people are friends or foe. None of these are easy, and together they might be too much for me to resolve. At least, I always have direct contact with the agency and can receive their help. That reminds me, I need to call them back and make sure they have someone working the problems there.*

That being decided, Axel called Kim and told him to contact the right people in the agency that would understand how to do the first two of these. "And as far as Ishler is concerned, we can compare their inputs with the information Ishler will unveil with his method. Maybe you will find a better way to do it than Ishler found."

"I doubt it," said Kim. "He probably has worked on this for years and is ahead of our people, but we will check."

The next day, Axel was back at the lab and setting up an experiment where he would take one of the Petri dishes and place it in a sealed incubator with a sealed vial. He set the temperature at 98.6 degrees Fahrenheit and waited for the dish and its inhabitants along with the sealed vial to reach this temperature. His setup included a microscope inside the chamber, so he could watch the stem cells. He wanted to see if they stayed unspecialized if he opened the sealed vial and left them in there for a few hours. After preparing this scenario, he was able to move a remote joy stick that allowed him to grab the vial inside the chamber and break it open above the Petri dish. He believed with it open the virus would rain down on the Stem cells and do what they normally do. With these thoughts in mind, he completed this task and watched very intently for fifteen minutes, and then he went to get a cup of coffee out of one machine and a roll out of another machine, sat down at the cafeteria table, and enjoyed his first food of the day.

He thought about how to remove the Petri dish from the chamber when he was convinced it had completed its function. He came to the conclusion that, after three hours, if he didn't see any change in the appearance of the cells via the microscope, he would place a glass dish over the Petri dish using the remote control. He needed to put a special mask over his nose and mouth that would filter any particle out that was over a tenth of a micron in size. The filtering system also included a carbon filter that would trap any virus that came out of the system. This would protect him from the virus, even though it probably wouldn't harm a human. After removing the dish, he needed to remove one or several of the cells and give each a thorough review by microscope and then by electron microscope. He believed he should be able to review the cell and determine if it had been entered by the virus and if it had remained unspecialized. If he found this to be true, then he would take the Petri dish full of stem cells and inject it down the nose of one of the hogs that had a partial lung removed that day.

He proceeded through these thought-out steps and came to the conclusion that things looked promising relative to the Petri dish and its contents. He decided to complete the task by injecting the examined dish and its contents down the nose of the hog. With that done, he decided he would check the hog twice a day to determine if it was in good health. Some of the checks would relate to listening to the hog's lungs, taking his temperature, and noticing if he ate his meals without a problem. He had a baseline to work from, since he had listened to the hog's lungs that morning before the removal and again after the removal. He knew its lungs sounded sort of raspy since the removal of the lower part of one lung. If it was in good health at each check and his lung sounded the same, then he would have a strong feeling that he at least had done no harm. If the hog continued to check out, he was hoping to hear an improvement in the sound of his breathing and perhaps even a better appetite.

If it showed an increase in temperature, then he knew it had acquired an infection. If this happened, he needed to determine whether to give the hog some type of medication or put it out of its misery. He felt good about this whole approach, and, after he initiated this whole act, he decided to call the agency on his inner phone. He needed to bring them up to date and determine if they agreed with this procedure and if the hog contracted a temperature gain he needed to know what he should give it. Kim said they would find out about any medication and told Axel that he hadn't received any solid inputs from his contacts to date. "Keep me apprised of the results," he told Axel.

Fortunately, the steps proceeded as he had envisioned. After a few days and no problems with the hog, he contacted the agency and gave them his update. They told him, if the hog had a temperature gain, that he should treat it like a human being and give it aspirin for the fever. They recommended ten aspirin, and, if the fever persisted, to try another ten in two hours. Meanwhile, they would leave a filled prescription for a Mr. Michael Kasian at the drugstore that was only a few blocks away.

By this time, Axel had his assistant, Manny Judit, informed on what he was doing. He wanted him to know all the steps, so he could help if this worked out, since he wanted Manny to do it on the other four hogs, all of which seemed to be enjoying their stay at the lab. They hadn't been touched yet and wouldn't have their lungs invaded until Axel felt he knew the answer to the questions he had in his mind and the answers he received from this first hog. Meanwhile, he had Manny monitor the amount of food the four hogs ate at each feeding and how the patient hog's appetite compared. These procedures continued for a week, and there was no indication that the hog was ill from the procedure, and there was no indication that what had been performed worked. Axel kept Ishler updated on his progress, and Ishler was surprised he had gone ahead without any of his inputs.

On the eighteenth day, while Axel was checking out the patient hog, he noticed an improved breathing sound coming from the animal. This excited Axel. He went back an hour later to check and see if it still sounded improved. He was elated that it sounded better to him, and he called Manny in to have him check. Manny listened intently, and a smile came across his face. "Sure enough, boss, that is a better-sounding hog. He is not as good as the others, but he is better than he was eighteen days ago." This progress continued, and, after the fourth week, Axel decided that the sound was so good that he should take an x-ray and a CT scan to see how the lung looked. He got on his internal phone, called the agency, and provided them with his findings to date. He was excited and told them he would call them back when he had viewed the films.

Manny and Axel slipped a long table that contained a jack under the hog and tied its legs to tie-downs on the table. Then, the table was jacked up and wheels released, so they could roll the hog down to the lab containing the equipment they needed. When they get the hog in position under the equipment, they took duct tape and wrapped it around the hog and under the table and then around several times, so the hog would not move while they were taking the pictures. They tried to take the pictures, but the hog seemed to always know when they were going to do something, and it moved. Manny and Axel kept going back and forth from fixing the hog down tighter and going behind the barrier to take the picture. On the second try, they got the x-ray, but it took six times before they got a clear CT scan. They were elated at what they found.

They placed these pictures next to the ones that were taken before and after the lung had been partially removed. Now, they saw a lung that was not as good as the initial picture but better than the one with the lung partially removed. This was remarkable, and they danced a jig around the room. This was a major advance as far as they were concerned. Axel said, "There is no doubt in my mind that the hog will have a full workable lung within a six-month period. With these results, we might not have to do anything to the other four hogs. If these results continue on this hog, it is definite feedback that the method works. How often, we don't know, but it is a game of statistics. We have so many unspecialized stem cells that it would be a matter of mathematics on how many hog lung problems would be relieved by this approach. We need to provide this information to Ishler. This proves the stem cells remained unspecialized with the virus in them, and they became specialized in the hog's lung and began to repair the damaged lung."

"Looks like we are in business," said Manny.

The Virus
and the Stem Cells

"Right on!" shouted Axel. "We will have to see what Ishler has to say about this. He might want to see it repeated or he might decide to go to the next step that he has in mind." With that, Axel looked at the hog and said, "I am going to call you Henry; Henry the First; Henry the First Hog. You deserve a name for what you have achieved." With that, they took Henry the First, back to the pen that had been constructed for him and gave him a good meal as reward for his progress. Henry ate a hearty meal.

Before contacting Ishler, Axel decided to make the agency aware of these preliminary results. They were impressed. Both Kim and Adam and others within the agency were surprised at this sudden turn of events. All of them were quite interested in learning what Ishler had to say about this and his decisions. Kim said they would spend more time on these results. They had to keep the information at a low silhouette within the agency, since information like this spreads like wildfire even within an organization that was proud of its ability to keep secrets as secrets.

Kim remarked, "Before you know it, the media would get the information, and the newspapers and TV would be saying a complete hog was morphed from some stem cells from a mouse or something to that extent!"

Immediately after making the agency contact, Axel contacted Ishler and made him aware of all the details. Ishler was probably more amazed by the rapid results than the people at the agency. "I had expected these results eventually," said Ishler, "but I didn't expect these results this early in the program. We owe much of this to you, Michael, and your attention to detail. You must have made the right steps one after the other." Ishler had been made aware of the various steps being taken by Axel as the experiment began.

Axel said, "I think the results indicate the high level expected of this approach, and I wonder if we have to continue the experiment on the remaining animals."

Ishler said he would think about the results and get back to Axel on how to handle the rest of the plans on the other animals. "You have to keep monitoring Henry (since Axel had told Ishler they named the hog Henry) and determine if there are any side effects related to the experiment. Since this is going to take a couple of months, I believe you should begin the same procedure on a second animal. This will give us a backup if something unexpected happens to Henry. My first thought is that the results on Henry were sufficient to stop this part of the experiment, but only if Henry shows no side effects and continues his progress. If you take a scan of Henry every two weeks, and there continues to be positive results with no side effects for the next two months, then I will accept this as a valid reason to consider stopping the remaining steps on the other three hogs. The second hog's results after a month or two will give us substantiating evidence that this is the right direction."

This was a very positive response by Ishler, and Axel finished the conversation with the question that continued to haunt him. "If we see these results continuing for two months, what will be the next step of this experiment that we have been doing all this preparation for?"

Ishler was quiet on the other end of the phone. Then, he broke the silence and said, "I will report these findings to my superior and ask that we make you privy to the final objective. I personally believe that you have shown the intelligence, the patience, and the true desires of an Iranian citizen and will recommend this take place. I will be contacting you."

With that, the conversation ended, and Axel sat quietly absorbing and analyzing the entirety of the conversation. He was satisfied that he had done a good professional job of this and felt proud. *Maybe,* he thought, *this will bring out the beast that must be hiding in the closet of this group.* It was the first time Ishler had mentioned his boss. *We will see*, he thought.

The next couple of weeks went fast, and he and Manny had gone through the same procedure with a second hog. At the same time, their second scan of Henry showed the lung to be even more advanced. These results were forwarded to the agency as well as to Ishler. Henry continued to be healthy with no fever and ate like a "hog." *Why not?* Axel thought, *That's what he is.* By this time though, Henry was considered one of the family and had been raised above the hog status. It was a happy thing when Axel looked at Henry the hog and saw him in his healthy ways and seeming to enjoy the attention he got from all the operators in the lab. Two weeks later, the lung continued to show advancement, and the second hog showed the same results that Henry had shown at this stage of his procedure. In some ways, Axel began to feel like a veterinarian, making animals feel better and enjoying the results of his commitments.

These last results on the two animals seemed to buoy Ishler's hopes for a meeting with his boss that would be positive. However, Axel's latest conversation over the phone left him puzzled. There was something different about the tone of the conversation, not that it wasn't positive about the results and Ishler's comment that his boss would be glad to hear these results, but the tone indicated to Axel that maybe Ishler didn't want this day to come. Axel had a strange feeling about this. Maybe he didn't want this day to come either. Things had been so positive and so much in the right direction that he enjoyed these days of praise. But now, Ishler's tone hadn't sat well with Axel. He called the agency and discussed this with them. He wanted to know if they had heard anything to the contrary about the results through any of their contacts. He wanted to know if they really had contacts with whoever was Ishler's boss.

Kim and Adam told him that they had feelers out, and there was some response coming back. "Something about a different virus being toted somewhere in the Middle East," was Adam's comment. They couldn't tell for sure if it was related. They continued their advisement to Axel that he should just keep following this through. The only positive thing they said was, "We believe we are on to something big, and we believe it is coming down the pike very soon."

Axel was concerned that they were hearing this second hand and didn't have a more positive input. *Rumors are always full of fantasies, as much as truth*, he thought. Pulling the truth out is an art, and he hoped the agency had the art. Then, he thought to himself, *Maybe I am making more of this than there is. I am only going on gut feel at this time, and that is no better than what I just heard from the agency. Maybe Ishler was just having a bad day when we talked, and that is what came through in the conversation over the phone. Maybe I am being paranoid.* He sat back and thought about it some more. *We shall see. What is to be will be?* His job was to halt the final move if it was bad. *We shall see*, he thought.

Axel didn't have to wait long. The next day, he got a call from Ishler. "My boss wants to come out and discuss things with you. He will be there in three days. Do the results still look good?" asked Ishler.

"Yes everything is moving in the right direction. All the tests on Henry look quite good, and the second hog is moving in the same direction as Henry did at this stage in his progress. I will prepare for his visit. Can you tell me who he is?" Axel asked.

"I am sorry, but he wants to keep a low profile till he is confident of the results and what to expect in the future," replied Ishler.

The next couple of days were spent working with Manny and the other operators to make sure things were buttoned up tight and the progress continued in this direction. On the third day, Axel got a phone call at six in the morning from Ishler. "The boss is in town and will be at the lab with me at ten this morning. Make sure everything is ready for an inspection," he said. With those comments, he was gone, and Axel hurried to the lab. He didn't even stop to have breakfast.

He called Manny and told him to be at the lab as soon as he could this morning because Ishler would be there with his boss. Axel checked everything at the lab, and Henry was in good spirits for a hog, and the other hog ate his meal like it was his last. Before long, Ishler arrived with a man who Axel assumed was his boss. He was an unassuming person of medium height with gray hair, and he looked like a college professor from Germany or some Eastern European country. He didn't look Iranian or sound Iranian. Ishler introduced Axel to the man, "This is Michael Kasian, our star performer," he said, as he extended his hand toward Axel. "And this is my boss, Max Howchev," he said, as he directed his arm toward the boss man.

Axel commented, "Nice to meet you, sir," and he extended his hand in a handshake position toward the man. Max extended his hand to shake hands and said something in Russian that Axel understood but nodded his head back and forth like he didn't understand the comment made.

"You don't understand Russian?" Max asked in English.

"No, sir," responded Axel, I understand English and Iranian, but never had the opportunity to be around any Russians or Russian areas to pick up the language," (even though he understood exactly what Max had said).

"That's too bad," Max commented in English. "I speak and understand Russian, Iranian, Iraqi, English, and some German. It comes in handy at times."

"Yes, I am sure it does," replied Axel.

With the introductions done, Ishler suggested that Axel take Max on a tour of the facility and show him Henry and the other hog along with his results to date. This, Axel commenced immediately, being quite proud of his results to date. He was excited to show a new person (*even if he is the enemy*, he thought) the results of his work. As they went around the area, Max asked him a question here and there, and Axel responded.

At times, Max asked why Axel had done the things in the direction they were done and seemed satisfied by the answers that Axel gave him. When they got to the hogs, Axel pointed out Henry and the second hog. From all appearances, the two hogs that had received the treatments looked no different from the three that had not been treated. Max looked at the x-rays and CT scan data as they were shown to him, from the first x-rays and scans taken with the lungs partially removed, and each taken in chronological order after the stem cell implants. Max seemed quite impressed, but he kept asking questions about the procedures that Axel had followed.

Then, Max pointed to Axel's office and said, "Let's go in here and talk." Once inside the office, along, with Ishler being present, Max asked Axel if he felt his process would work with other viruses.

Axel responded, "The approach was very straight forward, since we had the three necessary ingredients for success. We had unspecialized stem cells, a virus that was from the hogs' lungs to serve as a pointer, and an approach we developed that kept the stem cells unspecialized while providing the virus to the cells. It is important to understand that the key relates to the fact that the unspecialized cells we produced had no defense mechanisms built into them and , and they had no previous history to have established their own antiviral defense against these antigens. If we can continue to have these elements present, then we should be able to work with other virus types. I believe the cells provide the ideal host conditions for the virus, but I believe we must then immediately submit them to the area we want to repair. It is now known by our test results that the stem cells will only remain unspecialized with the virus for a maximum of three days, and, if we are lucky, they might last another day."

"After three days, the unspecialized stem cells begin to build up an antiviral response and lose their unspecialized characteristics. We were fortunate that we immediately placed the unspecialized stem cells containing hog lung virus into the noses of the hogs, and the virus acted as a catalyze in pointing toward the lungs. The lungs provided the ideal final host, and the stem cells began to be specialized to become lung cells. If you want to use a new virus, we must know its final resting place, so we can determine how best to handle the stem cell, virus connection, and the means of pointing it toward our final specialized resting place."

Then, Max asked a profound question, "What if we want the unspecialized stem cells to only act as the host for the virus to keep the virus alive, and then the stem cells and virus act as a specialized source of this virus?"

This question shocked Axel. "Do you mean that we work this thing in reverse?" he asked.

"Yes, in fact your comments that the stem cells can only provide an unspecialized source for the virus for three days more or less answers that question. It would seem if you waited three or four days and injected the cells containing the virus into the nose of the hog that the lung would not be repaired. Only more viruses would be formed in the lungs of the hogs, and it's possible that the virus would no longer be harmless in their lungs. It might even more or less drown them in viruses by clogging their lung cells with virus and therefore making it impossible for the lungs to perform their normal functions."

"But what good would that do?" asked Axel.

"No good for what you intended for these hogs. But what if our intention was to do the opposite and cause our final host to carry more viruses?"

Axel remained quiet in his thoughts. He made sure the internal Internet and cell phone were activated, and they were listening to this back at the agency. He thought, *This is what they are after. This is the bad news. I know I must follow up on this to see where it leads, but I am concerned it is for no good. I know I have a connection with the agency, and I will be asking them where I should take this when the party is over tonight.*

With those thoughts in mind, Axel answered, "I believe we could achieve the same success if we decided to aim this in the opposite direction. However, I believe the stem cells carrying the virus should be injected within the two or three days. During that time, the virus is healthy, and the stem cells are unaffected. During this time, if a potent virus were carried by the stem cells, it would be like a bus full of people that get off when they want to. For example, if the virus was one that the hog didn't contain in his stomach under normal circumstances, it would infect him and cause the virus illness to take its toll."

"That's an interesting comment," said Max, "and it makes sense to me."

Axel continued his comments, "What we would need to know is the final direction and the type of virus we need to transfer. By the final direction, I mean the animal to which you wish to aim this virus. If we knew the animal and the virus type, we could figure out how to introduce the virus into the stem cells and the timing for sending it to the final host. Can you provide us that information?"

"We will be able to provide you this information eventually," commented Max.

"Why not now?" questioned Axel.

"Why do you need to know now?" asked Max.

"Because we might not feel confident that we can carry out the task, or we might not want to do what you want. There might be ethics or ethnics involved," commented Axel rather strongly.

"Let's put any further discussion of this off for tonight," said Max.

"Before cutting off the discussion, let me ask you one more question," Axel responded. "What if I said, yes; do you have the authority to carry this out? Would the people you report to allow this to be carried out?"

Max looked at Axel and said, "I have no higher authority to ask for permission to have this done. I have the money to support this program, and I have everything I need to put it into effect. I am the boss on this program. I am the prime mover. I have been working on this for over five years, with only the top government people in Iran being privy to what I am going to accomplish." With that final outburst by Max, he motioned to Ishler and said, "Let's go in the office. There are some things I need to discuss with you."

The two of them went into Axel's office. Axel had been sending this whole conversation to the agency, so they would be aware of the immediate possible danger from this program. Now, Axel wanted to hear what was going on in the office between Max and Ishler. He immediately gave the internal signal, "Axelvation two." He knew his hearing improved significantly when he was in this mode. Then, he went into the men's room, which was immediately adjacent to his office and shared a common wall. He locked the door of the facility and placed his ear next to the wall. They were talking in Russian, and Axel had no problem understanding what they were saying.

Max said, "I am concerned about Michael's sensitivity to what we intend to do with the stem cells. He is a biologist and might not take highly to our intended use of the virus."

"I don't even know what virus you have in mind," Ishler commented.

"I will give you a short synopsis of my choice of the virus," said Max. "I wanted to provide a virus that would hit the United States hard. I am sure you have heard of the Spanish virus or Spanish flu. It hit most of the world in mid-1918 to mid-1920. It is believed that one third of Europeans died of this virus in that two-year period. Whole cities were eliminated in many parts of the world. It came and went before anyone knew what hit them. Keep in mind that the world did not have the technology we have today. The interesting thing about this virus is that it hit young people in the prime of their lives. Most of the damage was done to those between twenty years old and forty years old. Not many young children or older people were hit with this virus. This was puzzling, and the science world has been looking for the reason since then. More recently, a woman doctor from the States went to an Alaskan town where all the occupants of that city had died from this virus. She had bodies exhumed to see if she could determine the cause of this virus. A report later came out that said the people that were vulnerable to this virus were those with the highest immune systems. The people that died were killed by a cytokine storm."

"A cytokine storm is one where the body's immune system reacts so violently to the antigen that it floods the lungs and essentially causes the person to drown from his own defense system. This pandemic is believed to have been started by the virus passing from birds to humans. In two years, it killed more people than all of the world wars to date. It killed more young people in two years than AIDS has killed in thirty years. It has been believed that small amounts of the virus was being held by two countries, Russia and the United States, and was being isolated from the world. The only reason for them having this virus was in case another pandemic hit the world with this type of flu. They thought they could develop an antibody against it. I was able to acquire some of the virus through contacts about two years ago, and I have seen it work in controlled cases. My intention with this program was to have the virus applied to the large number of stem cells being produced in this lab. We had approximately one hundred thousand stem cells several months ago, and we should be close to one million by now. I had intended to wait till we had ten million, but I think I now have to put this program into effect immediately."

"I didn't tell Michael (Axel) today because I think the program might have been culminated today. I am going to contact my muscle crew tonight and have them come in tomorrow at noon to make sure we have control of the lab. I will have the virus brought in at two in the afternoon. We can have Michael (Axel) start working on the application of the virus by day after tomorrow. If things go right, we will have several thousand Wrens and some other birds that are native to this part of the country brought in early next week. They have been collecting them now for a couple of months from sites in the Philadelphia and New York areas. The intention would be to apply the stem cells containing this virus to these birds and release the birds in the New York, Washington, and Philadelphia areas to begin the flu pandemic. It is quite contagious, and we should be hitting areas that have twenty-five to fifty million people that could contact the flu, either directly or from person to person. I would expect ten million young people to be eliminated within a year and maybe more."

"Where are you getting the money to support this program?" asked Ishler.

"From my friends in Iran that I have worked with over the years," Max replied. "They want the infidels in this country eliminated. You saw what happened when a couple thousand people were killed in the 9/11 incident. This will make that look like child's play."

Ishler smiled and said, "I am so glad to be a part of this program. I have been waiting years to impact this country."

With that last comment, Axel heard them rustle around and start talking in a combination of Iranian and English. Axel thought, I have to get o*ut of this room before they arrive in the conference area. I wouldn't want them to see me coming out of this room. They would think I heard something.*

A few minutes later, Axel met Max and Ishler as they came out of his office. "Everything okay?" he asked.

"Certainly," said Max. "Things are going better than I thought, and you will be proud of your work when you see the final theme. We will be telling you about it soon."

With that, both Ishler and Max left the lab. Axel had not eaten, and, right then, he decided he had better things to do than to eat. On his way home, Axel called the agency and told them what he had heard. This got their adrenaline flowing. The key thing they needed to do was to intercept the virus before it made it to the lab. To make it into this country, they must have a high-level person in the ambassador level to bring this in. The discussion was centering on Iraq, Israel, Russia, or even Saudi Arabia. An ambassador from any of these countries surrounding or close to Iran might be the logical carrier.

While this discussion was going on, Axel interjected, "Check and see what ambassador is scheduled to leave the country in the next week. I would imagine the person who knows what is going on will make sure he isn't in the Washington, DC, area for the next month or longer. He wouldn't want to be one of the casualties."

"That's a good point," said Kim. "However," commented Kim, "we cannot interrupt this scenario at this time. We must let it move along its course while keeping close tabs to what is happening. We want to make sure we nail the top-level people involved. Right now, we have Ishler, Howchev, and probably some of the smaller fish in this terrible plot. Tomorrow, we might find out the others. The first priority is to stop this whole program from happening. If they ever get the virus into the stem cells, and then into birds, it could result in the biggest catastrophe to ever hit this country. Another priority that is just as high is to not allow the virus to be released, even if by accident, while bringing the virus to your lab. The next priority is to make sure these sick individuals never have another chance to do something like this. We know that Axel has the key part to play in trying to suck out any of the top-level names, while remaining on the knife's edge with these people. They can't find out your part before this is over or they might take drastic actions against you before we have a chance to end this. But, I know no other way but to continue the program until we have the top culprits. Do you agree with this Axel?"

"Yes, I understand," Axel replied.

Smashing the Terrorist Cell

When Axel arrived at his motel, he was too excited to eat and to think about what he could do by tomorrow, knowing that he couldn't allow this to proceed, but understanding the agency's stance. *This is tough*, he thought to himself, *but I still have the upper hand. There must be something I can do.*

He spent the rest of the night trying to get some rest, but coming up short. There was no way he could sleep with this on his mind. Early the next morning, he headed to the lab and walked around trying to decide what actions he might be able to take. He knew that he could just scuttle the stem cells, and the program would be dead, but this wouldn't serve the agency's purpose of trying to catch the big wigs of this program. He decided to look at Henry and the other hog to see if they were still progressing well. This would help pass the time until Max and Ishler arrived, and he could see where this whole thing was headed.

Henry looked great, and his lungs were normal, and the other hog was following in Henry's footsteps. He thought about the irony of this situation. He never would have had the chance to do this stem cell and virus work without this program. He was actually proud of his accomplishments with these hogs. No matter what happened, the agency had his work documented on the stem cell—virus work, which would help on any programs being pursued in the country. Axel thought, *This might help not only hogs in the future but people with certain sicknesses. It turns out that the pig has many things in common with people. People that are diabetic can use insulin from hogs that have been treated. People with heart valve problems can replace them with the valves from pigs. So, my work on improving the lungs of hogs might someday help people with lung problems, maybe even lung cancer.*

Axel found Manny and told him to have all the operators go home. "Tell them they will be paid for today, but we want to have the place cleared before visitors come." Axel could tell Manny what he had heard, but he was concerned that Manny might be a double agent, so he kept the information to himself. Axel activated his internal Internet and phone system and told the agency to listen closely to the conversation he would be having with these people when they arrived. "I don't want anything to go wrong with this whole setup. Even if we don't find the other people involved, we must stop this before it goes any further than today." Kim and Adam listened and commented that they agreed with his actions. With that done, Axel waited.

It wasn't long before Max and Ishler arrived, and six other men came with them. Axel felt this was going to be a muscle play by them to make sure that he continued to play the game they had set for him in their scheme of things. Axel felt he should take the first step to see where things might be headed. He greeted Max and Ishler with a smile and the comment, "Everything seems to be in good shape. I checked out the stem cells, and they look prime. I checked Henry and the other hog, and they are in great shape so the virus/stem cell exchange seems to be working perfectly. How and when will the virus arrive here? That can be a very dangerous virus for us to be working with, and we must make sure it is handled properly."

Max looked around and said, "Yes, Michael (Axel), the place looks in good shape. The virus will be arriving today. It will be carried in a special metal box with a glass lining, and the viruses are in separate sealed vials, so there shouldn't be anything to worry about."

Axel continued the probing, "About when will the virus arrive, and what kind of virus is it? You haven't told me yet what the virus is and how you expect to use it."

With this comment, both Max and Ishler look a little uncomfortable. Max spoke up, "The virus will be handled just as you have done with the other virus. You will transfer the virus to the stem cells. When you are convinced the transfer has taken place successfully, you no longer need to be concerned. We will handle it from there. You forget, I am a doctor and understand the various methods."

Axel continued the discussion, "I am sure you know some of the things we have done here and know some of the procedures, but there might be some steps that are different from the past. It depends on the virus. What kind of virus is it?" Axel continued.

"It is a rather dangerous virus," Max stated. "We would rather you be concerned about keeping it isolated from yourself and the operators. You should do the transfers in a sealed chamber and wearing the proper breathing apparatus."

Axel disclosed to them that he had had the operators go home. He had felt the transfer of the virus to the stem cells could be handled by only a couple of people and didn't require the operators. "We have the latest equipment in isolation chambers and in breathing gear," Axel related. "But why should we be working with dangerous viruses? We haven't done anything to date with viruses that were really dangerous to human beings."

This type of banter continued between Axel and Max as he tried to gain more information for the agency. Before he knew it, time had passed, and it was almost one o'clock in the afternoon. Axel knew he had to press this past the limit at this time. He spoke out, "I will not do anything with the virus unless you tell me what kind it is and the use of the virus."

Max responded in an irate manner, "The virus is the Spanish flu virus, and we are going to use it to infect birds that will then be released in highly populated areas. This will be a major attack on the American people. You should be proud as an Iranian to see us take that step," Max said in a rather cold tone.

Axel tried to remain calm and cool and continued to dig for more information out of them. "But how can you have the Spanish flu virus? I thought it was only held by the Russians and the Americans, and they keep it quite isolated. There is no way you could obtain this virus. Even if you got it, how would you get it into the country, and where would you keep it that makes it available to us today? I think you are bluffing. The Americans would not let this get out of their control. I think you are just trying to steal my method I developed for proliferating stem cells and contaminating them with a virus without having them be specialized. You are just thieves. That is what I think now!"

"Oh, you think so," Max shouted. "Well our man from the Iraqi ambassador's office will arrive here today with the virus. In fact, he will be here in an hour or so. Not only do we have the virus, but we have several thousand birds in an isolated set of buildings not far from here. We will take the stem cells with the virus they will be carrying and will transfer them to the bird sanctuaries and release them with a method I have tested out. There is someone besides you that knows how to handle this kind of maneuver."

With that comment, Max asked Axel if he had any problems with this plan of attack. "I am afraid I do," said Axel. "I am not going to let you infect the stem cells with that virus. I will not be a party to the killing of innocent Americans. You will have to take those cells over my dead body, and that isn't going to happen today or any day."

Max turned and shouted to his men. At about the same time, Axel relayed his message to his body, and Axelvation two went into effect. As the six men approached, Axel grabbed one, threw him against two of the others, and turned and whacked one across the jaw, and he went flying across the lab to the office wall. In several minutes, it was obvious that the six men were not going to be able to handle the situation, but, rather abruptly, things began to change. Axel felt a change in his body. He was losing his power. Max shouted to one of the men, "Shoot him." With that command, the thug pulled out a gun and shot at Axel, but it had no apparent affect. Axel's body was completely protected except for his head. Axel tried to release his hood with his normal command, but it didn't work. He now realized that he hadn't eaten anything since breakfast the day before, and he had no extra nutrients to allow his ATP to take effect.

As he tried to grab one of the thugs, he was suddenly struck across the head with a heavy object and fell unconscious to the floor. Max looked around and found some rope. "Tie him up in that chair over there. I don't want him killed at this time. We might need some of his biological experience as we proceed. I am amazed that a biological school teacher has the strength he showed. I can't understand why the gun shot didn't seem to faze him. You must have an inferior weapon or inferior ammunition in that pistol."

With those commands from Max, two of the thugs pulled Axel over to the chair, lifted him up, and tied him tightly. Axel's upper body and his legs were tied tightly to the chair. They had no sooner got him tied than the phone began ringing. Max turned and told Manny to answer the phone. "It is probably someone who knows you from your work here in the lab, and I don't want anyone to suspect that anything is out of order," he said.

Manny picked up the phone and answered, "Hello, this is Manny. What can I do for you?"

A voice on the other end of the phone said, "I want to speak to Mr. Max Howchev."

Manny turned and said, "The phone is for you, Max."

Max took the phone from Manny. "Yes, this is Max."

"Max, this is Hassein. I am going to be about two hours late in bringing the package to you. I got a little delayed in picking up the package, but things are proceeding as planned."

"Are you sure?" questioned Max.

"Yes, it's just a delay. I will arrive there at about four this afternoon. Is everything there in position for your part of the plan?"

"Yes," replied Max, "I have everything under control here. No sweat, just come as we planned. Be careful with the package. It's like carrying a bomb; only worse."

With that said, Max hung up the phone and directed the men to follow him to the lab and get everything ready for the package. "Manny, you stay here and watch Michael (Axel). Make sure that he stays contained. I believe he is out of this at this time. You might have to help us later when the package arrives. I think you know as much about the steps we need to take to have the virus transferred to the stem cells as Michael did. We will depend on you." With that said, Max turned and motioned for his men to go to the main lab.

Axel aroused from his semiconscious state and looked up at Manny standing off to the side. He looked around and saw no one. "Manny," he whispered, "I need your help, Manny."

Manny looked around to see if Ishler and Max were out of sight. Then, he looked at Axel and said, "You know I want to help you, but, if I do, they will kill me. Right now, they think of me as part of their crew, and there are too many of them for me to handle."

"I know," Axel replied. "Just go to the automatic vending machine and get me several candy bars and a Coke to drink. I will handle things if you just get those and feed them to me."

Manny didn't know what candy and a Coke had to do with relieving this dire situation. He thought Axel was just out of his head from that pounding he took, but he believed there was no harm in getting those for him as long as he didn't release him from his bonds. In about five minutes, Manny was back, and Axel told him to take the rappers off the candy bars and feed them to him. "Also, open the Coke can, and give me a drink. Hold it to my mouth until it's empty."

Manny did what Axel asked. With the candy in his system and the coke wetting his body's insides, Axel began to feel the power come back to his system. He signaled himself internally, "Axelvation two," and began sending a message to the agency. Manny didn't know what was going on, since this was all done in silence. Axel warned the agency that the carrier was coming from the Iraqi ambassador's office and would be here by four this afternoon. "You must intercept him, take the metal box he is carrying, and take it to the Medical Center at Bethesda, Maryland. Tell them what is in the box, and they will know how to handle it. When you get the box, send me a message, so I know that I don't have to stop it here."

With that message safely on its way, Axel, with his energy level back to normal, began taking deep breathes and burst away the bonds that held him. He was now safely in energy level two with the energy level of fifteen or more men. He immediately sounded off, "Hood down," and the hood covered his head as he shot down the corridor leading to the main lab. He burst through the double doors and directed his energy in the direction of the six thugs, Ishler, and Max.

Max hollered out, "Shoot the son of a bitch," and the thugs began to pull their pistols and fire. But Axel shed the bullets like snowflakes on a winter day, and he grabbed the first man he could grab and twisted his head like spinning the top on a bottle of beer. As he fell, he grabbed another man by the arms and swung him like a hammer thrower in the Olympics and flung him through the air toward the main second story window. The body smashed the window like a small explosion. He grabbed the rifle of one of the thugs and pulled the man with the gun. He then flung him against another who was emptying his gun out and firing at Axel. Axel ran and grabbed another who was trying to run away from this impenetrable force.

At the same time, he saw Max running down the corridor, and he threw the man like a sack of flour at Max, and Max went down. Another of the thugs smashed his gun across Axel's head, and it had the same effect as the bullets had. *The hood has passed its test*, thought Axel, as he turned around and punched this combatant in the chest so hard he heard his ribs crack, and the man's spine was pushed through his back.

Meanwhile, Manny, who had been watching this chain of events in shock, stirred into action. He ran into the large room, grabbed one of the guns lying on the floor, and shot one of the bastards. Axel grabbed the gun hand of the thug who had just crushed it against his head with no results and broke his wrist, and then he leaned down, grabbed him by the legs, and threw him against the main metal stanchion of the lab, breaking a few other more critical parts of his body.

He then turned toward the two other men and Ishler, and Ishler cried out, "Shoot the bastard; don't just stand there. Shoot the bastard." That was about all that Axel needed to hear. He was hoping that Ishler would be more civil when it got down to brass tacks, but he was just another one of these rotten terrorists that was more than willing to have American lives destroyed. Axel rushed the two thugs and then leaped in the air, and he was on the other side of them before they know what had happened. He reached down and grabbed the right leg of one and the left leg of the other and whipped them off the floor and toward the ceiling above. They smashed head first against the ceiling and dropped like two autumn leaves falling from the trees.

Then, he turned toward Ishler who had drawn a gun. Ishler shouted, "It wasn't me that planned this. It was Howchev." Axel turned and saw Howchev aiming his gun at Manny, and he leaped in front of Manny and took the blow of the bullet, and it fell useless to the ground. With that, Axel aimed his fist at Howchev and took a flying leap toward him. Axel's fist met with the gun held by Howchev and jammed it through the chest bone and out the back of Howchev. As he withdrew his fist, he turned toward Ishler. He didn't want to kill Ishler. He wanted him, so the Agency could derive some information from him concerning any other cell sites.

Axel looked at Ishler and said, "No, it only proves you would kill anyone to save your skin. Where they are going to take you, your skin will be old and worn out in the number of years you will get for this terrorist attempt on American lives."

With that comment, he walked quietly toward Ishler to relieve him of his gun, but, before he got there, Ishler took the gun and started to put the muzzle up to his mouth, but, before he could pull the trigger, Axel's hand intercepted the muzzle and plugged the end of the pistol with his finger. Ishler was taken aback by this. "There is no way I am going to let you take the easy way out," shouted Axel. He had wanted to take Ishler in and see if they could determine if any others were involved in this terrible planned murder of American lives.

Axel walked around, picked up the guns, and threw them toward the area where Manny was standing. Manny was standing as if in shock. He was immobile, frozen in his tracks at what he had witnessed. "I can't believe this," he said. "What kind of man are you? Ten minutes ago, I would have believed you were a dead man, and I was in need of a way out of this and back to the agency. Man, what kind of man are you?"

"A fortunate one," Axel shouted; "fortunate that my mother was able to survive through a couple of very tough days when I was born." But he looked up at Manny and said, "Thanks for the candy bars and Coke; that's all I needed to clean up this mess." He directed Manny to bind Ishler until the agency arrived.

Axel then contacted the agency, but he did it by using the standard phone, since he didn't want Manny to know of his hidden powers. "Kim, how is it going with the package?" he asked.

"No luck here, Axel. We have been watching the Iraqi embassy but have seen no activity in or out of the place in the past five hours we have been watching the place. We also have officers located around your lab and haven't seen anyone come in."

"Okay, Kim, I will be on the lookout here. I have everything under control here."

He hung up, went over to the vending machine, put in some coins, and took out a couple more candy bars. "No sense in running out of energy again," he muttered to himself. As he unwrapped one of the candy bars, the phone rang. He turned and told Manny to take the phone. "Answer in Iranian," he said, "in case it's someone wanting to get

Max. If they want him, tell them he is working with me getting the cells ready."

Manny picked up the phone and said "Manny here." Axel saw him listening to someone on the phone, and then Manny spoke again, in Iranian. "Max is in the main lab working on getting the cells ready. Yes, everything is going as planned here. Max told me to tell you to bring in the package. You'll be here in thirty minutes. That's fine. Just drive up to the main entrance, and I will be waiting to let you in. How many guys are with you? Take care of the package. We are close to completing this significant step in history." Manny hung up the phone and turned toward Axel. "You heard all of that. They will be here in about thirty minutes. There will just be the man and his driver. I never did get his name. It doesn't seem like they have had any problems getting here—no mention of any problems anyhow. I wonder how the agency guys missed them. I think they must have come from another location besides the embassy."

Axel thought about it and told Manny to go stand beside the door. "When they come and you see they have the package with them, close and lock the door after they enter. If they ask you why you are doing that, just say that you want the place isolated from any other outside disturbances. Let me take care of the problems from then on." Manny nodded and went toward the front entrance. "Before you do that, go to the lab and make sure there are no operators, and then we will lock the thugs that are unconscious and still living in the equipment room. I don't want any of them screwing things up. Also, if the people arrive and don't have a package, you tell them they can't enter without the package. That's an order."

With that command, Axel called on his internal system to the agency. "We had contact from the person carrying the package, and they are going to be here in another twenty-five or thirty minutes. Contact your people outside the building, and tell them to let the two people enter the building without provoking them. After they enter, have your men move in and surround the building. I will take care of things in here, but you should ensure this by having the place surrounded. I believe I can secure the package better than anyone that might be surrounding the building. If I have any problems, you will know because I am going to keep my communication system on till this is over with."

Manny positioned himself next to the front entrance and watched through the window, and, not long afterward, he shouted to Axel, "They are here."

"Good, let's hope things go our way. Don't forget to speak in Iranian. If they speak in Russian, you can answer them in Russian. If they don't have a box with them, don't let them in. Tell them they must bring the box directly in, so Max can start the operation immediately. If they give you any problems, tell them that Max said to not let anyone in unless they had a box with them."

Manny nodded and continued looking out the door. He saw the driver get out of the long executive vehicle. He opened the back door and let a man out. Then, he reached in and grabbed a shiny metal box and handed it to the man. They began their walk toward the entrance. Manny opened the door just as they arrived, seeing that they had the box and making it obvious that everything was okay, and they were welcome. The well-dressed man had a European-type hat on his head and a white scarf smartly wrapped around his neck and tucked into a light overcoat. He remarked in Russian, "And you, I assume, are Manny."

"Yes, sir," said Manny.

"I am Rudy," the well-dressed man introduced himself. Manny pointed toward the lab and said, "Let's go back to the lab where Max and Ishler are working with Michael on the stem cells."

As they entered, Manny noticed that Rudy now had the shiny box chained and connected with metal cuffs to his wrist. Axel stayed hidden and watched the men approaching, and he also realized that the man had the box cuffed to his wrist. He noticed the large man with him had his hand in his pocket like he was ready for action. Axel commented internally, "Axelvation two" and "hood up," and then he awaited their approach. As they approached the lab entrance, the large man moved ahead of the well-dressed gentleman in a position to protect him in case something went wrong.

Axel waited till they both entered the lab, and then he leaped out and pounded his fist against the side of the large man's head, and he went down like a ton of bricks. *No problem with him today*, he thought, as he turned and reached for the well-dressed man. He had jumped to the side and pulled out a gun. He shot three shots off rapidly at Axel and was astonished to see them bounce off his chest and face. He pointed the gun toward the shiny box, hoping to put a hole in it and free the terrible force inside the box. With a quick move, Axel shoved his hand across the top of the box, and the bullets fired just bounced backward off his hand, and one struck the man in the face, and down he fell. While he was falling, Axel immediately grabbed the chain connecting the wrist to the box and pulled. The well-dressed man's hand came off, and he was no longer well dressed as the blood squirted from his face and his handless arm.

Axel held the box at arm's length and hollered to Manny, "Grab the box, and don't let it go." Manny reached for the box and cradled it to his chest, blood and all. Axel turned and checked the big man and ripped the coat off of him and checked his pockets. "Yes, there's a gun in each pocket," he commented to himself. Axel quickly checked the pockets of both men to see if there was anything else they should be concerned with. "Looks good here," he shouted to Manny. "I am going to drag them into the equipment room and relock the door."

With that shout, he grabbed the one man by his leg, and, as he passed the big man, he grabbed him by his leg and dragged them both to the equipment room. As he opened the door, one of the thugs previously submitted to the room hit him in the head with a chair. Axel responded by dropping the one man he had been dragging and swinging the body of the other in the air like a whip and smashed him across the face of the pug, and down he crumbled in a pile of lifelessness. With that, Axel wiped his face with his hand and looked around to check for other possible offenders. *Nothing moving; must be okay*, he thought, as he turned and left the room, locking the latch as he left.

Manny was still standing in the middle of the room with the box held closely to his chest. He was almost in a trance, with his eyes staring ahead from his motionless face. "How did you do that?" he asked. "I thought I was seeing things when you handled Max, Ishler, and the other men, but you just did the same thing. How could you do that? I saw bullets coming off your body. Is this a joke?"

"No," said Axel, "it's a government secret." With that comment, he turned, went to the phone, and called the agency. "Kim, you can send in your men now. We have the place secured, and we have the virus. We will need some medical help for some of the thugs. I am afraid the top operative, Max, is dead. I was able to hold Ishler and have him tied up. Perhaps, he will be able to give you some additional information about the cell and any others. The operative who delivered the virus needs medical help immediately. One of the bullets ricocheted off and struck him in the face, and he lost his hand during the combat. I think he will be in good shape to interrogate and find out anything else you might need to know. If he isn't cooperative, you can tell him you will send your 'robot' back in and have him pull another hand off. That might scare something out of him. You know I would never do anything like that unless it was in the course of the battle."

Axel could hear Kim laughing over the phone, and Kim said, "Good work, unlatch the front door, and my guys will be entering the building and taking care of everything. We brought a medical group with us, since we often find these types of actions end up with injuries. How many casualties are we talking about?"

Axel responded, "Altogether, there are a dozen or so hostiles in here, but I believe there are only a few that would respond to any medical treatment."

"That's a heavy day of work," Kim kidded. "After the troops take care of everything, and you are satisfied that things are under control, you should return to your motel and get some rest. Tomorrow, I want you to drive up to the agency office, and we will review everything that occurred. If things go well, you can plan on returning home day after tomorrow. How does that sound?"

"That sounds like music to my ears," said Axel, "but I want to make sure the box with the virus is hand carried to the agency. I want to leave here with it and drive to your office immediately. You should have someone there that you trust who can make sure it is put in safe keeping. You might want to call your man at the Bethesda Naval Medical Center and see what he recommends. This is a very dangerous box even when it is within our control. Any accident and it's possible that we would have done for them what they couldn't do for themselves."

"Okay," said Kim, "I will be here when you arrive. It should take you about an hour to get here."

"One other thing," said Axel. "Find out where the birds are being kept by these people, and release them. When you find that out, you will also find some more members of this terrorist group. The more we gather the merrier. Also, your man Manny did a good job here. I am going to leave him here to take care of the facility. It's in good shape and should serve the government well for stem work or some other work requiring these super clean conditions."

Axel hung up the phone and turned to Manny. "Let the agency people in, and they will take care of cleaning up. I need you to stay here and make sure the place continues its operations. We should be able to continue this operation and have it produce something of benefit to mankind." Axel relieved Manny of the box and shook his hand. "You did a great job here, Manny. I have been happy to make your acquaintance and to realize there are people like you protecting our country. You went through a lot to carry this as far as you have without being caught, and I am sure it deprived you of your normal life. Do you have a family?"

"Yes," replied Manny. "I am married and have one boy that is five years old. It had been tough at times, but I guess I like the adventure of it all. I am very pleased with the way this went. All my work paid off when you entered the scene. I can't believe the agency has someone like you to put a finish to this kind of terrible danger. These people won't stop at anything. I am from Iran, but I am an American citizen, and I love this country. Don't worry about the lab. I will keep it going until they send someone that is more competent to handle these biological miracles. Good luck to you on your next assignment, whatever it is. I have never seen anyone like you, and I am glad you are on our side."

They shook hands, and Axel was on his way to Washington and the agency. After a few steps, he turned and shouted at Manny, "The good news is that the United States now has a perfect lab for any work they want to do on stem cell research. The great news is that the Iranian government paid for it." With that final word, he laughed and went on his way.

While driving to DC, Axel decided to give Tori a call. He hadn't talked to her for the better part of a week. The other day, he tried to get hold of her and couldn't make a connection, and he got her answering service. He decided to send her a record over the airways that he had heard a few days before. It reminded him of her. It was a song that was made by the blind singer Stevie Wonder called, "I Just Called to Say I Love You."

It was an old song and reminded him of what he wanted to say to her. I hope she got the message and liked it. Then, he heard that nice voice again. "Hello, this is Tori," sounded the voice over the phone.

When he heard that voice, his heart started pumping. He thought it had been pumping hard when he was going through that action today, but it seemed to be pounding away faster now like it was playing a different melody. He thought, *Maybe it's because I know I am going to see her in a few days. Maybe it's because I'm afraid that she won't agree with the song.* "Tori," he said. "This is Axel."

"Well, stranger," she remarked, "I thought maybe you had given up on me. Where have you been?"

"I got stuck with some tough and long-lasting jobs for Adam and his friend out here. I was calling to see if you are going to be around for the next week or longer. I am cleaning my job up here and will be home in a day or two. How does that sound?"

"That sounds great," she responded. "I finish the semester day after tomorrow and have a couple of months off. The timing is great. I look forward to seeing you. I miss you."

With that last comment, Axel's heart skipped a beat and began to pound away again. "Boy does your voice sound beautiful," said Axel. "It's like music to my ears. Maybe we can go down to Monterey for a couple of days and celebrate your junior year being completed."

"That sounds nice," Tori almost sang out.

Axel wondered if she was trying to tease him with that melodic sound to her voice. Maybe she enjoyed hearing the song he sent. He was afraid to ask. "Tori, I will call you some time tomorrow and let you know what my air accommodations are. Is that okay?"

"Sure thing; I have to run now and catch my next class. I will look for your call tomorrow. See ya!"

With that, she was gone, and Axel was left with some questions on his mind. His mind returned to the road and driving to see Kim and maybe Adam as well as delivering that shiny box next to him on the passenger seat of the car.

Axel arrived at the agency, showed his pass, and headed toward Kim's office. As he arrived at Kim's office, he was greeted by Kim, Adam, and a stately looking man. "Axel, this is Mr. George Bealor, the head of the agency; he wanted to meet you."

Axel turned and extended his hand. "Pleased to meet you Mr. Bealor," Axel said.

"The same for me, Mr. Tressler," Bealor said. "I am very impressed by the work you have done on this terrorist threat. This will end up saving many lives, and it puts us in position to follow up other leads that will also bring us closure on other cell levels of these people. I intend to send a message to the president and tell him about your successful mission. You know that this cannot be given to the press, so you won't be hearing anything about it. I am hoping the president will call you and thank you personally."

Axel was stunned and took a few seconds to comment. "I consider it an honor to have been able to help in this situation. When this got started, I didn't know if I would be of help, but your people provided me with some tools that allowed me to carry this farther than I thought possible. You have some great people working for you, sir."

"Well, the way I heard it, you had some things going for you that we at the agency were not able to duplicate; looks like we coupled your personal abilities with some of our capabilities to send a man out in the field that was hard to duplicate. That's astounding, and I am sure we will be asking you for some more help in the future. I must be on my way now, but I surely wanted to stick around and meet you and thank you for a job very well done. I hear you are going back to California in the next day or so. Have a safe trip." With that said, he started to walk away, but then he turned and said, "I don't think a man like you could have anything but a safe trip after what you have done," and with that comment, he was gone.

Axel looked at Kim and Adam and said, "That was really nice of him. It seems everyone I have met in this agency is a professional and a good human being." Axel sat down and handed the shiny box to Kim and commented, "I am glad to get this out of my possession and to someone I trust. I hope this box supplies some information to the people who receive it. This is a rare antigen that is not easy to come by."

Then, Axel spent over two hours going over all the details about the happenings at the Baltimore lab, even though they had most of this information from his silent communication with them over the last few months. When they were done, Kim asked Axel if he was heading back to California tomorrow. "I certainly am going to try. As soon as we are done here, I am going to go and try to make accommodations."

"Well, Axel, here is something to make your home stay a more enjoyable one." He handed Axel an envelope and said, "Don't spend it all in one place and not all of it on Tori. You probably want to spend a little time with your brother. I know he wants to spend some personal time with you. Again, I want to say that I appreciate what you accomplished. I don't believe it could have been done by anyone else. The capability you have and we used is a powerful capability that no one possesses. I am sure we will use that talent again. Good fortune to you and your girlfriend."

With that said, Kim left the room to Adam and Axel. Adam looked over at Axel, and he said, "Hey, "**Follower**," You did a great service to your country, and I believe the people you met today expressed that better than I can. I am proud of you and proud to be your brother and twin. Your experience has probably raised my standings with the agency, and it's a debt I probably won't be able to pay back."

"No problem," was the answer back from Axel. "The people I have met with your agency are a cut above any organization I have come in contact with. Each and every one of them had something to bring to the party, and there were no politics with one person trying to get noticed for his effort over others. They also gave me something physical that no one on earth has, and I didn't get to ask Kim some questions before he left. I have this body coating that is a tremendous gift, and he didn't say I had to return it. Do you think he wants it to stay that way?"

"Yes, I am sure he does," Adam commented. "I believe he wants you to do something for him and the agency in the future, and he would be nuts to take that away from you. As long as you remain in good standing with the agency, the body armor is yours to use as you see fit."

Axel looked at Adam and said, "Did I ever tell you Adam that I can swim under water with this on and the hood on and can see without blinking my eyes? Under water with this gear is as good as any underwater gear. A person's body has less resistance in the water, which gains you speed. The covering over the eyes allows as good a vision as one can obtain with normal deep underwater gear. There is another benefit that I haven't been able to explain. With my mitochondria capability and this gear, I seem to be able to pull more oxygen directly from the water through the pores of the material. Without this gear, I could normally stay under water for about two to three minutes. With this gear, and the added oxygen getting to my mitochondria, I can stay under water for about ten minutes. At the same time, my energy level is high because of this added oxygen, and, therefore, I can cover considerable distances under water. The key thing I must keep in mind is that I have to keep my nutrition level up. I learned that on this job."

"Without Manny supplying me with candy bars and cola when I was tied up at the lab, I would never have been able to accomplish the task at hand. I carry candy bars in my pockets everywhere I go now. I never know when I am going to need them. Normally, I don't have to be concerned because I have a good, full nutritional diet. I am going to write up the benefits of this gear as I find new achievements and send them to you and Kim. Eventually, the agency will want to supply this gear to your underwater units and your land lovers. Although they won't be as fortunate as I am with my organic capability, they will be a force to be reckoned with on land, on the sea, and in the sea."

"There are two main ingredients that I need, oxygen and sugar. I am fortunate that I have extra-sized lungs and am able to afford a good, rich diet. The key it will bring to a normal person is the protection from foreign objects like bullets and knifes, plus the ability to see better under water. It's possible it might bring other benefits like being isolated from certain bacteria and viruses. Tell Kim he should do a controlled experiment on animals and see if this coating protects them from certain contagious elements."

"Those are good inputs and a good thought about immunity against contagious elements," said Adam. "I never thought of that. We can use our laboratory animals to see if they are protected in various ways. I better let you go, so you can make plane reservations for tomorrow. Let me know what your itinerary is as soon as you find out. One of these days, I am going to meet this girl, Tori that you are all ga ga about."

Axel nodded and bid his brother good-bye for now. "I will keep you abreast of what's going on with me," said Axel.

Axel was able to schedule a flight out of the Dulles International airport to San Francisco via Dallas Texas International airport. It would leave Washington at 1:15 PM and get into San Francisco at 6:20 PM Pacific Coast time. He gave Tori a call, and she said she would meet him outside the baggage pickup between 6:45 and 7:00 PM. She was excited and couldn't wait to see him. This blew up his hopes more than anything he had heard in the past few months. *That's great that she wants to see me,* he thought. *I want to see more of her, and I am not talking about just her face, although I might have to be satisfied with that for the near future.*

Axel Returns to sanity and love

As Axel approached the baggage pickup area at the San Fran airport, he looked anxiously around to see if he could see Tori. He had been hoping that she might park the car and come into the baggage claim area to meet him, but he didn't see her. He continued waiting for his bag and looking over his shoulder to see if she was there, but no soap. His bags arrived at the carrousel, he grabbed them, and then he went outside to check for the car and the girl. *No car yet*, he thought, *but I am sure she will be here soon.* The thought never left his head for a second until he saw her car coming down toward the baggage pickup area. His heart beat like a drum. *Maybe she won't be as good looking as I have remembered her. It has been about six months since I saw her. Maybe she got fat,*

Then, the car stopped, out she jumped, and she was more beautiful than he had remembered her. "Hi," she said, and Axel didn't wait to say anything; he grabbed her, squeezed her, swung her around in the air, and gave her a big kiss right on the target area. "Wow," she cried out. "Is that the way you meet all your girls?"

"No, just you," Axel quietly whispered in her ear as he hugged her. "I missed you so much, and I have listened every night to that song I sent you when I was in the motel. It always leaves me missing you and wishing you were there, so the outburst was spontaneous and meaningful. Remember, absence makes the heart grow warmer," he shouted, as he jumped in the right front seat of the car. *God, she smells good*, he thought to himself. *I could eat that like candy.* Before he could literally take a bite out of her, she was away with the car and on their way to his house. They talked small talk for a while, and then he asked her if she would like to go to Carmel or Monterey with him the next day.

"Sure," she said, "as long as it's a two-bed deal like we did before."

That hurt, he thought, *but I can tolerate that for a while longer. I want her to believe in me for what I am and not for what I want from her.* "No problem with the two-bed deal. I just want to be around you and enjoying life with you," explained Axel.

The next three days found Tori and Axel having a great time together; they had been walking around on the beaches and going to great restaurants for lunches and dinners. There was a great bake shop in Carmel, and, every day, they stopped there and got some of their elephant ear cookies and some walnut rolls with coffee. In the evenings, they found places to dance at the various large motels in the area. As they slow danced, Axel would whisper his feelings in Tori's ears, how much he missed her while in Washington and that he loved her. She smiled and would give him a squeeze with her arms and sometimes give him a peck of a kiss on the cheek. They danced till one or two in the morning whenever the band stopped playing.

Back at their room, there were hugs and kisses, but it never got as far as Axel would have liked. Tori would ask Axel what he did in Washington with Adam, and Axel would have to come up with some story that was made up on the spur of the moment. "Seems like you spent a long time and don't do very much, or you don't tell me much," said Tori one evening.

"Well, remember, Adam is married and has a kid that is two years old, so we spend time together enjoying the whole family every time we have a few minutes from the job at hand."

"Are you sure you weren't out having a good time?" she would ask.

"No, our days were full, and I was tired at night," Axel replied. "We set up a lab for harvesting stem cells," was one of his responses that was the truth.

"That must have been interesting. Where did you get the stem cells to start the expansion of the cell base?" she asked.

"Adam is associated with a group in an agency that works on trying to find answers on biological issues like stem cells," he said. "Seems like he is in the biological field more than I am," joked Axel. "That's one of the reasons they wanted me out there with my biological experience to assist them on solutions to problems. I guess I provided them a lot of answers, and I learned a great deal while doing this for them. That's the best of worlds when both sides benefit," he continued. "They will probably ask me out there again in the near future. Maybe you could go out there with me. You would enjoy Washington. There are a lot of historical sites there, and they are beautiful to visit. It's one of those ideal times where you get to enjoy history and the beauty of the area at the same time. Besides, Adam and Laura would like to meet you. They probably know you already just by my discussions with them about you. They got tired of hearing about you when I was out there."

"Oh, you are just kidding me," teased Tori.

"Not on your life," Axel responded. "If you don't know how much I love you by now, then you are not a good judge of people."

With that said Tori looked at Axel and said, "I know you love me, and I know I am a pain in the ass at times, but I got burnt before, and I tried to loosen up, but it is hard. I love being with you, and I love the way you treat me, and my heart beats some extra beats when I see you, whether it's the next day or after being away for a while. So, my heart must be on your side, even if my brain is stubborn or scared."

She walked over to Axel and gave him a big hug and a kiss like she had never given him before. Her mouth was open, and her tongue was playing music on Axel's mouth and tongue. His heart was beating, and that thing between his legs was getting hard. *This is the way it should be*, Axel thought, as he pushed her down on the couch and pressed his body against her body. He took his hand and began to softly rub her breasts hidden beneath the smooth white cloth of her blouse. Tori squiggled beneath his hands, but she didn't resist his advances. Axel took his hands up beneath her blouse and unsnapped her brassiere in the back.

He now could take her breasts in his mouth and rub his tongue across her nipples. He knew they would be nice, but these were beautiful breasts that were better than he ever supposed. As he licked and sucked her breasts, the nipples got hard as he continued, and he knew she was getting hot and responding to his caresses. Axel placed his face between her breasts and smelled her body. *How can one person smell so good?* he thought. This continued for several minutes with Axel getting bolder by the minute. He was in heaven and loving his angel as he kept caressing her breasts, and now his hand moved down toward her female part between her legs.

She was now moaning and enjoying what he was doing, and he wanted to carry it further. Just when he believed this would go all the way, Tori whispered, "I think we better stop." He had a hard time believing she would let this go this far and not allow it to go to completion. She knows enough about biology to know what this does to a man.

He let a big puff of air escape from his chest as he disappointingly lay backward on the couch. "I am sorry," she said. That was all that could come out of her at the time, and they laid there exhausted.

Axel was now hurting in his groin area, sometimes called the disappointment of a male, and he was really disappointed. A little later, they get ready for bed, and each crawled into their own bed without saying much. "Good night," Axel said.

"Night," she said.

Axel was soon falling asleep when he heard the shower running. *I wonder what she is up to now*, he thought. He closed his eyes and tried to sleep. Before long, he heard her come out of the bathroom, and, as he lay there, he felt her crawl into bed with him and push her body up against his back. *And I thought she smelled good before*, he thought, but, now, it was not only a great smell, but her body was still a little moist from the shower and felt cool against his body.

She was naked, and she put her breasts next to his back and moved her body up against his. Axel knew what was happening and so did his penis as it began to harden. She kissed his neck and kept rubbing her body against his. Just when he thought he couldn't feel any better or more excited, he felt her hand reach around and grab him by the penis and start to rub it up and down. "Unbelievable," he moaned out loud. "This is better than heaven." He turned in the bed and caressed those beautiful nipples in his mouth and rubbed her, and his hand now reached her clitoris, and he began to stroke it. This brought wonderful moves from her full body as she spread her legs to invite this movement further. Her clitoris was wet and moving to the tune of his hand as she made nice little cute sounds and breathed hard in his ears.

Axel began kissing her body and worked his way down to that clean clitoris that he knew she had just bathed. He invaded it with his tongue, and she moaned and loved it as if it was a virginal move, like it never happened before. She took her legs, wrapped them around his body, and helped the rhythm they had developed together. He pulled his body up and took his dick and rubbed it against her clitoris, and she reached down and directed it into her body. *Oh, what a wonderful feeling. It's warm and fits like a glove. It's like it was made to be in there.*

They were both in synch now as they moved against each other and enjoyed the love they were making. It didn't take long, and Tori let out a loud moan, and he knew she was climaxing. It was like a switch, and, as he heard her loud moan, his sexual feeling was aroused even more, and he began to come. His body jerked as did hers, and then they laid in silence like they were out of breath. He looked at her and whispered, "That sure beats kissing."

"It surely does," she responded. "I love you, Axel," she whispered. These were words he had wanted to hear for months, and there was no better time to say it than now. "I think I loved you the day you ran down the hall at the school and saved Ellen and me, but I didn't want to accept it. I was scared from my previous experience and didn't want to get hurt again, but you have been a jewel. I have been attracted to you so much that it scares me. So, I went out of my way to put it off. While you were gone, I realized how much I missed you and said to myself, 'Don't fall for a guy again that won't return the love,' but, the longer you were gone, the more I missed you. I loved that song you sent to me, 'I Just Called to Say I Love You.' That was important to me. I think that's when I started to realize that you were for real. I wanted you to be for real and kept my distance from you to make sure I didn't make the same mistake I had made before. But then, I realized that you were better than the man before, better in many ways."

"You are not selfish. You are giving. You are sensitive. You are easy to communicate with. You are good looking and smart. Maybe I also love you because you are strong. I have never seen a man like you that has the strength you have, and you never boast of it. You only use your strength at crucial times. There I go; I am confessing all my weaknesses to you and hoping you won't take advantage of them."

Axel laid there and took this all in. Then, he said, "Those were the most wonderful words I have ever heard from anyone. My brother would not even say that about me. I have loved you since I started taking you from the school to your car. As much as I loved you—and I didn't think I could love you any more than I did—at this moment, I love you even more because of your love for me. If I could craw inside of you, I would, so I could be closer to you. I have had sex with women in my life, but you are the only one I have made love to. Tonight was a total love. I have never kissed a woman where I kissed you tonight. It was like I was in a trance and couldn't love you any more than I was trying to love you. I wanted to satisfy you. Maybe it was because I knew that you had been with another man, and I wanted you to feel true love and not just sex. I think tonight I learned what love is all about. It is wanting a person more than what you can see in that person. It is wanting to be part of that person. It is wanting to be inside that person, not only sexually but truly a part of your body and mind. Tonight, I felt that. I have come before with women, but, tonight, when I came during your climax, it was something unbelievable, both in feeling and mentally. Do you understand what I am trying to say?"

Tori whispered in his ear, "That was a beautiful description of how I felt, and I wouldn't ever be able to find those words to describe it. I love you, Axel."

The remaining days at Carmel and Monterey were even more enjoyable for the two love birds. Now, they not only had the days to enjoy but the nights also. But when you are having fun, the time seems to go faster, and, before they knew it, they were in the car on the way back to home and some more wonderful days and nights together. Axel said to himself, *Now we are going to be one, and it doesn't have to be in Carmel or Monterey; it can be anywhere.*

Adam's Mexican Assignment

Back at the agency, about a month after Axel had left to return to California; Kim called Adam into his office to discuss a problem the agency wanted solved. Kim felt that Adam was the person to carry out this assignment. As Adam walked into Kim's office, he knew something was up, something important. "Have a seat, Adam," said Kim, as he pointed to one of the office chairs. As Adam sat down, Kim hollered out to his secretary. "Bring Adam and me a coffee please." Then, he turned to Adam and said, "Adam, the agency has a problem to solve, and it's a tough one. I have thought it over and think you are the man to carry it out. There is a huge drug cartel operating in Mexico. It is near the country's border, and it has been extending its operations over the border between the two countries. We have had several drug agents come up missing, and we haven't heard from them for over three months now. It is believed they are dead. We have been trying to determine whether the drugs have been coming in from Afghanistan via Iraq or from Columbia. If we can find where they are coming from, we might be able to do something about it. I have discussed this with the agency, and we came to the conclusion that the ways to find the source of the problem is to have an agent infiltrate the cartel."

"We have two basic ways to do this, a short way and a long way. The long way is to have an underground agent work his way into the cartel and up to the top of the cartel. This is a risky approach and takes years to accomplish. The short way, and the way we prefer, is to have an agent act as a heavy buyer—one who wants to buy a large amount and move it into the States. This approach can get to the top of the cartel more rapidly, if it indeed works. We feel you have the right credentials to carry this off. This person must look smart, look wealthy, and have the gift of gab. By the gift of the gab, we mean 'talks their language.' You look smart. You look intelligent. You can be made to look wealthy, and we can teach you the gab they use."

"We have good contacts in San Diego that have contacts in Tijuana. We believe the center of one of many cartels is located in Tijuana. What we would do is send you to San Diego and set you up with a million dollars in a local bank of San Diego and a decent batch of cocaine and some heroin. We believe the best way to catch a rat is to play the part of a rat. The worrisome thing about all this is that there are many officials in the local areas of Mexico that are being paid off, and we can't depend on them. The feds of Mexico have been fighting this battle also. They made some great catches, but, before you know it, another cell pops up, and they find another dirty official."

"There has been killing at all levels. Both the Mexican government and our government keep fighting this, but it is insidious. It seems like hard times breeds these problems more than good times. People in both countries lose their jobs and are depressed, and, before you know it, they are taking drugs to make them feel artificially good. But they have no money, so they next thing that happens is either they start stealing to get the money they need to buy the drugs or they start peddling the drugs, so they can make money to support their habit. The peddling is what spreads it to the States. Either way is bad news. It seems this problem had a huge increase about a year after the war in Iraq began. This might just be a coincidence, but it might be the means by which the drugs are making it into the country."

"Let's face it; Afghanistan is the biggest grower of poppies for opium in the world. Then, there's Columbia, which is not far from Mexico, and could be the major source of cocaine. There's also a problem with marijuana, but this is the least problem of the batch. We would like to set you up in San Diego. It will take at least several months and maybe a year. So, what do you think?"

Adam sat there and stared at Kim, and then he said, "This is a big assignment. Why do you think I can carry this off?"

"Because you can look the part, and you have a strong character," said Kim. "We can make you look the part even more than you do. You will be provided suits that are two thousand dollar suits, shoes that are three hundred dollar shoes, and all the other garb that high-level dope peddlers seem to prefer. You will have a 500SL Mercedes Benz hardtop car that is the pick of the lot. We will give you a home in San Diego that is a rich man's home. We have underground agents in San Diego and Tijuana that can mention your name every once in a while. We can teach you how high-levels dope peddlers talk and act."

"We can sell you. We can spread some propaganda before you get there. You would have a different name, and we will have records that show you as being arrested several times for peddling or taking drugs. We could set you up to sell some drugs to our undercover agents. As soon as the 'Toppies' or 'Biggies' of the various drug rings hear that someone is selling drugs to their customers, the word will get around. This is the critical point. They will either want to snuff you out or think of you as a major conduit into the States. If you remain in the San Diego area for at least a month before trying to contact the Tijuana Toppies, it won't look like you are trying to take their game. We would depend on them thinking you are a natural conduit for them to spread big time into the States. This is where the money is. They know that, and they have been trying to find a way to bring large amounts into the southern part of the country and spread to the northeast and the Chicago area."

"What if I want out?" asked Adam.

"Don't worry; we will set up a means to have you communicate that to us," said Kim. "As soon as you feel you are in trouble, one way or another, we will get you out."

Adam thought about it for a little while and then asked, "What about Laura and my son? Do they go or stay here?"

"We thought about that," Kim replied. "We think it would be best if they stayed here. Being out there might end up compromising you in some way."

"How long do you believe I will be out there and away from my family? I could only take that so long," said Adam.

Kim thought about it, then looked at Adam, and said, "I would be lying if I said it was less than three months. It is more likely six months to a year."

"I could take three months and maybe even six months, but any longer than that would be untenable by me and probably my family," Adam replied.

"We could probably set up trips for you back east to visit them. We would do this in a manner that wouldn't disrupt your operation out there. They would be like business trips, and we would route you via a city or two before arriving at your final destination. Another way would be to have you meet them in a town away from your home. I think we could arrange this for a couple of days every month you are away. We could hire a nanny for your kid, so your wife could be free to meet you in an offsite location. The only reason for these visits to be offsite would be to keep anyone from relating to your family and causing any issues. We want them to be safe at all times. We believe we can handle the San Diego place of operation without any trouble and keep you in operation without trouble, but we would need to take these precautions, so your position wouldn't be compromised by their doing something to your family. You would be set up as a single man with no family. How does that sound?" asked Kim.

"That is more palatable than being away long, but I still believe I could only commit for six months at the most. I will have to talk to Laura about this. She will know it is for the good of the country, and I believe she will go along with the time spans I mentioned, but no more. I wouldn't want it any longer than that," Adam declared.

"Okay, let's assume she will go along with this and start in that direction today. I have a person to tutor you on the language used by a person of this type. They have their little phrases that seem to be common among them. The air of superiority that you must portray is up to you, but you must have this superior demeanor. They all have it," remarked Kim. "Another key thing," commented Kim, "your name will be Adam Martel while down there, and all your paperwork will be made this way."

"The emergency key we are going to provide you with is a secondary ID card. We believe you will be passing the border and meeting at their site sooner or later. During these visits, use the normal card supplied. However, if for some reason or another they are taking you through the border check against your will, you should use the ID card that has a small dot at the top of the 'L' in your last name, Martel. If this card is used while going through the border check, it will automatically tell us you are being forced to go across the border, and we will take steps to get you out of there. Don't forget this identity card. The dot on top of the 'L' is barely visible. You should take it out and view it every once in a while to make sure you know what it looks like compared to the original. If you intend to use it because you suspect trouble, drop your original card in your office desk right-hand drawer. That way, we have two checks against you. If we don't hear from you in a twenty-four-hour period, I will have them check the right-hand drawer. You got that?"

"Yes, I do get it, and I think that is a good approach and will keep it in mind," Adam remarked.

"One more thing," said Kim, "if you use the ID card with the dot on it, we can follow you via satellite. What we would do is interrogate your position every hour. So, the signal will only be on for a few seconds per hour, and we will know where you are being kept or where they are moving you."

For three weeks Adam was debriefed on what the language of the trade was, and then he was ready for the flight to San Diego. He took a flight to San Diego and was met by Dred Pollack, who was to be his initial contact man during the operation. Adam rented a car and followed Dred to a house just outside the city limits. It was a great house that represented a person who was in the bucks. Once inside the house, Dred introduced Adam, who was now known as Adam Martel, to the four men who would be taking care of the facility as well as any business he was to conduct. There was an ample supply of cocaine stalked in three different wall safes, so they could begin business. In addition, the local bank showed four deposits of five hundred thousand dollars over the course of time, adding up to the two million dollars the agency wanted Adam to work with. This was the seed money. Drugs were not dealt for nothing. They were dealt to make money, considerable money.

Kim had told Adam that the two million dollars in seed money should be leveraged to over ten million within a few months. Eventually, the bank deposits would add up to monies approaching fifty to one hundred million dollars. Some would come from the agency and some from business transactions of selling coke at a profit around the San Diego area to local users or local peddlers. When it was at this level, it was a position of strength and gave Adam the opportunity to flush out the big hitters, especially the ones driving the Tijuana cartel.

The idea was to have contacts with some small dealers of drugs, hoping that eventually the word would get out that there was a new dealer in town. This usually would happen very rapidly and cause a ripple in the local dealing system. This would usually be followed up with other major dealers wanting to find out how much the new crew was dealing or buying and, in some cases, whether they were a detriment to their business. This was usually a short hunt by the dealers who deal in the ten-thousand-dollars-a-week level. They usually don't want to get any bigger and live with the pressure that follows the bigger guys. If they see the new guy doesn't bother their weekly business, they pull back and just keep watching. They also look at the new dealer as a source for their drugs—a source that is better in quality of product or ease of dealing with than any previous source they had. The dealers that would be the ones that might take issue with a new "Biggy" were the ones that deal to the ten-thousand-dollar peddlers or above. Beyond this were the really big bosses that controlled a larger area and a larger amount of weekly turnover. In order to deal, you have to buy.

Some dealers were the ones working in the one- to ten-thousand-dollars-a-week level. Adam, as a buyer and dealer, was to get past this level and get to higher levels. Where he was buying would be kept a secret. As long as he wasn't buying from the peddlers who fed the ten-thousand-a-week guys, this wouldn't decrease from their weekly buys. This would relieve any pressure that he might have from the ten-thousand-a-week local dealers. In order to cause some commotion, the Adam group was to push for deals where he bought at the one-million-dollar level and sold at the two- to four-million-dollar level a week. This would get him in the main flow of the stuff. This would bring out the bigger guns who would either want to sell to this new bigger dealer or kill him off if he looked like he would be a danger and would infringe on their business.

It was Adam's objective to show them he wanted to deal in the United States and would keep out of their territory. He was to fish them out with bigger and bigger transactions. As the transaction levels increased, and there appeared to be sales within the States, it would increase the greed of the dealers. When they saw that he was buying and not dealing in their area, it would be cool.

Meanwhile, a level of mock contacts was set up in the United States, such that, as Adam bought, he sold to them. They would not be transparent to the big dealers that Adam was buying from but would serve as an outlet for his drug sales. Several levels were set up for these mock dealers to send money to various drop-off banks as payment for the drugs. Eventually, these deposits would be withdrawn and made their securitas routes to Adam's bank location. In this way, Adam's local bank location would be growing rapidly and put him in position to be well known in the drug world and the banking world. Eventually, it was expected he would hit pay dirt and find the dealers who were working at the multimillion-dollar level. It was hoped this would fish out the big Tijuana dealers and the main Mexican drug cartel. This whole thing was like a pyramid that went from the small dealers to the larger ones and eventually to the biggest in the area. There was no doubt that the biggest dealer in the San Diego–Tijuana area was the Mexican cartel feeding Tijuana as its major location.

It didn't take long for the strikes to happen, and it didn't take long for the ten-thousand-dollar dealers to know this was a big dealer that worked the States and wasn't interested in penetrating their business. So, that particular pressure was relieved, and Adam's troops were not dealing to these unless it was found that the seeker was just a dealer having problems with his normal sources. Adam wanted and needed this group to appear. After buys, they usually would end up talking to their ex-sources, and this led to the word moving up the pyramid that a new and big dealer named Martel was in town and was more interested in buying large amounts and shipping back to the Eastern part of the States rather than selling large amounts in the local area.

Adam's troops were told to pass the word to these small buyers that they were looking for their own big buys to peddle to the States. These were transactions in the millions of dollars a week through their U.S. contacts and their sources. So, the action had been started, and Adam and his crew could feed the energy being generated by their presence. A big dog needs food, and the big suppliers look for the big dogs. It wasn't long before Adam's crew was bringing him news that there were rumblings that the big Prima boss wanted to talk to the big Martel boss. Adam told his crew that they should play it cool and wait till they really get a contact they knew was real; meanwhile, he told his crew to start making buys at the ten-thousand-dollar level, so those suppliers knew there was a real entity in town.

This worked; as his crew began to bring back more quoted statements, and these ten-thousand-dollar-per-week people said the Prima boss wanted to meet with him. Still, Adam kept his constant silhouette awaiting a more direct line and direct contact. Finally, after being there for a little over a month, Dred brought Adam the news that an intermediary representing the Prima wanted to meet with him. Adam discusses this with Dred and the rest of the crew, and their recommendation was to set up a meeting at the Long Shore Restaurant down on the ocean front. It was a very famous restaurant but was remote relative to other business. They believed this was an ideal meeting place. Adam gave them the okay to relay this message to their contact.

By the next night, the date was set for them to meet the following Monday at the Long Shore Restaurant for dinner. The time was set for seven o'clock in the evening. The reservation was made with a given private room for their dinner. In this way, Adam knew he would have the privacy he wanted, and it served as a first meeting with someone they didn't even know. "Whoever shows up that night in that room better be ready to talk 'turkey,'" said Adam.

Adam and Dred arrived at the Long Shore Restaurant at 6:45 PM on Monday evening, ready to discuss business with an intermediary. Adam told Dred that he didn't intend to make a commitment during the meeting. He only wanted to set the atmosphere of one who was in business and looking to talk to the top guy in the area about purchases. At five minutes to seven, a well-dressed gentleman along with one who looked like the assistant entered the private room. Adam was slightly surprised by the suave appearance of this man who promptly introduced himself as Dijon LaCount and introduced his compadre as Ramon Dias. Adam introduced himself as Adam Markel and Dred as his assistant.

They exchanged pleasantries for a few minutes, and Adam asked if they would like to order wine before dinner. Dijon said, "It would be a pleasure to imbibe with you in a good bottle of wine during our discussion. I find it very warming to start any discussion with a good bottle of wine." Before long, they were indeed having a glass of good wine and talking about everything but the purchase of drugs. As time passed, they made their choice on the menu, and, as the waiter left to provide this service, Dijon broke the ice with a soft comment. "I understand you are working the States and looking for volume. Is this true?"

"I am indeed looking for volume," said Adam. "Are you in the position to handle this matter?" questioned Adam.

"It depends on the amount we are discussing. The person I represent doesn't want to bother with accounts that are small. Do you have the muscle to take on big buys? If not, then we should have a great dinner and go about our business," replied Dijon.

"The amount I am interested in would probably put a dent in your boss's supplies. I have contacts in the States that are spread all over the States and can handle anything you can supply. We also don't want to discuss business with anyone that isn't big enough to handle our business. I don't want to peddle pouches of material to the locals. It takes up too much of my time. There seems to be an ample supply of dealers locally that are handling this business today. I don't want to fracture their business, and I don't want to sample the States. I want to handle big buys that cover months of supplies to my contacts in the States. I am talking about millions of dollars per week. If your boss can't handle this without it infringing on his supply, then we should have a nice dinner and go about our business," commented Adam, in a low but authoritative voice.

At that point, the waiter arrived with their meals, and both sides of this conversation remained quiet as he spread out the meals. Upon his leaving, all at the table remained quiet and began to pursue the food on their plates. There were pleasantries discussed as they ate their food. They discussed the Super Bowl that would be coming up soon, and some commented about soccer. Adam said, "I think the Steelers from Pittsburgh look good for the Super Bowl. They have a great defense and enough of an offense to handle the Arizona team."

"Yes, I have been watching the games," said Dijon, "and they bring out many surprises. I am quite entertained by American football. I began watching when I was a youngster living in France. Then, when I came to Mexico about twenty years ago, I began watching the Dallas Cowboys and their team. I followed their results each week on television if they were being televised. But, deep down, I am still a soccer nut, since this was the game of my growing up years and continued here in Mexico. The problem is that soccer is not on television very often, and the teams seemed second class compared to what I watched in Europe."

Adam continued by remarking that soccer was too slow a sport for most Americans, and they were wild about football. These talks during the meal were seen as premature remarks to the main subject. Both sides knew this, and each wondered when they would get back to the main topic.

As they were finishing and having a cup of coffee, Dijon mentioned quietly, "My Primo will handle anything you need for this market, but I am sure he wants to personally talk to you. I usually make the first impression and determine whether it is a waste of his time or not. What am I to say to him concerning the volume we were talking about?"

Adam paused before speaking. He looked up at the ceiling and said, "I want to know if he can handle buys that are five to ten million dollars a week for the next several months. I want to know if he can handle buys in the ten-to fifty-million-a-week category in the months following that. Tell him I don't want to go to a second supplier. I want a supplier that is the 'numero uno' in this land. If this is not his cup of tea, let me know now, so I can go and find who is 'numero uno' in this area."

With that comment, Dijon arose from his seat, took the napkin and slowly wiped his mouth, looked at Adam, and commented, "I like the numbers we are talking about , and I believe my Primo will be interested in talking to you. I think you two will begin a long and fortuitous relationship. I would like to talk to you about your ability to keep the business confidential and your means of doing that, but I think he would rather talk to you about these details when the two of you are together. I will get back to you through your man, Dred. Thank you for the wonderful meal and a fine wine. I hope we can do this again sometime in the near future."

Adam and Dred got up and shook hands with Dijon and his assistant as they left the table. Adam and Dred remained at the table to discuss things further.

"What do you think, Dred?" asked Adam.

"It appears to be the first step. This is the way they handle big business. You might not get to talk to the Primo next. They might send another intermediary to get a little more information. On the other hand, they are very interested in getting into the U.S. market without themselves being involved. You look like a big hog to them, one that could eat a lot of their products. If I am right, we will hear from them by day after tomorrow. I don't think we have to take the next step. We should just lay back and do what we have been doing. If they think you are real, they will take the bait. They don't have anything to lose at this stage of the game. They don't have to worry about American authorities, and the Mexican authorities are on their payroll. This is like a stroll in the park for them at this point. They might keep it a stroll in the park or they might be greedy enough that they will take the next big step. We shall see."

"I agree," said Adam.

"I want you to keep a low profile. I don't want them or any of the locals giving you any problems. If you feel heat, I want you to get hold of me immediately. We have people that can give plenty of heat if need be." With that, they called it a night and went their separate ways.

Dred was pretty close to being right as two days went by, and he got a call from Dijon saying he would like to set up a time for a meeting with the Primo and Martel. He said it must be in Mexico, and he would be making all the arrangements. "Find out from Martel when there's a good time for them to meet, and let me know, and I will contact Primo and see if the timing is okay," said Dijon.

"You got it," said Dred. "I have your cell phone number and will give you a call by this evening."

Dred no sooner got off the phone and then he was back on the phone with Adam. Adam believed they shouldn't respond with a one-day deal. "It would sound like we are too excited," he said. "It's now Friday, and I think the middle of next week would be okay. Let them pick the day and the time and give us the instructions we need to make the contact."

Dijon set up the day as Wednesday of the following week and said that they were to drive down to Tijuana and drive through on the main highway to a location about two miles down the highway. "Just on the outskirts on the southern side of Tijuana there is a restaurant used by many tourists called Mia Casa. You should arrive there about 10:00 .AM, but don't come in; just drive around back, and stay in your car, and, when I see you drive in the back, I will drive by and flash my headlights and drive out of the parking lot, and you should follow me. We will be driving about thirty miles, and I won't drive any faster than fifty-five, so you won't have any problems following me. After about ten miles, I will be turning off on a two-lane side road, so stay close enough so that I don't lose you on that turn off. After that, it is only about a thirty-minute drive."

Dred repeated the instructions back to Dijon and everything was set. Later, he provided the instructions to Adam who was glad to hear this and contacted the agency to bring them up to speed.

Kim was excited with this news. "This looks like the first big break," he said. "Make sure you don't push things too fast. You don't want them to think this is anything but business as usual. I will be anxious to hear what they come up with. This is a big outfit if you have struck the right chord. There are two major outlets in Mexico today; the one is the East Coast supply line and is called the Gulf cartel. It supplies Central America and Mexico City and up to Florida and the states along the Gulf. The other is the West Coast supply line and is called the Pacific cartel. It supplies western Mexico, Tijuana, and the resorts along the Pacific. It is able to get supplies into California, Arizona, and possibly Texas. It reminds me of the evolution of the African ants that migrated up from South America and made their way through Mexico and are now in the southern part of our country. It seems the more you kill, the more they come."

"These cartels are like those ants and find ways to get the stuff into the country. It is estimated that they do thirty to fifty billion dollars of trade each year from Central America to the southern part of our country. Don't think it stops there. Those drugs make it to Iowa and all the other states, but most of it makes it to the rich areas of the country. They won't be interested in you unless you can show that you will be able to do two billion dollars a year or more by three years from your first take. This being true, you have to talk about doing ten million dollars a week within a three-month period and doing up to twenty million dollars a week by year's end. This would have you going out of the year at a billion-dollar rate. That would have you doing about 4 to 6 percent of their business at year's end and with a promise of doing 12 percent of their business within the three-year period. This is 12 percent of the total Gulf and Pacific cartel business. But it would represent about double that for the Pacific cartel or about 24 percent of their business. That will make their eyes light up."

"Greed is what gets them high, and greed is what we must depend on to find their top guys and crack down on them. But this is like Al

Qaeda where you can knock the top guy down, and another one stands up. So, you can't get euphoric if we nail their top today. We will have to keep nailing the top guy and taking bites out of their trade. After a while, if the trade doesn't grow, the cartel will start taking their own guys out of it and replacing them. If we nail the top guy through your efforts, we will immediately take you out of that area and return you home. If you crack them, they will know there is some connection. I think the only way we could really stop all this drug traffic is to go to Columbia, buy all their drugs, take them to some remote place, and burn them all. It might be cheaper than all the money we spend trying to track them down and chopping off part of their business only to have them pop up somewhere else. But we have to make it hard for them to do business. That's the main goal; make it hard. Make them suffer."

"Meanwhile, it seems there is a good man at the top of Mexico's government at this time, and he is doing a yeoman's level of work on this issue. The Mexican president has made arrests at the high government level recently for their connection to the Gulf and Pacific cartels. If he can keep squeezing them at the high official level, and we get the top runner level, we can cause them a lot of damage and make it hard for them to do business. Now, that's a lot of talk, and I don't want to preach to you. I know you know most of this, but I am just sounding off because it sounds like you are making a good hit. The thing that might throw them off is the fact that it isn't the U.S. Drug Enforcement agents that are involved with this. It would appear they have some moles in that group, since they seem to know some of the moves the enforcement agents are about to make and cause it to fail. They seem to know in advance when these agents are going to do something. With our agency being separate from the DEA, it breaks whatever link they have or had with the drug enforcement actions of our country. The head of the DEA is the only one outside of a chosen few within our agency that knows what is going down there. We have done this to keep people like yourself safe, and, hopefully, we can pull something off and get you out of there while we set up something else."

There wasn't much that Adam could say after hearing that, and he felt good about his part in this so far. He nervously awaited next Wednesday.

Adam connects with the Mexican Cartel

When Wednesday arrived, Adam and Dred left early in the morning to ensure being at the meeting place on time. The idea would be to get there about a half hour before the meeting time, but to wait about a half mile from the pickup location until it was time to be there. They did this, and then they drove the last half mile and got there at the designated time. "Now, if everything goes well when we park in the back lot of the Mia Casa, a car will go by and blink its lights," said Dred.

Sure enough, they were in the back for only a couple of seconds, and a car went by with its lights blinking. Adam was not driving, and he looked toward the other car and recognized Dijon. Their trip to the turn-off road was uneventful, and this turn-off road was called Via Way. It was a two-lane road that winded back and forth and didn't look like it was used much. However, as they continued, they soon saw a large house off to the right about a mile away and suspected this might be the place. However, Dijon continued driving and passed the turn off to this house. About another mile down the road, he turned off to his right, and, after a couple of miles down a dusty road, they saw a very large and pretentious house sitting up on a knoll.

Dijon drove in the entrance and continued on this driveway to an area behind the house and parked. Dred pulled up beside and parked.

Adam left the car and extended his hand out for a handshake as he approached Dijon and said, "Good to see you again. Your directions were right on. No problems."

"Good, "said Dijon, and then he smiled and turned toward a back entrance. Adam noticed a person standing at the entrance, one on a veranda and another standing on a left-hand side porch. He assumed these were guards. *There are probably several in the house*, he thought to himself.

Once inside, he was led to the front of this large house to what looked like a living room or family room. There sitting on a large couch was a rather small man who was neatly dressed. He stood up as they approached and said, "Hello, I hope you had a nice trip," and he extended his arm for a handshake. "My name is unimportant, but they call me Punta. I am the assistant to the Primo."

"Pleased to meet you," replied Adam. "This is my assistant, Dred, and we haven't figured out a nickname to call him, since his name is short and easy enough as it is."

They shook hands, and Punta pointed to an indoor elevator while saying, "Primo is waiting for us upstairs."

When the elevator stopped, Punta led them down a large hall to a porch that extended out from the third floor. As Punta opened the glass door that led them out to the porch, Adam noted a tall, prematurely gray haired, and well-groomed man. His appearance was such that he looked like a "Primo." *If this isn't Primo, he sure fooled me*, thought Adam.

The well-groomed man stood to meet them and extended his hand while smiling and stating, "Buenos dias, gentlemen. I am happy to meet you on this fine day."

He didn't state his name, and Adam took the hint not to announce Dred's name and his own.

"Have a seat," the man suggested. "Would you like to have something to drink or eat? It is about your lunch hour."

"I never eat lunch," stated Adam, "but I would like a glass of iced tea." Dred commented that iced tea would be good for him also.

The four of them discussed several things for several hours, including the methods to be used to handle the bulk of the drug sales, including the methods of transportation of the money and the drugs. Adam was very interested in the method of transport. It appeared Primo had purchased a rental car operation just outside of San Diego. The cars had all been outfitted with special bottoms to one section of the underside of the cars. This false section could be removed, and either money or cocaine could be placed in the section, and then it was replaced back in the bottom of the car. When one looked at the bottom of these cars, they looked like a standard bottom on all these kind of cars. This special section allowed a metal container that matched the underside of one of their cars to be removed or put back in place via two slots that the container slid into.

Once the metal container was slid into position, the bottom of the car looked just like any other car. By taking a magnet and dragging it across the end facing the rear of the car in a direction from the driver's side of the car to the passenger's side of the car, it moved a locking mechanism, so the box would not be dislodged. In this manner, there were no screws or bolts to remove, and the mechanism matched any of these standard car bottoms. The fact that there were no screws or bolts seen by anyone inspecting the bottom made it hard to determine that this was a false bottom where these containers were located.

All a renter had to show at the car rental place was that the car was going to go across the border into Tijuana and what its final destination was. This was not an unusual request, and it was asked of each customer as he filled out the rental papers. Then, they had one of their "snatchers" go to that destination. During the night, the box was removed from the bottom of the car. The box contained the money for the next shipment. When sending the drugs from the Mexico side of the border, they had several alternatives. The "snatcher" packed the drugs in these containers, and they replaced the ones that they removed that had the money, with these that had the drugs. The drugs were picked up in a similar way.

There were two approaches that were used with the cars that were returning to the San Diego area with drugs from Mexico. The one used most was to advise the car rental person to stop at a certain gas station to fill up their tank prior to returning the car with a full tank of gas. The gas station was located on the U.S. side of the border just before San Diego proper and was owned by the cartel. The renter would receive a special price per gallon that was less than the standard price by one dollar a gallon if the car rental place filled up the tank and charged the customer for the gas. If they took a longer trip, such that they would need more than ten gallons of gas apron return, then they would receive a two-dollars-a-gallon discount. While getting the gas, the attendant would pretend to check out the car for damages. As he went around the car, another attendant talked to the driver and asked him how his visit to Mexico was to take his attention away from the box being slipped from under the car and was replaced by another empty one.

When the car was returned to the rental agency, the box was removed at their convenience. The advantage of this approach was that if anyone was caught, such as the parties renting the car, they were the ones that would face the issue. According to Primo, to date there had been no problems with this method of transactions.

During the discussions, Adam assured Primo that he would be handling volumes that would bring his level of business to approximately a billion dollars in a year and would continue growing after that. Primo indicated that the business would be monitored, and, if the rate didn't reach the expected monthly amount in three months, then it would be grounds to consider other arrangements. Primo asked Adam how he expected to handle this level of business without the feds making a hit on him. Adam described in general his method of making contacts around the States without describing in detail the subtleties of the method. Primo tried to gather the details from Adam, but they were avoided by Adam. Adam could tell as the conversation continued that Primo was smart enough to know that these details could not be divulged without Adam being compromised; if not now, then later when Primo wanted some other dealer for the States that would infringe on Adam's method.

At first, the discussion and conversation between Adam and Primo were somewhat strained, but, as the day proceeded, it was obvious that they were making points with each other.

After a couple of hours, you would think they had known each other for years. Their conversation was quite open and relaxed about other general subjects of the day. In fact, before the day was over, they had made a personal wager between them on the Super Bowl that was to be played February first of this year. Primo took the Arizona Cardinals and Adam the Pittsburgh Steelers. Primo thought the passing of the Cardinals would be the difference, and Adam believed that the Steelers had a great defense and must defend the wide receivers of the Cardinals, especially Fittsgerald.

"If they can keep Fittsgerald controlled, they will control the game," said Adam.

"Yes, but that's the point," said Primo. "They won't control him. He's too good and too strong with hands like magnets," he said with a laugh."

Before they knew it, the time had come to call it a day. They set up a schedule for the first shipment. It would be a one-million-dollar buy with the money delivered next Wednesday. The first transaction would start with the money pickup being done through Dred. A pickup messenger would arrive Wednesday morning, and he would have a reaccepted password to give to Dred. Later, Dred would have his man deliver the money at four in the afternoon to the car rental. A car had been previously reserved and scheduled to go to a location about fifty miles south of Tijuana for a business visit to a potential customer. This was ideal for a first transaction, since there was a known starting location (the rental) and a known final location.

While the man was making the stop to transact his business, the transaction could be made by their "snatcher." It took less than thirty seconds to pick up the money and transfer the drugs, since a drug-containing container was loaded and waiting for the pickup. A magnet swipe and the money cache could be removed and a magnet swipe in the opposite direction, and the loaded drugs were locked in. The salesman stayed the night, and, the next morning, he was driving back to San Diego. He didn't even stop at the gas station to take advantage of the several dollars he would collect. By Thursday evening, Dred delivered the first batch of drugs in a bag of groceries. So, the first transaction was complete, as it should be. Adam now awaited the word from within the cartel that business was on.

Business was not only on, but it was on big and moving smoothly for the first several transactions. Now, the agency wanted to take this one step further. In a call to Adam's cell phone, Kim talked about finding where the money went after it was picked up in Mexico. They were going to mark some bill of the money when they got sent on the next delivery to Adam's bank. There would be a small single frequency transmitter placed in two of the bills. They used the very latest in technology incorporating the transmitter in a small dot of the bill. It was located in a part of the bill where there was a large amount of printed material, and one had a hard time finding it even if they were told where to look. The transmitter would not begin transmitting until a signal was sent from a satellite.

In this way, there was no way that the dot would be noticed on the pickup. After a day or so, the transmitter would be activated and would begin transmitting. It would transmit for twelve days and stop, or it could be turned off by a satellite signal. In this way, the agency would be able to follow it for the twelve days, and then it would become void of signal. This should be good, since the money would probably be traveling for less time then twelve days, and then it would be deactivated, so it didn't come to anyone's attention. Adam thought this was a bright idea and just wanted to know when it would be happening. "When you receive a shipment at the bank, and the bills are wrapped with a green band around each ten thousand dollars, you will know that is the shipment," said Kim.

Adam was excited about this proposal, since he felt that when the final location of the bills was known that his service would have provided a great advantage to the agency, and he would be able to return to his normal duties and his home and family. It was only two weeks that passed when Adam noticed a deposit in his bank that was wrapped in the green bands around the money. That week's shipment of money to the cartel via the rental car carried those bills. He knew that the bill would be activated the following day or two, and he continued business as usual. The next evening, the drugs were delivered via the rental car and Dred. So, Adam now knew that things were going as planned. The pickup and sale were made without incident as far as he could tell. The next thing he could expect was a call from the agency concerning the destination of the money.

That evening, Adam received a call from Kim. The money had gone to a place that was about a mile beyond where Adam had made his first contact with Primo. This would indicate the house that Adam had made contact was just a ruse to lead them to think this was the main house. This corresponded to how Adam and Dred had felt. They felt the house where they made contact didn't show the normal armed site one would expect. Yes, there were some guards around the place, but it was fairly simple protection for someone that was supposed to be as big as Primo. "Let's see where it goes from here," said Kim, and Adam was in agreement with him.

The next night, Kim called again. "We followed at least some part of the money, and it went to a place just outside of Nogales. We feel that this is where the arms are being purchased for the Mexican band of guerrillas that have been attacking the Mexican police in most of the key places in Mexico. They are buying arms from legitimate dealers of guns in Arizona and New Mexico. The guns are being purchased in Phoenix at several gun shops, as well as weapons dealers who bring the guns to the Phoenix and Tucson, Arizona. These arms are smuggled across the border from weapon dealers that are supplying the Mexican cartels for their protection. We have contacted the top person at the U.S. Bureau of Alcohol, Tobacco, Firearms, and Explosives in Arizona and New Mexico, and they contacted the highest level of trust of the Mexican authorities, and it has been decided that they, along with some U.S. support, are going to hit this area immediately while we have the location with the money, and the arms have not been dealt yet."

"As we speak, the Mexican government forces are moving in on this location with police, soldiers, and helicopter forces. You won't hear any more from me on this. If the transmitting money stays at this location, and it is hit with success, you will know by me calling tomorrow and just saying, 'The mark is gone. We have erased it.'"

The next night, Adam got a call, saying the mark had been erased, and that was the extent of his message.

As luck would have it, another mark had been sighted at the house mentioned a mile beyond the Tijuana-related visit. This mark made its way down the Baja Peninsula to La Paz where it moved around for a day and then was placed on a boat of some sort. This boat went down the coast to Manzanillo and was there for several days, and then the mark disappeared. It was expected this was due to the time span before it shut itself off. It was now known that the Pacific cartel on at least this one occasion made a rendezvous with whoever was the supplier of the drugs. The guess was that they came from Columbia and not Iraq; time would tell based on future shipments.

"In order for you to have a better feel of these locations, I am faxing you a map of the main areas of Mexico. Keep them in mind as we continue our discussions." When the conversation was over, Adam went to the fax machine and waited. Soon, there was a printed map arriving. He looked it over and related to the locations.

As Adam examined the map it became quite apparent to him how the Mexican Cartels evolved into two main ones. The area around Tijana is just like San Diego. It is not as warm as most of Mexico, having the Pacific Ocean bringing in cool breezes. As one moved to the East or South of Tijuana the weather changes as did the scenery. It got much warmer as one approached the Tropic of Cancer area. Meanwhile there are two major arteries of mountain ranges that run north and south;; The Sierra Madre Occiddental and the Sierra Madre Oriental. These two mountain ranges split this beautiful country into major segments that follow the split of the cartels of the country. The Sierra Madre del Sur provides a range that splits this country from Central America. The capital, Mexico City sits high on top of the mountain range of Sierra Madre Oriental. The Cartels are on the left and right of the capital. Although the one cartel that leads up to Tijuana is called the Pacific Cartel, it easily could have been called the Occidental Cartel since most of the action is up through that corridor. The other cartel has a natural lead into the gulf states of the U.S. and extends over to Texas for some of its action and probably some of the major fights between the two cartels takes place in this location.

The money being received for the next couple of weeks had green bands on it and followed the movement to Primo's location and then the route from Baja to La Paz to Manzanillo. This brought two points to the agency's notice; one that the major supply of the drugs was coming through the Manzanillo supply center, and the other point related to the fact that the mark was eliminated abruptly without any signal by satellite. This was concerning. It meant that either the mark was accidentally eliminated or they found it and eliminated it. Because of this, Kim made contact with Adam and informed him that the next money supply would not be marked. The one after that would be marked. Since these shipments of currency were being done on a weekly basis from different points in the United States, it was believed Primo's people had not found any fault with the supply coming in. They believed Primo felt he had a great contact with this American big-time dealer. They intended to find out with the second shipment and see where it took them next.

Adam was now aware that the next week was okay, but he knew the following week could be a problem. This thing was coming to a close now, and, if they could make it past the next two weeks, they would probably start actions to hit the Tijuana site and the Manzanillo site to begin taking the Pacific cartel down or at least part of it. However, he believed they needed to determine if the Manzanillo site was still in operation, since they might have been the ones who found the mark. They might have not only found the mark but made the decision to change the route. They needed to find this out.

With this in mind, Adam called Kim on his private cell phone. He told him to change the mark and its frequency. That would give them a chance to make it past Primo's point and make it to wherever the money flowed. Kim agreed and said the next shipment of money would come from a different bank than the previous ones and would have a completely different mark located on a different point of two of the bills.

Kim continued, "In this way, if they look for whatever they might have found on the previous shipment, it won't be there. These marks will generate a different transmitter signal frequency in case the smugglers have picked up the previous signal and were looking for it. We can't promise they won't find it again, if indeed they had found it on that past shipment, but this should make it very difficult. We won't activate the signal from the satellite until we feel the money has left Primo's location, so there won't be a transmitter putting out a signal if that happens to be the way they found it in the past."

"We will wait four days before activating the signal. That way, the money should have left Primo's location and be well on its way to the drug pickup location. Keep in mind that we will warn you if we find anything happening during the twelve-day cycle. Keep in mind that these people need the money coming in to purchase the drugs. They can't afford to hold the money for any length of time or they will be getting bugged by either the Columbian supplier or Iraqi supplier. These suppliers don't wait long before they start getting things moving from Primo or they will get rid of him and find another contact. You also must keep in mind that Primo keeps a certain portion of the money, and we might be unlucky enough that the money he keeps contains both of the transmitter marks. If this happens, we will know it and will know that we need to cut off the transmitters, so his guys don't find the signal someway. We then would have to go with another money supply the following week and hope we find whether Manzanillo is still in action."

As luck would have it, the following supply of money didn't make it out of Primo's location. When the signal was activated after the fourth day, it showed two signals coming from Primo's location. With this information, the agency had the signal cut off, and Kim contacted Adam and made him aware of the status. They decided to go with plan B where the following week the money would be marked again with these new marks and new transmitter frequencies. They again would wait for four days and hope they found that the two transmitters were on their way to Manzanillo. With this final word, Adam was playing a waiting game with the hopes that this would soon be over, and he could go home to his family and normal life.

Major danger for Adam

Two weeks went by, and Adam got a call from Kim. "I have good and bad news to report. The good news is that one of the transmitters made it to Manzanillo, so it looks like the route is still valid. As soon as the money arrived, there we turned the transmitter off, so they couldn't find anything to suspect there was anything corrupt with this shipment of money. However, the money that stayed in Primo's location was there with no signal till it was there for four days. When we turned on the transmitters and saw the one was on the Pacific route, and the other was in Primo's location, we kept the signals going till we were sure of the Manzanillo route and then turned off the transmitters."

"This means the one in Primo's location was transmitting for three days before it was turned off when both of them were turned off. This was a flaw in our methodology. We should have had a means of turning off each of the transmitters separately. We don't know if they found anything at Primo's location when the transmitters were both on from the fourth till the seventh day. We needed those three days to verify the Manzanillo location. Contacts have been made with the right people in the States and Mexico. The Mexican government is going to make a raid on the Manzanillo location. They will probably do this on Wednesday, day after tomorrow. What we will do is turn on the transmitters again when they are a mile from Manzanillo, so they can find the exact location and nail the cartel suppliers."

"This being so, on Wednesday, the signal for the transmitter in Primo's location will be activated. If it is still at his site, we will know they probably didn't find the transmitter. If we find that the money has moved toward some other location, this will be great news because it will mean they haven't found the transmitter, and the movement of the money will show us where it goes after Primo. This is a critical period, and we will be watching. I am activating three more guards to be at your site in San Diego by tomorrow. I want to be sure you are protected." Adam understood all this and believed he had a few days from completing what he was sent out to accomplish.

Adam had only been off the phone with Kim for about an hour when he tried to contact Dred to debrief him on what was going on. However, Dred didn't answer his phone, private or cell. This bothered Adam, and he decided to take one action that had been in the back of his mind. He took out his wallet and took out his ID card. He put it in the top right desk drawer and took out the one with the dot on the end of the "L." He wanted to be sure if things didn't go down right that he had at least made this move to make others aware of where he was.

With that done, Adam went to find Dred. He went down to the first level and toward Dred's office area. As he entered the office, a voice shouted, "Don't make a move. We have two guns aimed at you." It was at that point that he saw Dred's body in the corner. Blood was rolling out his neck, which he saw had been slit. He decided to not talk at all. The two men walked up behind him, and one tied his wrists behind him.

Adam's heart was beating at a rapid rhythm. "Let's go out to your car. We are going to take a ride," said the tall guy. As they reached Adam's car, the tall guy told him to get in and drive. "Where are we going?" asked Adam.

"We're going to take a little ride down Mexico way," said the shorter guy.

It didn't take them long, and they were at the border gates showing their ID information. As Adam showed his, he was glad he had at least changed his card. *If things go right, they will see I went under duress,* thought Adam.

Not a word was spoken as they rode down through Tijuana and came to the turnoff that went to the Primo house. Adam turned and drove up toward the house, but, as he approached the house he and Dred had gone to originally, the tall guy said, "Keep driving. I'll tell you when to turn off."

They had gone a little over a mile, and the tall guy told him to take the next left turnoff. As Adam made the turn, he remembered that Kim had said that there was a house beyond the one he and Dred had gone to. As he thought about that, he thought about Dred's body lying back at the San Diego house, and a big lump was in his throat. *He was such a good guy*, he thought. *I wish people would know what these kinds of people are doing for the country to control a sickness like doping up. It's a silent effort. It's a war without the thrill of a war or the broad media hipping it up.*

Just then, he saw a large house looming up in the distance. It reminded him of the castles and moats he had read about when the Knights of the Round Table were fighting in England. It was a large house surrounded by a lake on three sides, including the front. They had to drive around back to park the car. As they got out of the car, the small guy took a rope and tied Adam's hands behind his back. "What's that for?" he asked.

"That's so you know that you are not here on a friendly visit," remarked the tall guy.

As they approached the house, Adam could see guys all over the place walking around with shotguns or the guns like the infamous AK-47 used in terrorist's mobs. This time, when he entered the house, they took him down the stairs toward a cellar. They proceeded down a hall that went to a door with a large latch on the outside. They literally threw Adam in the room and onto a chair. Once in the chair, one of them took a small chain and hooked Adam's wrist bond to the chair. The other guy picked up a chain and wrapped it around his feet and hooked it to the chair legs, which have places to hook to. He was not comfortable, and he knew they knew it, and he knew they didn't care.

They both left the room, and it was very quiet. As Adam sat there, he wondered about his fate. *This is something they can never train you for,* he thought. *I guess I'm about to find out what they know and what they don't know. I know it's no good because they already killed a man about the problem.*

During his life, Adam had experienced times when time went slow, and he would get anxious about some event beginning or ending. This was the worst of them all. The time seemed to go very slow. There was one around, it was quiet, and he had an itch on his left shoulder blade. It seemed like he was in there a day when he heard the door being unlatched. *Thank goodness the lights are on in this room*, he thought. *I can at least see who the enemy is that is coming in the door.*

Again, the time seemed long as he waited to see a face come through the door. It was like they were teasing him as one of them stood at the partially open door and looked back at someone behind him and made some comments. And then, Primo entered with a large guy behind him. "Hello, Mr. Martel," Primo spoke. "Not exactly like the last time we met. We have made a lot of money off you, and now we are coming up with some strange happenings. Let's see if we can make some sense of them." With that comment he pulled up a chair and looked Adam square in the face. "Who's the joker that is putting transmitters on our money?" he asked.

"I don't know what you are talking about," answered Adam.

"Don't give me that crap. We have been seeing 'money that talks' down here. That money comes from you, and now Dred has paid part of the price for playing with us. Do you want to pay the rest for playing around with us? What group are you working for?"

Adam looked up and said he didn't work for anyone except his own bank account. "I don't know what you are talking about or who you are talking about. I can't believe you had some kind of hiccup, and you went and killed my boy for that. Is that how you treat your best buyer? I can't believe this is happening."

With that comment from Adam, Primo looked around at the big guy and nodded toward Adam. The big guy took two steps forward and slapped his large hand across the face of Adam. Adam felt like his head got taken off with this one slap. This went on for about an hour, and Adam's head was drooping from the punishment. He mumbled out a comment. "Why don't you check my bank account and see the money I have cornered from this operation. That should give you some idea who I am working for. I can't believe you have taken a good thing like this and want to blow it because you got a headache or some small thing happened to you. You aren't going to be finding another contact like me that is putting you in the big time. This sucks!"

Primo got up and nodded to the big man to follow him. The two left the room, and Adam hoped the time really went slow now. He didn't want to see that guy's hand any more. As he slumped in the chair, he thought to himself. *Maybe they don't know who the culprit is. I wonder how long I can continue this without breaking. This is not fun, but I have to keep playing this game and hope they buy my story. I can take the slapping around as long as they don't start breaking bones or doing the things I heard they do to people in my position. I assume that the agency got my signal, and they will take some course of action in the next couple of days. I wonder if I can hold out for a couple of days.*

Meanwhile, as Primo left the room he talked to his guys. "Maybe he doesn't know anything about this. He has given us good service for a couple of months, and we never saw any problems. Now when the gun dealers get hit, I get pressure, and it might not have anything to do with 'the money that talks' or the strike on the gun merchants. Remember, we didn't see anything wrong with the money before or after the gun dealers got hit. Then, we had a find on one of the money piles that gave out some kind of signal frequency. Our people didn't even know what was causing the frequency. What if someone from the U.S. Drug Enforcement Agency had one of their agents make the mark? What if someone from the U.S. Bureau of Firearms made the mark? We have contacts within both of those agencies, and none of them have heard of Adam Martel. What if one of those agencies found out about the Martel business and found a way to put a mark on the bills that were moving around the banks in the United States?"

"Their best way to stop the Martel business would be for us to find a mark and put him out of business. We might be doing them a favor. I want you to make contacts with our people and have them search this thing out. I will talk to my super and see if he has any inputs. We have seen one problem, and we have knocked off a guy today and might have done the U.S. drug or gun agencies a big help. I want you to take Martel up to the third floor bedrooms, pick out one, and lock him in it. He doesn't need to be cuffed. He ain't going anywhere. We can wait out a few days and see what we find out. Meanwhile, we are going to miss at least one big shipment and probably two. This is hurting us, and I don't want to be hurt if it doesn't compute."

The Follower to Mexico

Back in the agency, Kim had seen the new ID card pass the border patrol and knew there was a problem, and he knew that they had taken Adam into their lair in Mexico. He knew that Dred took a hit. He hoped that Adam hadn't taken a hit. He had the satellite people activate the signal on Adam's ID card, and they confirmed he was in the Primo location. He discussed this with his people. He wanted to determine if they should make a hit on the Primo site and risk the killing of Adam or to hold off and risk the killing of Adam.

"We do not have more than a day to make the decision," he said.

Less than an hour went by, and his staff came back with some surprising recommendations. They felt that making a hit on the Primo site would probably end up with Adam's death and take away any chance they had in the future to use their contacts they had developed and wanted to keep developing till they could make a closure on a bigger portion of the Pacific cartel. They recommended contacting Axel and having him go down posing as the twin and partner of Adam on the business they had been moving.

"He could call Primo and explain that he wants to come down and discuss what has happened. He can try to convince Primo that any problems they have had is not due to anything the two of them have been doing. When they see Axel and see how much he looks like Adam, it will immediately take away any thoughts they might have that this is a rouse. They would also be convinced that Adam's brother would not come down there and give them two hostages to work with. It would show that the twins have a good business going and don't want to stop it.

We know that Axel with his energy levels and his armor could devastate the whole Mexican lair if it came to that."

"He might be able to take this past the Primo location if he can make a viable pitch to the Primo location. We think the cartel would like to see the business pick back up or they lose a big portion of their present and future business. We believe they would bend their backs to make Adam look good. We believe that's what they would be hoping for."

Kim spent almost two hours discussing the details. What he would tell Axel was that he should convince Primo's people that he represented the banks that his brother had been working through and wanted to know what the problem was. With Adam being held, he wouldn't be able to complete the loop that had been developed. Knowing that the West Coast was three hours behind the agency, Kim decided to make a call immediately to Axel.

Axel was just starting his lab class when the call came. He instructed the lab to continue their work, and then he went in his office and listened to the dreadful tale that Kim told him. "You mean they have Adam down in Mexico, and it's a possibility they might kill him, and you want to know if I will go down and try to work the problem. You know I will. I will jump in my car and drive down to the San Diego area and into Tijuana immediately if you give me enough information to handle the problem." Kim spent almost an hour bringing Axel up to date on the business that Adam had developed.

"You can't go until you get the proper ID card and any other things you will need. We felt 100 percent sure you would take this on Mineta, so we sent all this information on a U.S. Air flight that arrives in San Jose, California, in about five more hours. You will need to go to the San Jose International airport and go to the U.S. Air counter and show your identity, and you will have the information you need."

"The paperwork will call out your name as Axel Martel on your ID card. I will give you Primo's cell phone number, and you should call him immediately and make arrangements with him to accept you at his location. You can tell him you are the other half of the team your brother and you started some time ago. Tell him you are the one that arranges the sales in the United States and has the money sent via several safe routes. Explain to him that you are aware of Dred's being shot and wanted to know if he knew the whereabouts of your brother. Tell him that your brother had told you that anytime there appeared to be a problem, and you couldn't get Adam, that Adam had told you to call Primo. Tell him this was given to you in confidence, and no one else has his number. Ask if he will have someone meet you in San Diego."

"There should be a flight that goes out of San Jose about two hours after the flight you are to meet in the Mineta San Jose International airport. You must make sure you don't take your real card with you. Your ID card will have a special mark on it that we will activate when we see you pass the border gate and enter Mexico. The mark will be picked up automatically as they scan your card entering the country. When it is activated, we will be able to follow your route. You have a major advantage. With your internal Internet capability, you could actually talk to us anytime you want."

"Make sure you take a lot of candy bars and lozenges with you, so you can always be 'sugared up' and in good fighting condition. Don't think a second time about activating your hood. This is a dangerous crowd, and it won't take much to get angry and start shooting over nothing. We believe you are the best bet we have of getting Adam out of there alive and keeping our contact with the Primo location valid. At this time, we don't know what they have on Adam."

"They did kill Dred at the San Diego office. It has been described as a shooting that resulted in some bad business that Dred had been in and had a huge debt with. They reported that they are still looking for the owner of the place who is missing. We wanted the story to go out that way. With your armor and strength, we believe you are better than a band of thirty Mexican patrols hitting the location, all without your special body protection. That would guarantee Adam's death. You can get in there and be close to the subject and make the right decision. Any questions?" Kim asked.

"No," replied Axel. "I believe I understand the situation and am prepared to carry out your plan. I will keep you advised once I get beyond the border gate. I imagine someone will meet me in San Diego, but I will keep you advised."

Axel didn't have much time and decided to contact Tori at her class to see if she could leave it and help him out. He decided he better determine if he could contact Primo first. He called on his internal phone with a contact to the Internet, so the agency could hear what was transpiring.

He heard the phone being answered, and a voice said, in Portuguese, "Hello," and there was silence.

"Hello," said Axel. "My name is Axel Martel, and I would like to talk to Primo. He knows my twin brother, Adam, and I believe it is important for him to talk to me."

"Wait," said the voice on the other end of the phone. Axel heard some voices and picked up some of the comments that indicated that no one was supposed to talk to Primo. There was more rumbling about, and a voice came back on the phone again. "Who are you, and what do you want of Primo?"

"I am the twin of Adam Martel and the other half of the business Primo is transpiring with my brother. I need to talk to Primo about my brother." Axel heard a phone buzzing as if someone was trying to transfer the call to a different phone.

"Hello," said a voice in pure Spanish.

"Hello," said Axel. "I am Axel Martel, and my brother told me to get hold of Primo if I thought there were any problems."

There was a pause and quiet for a few seconds. Then, the voice was back. "I am Primo. What can I do for you?" he asked.

Axel began his communication. "My brother and I have been doing business with you now for several months. Things have been going quite well. Then, today, my brother's right hand-man got shot and killed, and my brother is missing. He had told me several times that if a problem came up, and I couldn't get him, to give you a call to see if you knew his whereabouts. Do you know where Adam is?" Axel asked.

Again, there was a quiet period, and then a rich, bold voice responded, "Sure, I know where your brother is. He is down here with me. We are seeing some problems with the operation and had him come down to see if we could ration them out."

"I don't understand what problems you are talking about," commented Axel.

"There seems to be some problems with marked money," said Primo.

"That can't be," commented Axel. "I have been handling the money and have fed it through security routes to ensure the money doesn't always flow the same routes. You haven't seen any problems before have you?"

Again, Axel was met with silence for a few seconds, and then the voice said, "What would you like to do?"

"I would like to fly down to San Diego this evening and have one of your people pick me up and take me to where you have my brother. We can listen to the problem and try to decipher where the problem is entering. We don't want this business to stop now. It's really making a lot of people happy in the States."

Again, there was silence for a few seconds, and then the voice was back. "Let us know the flight number and when it is expected to arrive in San Diego. I will have a couple of my people meet you. Do you look like your brother?"

"Yes" replied Axel. "We are not identical twins, but we look a good bit alike. Adam is about an inch taller than me, and I weigh about ten pounds more than he does. He is kind of skinny, but we look alike. Your people will have no problem picking me out of the crowd."

"Okay, it's all set," said Primo. "I will see you late this evening."

With that, he was gone, and Axel began to make the air travel arrangements. He had to make them for Axel Martel and almost forgot that. He mentally told himself that he could not afford to make that mistake with Primo or his hoods around. He found a flight that was leaving almost an hour after the package should arrive from the agency at the airport.

Then, he leafed through his small black book to see Tori's schedule for the day. Finding the classroom she should be in, he went and knocked on the classroom door. Mrs. Fleming was teaching the class and came to the door. She knew Axel and knew he taught some labs and freshmen classes.

"What can I do for you, Mr. Tressler?" she asked.

"I need to talk to Tori please," he commented.

She turned and said, "Tori, someone wants to talk to you."

As Tori got up and walked toward the door, Axel looked at the beauty of her. *She even walks beautifully*, he thought.

Tori proceeded to outside the door and closed it. "Axel is there trouble?" she asked.

"Sort of," he replied. Then, he began to describe his brother's situation and what he had to do. "I need to meet a flight in a few hours and then fly out of here a couple hours after that. I would like to spend some time with you before I leave, and then I want you to drive me to the San Jose airport."

"I don't understand," she said. "What do you expect to do? Do you want to become another captive of these guys? What part are you playing in this? Are you keeping secrets from me?" she rattled off the questions before Axel had time to answer any of them.

Axel had felt she would react in this manner and considered whether he should tell her of his part in the agency and of his unique capabilities. He had decided to downplay that and say that he thought there would be no problem. He had decided to not tell her of his unique situation. He had promised the people at the agency and promised himself that anyone knowing this could possibly result in some future compromise of his strengths and possibly their good fortune.

He looked at her for a while and then said, "I knew you would be upset by this, but I need to go and try to help my brother out of a problem. I hope to convince his captors that they have the wrong facts about our company and especially about Adam."

"But, what if they don't believe you and both of you end up in their possession?" Tori asked.

"I have to take that chance. There is nothing else that anyone can do. I need to give it this chance. I had a good phone conversation with the head man down there about a half hour ago, and he will have someone meet me at the San Diego airport. Can you leave class now? I need to spend some time with you. I need that. I love you and will miss you each minute I am away," Axel pleaded.

"Certainly, I can leave class and want to be with you. It's doesn't have anything to do with me, only with you. I love you and don't want to lose you, but I understand how you feel about your twin. I guess I would do the same thing if I had a twin sister, and she was being held against her will and I had a chance to save her." With these comments, Tori grabbed Axel by the arm and led him toward the parking lot. "I will follow you to your house in my car," she said as they split in the parking lot and headed toward each car.

Once they were in Axel's apartment, Axel put his hands around Tori's waist and raised her in the air and pulled her close to him. They both let all their emotions out and began pulling their clothes from each other. Axel took her breasts to his mouth and began sucking the nipples and her stomach and her hips and down to her clitoris and the wonderful fur that surrounded it. He could not express his love any more than this move, and she loved the feeling. Her moans told Axel that he was in the right spot, and her legs surrounded his neck as they rocked back and forth in heavenly bliss.

He moved her to the couch, and as he sat down and brought her to a position just above him, and his rock-hard dick was placed in the spot just abandoned by his mouth. With a shove by both, they were soon riding each other toward that final feeling that comes with the passion borne by both. It seemed he could not get enough of her and the warm feeling that greeted his hard dick. She was moist from the combination of her sexual response and the wetness he left there with his tongue. Then, she shouted in a low moan that she was coming, and this was the only signal he needed to begin his climax. They both moaned and exchanged love whispers in each other's ears as the juices flowed from each.

"God, this is a wonderful feeling," whispered Axel. "I can't find a better way to show my love to you. As I embrace you and feel your body touching mine, I think there is nothing that feels like that. It isn't velvet or any other cloth, and it has a feeling all of its own. It sure beats kissing. There are nights when I don't have you around me, and I miss that feel of your firm but soft body against mine. I don't believe the people that take cocaine can achieve a better high than this. Maybe that's their problem. They don't get laid enough."

They laid next to each other for an hour talking about life and their feelings for each other and then returned to the lovemaking. This time was just as good as the time before, and they lay beside each other and kissed different parts of their bodies. Axel believed he was in heaven and hoped Tori thought the same. Life was wonderful.

Before long, Tori was driving Axel to the San Jose airport. When they arrived, Axel went to U.S. Air and picked up the package sent to him by Kim and the agency. He took it out to Tori's car, opened it, and searched through its contents. The agency did a nice job of sorting out the contents. They had marked the material he should take with him and the material that he should be aware of but not take with him. He told Tori to take the material back with her that he wasn't to take with him.

They went back in the airport, and he picked up his ticket for the flight to San Diego. It was not long before he had to go through the security check and leave her on the non passenger side. Before entering the security check, he took her and hugged her and said he would see her soon. "I will call you every night, so you know I am okay, and I want to hear your voice. After that, I can go to sleep in a better mood." They hugged again, and he passed through the security check. He was now not Axel Tressler but Axel Martel.

The Follower within the Mexican Cartel of Primo

It was a rather short flight to San Diego, and there were two men waiting to meet Axel.

"I am Bono Fernandez," said the one greeter, and the other introduced himself as Sergi Mendez.

"We are here to take you to see the Primo," said Bono.

The discussions stopped there, and only a few words were spoken as they approached the border crossing security gate to Mexico. Things moved smoothly through there, and, shortly, they were on their way through Tijuana and on a road unfamiliar to Axel. They made a turn off the main highway and traveled down a rather quiet stretch of road. Axel saw a well-lit house along the side of the road off in the distance that Axel thought must be the place they were headed, but they were soon past that.

They traveled a mile or so down the road and took a turn off, and soon, he saw a miniature castle. At least, it looked like one. It was night time, and the moon was shining off the water that surrounded this house on the front and part of the side they were approaching. They took a left turn and went behind this house and parked in the rear. Axel got out of the car with the other two, and they only took a couple of steps, and they stopped and said they had to search him for weapons. Axel held his hands up in the air and allowed them to check his clothes and feel around his body to see if he was carrying anything.

"Nothing," said Bono.

"Likewise," said Sergi in Portuguese, and they proceeded to the large door in the back of this impressive house.

They proceeded and reached what looked like a living room, and there was a man there, and he said, "Primo said to take him up to the third floor." There was an elevator to take them up. Upon reaching the third floor and disembarking, they proceeded to a large, open room where there were three men. Axel viewed the three and knew that one of them was obviously Primo. He was the well-dressed, tall, and business-like-looking man. The other two must be there to protect him, his bodyguards. "Good evening," greeted the tall man. "I am Primo," and "you are Axel, I presume."

"Yes, I am Axel and pleased to meet you. I have heard a lot about you from my brother. I knew you as soon as I saw you."

"Same with me," said Primo. "You look just like your brother."

With the introductions done, Primo told Bono and Sergi to go downstairs and have a drink. "And what will you have to drink, Axel?" he asked.

"I think a nice glass of wine would be refreshing," Axel responded. "I haven't had anything to eat since breakfast. Do you have any sandwiches or anything available that doesn't require a lot of preparing?"

"Hell yes," replied Primo. "I never let it be said I didn't treat a guest to the finest of foods.

With that, he pushed a button on the table beside him and a voice echoed out. "Yes sir, what can I do for you?" asked the voice.

"Let's have a bottle of cabernet wine, the spinach salad with the chicken breast strips, a bowl of soup, and a nice dessert for our gentleman guest."

"Right sir; it should be ready in about fifteen minutes or so."

With that, Primo turned in his chair and invited discussion. Primo said that he was trying to determine the truth concerning something that happened during the last several weeks. "More than the truth," he said, "I am looking for the source." He then described in detail what had occurred and what actions he had taken. "The killing of Dred and bringing your brother down here might have been the right thing or the wrong thing to do. If it was the wrong thing, I apologize for the reflex action. If it was the right thing to do, then I believe you are in trouble along with your brother. So, which is it?"

"I don't know what you are talking about," replied Axel. "My brother and I have been running a hell of a show for you and ourselves. We have been doing millions a week and were looking at going out of the year at a rate of two billion a year. Why would we screw that up? We were living high on the hog, as they say in the States. Now, all of a sudden, you get a frequency signal that appears out of nowhere, and, bang, you kill a guy and bring my brother down here. What kind of game is that?"

Primo looked at Axel for a few seconds without saying a word. Then, he began a fairly long, soft-spoken tirade of sorts. "Young man, we are running a very large business. There are other parts of our business that you don't engage in. We cannot afford to overlook just the slightest of hints that something might go wrong with it. I don't sit in an armed fortress, and my body is not surrounded by armor. (This took Axel's ears. *If only Primo knew what he just mentioned and how my body is surrounded by armor*, he thought.) Every day of my life is one sitting on the edge of disaster. I can't afford to allow anything to slip by without it going unnoticed. I didn't get to this level of this organization by taking things for granted. Do you understand where I am coming from Axel?"

"Yes, my brother and I know you are in a tenuous position. We are too; maybe not as delicate as yours, but not an easy situation either."

"Well, what do you recommend?" asked Primo.

The room was quiet for several seconds as Axel looked as though he was rolling that question around in his brain. "For one thing, you can give us a chance to prove ourselves. Let us work with you to try and determine the source of this problem. You know it might not be a problem. It might be some coincidence that occurred, unfortunately while we were doing business, and it might never happen again."

"What do you mean by me giving you a chance to prove yourselves?" asked Primo.

"I was thinking that you could leave my brother and me to return to work providing you the weekly business, and you can monitor it to see if the problem reoccurs. If it doesn't happen on all of our buys except the one you are mentioning, it could be a fluke. You know that if you take the problem as ours and keep us out of the loop that you will be losing a couple billion dollars a year with business growing. We are lining up considerable business with high-level rollers and many sales directly to wealthy buyers. You don't want to lose that do you?"

The room was quiet again as Primo took in the comments by Axel. Just as it looked like he was going to talk, the lady with the food came into the room. "Here you are sir," she commented. "I believe you will like what I jimmied up for you."

The food looked delicious as well as the bottle of wine and two lovely wine glasses. The conversation stopped, and Primo told Axel to make a plate. For the next half hour, they were busy eating, drinking, and talking in general about the economy. "Things have slowed down around the world," commented Primo.

"Yes, it has," said Axel. "But the odd thing is that business at the high-end level for coke has increased, as well as at the street level. It looks like they are fluffing off the economy and taking hits to keep it out of their minds. Coke can do that. The wealthy have a way of doing away with problems. Some take marijuana to put them in la la land, some take heroin that takes you further into the la la land, and the smart and wealthy take cocaine to relieve the pain of life. We work with coke because it keeps us away from some of the low-level street activities. We only work with people that are known high-level users, those that can afford the stuff and are above the level of the riffraff. I think the problems with the economy are an open road to the high-end users we service."

As they finished their food and wine, Axel could see that Primo wanted to open the discussion back to what they were having before the food arrived. He picked up the bottle of wine and poured another glass for Primo and another one for himself (thinking about the great nourishment this fine food was providing his ATP energy suppliers) and set the bottle down.

"Do you want to get back to the discussion we were having before the food arrived?" he asked Primo.

"Yes, I believe there can be several alternatives we could follow," replied Primo. "We could let you both go back to San Diego and continue with the purchases while we monitor things more closely. But that wouldn't be very smart of me, would it?"

"Why not?" asked Axel.

"Well, it leaves me with my ace in the hole I have now," commented Primo.

"What would that be?" asked Axel.

"You and your brother are my aces," Primo smiled.

"How is that?" asked Axel.

"I would say that at this point in time I have you as hostages and believe that anyone you might be working with in the States would not risk your lives, would they?" Primo stated with a smile across his face.

Axel looked at Primo and said, "I don't think you understand. There is no one in the States that knows we are here. If they do, it's an accident. If you kept us here for a month, nothing would happen, and I mean nothing. You wouldn't have the large sales you have through us because there is no one else involved in the transactions since you killed Dred. He was the only one who knew this was going down, and he got paid well to keep this quiet. Adam had the connections, and I had the money flow from them to me and the banks. I guarantee the banks didn't know where the money was coming from or going to. So, I think you have a great poker hand with four aces in it, and there is no one across the table for you to play against. Two of your four aces are Adam and me. How can you play with no one on the other side of the table? You have all the elements, including two of the players as the aces in your hand. A winning hand with no players," smiled Axel.

"That's interesting," commented Primo as he looked up toward the ceiling as if to find an answer somewhere on the overhead. It was quiet again, this time for several minutes. Then, Primo said, "I'll tell you what, Mr. Axel; we are going to send you up to bed and talk a little more about this tomorrow when we both have a good night's sleep. Rest is good for the mind, and right now I have a hand full of aces I have to think about."

"Can I see Adam before I go to bed?" asked Axel. "I want to make sure that all of your aces are accounted for."

"I don't think so," replied Primo. "I don't need two of you making up stories. One at a time appears to be enough. Besides, you can see him in the morning at the breakfast table."

With that comment, Primo pushed another button beside his chair, and out of one door popped a hood. At least, he looked like a hood. "Yes sir," he asked.

"Take Mr. Axel to bedroom five," directed Primo. "It has all the accommodations one would need for the night, but if you need something else, just push the service button, and they will ask your needs. Have a good rest. We will awake you at eight in the morning, and breakfast will be at nine."

With those comments, Axel was led off in the direction of room five, and Primo got up from his seat and walked toward the window as though he was going to cogitate on the issue.

Axel got a wakeup call at eight and found a package of toothbrushes unopened that fit on the battery-operated toothbrush supplied. As Primo had said, there was everything he needed to start his day. They had taken the briefcase he carried when he got off the plane in San Diego. They obviously had opened it and found his pair of shorts and an undershirt and a clean dress shirt for him and placed it on the dresser the night before. There was also a clean pair of socks, so he was in good shape when they came to take him to breakfast. There was no doubt in his mind that they considered him a hostage but were treating him well so far.

When he sat down at the breakfast table, there was no one else at the table. Next to the plate on the table where he was sitting was a menu. It was almost like being in a restaurant. He picked it up and peruses the listing. *Just like home*, he thought. Just as he was prepared to order something to eat, he heard the sound of footsteps, and as he rose up from his seat, Primo and Adam came into view. *Wow*, he thought, *Am I glad to see Adam*" "Hi Bro," he said as he raised both his arms in the air and moved toward Adam.

Adam got a big smile on his face and said "Hey, where did you find this ugly guy?"

Primo smiled and said, "We found him loitering around the San Diego airport and thought you might like to see him."

"Yes, he's a sight for sore eyes," Adam said while giving his brother a hug. "How long have you been here, Bro?"

"I just came over last night and had a chat with Primo. I had called him yesterday afternoon asking about you, and we came up with an arrangement where I would fly to Diego and his guys would meet me and deliver me here."

At that point, Primo asked them to look at their menus and pick their breakfast out. "We want to get moving on whatever plan we will be moving on, and I don't want to be wasting time. Time is money in this business just like all businesses, but maybe more in this business, since we have to set up schedules that have to be met."

They all reviewed their menus and gave their orders to a nice-looking young lady who awaited their demands. As she walked away, Adam looked at Axel and asked if he knew about Dred. "Yes, I heard about it on the television, and when I called your place and no one answered, I remembered that you had told me to call Primo if I couldn't make connections with you. I certainly was happy that you hadn't followed in Dred's footsteps and that Primo had you down here. I then made the arrangement to come down and see if I could clear up any issues that Primo might have about our business practice. We discussed a few things last night over wine to see if we could come up with some resolution. We discussed several alternatives, but Primo wanted to wait till we had breakfast this morning."

They both must have decided independently to not talk about Adam's wife or Axel's girlfriend, and so far, the subject had not come up. They talked about everything but the important thing till the breakfast finally arrived. After completing the meal, Primo decided to break the ice with a declaration. "I have decided that we will do nothing for a week, just to see if anything happens."

"What would you expect to happen?" asked Adam.

"I don't know, but I want to give this a little more time to see if it resolves itself," said Primo. "Besides my boss, El Encima, would like to talk to at least one of you and see if he has more convincing methods to find out whether you are involved in some way with the blitz on our weapons site. It happened about the same time as we heard the signal transmission coming from the money you sent. Some of that money made it to our weapons location, and then it was followed by the raid by the Mexican police. About the same time, our systems picked up a signal coming from some of the money that made it to southern Mexico. You two say you haven't been involved. I have to find out for sure. I have a tendency to believe you or you wouldn't be around today. However, El Encima isn't so sure. We haven't had any problems since then, but this might be your, or someone's, strategy. We will keep you here or at El Encima's place for a week and see what happens."

"I guess I don't understand," questioned Axel. "If we stay here for a week, you won't have any activities between you and anyone in the States. We are the connection, and this whole thing is just going to stop. This doesn't make any sense."

"If we keep you here for a week and see the problem popping up, then we know that you had nothing to do with it. If nothing happens, it means that maybe you had something to do with it. After a week, we will have more information so as to make a better decision. So, we will make you comfortable with good meals, and you can play tennis right here on site, and you can play golf just five miles from here. We will keep everything from you just as we have so far; no cell phones, no IPhones, no access to a telephone, no access to a computer, no pen or pencil, no mail, no car, and you will have several people escorting you twenty-four hours a day, seven days a week. We feel if you can't communicate with anyone outside of this site that it will be like an open loop as far as you are concerned. Then, we will watch for any indications that something might happen elsewhere. If it does, it helps your case. If it doesn't, then your case is questionable, and we will decide what to do at that time. Do either of you have a wife or fiancé that might be looking for you?"

Adam looked at Axel and then turned to Primo and said, "I have no wife and no fiancé, and I know that Axel doesn't have a wife or a fiancé or I would know about it. Even if we did, they wouldn't know about our business or our contacts or any locations in this country. I think you picked a poker game with no players. This is unfair to both of us. We have had a lucrative business deal with you and your people and have followed your directions at all times. Then, all of a sudden, you get paranoid and kill one of our good friends. Is this the way to run a successful business, where you kill off all your clients? This is the shits. I like to play golf and tennis, but I don't believe I would enjoy playing in this coming week. This doesn't make sense. Can't you think of something more constructive? I don't want to do this."

"I am sorry, Mr. Axel, but you have nothing to say about this," said Primo with a smile on his face. "You are our guests in our country, and I make the rules while you are here. Does that make sense to you?"

With that directive, both Adam and Axel sat back and breathed out a big puff of air as though in disgust or relief. Axel thought, *Things could be worse than this. At least, they know which side of the bread their butter is on. They hope we aren't involved in any of this. It would reflect back to El Encima that they don't know how to control their responsibilities. It also would turn their business back on. Greed will overcome competence in the end; it always does. There's a question in their mind, and I can solve that problem. When we get done here, and I think about it a little longer, I will contact the agency and see if they can quietly get some "talking money" to the agency that has drug control as their charter. If they can get that into circulation in Mexico, it will diffuse this situation. We need there to be a happening that comes up in one of the cartels and makes it clear that this can happen even if we are quarantined. That would take the whole argument away from Primo and his Pacific cartel.*

As Axel continued his thoughts, he was suddenly awakened by the fact that Primo was asking him or Adam or both something. He cleared his head and paid attention to the words being shouted out by Primo. "If I find you two have been playing me, I will make your last hours on earth ones you would want to forget. I have no patience with treason," he shouted. "You better make this week a good one and hope this event passes in your favor. You might be victims of your government's games they play. If they are the culprits, and this week goes by without an incident, you will hope that they had played their games a little longer. Each evening, we will have a meeting to cover what has or has not occurred that day. As the days approach, next Friday both you and I will wait anxiously to see if we get another attack. That's what it is, an attack."

"I now introduce you to your escort for the next week. This is Jake Maldonado, on my left, and this is Luke Juarez on my right. They will be living with you every minute that you are out of your rooms. That means if you have to go to the bathroom for anything, they will be with you. I want you to take note of the big guns they each have on their bodies. I hope they stay in their locations. Movement of the location means you will be removed from your locations. Don't take me wrong. I hope you are both vindicated, and we can continue our big business together. In fact, if you are vindicated , and I find that these two escorts caused you any problems, they will pay the pauper. Now, with that out of my system, it is early in the day, and you two might want to play tennis, or go golfing, or go swimming. There are booklets that were left in your rooms while you were having breakfast. Look through them and pick what you want to do with the rest of this day. I'll see you tonight."

With that, Primo got up and walked away from the table and toward his office. Before he could take two steps, Axel spoke out, "I want you to know that I am hypoglycemic and therefore need to eat a little every couple of hours. Please have your men stock up my refrigerator in my room with candy bars and soft drinks. I can eat a candy bar or something like that every couple of hours to balance my system."

"I understand hypoglycemia and your need for food on a regular basis," stated Primo. He turned and looked at one of his men and told him to take care of the problem. "If you are not getting enough food, let me know, but I believe my people will take care of your needs. When you are at golfing or tennis or whatever activities you are inclined to participate in, your escorts have their orders to take care of your needs. You can have everything, but communication with the people of the States."

With that said, the two escorts walked over to Adam and Axel and escorted them up to their rooms, so they could clean up after breakfast. On the way up, Adam asked Axel what he would like to do for the day. "I think I would like to go over to the golf course and just watch the players and walk around a little and blow off some of this anxiety I have," said Axel. "I need to relax more than play some games. I don't feel like I am in that mood. What about you?"

"That sounds good to me too. I'm with you on that. After hearing that guy get up and preach us a sermon, I am in the mood for leaving this place and going out and seeing the world pass me by. Standing on a golf course and watching players might just be the thing to take my mind off this. I would normally want to golf, and maybe I will one of these coming days." Then, he whispered to Axel, "Meanwhile, I assume you will make the right calls to the guys to get us off the hook. Also, when you call Tori, make sure she gets hold of my wife, and tell her we are enjoying ourselves in Mexico."

Back in his room getting washed up and ready to go to the golf course, Axel decided to call the agency on his internal phone/Internet system. As he was washing his face, the calls went through, and he talked to Kim. "I hope you got the drift of things last night," said Axel. "You need to get some of the marked bills to the U.S. Drug Agency and hope the mole knows they are there. When a sale goes down and the bills pass over, we want the word to get out. This time, they won't have to hear the 'money that talks,' since they will get the word from the inside man to the right people down south. We just hope it gets out in a few days. I think if they don't get the word by a week from now that we will have to find our own way out of here."

Kim listened and said, "No problem; we will work on this immediately. A million dollars will go out by tomorrow morning. It will be a million spent well. When you guys get free from that place, we will clear it up and save our country's people billions of dollars. They will be spending money recovering from the bends and the sweats. You keep us abreast of what's happening. We flash on the satellite every couple of hours for five minutes to see where Adam is. Fortunately, they let him keep his driver's license and ID card. We can at least see where he is, even if we can't help him at the time. We are depending on you to find the way out for him. Maybe the funny money going out and the mole giving us away will free you guys up without needing to bust some balls. Nice job so far."

With that, Kim and the agency were off the line. Axel then phoned Tori, and they talked for several minutes. He didn't want anyone to suspect he was capable of this type of communication. Although that wasn't probable, he didn't know what kind of technology they had here for picking up phone or Internet signals. Besides, when talking to her, he got emotional, and it was almost impossible for him to not show that he was dreaming about someone or having a seizure.

He told her he was okay, Adam was okay, and he missed her and loved her. He said that in many nice words and finished by telling her to get hold of Adam's wife and tell her that he was okay too. "I will call you every night," he said and sent her a kiss across the phone lines. With that, he joined his brother, and they went with their escorts to the golf course.

The meeting that night was not a friendly one as Primo got up after dinner and informed everyone that he hadn't heard any "'talking money'" today. He was pretty cool about it and made comment that he hoped something would show up and save the good business they had been enjoying with these gentlemen while pointing at the Martel brothers.

Adam sat there and absorbed the words from Primo. *I think he really would like to find some "talking money,"* he thought to himself. *He wants to get back into business. Well, one way or another, we are going to put him out of business.*

The second day was some of the same, and the evening session with Primo went a little worst than it did the day before. Both Axel and Adam thought he was taking this thing harder than they were. The pressure seemed to be building up in Primo, and he no longer looked the picture of confidence he possessed when first they had met him. Of course, they thought they were going to get out of this, one way or another.

Later, in the rooms, they discussed the fact that the agency hadn't made a hit yet. "They better hurry," remarked Adam, "or we have to fight our way out of here."

"I have a plan," said Axel. "They are greedy, and we have to make that greed work against them. We have to convince them that the only way they can start the money rolling again is to have one of us back to San Diego. They will want to keep one of us as a hostage to protect their position. We have to convince them that you should be the one that goes back. We can do that by convincing them that you are the key guy. You have all the contacts, and you tell them you can get someone to handle the money flow from your clients to you until I get back. They will buy that. You and I know there is no way they can hurt me, so we have to work a deal where you go back to the States, and I stay here. When I know you are safely back in the States and safe, I will go to work here. Let's see what happens. Maybe they will find the 'money that talks,' and we both can go back. We shall see."

The next day went the same as the first couple except Adam and Axel played a few sets of tennis instead of watching golf. Later that evening, after having dinner, they were taken to the office area where Primo and some of his goons were talking. "Sit down," Primo said as he pointed to two chairs by the large conference table. They had no sooner sat down when Primo started back to his normal tirade of talking. Only this time, he seemed a little less tense than the prior days. After a few minutes of dialogue that wasn't going anywhere, he broke out into a big smile and said, "The money that talks has spoken. Today, I got a call from the head of our Gulf cartel. He got word from our contact that the drug agency was sending out money with marking on it. Later, we got a call from Monterrey that they got paid off with money, and one of the bills gave out this frequency that we had advised them to look for. It was only on one bill of the total buy. They told us the good news was they found it, and the bad news was that the drug agency had a location that they probably didn't have before. So, that is good news for you people. We are getting closer to resolving this problem. Maybe we can get back to working our business after all and maybe sooner than I expected."

Adam and Axel looked at each other with big smiles and gave each other the high sign. "That's great," yelled Adam. 'It's what we have been saying all along. Thank goodness someone else found the same problem before our week was up."

"Don't get excited too early," said Primo. "We want to make sure this is not a fluke. Let me sleep on this, and we will talk in the morning at breakfast. I have to talk to my boss, El Encima."

Adam and Axel went to bed that night thinking that things had worked their way out, and things would be good in a few days. They were wrong. After breakfast, Primo began discussing the situation. "I talked to El Encima last evening. He wants us to wait to see if things continue as they did yesterday. He wants to keep the situation as it is now to make sure. What we expect to find, I don't know, but he's El Encima (the top) and my boss. So, you guys are going to be sticking around until we decide which way to go."

With that, he ended his speech making and walked away. The escorts took the two of them up to the rooms again. This night, they didn't let Adam and Axel spend any time together saying that was the orders from Primo. So, each was taken to his room. Adam knew that Axel would take care of the situation without their talking about it. Once in his room, Axel contacted Kim on his internal phone/Internet system. He told him of the happenings of the evening and asked him if he had any inputs. Kim didn't want to send out any more marked bills immediately. He thought it might be good to send a marker out in a week if nothing else happened to Axel and Adam over that time span. Axel told him about the suggestion he had discussed with Adam, and Kim thought it was a good move if they couldn't get out of there any other way.

Kim said he would like to find out a little more about El Encima. "He appears to be the big guru of the Pacific cartel," said Kim.

"I will see what I can do to pull that out of Primo or one of his goons," responded Axel.

Kim continued, "Maybe you can sort out El Encima's location. I know you won't get his exact location, but the town would be a good start."

Axel answered this with, "If I get them to take me to his location, it will be like you are there. You will be fully informed. I guarantee you. Before we cut off, I think you better have the marked bills go out in about three days, not a week. I don't want to be sticking around here that long." With that comment, Axel completed his dialogue with Kim.

Several days went by with no other actions taken. Then, during breakfast several days later, Primo shocked them with the comment, "El Encima believes that I should send one of you to his location. He believes he has better means of getting to the facts than I do. Adam, I want you to go. One of my guys will fly you out of our local airport, so I want you to be ready to fly by noon today. Do you understand?"

Before Adam could respond, Axel made a comment, "I think you can have your cake and eat it too. Adam is the main guy in our business. You should send me to El Encima and allow Adam to go back to San Diego and start the business up again. You will have me as a hostage, and I would take the flight to El Encima. This gives you the best of worlds. You will start selling your trade within a week. Adam will get it flowing. El Encima will have me to enforce the deal. If things go well, you will be shipping in a week or so. Let's say these shipments start and run for a month or so with no incidents; this should be reason for you and El Encima to see that this works, and then you can release me."

Primo picked up his cup of coffee and said, "Let's drink to that. Let's hope that El Encima agrees with this. I buy it, but don't know if he will. You guys go to your rooms, and I will call him and see what comes of this." Primo got up from his seat and headed toward his office. Then, he turned and said, "Take them up to their rooms right now till I find out the way we are going to go."

Back in their rooms, Adam and Axel awaited the outcome of this suggestion. Before long, they were returned to Primo's office. When they get there, Primo was not there, and their escorts, Jake Maldonado and Luke Juarez, told them to take a seat and Primo would be coming soon. Jake laughed and said, "Primo is probably trying to convince El Encima to go along with this plan."

"No doubt about it," said Jake. They sat down and picked up the morning paper and began to read.

They were waiting longer than they expected, but Primo finally made his appearance. He sat down and looked up at the ceiling for a few seconds and then began his normal preaching. "Well folks, you will get half of what Axel suggested. El Encima agreed that Axel will be the one that is transferred to him; however, he wants Adam to be held here for at least another week. He wants to get a better handle on the situation and believes it will take at least a week for that to reach fruition. He will be talking to the Eastern cartel (Gulf cartel) while Axel is there. He will see if any other talking money comes along. If it does, he might allow Adam to return to San Diego and begin the flow again. If nothing happens, I don't know what will happen. We will have to play it by ear. I think this is a start toward returning to our normal high-level business."

"I will tell you now that if this wasn't high-level business, you guys would be sucking up dirt by now with no one to find you. We don't believe in playing with little players. It's only because you are viable that you have a chance to continue to be viable. Get ready to go, Axel. When you are ready, my pilot, Simon Perez, will fly you to the working place of El Encima."

"How long a flight is it?" asked Axel.

"Not long," Primo responded. "If the winds are right, you will be there in two hours. It is just outside of Nogales."

"I will need to get some underwear, undershirts, and socks to carry me over for a week, or do you think it will be longer?" asked Axel.

"Maldonado will take you to Sears, which is on the way to the airport. You better get enough clothes to last you two weeks. I don't believe you will be there that long, but you never know," said Primo.

The Follower infiltrates the two cartels

The pilot, Simon Perez, was a tall man for a Mexican. He met Maldonado and Axel at a small airport that was just outside of Tijuana and led them to the plane. It was a single-engine plane that carried four, including the pilot. On this flight, there would be three, counting Maldonado. With little fanfare, the plane was soon taxing down the runway and was off on the short flight. (While taxing down the strip, Axel contacted the agency and told them of the flight, and he told them he would keep the channel open, so they could listen and gain as much information as possible.)

Simon was a cheerful person and talked the whole time they were flying. They were only in the air for about an hour and fifteen minutes when he started his descent to a small airport that Simon said was just outside of Nogales. After landing and parking in a reserved parking spot, they were met by two men who Simon knew. "Here's the package," Simon said with a smile. Maldonado obviously knew them and stood aside and talked to them.

Then, he turned and said to Axel, "I will be flying back with Simon. These two gentlemen will be your escorts while you are here. The tall one," he pointed out, "is Jose Reyes, and the other is Romeo Sanchez. They will take good care of you. I wish you the best of luck while you are here. Hopefully, I will be back with Simon to pick you up in a week or so."

"Thank you, replied Axel. "I hope you and Simon have a good flight back, and I hope we see each other in a week."

With that, the two of them got in the airplane, and Axel went with Jose and Romeo. Their car was parked in the parking lot, and they were soon on their way to wherever, "How long a drive do we have?" asked Axel.

"Not too long," said Romeo who was driving.

It takes about half an hour, Axel thought to himself and via his internal cell phone to the agency. *Well, now we know it's about half an hour outside of this small Nogales airfield. I assume the agency will get a fix on this airport. It looks like we are going south to their lair.*

"We already have a fix on the airport, and it does look like you are going south. Keep your internal phone on, and keep eating those candy bars. We'll keep listening to your conversation. Keep talking."

Axel then started up a conversation with his two escorts. Before long, they were on a small side road that was a nice road made of black top. They had only traveled on it for about three or four miles when Axel could see a large house sitting on top of a hill in the distance. "Is that where we are going?" he asked.

"Yes, that's where we are heading," said Jose, "pretty nice, huh?"

"Yes it is a great looking house," and in a short time, they were parking in the back lot of this huge house.

Beyond the back parking lot was a forest of trees, and it was lucky they were on a hill or you couldn't see much. Even now, all you could see was the tops of the trees. "Boy, this is beautiful," said Axel. "It's lucky this house is on a hill or you wouldn't be able to see beyond the trees in the back. Even at this height, I can't see another house in the distance in back."

"Yes, that's true," remarked Romeo. "I believe the cartel owns all the land from the first house you saw on this road to a couple of miles beyond this house where you see all the trees."

Shortly, Axel was inside the back entrance to the house with his two escorts. They took him to an office like room and told Axel to take a seat. "El Encima will be here shortly."

Axel picked up a magazine next to the chair and began to glance through it. Not long afterward, a tall, well-dressed man entered the room, and Axel was surprised. He looked like he was from Europe, not Mexico or any of the Central America or South American countries that Axel expected. Axel stood up to greet this surprise person, and before he could say anything, the man said in English, "Well, I am glad to see you made it in one piece. Welcome to Nogales supreme. I am El Encima, and I assume you are Axel Martel."

"Yes sir," replied Axel; surprised that he had addressed this mob leader with a "sir" notation in his greeting.

"Take your seat," said Encima. "We will talk a little bit about your business with us, or not."

They then began their discussion on how the Martel twin brothers conducted their business, especially as it related to supplying this cartel. After talking about this for a couple of hours and seemingly covering the subject as well as he could, Axel decided to turn the conversation around and see if he could get Encima to discuss how he got to this position. El Encima was more than happy to discuss his rise to this position. He was from Russia, and his real name was Mercia Bratovitch. The Russians had invaded Afghanistan about twenty years ago, and there was a war effort by Russia and a guerilla effort by the people of Afghanistan. This went on for several years before Mercia got sent to Afghanistan as a sort of envoy by Russia. Later, when the Russian armies retreated from Afghanistan, Mercia decided to stay. His reason was that he had made contact with the poppy seed–opium world of that country.

His contacts were made with the people growing the poppies as well as the rulers of the opium trade. When the United States invaded Afghanistan shortly after September 11, 2001, Mercia found a way to become one of the traffickers of this trade to places outside of Afghanistan. This brought him to South America where he consummated some of the opium trade with the cocaine traffic of Columbia. He now had a routine business of bringing in opium to this juncture. Eventually, this opium trade opened up some contacts with the people that controlled the cocaine smuggling from Columbia via the Gulf cartel. After a couple of years, he rationally looked at the trade for cocaine versus opium and decided the cocaine business was easier to conduct. The traffic from Columbia through either the countries of Central America or by sea up to Mexico was well established and, and he became a major director of some of this traffic.

When they wanted to establish what was now called the Pacific cartel, the drug lords decided he was ideal for establishing and handling this business, and he was established as El Encima (the top) of this trade route. He obviously had done a good (or bad, depending on how you look at it) job of establishing this cartel as a major one. He opened up some of the cities to this trade in the southwestern part of the States. He established smuggling routes into the States via the cities of San Diego, Phoenix, Tucson, and El Paso. The San Diego route was becoming a major one with the business set up by the Martel twins. That's why he and his troops were playing it gently with Adam and Axel. If they weren't a part of some sabotage scheme, they would be his major contact into the States and make a major impact on this trade. As it was, he was having more trouble running his business inside of Mexico than the trouble he was having with the American government. Small smuggling groups kept popping up in Mexico that wanted the trade both inside of Mexico and the trade with the Americans. This brought them in contact with El Encima and his trade, where they were trying to whittle in on his customers. This meant internal war among the groups of central and northern Mexico. El Encima had been able to overcome this by having a well-armed group of "citizen soldiers" that killed off the competition.

During the conversation, El Encima told Axel that he had skirmishes and bloodshed almost weekly, and through this, he had built an army of trustworthy troops that he paid well. About 10 percent of the revenue his cartel received was going to these good Mexican troops who protected his trade. Over time, he had become so strong that he now was having volunteers coming from the other camps who wanted to joint his cartel. They wanted to be part of the winning hand, so to speak. Through this mentality, El Encima had built a large civilian force of bandits who watched over his trade and openly bragged about belonging to the leading trader in Mexico. This was impressive to Axel. He almost felt sorry for El Encima, since he knew that eventually he was going to take him down. *Let's wait and see what comes of all this*, he thought to himself. Axel found it interesting talking to El Encima and hoped they would spend more time together discussing philosophies.

Axel's day had gone well, and when he was in his room, he contacted the agency to make them aware of his findings. "This is a large group, and it will be difficult for the Mexican government and the United States to come up with a plan that eliminates this kind of force. This is not an incompetent and small group of people we are talking about. It is a well-educated group at the top level and well-disciplined group at the lower levels; trained, not only on smuggling, but on how to handle this business and keep the morale high here in Mexico. It is like a well-organized and disciplined army that will not be easy to dispatch," he related.

The people at the agency now were made aware of Primo and his group and how they were a part of El Encima and the whole Pacific cartel. If Adam and Axel did nothing more, they at least had supplied a vivid picture of the Pacific cartel and how at least part of it was run. Axel told them that he didn't know how his visit to Nogales would end. He would have to see what El Encima made of his "capture" over the next few days. He knew that El Encima felt he had the upper hand, since he could eliminate Axel any time he wanted (little did he know), so there seemed to be no problem for him to openly tell Axel of how things worked in Nogales and the whole Pacific cartel. If Axel proved to be a real trader, then knowing these things would help him in his working with the cartel. If Axel turned out to be a spy, he could have him eliminated immediately. Axel told the agency that he believed that El Encima would do whatever he could to trick him into giving his true self away over the next few days. So, the next few days were critical.

Axel asked if they had heard anything from Adam or if they knew whether he was still at the Tijuana site. Kim broke in on the conversation to tell Axel that they had the satellite activate Adam's ID card every few hours to see where he was, and so far, everything was stable there. Of course, he could be dead and his ID card remained at the building. This they couldn't tell.

After this conversation, Axel contacted Tori. This was like going from night to day. After all the tension he had all day with El Encima and now going over details with the agency, he now was talking to someone with a soft, lovely voice that made him forget what had transpired today. "Boy, is it nice to hear your voice," poured out of his mouth. "It's like a bird singing to me after the storm has passed."

"Are things that bad down there?" Tori asked.

"No, they are not that bad so far, but things get edgy, and it's like waiting for a shoe to fall. But, so far, things are going well. I am not at the Tijuana site any longer. I flew into Nogales earlier today to discuss things with the person who can have Adam released. One way or another, I am going to get Adam out of here, and the earlier, the better. I am especially interested in this thing being a short-time thing, so I can come home and see you. I need some loving. When I come home, we are going to take a whole day off and make love the whole time."

"I'll buy that," she said. "I miss you, Axel. "When I go for lunch, it is like I never ate. It seems I got used to you being around when I ate lunch or dinner, and without you, the food doesn't taste as good."

"Man, that's the best compliment I ever had," returned Axel. "I never thought of me as food, even though I always thought of you as food. I love to eat you from top to bottom."

With that, it was quiet on the phone, and Axel could almost see Tori blushing on the other end of that line. They talked a few more minutes, and then Axel said he had to get ready to go somewhere with the boss man around there.

The next day, Axel was awakened early in the morning with a message to move rapidly and eat breakfast because El Encima wanted to take him somewhere. Axel moved rapidly and was down the stairs to eat along with his escorts in short order. After finishing their breakfast, the three of them awaited the arrival of El Encima. Soon, he came in the room while talking on his cell phone to someone. They could hear the conversation as he was directing someone to be at a certain location next to a creek or body of water somewhere. As he talked, he switched between Spanish, Portuguese, English, and maybe even some Afghan or Russian. It was like he was talking to more than one person, and each of them could only understand one of these languages.

El didn't know it, but Axel could understand all of these languages, and he was getting an earful. The one thing he was doing was directing each to meet him with a certain number of their cohorts, along with the firepower needed to beat the shit out of some band of guys trying to take away some of their business. As best Axel could understand, these were a band of guys trying to intercept the cocaine that came via this route from Colombia. He also could make out that it wasn't a small band of interceptors, numbering somewhere around twenty or so guerillas. *Sounds like an old-fashioned turf war*, thought Axel.

El Encima put the phone in his coat pocket. For the first time, Axel saw that he wasn't wearing the suit he wore yesterday. He had green army fatigues on and a green lightweight jacket and a military style hat making him look like he was ready to begin the fight for his territory. "Let's go," he waved at Axel and his escorts. "You can watch how we take care of intruders to our business. I don't want any of you to have weapons, including the escorts."

One of El Encima's sidekicks moved over to Jose and Romeo and took their weapons. While they were at it, they checked Axel who had been frisked the day before for weapons. Before long, they were in a jeep along with a parade of jeeps. Axel counted five jeeps full of readymade soldiers along with their weapons. They drove about two miles and picked up another band of vehicles; these were not jeeps, but were made up of four-wheeler trucks out of Japan, probably vintage nineties and a Ford Ranger. These all had warriors in the truck beds along with their weapons.

They came to a small river—maybe it could be a creek—and there were three trucks and one large army vehicle that looked like it was from the first invasion of Iraq. It was in good condition, like an owner had been proud of it and had taken good care of it. Altogether, they now had about sixty tough-looking guys ready for a fight. El Encima got out of his vehicle and waved to the group of vehicles from the two site pickups. Each then sent a person who must have been the leader of each of those groups, and they met with El. You could see he was talking to them about his plan of attack. He keep waving his arms in circles and then in a punching direction as he was probably directing them about how to flank the group of bandits they were about to hit.

Before long, the cars went to a site, and everyone got out of their vehicles except one vehicle that continued toward another reconnoiter site. They then gathered around El, while the two escorts and Axel were held in one of the jeeps with two people guarding them. As El took his band of warriors toward what was the obvious objective site, the guards allowed Axel and his escorts to follow about fifty or sixty yards behind. Evidently, El wanted them to see things up close and get a feel for the power of his wrath. Soon, they were quietly approaching a fairly large warehouse with a house next to it.

At this point, they were crawling through the jungle like weeds and shrubs that covered the land up to a point about fifty or sixty feet from these buildings. El quietly signaled his followers where he wanted them to go, and they spread out completely covering half a circle that covered this one side of the house. The house was next to the water, and this left just the far side of the buildings uncovered. El gave two of his guys a signal to go around through the bushes to that far side. He pointed to his watch and held up his two hands as if to say "ten minutes." That's the amount of time he would give them to get to the other side. They could now hear the voices of the men who were either in the house or in the warehouse. They were carrying out large packages of what Axel figured was cocaine and putting them in three of their vehicles, which numbered five in total.

El probably figured that his people that had run the warehouse were either dead or tied up in the warehouse. He also figured they should rush the place when several of the bandits were either carrying the packages or were returning to the warehouse for another package. This turned out to be six of the bandits. When this happened, and El was sure that ten minutes had gone by, he took his rifle and shot the one bandit who had left his package in the truck and was the closest to making it back to the warehouse. When his shot went off, guns began firing from all directions. It didn't take long till there were six bodies lying on the ground. Then, shots began ringing out from the house and the warehouse; they were shooting blindly, since they didn't see the forces that had shot their six men.

El moved his hands down in a ground-ward direction, as if to signal his men to stop shooting, lie low, and wait for them to expose themselves. He knew they didn't have to do anything for the time being. He could afford to let those people shoot at nothing and use up their ammunition. Meanwhile, it gave them a mental picture of where the bandits were located. They couldn't go anywhere. Their vehicles were right out in plain view, and that was their only means of escape. So, El waited. Soon, two of the bandits made a run for the one vehicle, and they only got halfway there before they were gunned down.

Every so often, there would be a gun that fired from either the warehouse or the house as if to try and get some gunfire from El's troops and show their positions. It didn't happen. It was quiet, and then El and his people heard two gun shots from the other side of the house., and then it was quiet again. El looked around at Axel, and he pointed toward the house and looped his hand as if to say, "We got the one guy who tried to get away from the other side of the warehouse." Then, someone in the upper level of the warehouse shot and almost hit one of the men not far from El. When that happened, about sixty guns fired at the spot near a large door in the second level and ripped the wood away from the framework and exposed a dead shooter. As fast as they had initiated their shooting, the guns immediately became silent. It was like a well-rehearsed orchestra playing a tune they had played over and over, *and maybe they have*, thought Axel.

It now became obvious to the remaining people in this hoodlum band that "school was out," and they had no choice but to give up. Things were quiet for about ten minutes, and then a white flag could be seen waving at one of the windows. El waved to his people to hold off and lie low. "Just be quiet until the waver moved out of the house." El shouted, "Come out with your arms up and with no guns in sight. Come out now."

A minute passed, and then slowly Axel could see the men coming out of the house and the warehouse slowly as if afraid of being gunned down. Nine men came out of the two buildings and stood in a group near the middle of the yard outside the house. "Get down on your knees," shouted El Encima. "If you move, you won't ever move again."

Then, El got up and slowly approached the group of men. As he did, about ten of his followers also moved toward them, while the remaining men stood their positions with guns aimed at the center group of men on their knees. Soon, the captives were standing with their hands behind them with ropes tied to their wrists. There was a large rope that tied the men in a string so that none of them were capable of moving on their own.

Axel looked over the group of men. Eight of them were obviously Mexicans, but one of them looked like an American. *What the hell is he doing down here?* thought Axel. It didn't take them long to realize he was the ring leader of this group of bandits.

El waved to one of his right-hand men and told him to take two guys and walk through the house to see what happened to the previous occupants. He waved to another of his guys and waved him toward the warehouse. "Be careful," he said in his excellent Mexican dialect. "I don't trust that all of them came out."

As the two of them looked for any remaining from the gang and were determining what happened to El's men who ran this warehouse, El had several of his men taking the packages that had been carried to the vehicles and returning them back to the warehouse and doing an inventory. Again, Axel was impressed with the discipline and organization of the group. It was like they each knew what their particular duty was.

The finish of the inventory of the cocaine and El's people who had run this particular distribution site found several interesting and stunning facts. The first was that only one of the three men who El had running this center was found dead, and the other two were not to be found. The inventory of packages found two missing. No matter where they looked, the two could not be found. This led El to believe that the two missing people from the distribution center had actually been part of the raiders of the place. He believed they were missing, and the two packages of cocaine missing must have represented their payoff. Further examination of the place showed the one remaining vehicle was that of the dead employee, and the vehicles of the other two were not here.

El turned to one of the men who must have been the secretary and asked him what the home address was of the two missing employees. El shouted orders, "Give the addresses to Benny. Benny, you take your five guys, and beat the way to those houses. They haven't been gone long, and you will probably catch them at these addresses. Take three vehicles. I want you to have enough car space to bring them back to me, along with the packages, and hurry!"

They were off like the disciplined soldiers they were. El turned and said, "Take the nine we have here, and take them into the warehouse where there is plenty of room. I want to find out how this all got started and who was the leader of this raid. Also, Benito, take three of your guys, and you will have to take over the supervising of this site. Make sure you all have cell phones that are working and batteries that are good. Also, pick up one of the chargers we have in the jeep, so you can keep your batteries charged. If anything happens after we are gone, I want you to give me an immediate call. I am holding you responsible. I know you can handle this."

Once inside the warehouse, El had the nine separated, and one by one, he interrogated each of them while the others remained in a separate room. His techniques were somewhat brutal with each as he tried to sweat the truth out of them. One of his henchmen would literally beat each one being interrogated till they almost lost consciousness. When they would pass out, he had another dump a bucket of water on him, and when he was alert enough, they continued. This lasted about twenty minutes with each of the first eight he had go through this interrogation routine. There was blood all over the wooden floor of the warehouse.

Before bringing out the American prisoner, El had a discussion with his top men to see if they agreed with what they had gained so far. Each, including El, was convinced that these eight represented migrant workers who were just trying to pick up some quick pesos. El asked, "Is there any of them that you think we should bring into our cause?" With this question, his top guys decided they should have a short discussion and return in ten minutes. When they came back, they had all agreed that there were three of the captives that they thought were sharp enough, strong enough, and hungry enough to be good additions to the cause. "Take those three into room 811, and I will be there in a few minutes. Meanwhile, Rick, take your guys and discuss what to do with the other five."

El pointed to Axel and said, "Come with me to talk to these three. Maybe you will have some suggestions." Axel was surprised by this last comment from El. It was like he respected input from an American.

Once in the room with the three "candidates," El began a sales job on the three. "You see how we operate and the morale of my men. They lead a good life and are able to take home good earnings, so their families can enjoy life also. My men think you three might want to join our cause." El continued on selling the advantages of his group, including telling them that, "The Cause" had gone for three years without failure." And we don't expect to see failure. Do you have any questions?"

The three were obviously working-level people that were out trying to earn a living when this opportunity came up. They didn't know the extent of it and that it included the theft of dope or they wouldn't have been part of this scenario. Each of them had a family, and they would enjoy the opportunity to join a group that had some stability to it.

El then followed with some conditions. "Each of you will be working in three different locations, so you won't be seeing each other for weeks at a time. Each of these locations will have men assigned to you, so they can grade your capabilities and your drive. Each of you and your family will be living with another family, so they can also determine your qualifications. We do not want employees that have family problems. These conditions will last for six months. At the end of the six months, your grades will be summarized and will determine your disposition.

There are three dispositions with the best one being that you will be free from these restrictions and be considered and treated as a regular employee with the same freedoms as the rest of the group."

"The second disposition is that you have shown some good qualities and some not-so-good qualities, and you will be given six more months to try to improve on the weaknesses that will be pointed out to you. At the end of those six months, you will receive a second review. This is a pass or fail review. The pass results are obvious. The fail category places you in what we consider the third disposition. You don't want to know what that involves. Just remember that I wouldn't want anyone to leave our group while knowing what you have learned during the time you have been with us, including some things we consider as secret and sacred. With these conditions, I want you to go into the room next door and discuss each of your decisions. I will let you know now that if you don't chose to join our cause, I will have my men drive you to the general area from where you originally came before joining this loss effort and free you. We don't want to take your lives from you. We don't want to ruin your family's lives. We also would not want to learn later that you provided any information to anyone that affected our cause."

With that, he let the three go into a room to discuss their alternatives. Needless to say, when the three came out of the room, they had each decided to join the cause. Axel thought to himself, *Now I know why this group of drug smugglers works so well. They have a good leader. Isn't it a shame it's for a cause like this? Here were three men who had the shit kicked out of them less than a couple of hours ago. They were beaten, bloodied, bruised, and weak from the interrogation flogging they took, and here they were turned around into followers of this El Encima; amazing.*

El had the five other invaders brought to him. He basically gave them option three whereby they would be taken to the general area of their homes and hope they picked up some work that was not related to this type of effort. "I am not in the business of eliminating good Mexican citizens who are looking for work. Consider yourselves lucky that you did not end up like so many of your party did. If I find out through a third or fourth party that you have taken any actions that might result in harm to this group, you will be sought out and an example made of you. Jose, get your guys together, and take these five to the general area from where they came. Give them each twenty pesos, so their families feel they earned their way today; now take off."

With this last command, El turned and told one of the men to bring the American forth. Axel had been waiting for this to see what would come of the obvious foreign captive of the nine. He had to be the leader of this foray. The American was led out to the center of the main warehouse room, and the questioning and beating began. "Who hired you to collect this group of men to hit this place?" This question kept coming back to this lily white beat-up captive.

After many minutes of no answers to their queries, he passed out from the continuous flogging; then came the bucket of water followed by more beating. Within fifteen minutes of additional efforts, the captive passed out again. With this, El said, "That's enough for today. Put him in one of the vehicles, and take him to our compound. We will see how he does after a night to think about it." With this last instruction, it was almost like El had said today was over, and everyone departed for their vehicles and began to return to their compound. It was obvious they were all excited. They hadn't lost a man, and not one was wounded. They were pretty sure they would end up with the same number of packages. The men El sent after the two packages and with orders to bring them back to be consummated. They knew the men that El left behind to monitor the warehouse would do a good job. It was a good day for these amigos.

El had Axel ride with him back to the compound, so they could talk about the activities that had occurred today. "What do you think Axel?" El asked.

"About what?" remarked Axel.

El seemed confused and then got a big smile on his face and said, "You know what I am talking about. What did you think of the events of today?"

"I was impressed," said Axel.

"What impressed you?" he questioned Axel.

"I was impressed by several things," responded Axel. "Your guys are very organized and very well disciplined. They appear to work well together and have a common goal. The goal is to be part of a successful cause and to please you, and they seem to do it by the numbers as if they had rehearsed this event before many times. I also was impressed by the way you handled the situation. You did a good job of separating out the competent from the incompetent bandits. I believe you were benevolent to those prisoners you took today. Offering them a position in your group was a grand gesture and leaving the ones go back to their families that didn't meet your standards."

"I believe you knew from the beginning who was the leader, and now you have him to interrogate. I don't believe you will be that benevolent with him. He is an outsider, whereas the ones you let return to their homes were just good Mexicans trying to earn a living. You obviously are not Mexican, but you are empathetic to their needs and their cause. You are a good businessman. It's too bad you didn't go to the States and become a thriving businessman for that country, but I can understand how you made your way here. I also believe you made a good choice to work with the Mexican strengths rather than the opium strengths you had in arriving here."

With that, Axel stopped talking and waited for a return from El. It was quiet for several minutes except for the hum of the engines of the car and the tires riding on the rough pavement. Then, El made comment to the summary made by Axel. "That's a wonderful complement you paid me, Axel. You have only been here a couple of days, and it seems we know each other to a great extent. I believe that was a very succinct summary of your thoughts on today's events, and I appreciate your perception of me and my motives. I will have to think about you and your motives over the next few days. No matter the outcome over the next few days, I believe that you spoke your true feelings about me and the events of today, no matter what your ulterior motives might be. I truly hope things work out well for you over the next few days. I almost think of you as a friend, and I would hate to be disappointed in my feelings."

When Axel went to bed that night, his thoughts were on the American prisoner. He knew they would continue their interrogations the next day, probably right after breakfast. *I have to remain calm and hope that he makes it through the day. I might have a chance to do something for him tomorrow night if things go right. I want to do it without tipping my hand. How will I do that?* His thoughts soon faded away as he fell asleep contemplating this issue.

The next morning, he was awakened the same time as normal as though nothing was going to be different. Breakfast also came and went without incident, but El was not going to disappoint him. About a half hour after breakfast, El appeared on the scene. "Did you have a good night of rest?" he asked Axel and his two escorts. They all nodded in the positive and sort of waited for the next volley of questions from El. El picked up an apple from the table and began to gnaw on it as if he was having fun with the three of them. "What do you think I should do with the American?" he asked.

The two escorts remained silent, and Axel offered the only comment.

"You seem to be able to handle these types of situations better than I, so I would assume you will follow whatever pattern you have used in the past. Do you believe in torture? Do you intend to torture him? What is his name anyhow?"

"Let's start with his name," commented El. "His name is Joseph Ringgold. He is twenty-eight years old. He comes from a city in Texas, and he has been in Mexico for about four years as best we can ascertain. He spent most of that time in Tijuana where he acted as a broker on a couple of drugs, including marijuana and cocaine. Somehow, he got word that someone was interested in him in Guaymas; who, we don't know. We know from interrogating the other captives we took that the gringo contacted them just a week ago. He told them it might require some fighting, and about fifteen of them assumed he meant using their fists, which didn't bother them."

"When they got together for this foray, they realized that there were six amigos, including the gringo, who had guns. When they asked why, they were told it was to protect them while making a raid on a warehouse. It's amazing, but those fifteen didn't know that the raid was to take cocaine. Now, when they look back, they felt the six with the guns knew. Those six with the guns were all killed in the skirmish except for the gringo. They had one additional gun that they had taken from the one they had overcome when taking the house. They told us that the two other watchers had left with a package soon after they had taken over the warehouse. What bothers me is that they had AK-47 automatic guns. This means there was someone organizing this raid with the American who had money and had access to weapons. My concern is who would be in that position of strength. I know that our cartel that handles weapons was raided recently, many were killed, and we lost much of our munitions."

"I am wondering whether these weapons came from our own weapons group prior to the raid on their site by a combination of Mexican police and American agents. I am wondering whether there was a traitor in the weapons group that smuggled these guns to the contras that were being organized to take over my group. This would bother me more than if it was the Americans who set this up. We will see if we can get to the truth from the gringo. We won't torture him till we have to. We'll see what happens today. Hopefully, we can determine the truth from the gringo before we have to take drastic measures. We will take drastic measures if we have to."

El allowed Axel and the two escorts to attend the day's questioning of Ringgold. The sessions followed the same routine as the ones used at the warehouse raid site. Ringgold kept saying he didn't know who set this up. He kept saying he was part of the same pickup as the other members of the raid. He believed one of the killed raiders was the one who initiated the bandit gathering. He just happened to be in the area and heard about the possibility of the raid. He joined because he thought it was a chance to make a big hit. They kept asking and roughing him up, and he would lose consciousness. This continued for the better part of four hours and several buckets of water to bring Ringgold back to his senses, but El didn't get what he was after.

Finally, he said, "Okay, gringo. We are going to let you sit in your cell room for the rest of the day and let you think about what is going to happen to you tomorrow. It won't be as easy as we have been on you today."

With that said, El waved to two of his men to take Ringgold away. As El and Axel left the room, El said, "Too bad. He will wish tomorrow didn't come. I'm thirsty' how about a beer?"

"Sounds good to me," said Axel.

They went to El's office, and he reached into a small refrigerator and came away with two beers. He unscrewed the top off of one, handed it to Axel, sat at his office chair, and opened the other, while making the comment, "We will find out the truth tomorrow. I know what a man can take as far as punishment is concerned before they break, and he will get that punishment."

"What if what he says is the truth?" questioned Axel. It's possible that his story is real," remarked Axel.

"I don't think so," said El. "Things that we know about him don't piece together. As far as we can understand, he was doing well when he was at Tijuana. He was doing business with Americans that came into the Tijuana area. This is fairly safe business. It doesn't make you rich, but it beats most jobs. The Mexican police don't like to hit on Americans in that area. They know that most of the Americans are in the area to have a good time, get something done cheap, or are just passing through to one of the warm tourists areas along the coast. That is good business for this country. They will hit on an American if it is obvious he is up to no good. Ringgold probably made many good connections in that area and had no reason to leave that area and go to Nogales, or Hermosillo, or wherever he ended up as a gringo-led band of coke busters. He was part of a gang that organized this raid. They knew where the coke was located and how to get to it. You saw that we only had three men there. What you didn't see is that there are normally five times that many picking up their business. This goes on for five. or six days out of a week. It is rare there is no activity there and only three of our compadres there. Whoever planned this knew that this was the best day to hit the place."

"Those packages just arrived early yesterday morning, and they knew it was the best time to hit it. By today, the packages would be gone, and there would have been a high activity level. They knew when to hit the place. This is a local group that wants to take my trade away from me. The gringo was just one of their tools they felt they could trust and had faith in his ability to handle the raid. They underestimated my group. We will find out tomorrow."

Axel asked El, "How do the packages find their way to the customer and how do you get the money back?"

"We have a good system," responded El. "We have a computer set up at the house next to the warehouse. The deliveries are numbered as to who they go to and when the pickups come; each signs for their delivery and receipt. They deliver the package to the known customer in their area. The packages are parceled out so that certain ones, 75 percent, go to customers that send their payment to the client's bank account. That takes care of the payoff for 75 percent of the total packages that are delivered to me. Twenty-five percent of the packages are delivered directly to my clients, and they send their payments to my bank in Nogales. So, that is how I get my take. Incidentally, Benny and his boys got the two packages that were missing, and now, those two shit birds that stole them are missing. I don't know the details on how they got away, but I will find out."

The rest of the day went as the other days had, and Axel began to wonder when he was going to be the center of their attention. *El doesn't have me here to keep him company. He has been sidetracked by this raid, and as soon as he feels he has the time, he will be on my case.*

As the evening moved on, he was at dinner, and El was not there; why, he didn't know, but he was happy because it gave him time to think about Ringgold. He did ask the cook where El was, and he said, "This is his day to go to the bank in Nogales."

Axel now knew what day El went to the bank. That would probably be a good day to know. Now, his thoughts went back to the gringo. He knew he had to get his fellow American out of this place tonight, so his thoughts were about how to do that. He realized it must look like it was done by an outsider. He had been reviewing the place and the guards ever since he had arrived. He knew he would have to take out the guard that sat on the knoll outside the gate.

For this to look like it was done by someone from the outside, he must take this man down and then get to the guard that watched over the main iron-barred gate that led to this fortress. He would have to take two cars out of the car parking area to make it look like there were at least two people involved, including Ringgold. He thought about how he would do that, and it included taking out the guard that stayed in the "key holding house" next to the parking area. He knew the room where Ringgold was contained had barred windows, and there was a hall outside this room that went in one of three directions. One of the directions ended up at a barred gate that was ceiling high. He knew he would have to make it through that barred gate to get to the prisoner's room. These thoughts kept coming to his brain and rolling around as if to find a better way. The escorts normally took him to his room about 10:00 PM. His guess was that a good time to do something was around midnight.

Later that evening, Axel waited anxiously for the clock to report with all its hands pointing upward, toward midnight. Soon, midnight arrived, and he moved into action. His room was on a floor that was about twenty feet from the ground. This height must have made them feel comfortable about not having to bar it. He opened the window and looked around outside. He saw no one at first glance but continued to survey the whole area. He could see the parking area off to his right about one hundred yards away. He remained in this position of reviewing the land below for about ten minutes and then decided it was time to take the leap. He alerted his internal system by "Axelvation two" and began to feel the energy immediately. He then jumped toward the ground below and gave the signal "up" to his internal system to allow him to hit the ground softly and bounce up about two feet. These movements were done quite softly, and he remained in a frozen state as he reviewed the area around him. *Coast is clear*, he said to himself as he took several long strides toward the wall that he must elevate to and then take a small leap to the fifteen-foot wall.

He laid atop the wall to again survey the area he had just evacuated as well as the area he was about to enter. *Looks good*, he confirmed with himself, and he jumped to the ground on the other side of the wall. He knew the knoll that he must get to was about one hundred yards down the roadway. He stayed about fifty feet from the edge of the road that led to the gate that barred entrance to the building he had just left. Several long and swift strides took him to the knoll's edge away from the road. He looked up and didn't see the guard, but he knew he was up there somewhere. He began to circulate around the bottom of the knoll while peering up to see if he could locate the guard. "There he is," he commented to himself. He was about fifty feet up on the top of the knoll. Axel could only see the top of his head from his vantage point. He thought to himself, *I will crawl up to where I can see his whole body. That would be about thirty or so feet of crawling. When he is facing away from me, I will take one great and fast leap and nail him.*

With that thought in mind, Axel began his crawling. Soon, he could see the man. He was sitting on a large rock or log and smoking a cigarette with his rifle set next to him against the rock or log. Axel gave himself another command, "hood down," and then he made a dramatic leap toward the guard with his fist out in front of his prone figure. The fist hit the head of the guard, and it was all over in a split second. Axel didn't wait around to see anything further and headed back down the knoll and back toward the wall he must leap atop.

As he reached the top of the wall, he again made himself prone and surveyed the area inside the compound. *All is quiet*, he thought. With that recognition, he jumped to the ground below and moved toward the main gate and the next guard. As he moved swiftly along the wall, he could see the guard, and he was leaning against the wall with ear phones over his ears listening to music or something. It would be his last tune. Axel grabbed the guard by the earphones and spun his head in a circle. That ended the music and everything for him. Axel moved the body to the side and to the back of a shrub. He removed the key from the guard's waistband and unlocked the large gate. He then turned and headed toward the parking area. Once he arrived at the parking area, Axel could see the guard reading a magazine inside the guard shack. Axel got next to the knob that opened the door to the shack. He took a deep breath, turned the knob, grabbed the guard's head, and twisted his head in one swift circular movement that broke his neck. The keys on the wall rack had the numbers of the cars stamped on them. The numbers related to the parking space. *The number one space was for El, and the number two space was for one of his top men*, Axel surmised. Axel took those two keys and headed toward the barred side entrance that enters into the hall that led to where the American was kept.

When he stood outside the door where the barred entrance was located, he knew he had to get the door open to expose the bars. Axel gave himself another command; "Axelvation three," he said to himself. This would be the first time he would be using this third level. He had activated it several times to see if it gave him a boost in energy but had never used the energy it brought forth. He thought he would need this level to handle the bars once he got rid of the door, and he wanted extra strength to be able to rapidly and silently remove the door knob. Axel reached down and grabbed the door knob that contained the lock for the door. With one swift pull, the total knob and lock were ripped from the door, and it floated open. *Quite good*, he thought, and it had hardly made a sound. *Now the bars must be spread.* Axel placed his hands on the two central bars that made up the four bars of iron that made up this entrance. Axel put his chest against the bars and his folded arms and began to pull each arm sideways toward the sides of the gate. The bars spread like hard rubber rather than iron or steel, and he continued till they actually overlapped the other remaining bars. *That should give us enough room*, he thought.

He entered the hallway and viewed ahead at where the hallway made a cross with the hallway that led toward Ringgold's room. He continued in this direction, and when he got to that crossing, he took a quick glance down that hall to see what that guard was doing. He was in a chair that was leaning against the wall next to the doorway to Ringgold's room. He was preoccupied with a magazine. *Seems like these guards all like to read a magazine while on watch*, he thought. This guard didn't have a rifle, and Axel could see the pistol jammed in the waistband. *This should be no problem*, thought Axel. He gave a new command to his inner self, *Axelvation two*. He felt he didn't need the energy level of the third and most powerful level.

With that being established, Axel took one rapid dive toward the guard with his fist extended, and he literally flew through the air in a diving position, his fist met the guard's side of his face, and the magazine dropped to the floor. Axel immediately grabbed the key that was attached to the same waistband as the gun and moved to unlock the door. Upon entering, he wasn't surprised to see that Ringgold was not asleep. *Probably worrying about what he faces this coming day*, he thought. Axel put his index finger to his mouth to show Ringgold that he wanted him to be quiet. He whispered for Ringgold to put on his shoes and grab his clothes and not to worry about putting them on. "Just follow me," he whispered.

After that, Axel led the gringo toward the bent bars and the eventual parking lot. He handed him a key to car number two and said, "Follow me and take car number two. No lights till we get outside the gate. Then, I want you to follow me, and I will be in car one. I will drive in front of you till we get about a mile down the road, and when I blink the headlights on and off; you pass me and keep going."

That was the total conversation between the two, and they arrived at the parked cars. As Axel started the car, he was oblivious to the noise it made and hoped that the people inside the house kept on sleeping. He slowly moved down the driveway to the open gate and then began to pick up speed; he had gone about fifty or so feet when he saw the car behind him put on his headlights and Axel turned his on. When they got about a mile down the road, Axel blinked his lights several times, and the car behind became the car ahead of him and on his way to safety. He honked his horn once to thank his savior and was gone.

Axel pulled into a thinly bushed side of the road and drove the car as deep as he could. He left the care in "drive" and got out. He said the words out loud, "Axelvation three" and got behind the car and pushed it another fifty yards or so and then got back in the car and turned it off. He threw the keys out into the woods and began running down the road toward the compound. When he got past the spot where the guard normally stood up on the knoll, he ran off the road and continued till he had to scale the wall where he had scaled it before. In a matter of minutes, he was standing on the ground looking up at his room's window. He leaped and grabbed the sides of the window seal, and then he entered the room, took off his clothes, and got in bed.

He was lying there awake when he heard the alarms go off at three in the morning. *Time for the guards to change*, he thought to himself. The new guard had found the other one's body and set off the alarm. Before long, he could hear footsteps running around outside in the hall. About ten minutes passed, and someone unlocked his door. Standing there was El. "So, you are still here," he said. "Someone killed several of the guards and freed the gringo and took two of our cars. There must have been at least two or three of them. We still don't know how they got in and got the gringo out. I thought when I heard that the gringo was gone that maybe you were too. I guess I am kind of glad you weren't a part of that escapade," he said as he smiled. "I kind of enjoy talking to you."

While he was standing there and talking, one of his men came running down the hall. "You have to see this, El; you have to see this."

"See what?" asked El.

"The bars of the door barrier have been bent, and that's how the gringo got out. They must have had several men and a long bar of steel to bend those bars that way. So far, we have found four dead, including the road sentinel, the parking chief, the main gate guard, and the guard that was watching the gringo's room. There must be an informant inside for them to know which room he was in and how to get to it. We lost a couple of our guys about a month ago. It might have been them. They knew this place like they know their home."

"Keep looking, and report back to me if you find anything new to report," ordered El. "Hurry, we might still be able to catch that son of a bitch. It depends on how long ago this happened."

With that last command, the man was off running. El sat down on the edge of the bed and talked out loud like he was thinking to himself but was saying the words out loud. "I can't believe this. That's the first time we ever lost a keeper. They had to know we change guards at eleven. Both the sentinel and the gate guard shifted out at eleven as well as the guard of the gringo's room. The guard of the car parking stays there for twelve hours and sometimes probably falls asleep. They took my car and my top guy's car. They were the two best cars in the lot. Damn it, I liked that car." With those remarks out of his system he looked at Axel. "You didn't hear anything either?" he asked.

"No," replied Axel. "When I fall asleep, it is a good-bye sleep. I am gone till the alarm in the morning."

After sitting a while and not saying anything, El got up and started toward the door. "I am going to lock this door and go and see if I can find out anything about this. Something is fishy. Have a good sleep; I won't," said El, and he was gone.

After El left the room, Axel had to think about his position here at this Nogales home of the Pacific cartel. He had to make some kind of plan to destroy it and save his brother at the same time. He knew to do this required swift action once he put it into effect. He thought about the warehouse that was about five miles away and that it represented the major receiving point of the cocaine coming from the south. It would have to be destroyed, and this had to be followed by the destruction of El Encima's operation. He kind of felt sorry about that. He had learned to respect El, but knew this was only a short-term situation. He had to overcome these empathetic thoughts and come up with something concrete.

The Follower smashes the cartels

His thoughts went to the actions he had just created. These would bring more watchful eyes and more security beginning with today. Perhaps, while they were consumed with what they should do here it, would take their thoughts away from the warehouse. This brought the thought to mind that perhaps he should take action during the following night. No matter what their watch and security, most of the people of this compound would be sleeping at 4:00 AM. So, he made his plans around doing something at 4:00 AM This was after they made their guard changes at 3:00 AM

He would go down to the ground and over the wall and pass on the other side of the guard on the knoll. After passing that point, he would run at top speed to where he dumped El's car, try to hot-wire it, and use it to drive down to the warehouse. For one thing, whoever was on guard at the warehouse wouldn't suspect El's car when he got there and if he was spotted. He would have to do away with the guards there and someway destroy the warehouse.

He felt he had to do this and come back to the house by 6:00 AM. This gave him two hours, and if he was in his bed when they came to check in the morning, things would be cool. That became his plan. Hopefully, today would proceed in a fashion that would not eliminate the execution of this plan. With that plan accepted in his mind, he thought about the details of how to carry it out. Time passed, and the escorts that normally came around eight each morning didn't arrive at that time this morning. He thought it probably was due to the distraction caused by the escape of the gringo. He got out of bed and put his clothes on, and then he sat around waiting for things to relax to normal. As the time approached nine, he heard the door latch being unlocked, and his two escorts stood at the door. "Let's go to breakfast," they said.

Breakfast was quieter than normal. This could be expected. El was not at the table, and there was a great bit of moving around taking place outside and in the halls of the compound. *They are evidently looking for clues and trying to buckle down their security*, Axel thought. *If a strike force could free the gringo, they could also strike the compound when it wasn't under proper security. I bet the security here was much better a couple of years ago and then got more lax as time went on, and they felt more confident about their strengths and capabilities. Things will change now. I bet the magazines they found lying next to the four bodies didn't go over well with El. He probably banned magazines years ago, but they just got more lax and started to bring them to their guard positions. I bet he burns them today and gives strict orders to his compadre group to stiffen up their vigilance. There is too much at stake for them all. We shall see what actions are taken. I must find out before taking off during the night.*

The day was one of no smiling. He and his escorts were not allowed to venture to the tennis courts or to the golf course. Someone broke out some playing cards, and Axel found a foursome to play bridge, a good card game that he hadn't played for a while. Others gathered around and watched, and before a couple of hours went by, there was another foursome playing cards, probably not bridge. Before they knew, it the time had passed, and it was time for a short lunch and back to playing cards.

It seemed like they had been playing cards for an hour when the bell rang for them to get ready for dinner. Axel looked at his watch, and it was after five PM. Axel said, "Let's put our cards down, and after dinner, we can come back and resume the game." The others nodded, and Axel went with his escorts to clean up for dinner. *One thing about this place, they are orderly and remain committed to their schedules*, thought Axel. *The place is kept clean, and all the occupants except my escorts and me have their daily duties and carry them out without bitching. That is what keeps this place tolerable. A certain number of them get to take the weekends off, and the following weekend some others take the weekend off. It looks like they have every third or fourth weekend off in their routine. It's a good bit like I have heard the armed forces for the States have it; it works*, he thought.

After dinner, there was a lot of discussion about what happened with the gringo last night. Before long, El called a meeting in the main conference room with everyone attending except those on watch. El stood up on a platform in the center of one end of the room. Axel looked around and saw approximately twenty-five men awaiting El's word. It was more than he thought was in the compound. There were probably at least five or six men on guard and three in the kitchen, so the total compound occupants were above thirty. Axel thought about it and figured that he had come to a smaller number because he previously saw the number that attended the attack on the warehouse. He figured there were fifteen from the compound, and by the time they had gathered to attack the warehouse, they had picked up another forty five or so. This meant with fifteen at the warehouse from the compound that this was less than half of the total compound, and that the rest were left to guard the compound or take care of duties like making meals and keeping the compound clean.

He then thought about the four that he had eliminated the night before. *So, they must have had thirty-five to thirty-eight total and now have about thirty-one to thirty-four with those four being eliminated. The forty-five that came to El's call for the warehouse attack must be considered. They must come from about a five- to ten-mile radius around the compound and warehouse. I will have to be alert to watch out for them as I go down after the warehouse tonight.*

As best he could remember, they got to the warehouse by going down the road to just a little beyond where he ditched El's car and then made a left-hand turn onto a road that in a short distance ran alongside of a river or creek. It was only about three miles or so where the warehouse was located.

Axel's thoughts were broken by El speaking over a loudspeaker. "Now you see what can happen if you don't have your vigilance up. I am pissed at you. All of the guards that were found dead had a magazine by their side. This is intolerable and not what each of you was trained to do. Reading a magazine is not on watch; it is like being asleep. You are a prey when you don't have your mind on your duties. We have just lost the best source of information about how the enemy works and who the enemy is. That gringo was our source and key to considerable information, and we let it fly away. We should have been more aware when we saw him and his raiders that there was someone out there that wants what we have. This is partially my fault. I should have known there would be more of them. I don't understand why our outside perimeter people did not see this coming. The compadres who alerted us to the event at the warehouse should have seen more coming."

"As we look around today, it would appear this gringo was released by a small force of probably three or so of our foes, probably someone close to the gringo like a brother or friend that wanted to release him. What bothers me is that they knew more about this place than the average foe. They knew where our guards were, and they knew where our prisoner was. Maybe one or two of you used a cell phone to talk to these foes of ours. If we find out who you are, you will be eliminated. As of now, I want all of you to take your cell phones and place them on the floor next to you. Miguel will come along and take your phone and place your name on it. The only ones allowed to have a phone for the next week are the men on guard duty. In a week, I will determine if you get your phones back. If I catch anyone of you with a phone in the next seven days, you will be sorry. Does anyone have a problem with that?"

One of the men stood up and said that he calls his wife and kids once a day. "What am I going to do with this restriction?"

"That's a good point," commented El. "There will be a phone in the inside guard shack. Any of you that want to call home will go to the guard shack. Your home numbers are listed, and the man on guard will place the call and give you the phone to use for five minutes after the phone is answered. Each of you will only be allowed one call a day for the next week. This is a form of punishment that perhaps one of you has caused your friends. If any of you used your phone to free the gringo, this is the punishment to all of your amigos. Each of you should be pissed at whoever made a call that resulted in this escape. I must take this precaution at this time till we assess the problem better. All of you that perform guard duty must make sure you arrive to relieve the guard at least ten minutes before the relief."

"During the ten minutes, the guard that is being relieved must make the incoming guard aware of anything he heard that was out of the ordinary. Both of you will remain on guard till the actual time the guard is to be relieved. For example, this means that guards that are to be relieved at three will have the oncoming guard at your post at two fifty, and both of you will remain their till three, and then the guard will be officially relieved. Does everyone understand this? Be alert," shouted El. "Our foes are not many, but they are sly, and they are trying to take our dinner away from us." El stomped off the stage and handed the microphone to his assistant. The rest of the day was sort of quiet. There was a lounge room that had a TV set, and many of the men were watching TV this evening.

Axel was escorted to his room at 10:00 PM, and he heard the door latched behind his escorts. He didn't take off his clothes, but set the alarm on his wristwatch to make sure he was alerted at 4:00 AM He then continued his thoughts to make sure he knew exactly what he was going to be doing tonight. His one concern, besides being detected, was how to eliminate the warehouse. If he found some explosives at the site, this would prove invaluable. If not, he would have to use the gasoline from the guard's vehicles to douse the building and set it afire. This was a slower route to take but probably would work well, since there were no houses close and no fire stations to put out the fire. The river next to the building would prove a source of fire extinguishing if anyone got there in time. He would have to make sure it was well doused with the gasoline. He had to make sure he didn't get any of the gas on his clothes or it would give off fumes that someone at the compound would detect and know he was down at the warehouse when it caught fire.

At ten to four, he turned off the alarm on his wristwatch, so its sound would not alert anyone. Then, he went to the window and looked down at the grounds that were in his view. *Looks good*, he thought. "Hood down," he said to his internal friend, and the hood was in place. He leaped to earth and gave the "up" call as he approached the ground. He didn't even stop to look around. He took a leap that took him toward the wall, and he was soon atop it. Then, he was on the other side and running in long strides past the back of the knoll that had the guard and continued like a deer running and avoiding the trees along the way. Soon, he was in the bushes and trying to hot-wire the car he had left there. Now, he wished he hadn't thrown the keys away. "Oh well, I'll do it the hard way," he said to himself.

After hot-wiring, it turned out it was easy to back out of the bushes, since a path had been made when it was jammed in there. Soon, he was along the river and approaching the warehouse. Axel cut the engine about a half mile from the warehouse and began those long strides toward the house next to the warehouse. He looked in one of the windows and only saw one man sitting at a desk. *The others must be sleeping in their rooms,* thought Axel. He thought about the best way to enter and decided on just rapidly opening the door and whipping the head of the man at the desk. However, he had learned to like these men and the way they handled their duties. He had a method of pushing his thumb and index finger on a person's neck, and this rendered them unconscious for two to three hours. He decided to do this.

He whipped open the door and grabbed the neck behind the man's head, and he was out before he could see who did it. This worked well, and he continued on to the bedrooms and disabled the other two men in the same manner. He looked in one of the small closets and found a box of shotgun shells and a shotgun. He grabbed the box and ran toward the warehouse. *Better be quiet,* he thought. *There might be another one in here.* He set the box of shotgun shells next to the door, and he rushed in and hurried around looking for another guard.

Then, he heard and felt a shot hit him from the side, and he twirled in his stride and leaped in that direction. Sure enough, the guard sent another shot toward him with the same result, and he jammed the gun against his chest and into his lungs with one swift move. *Too bad,* he thought. *But I had no other choice, since he saw me.* This cleaned out the guards, and he went out and took the box of shells to an area where there were a bunch of old wooden chairs. He felt this could be a place where the shells would help to enflame this wood.

He hurried out to the cars with four cooking pans that were sitting against the wall in the house next to the stove. He didn't have time to start siphoning the gas into the cans. He took his thumb and jammed it into the gas tank under the car. This made a perfect hole for a slow release gasoline flow, and he placed one of the pans under it and went to a second car and repeated the action. Before long, he had four large pans of gasoline and a good bit of gasoline on the ground. He made three trips in and out of the warehouse, each time filling and emptying his pans of gas. To fill the pans on his last visit, he had to hit the third car's tank and empty it into the four pans and onto the floor.

With this job of emptying the pans complete, he took another gun from the guard inside the house and shot a bullet at the gasoline inside the warehouse. He expected it to burst into flames, but it didn't. This didn't work, and he went inside the house and grabbed the pack of matches sitting on the desk He ran to the warehouse and threw one of the matches at the gasoline-soaked area, and it immediately burst into flames. He ran outside and threw the whole pack of burning matches at the gasoline on the ground that soaked the ground and the base of the house. As he ran toward where his car was located, he looked back and could see a large flame in the warehouse and the flame crawling along the outside of the house. This bothered him, and he ran back and pulled the three men out of the burning house and laid them safely away from the flames. He knew the job was done.

As he started up the car, he could hear a thunder of explosions as the flame had ignited the buckshot, and he knew there was no way the cocaine in that warehouse would ever make it to the States. Axel drove rapidly down the road and soon came to the place where it had been stored before. This time, he went past it a little distance and into another slight opening along the side of the road. He completed the hiding as he had done before by putting the car in drive and pushing it. Soon, he had run beyond the back of the knoll and leaped to the top of the wall. Everything was quiet and serine, as it contrasted to the sight he had just left back at the warehouse.

Soon, he was in his room. As he took off his clothes, he smelled them to see if there was any smell to them—nothing, and just to make sure, he went to where he kept his shaving cologne and sprinkled some of it on his shoes and pants. He hung these in the bathroom, turned on the small exhaust fan, and moved to his bed. He looked at his wristwatch. It was only fifteen minutes past five in the darkness of night. He had completed all of that in an hour and fifteen minutes. He was sleeping in a short time after his breathing had slowed down from the excitement of the night's actions. He laid there feeling content about his accomplishments.

He was awakened about an hour later with alarms going off. He remained in his bed, since the alarms meant nothing to him. It probably meant he would be in the room longer than normal as the compound gathered their men and headed toward the warehouse location. He was there longer than he thought he would be. This was good news for any smell that might have been left on his clothes. Axel went into the bathroom and smelled his clothes. All he could smell was the aftershave lotion he had sprinkled, and he decided to now sprinkle some water on that so that it wasn't obvious that the smell of the cologne was sprinkled on the clothes.

Breakfast never happened. Soon, it was around lunch hour, and Axel knocked on his door to try and get someone's attention. He wanted to make sure he had plenty of nourishment in his system in case some action came up during the day. Soon, one of the escorts was at the door. "I need something to eat," said Axel.

"Yes, so do I," said Romeo. "I will go down to the mess hall and see if we can get something to eat."

"What's all the running around about?" asked Axel.

"Looks like the warehouse got raided and set afire," remarked Romeo.

"What?" cried out Axel. "I can't believe they hit that place again. How bad is it?"

"Pretty bad," answered Romeo. "El and his men have been there since early in the morning. Looks like they hit the place during the night and killed the men we left behind."

"Holly shit," cried out Axel. "It's after one in the afternoon now, and they aren't back yet. They must be trying to put out the fire and try to catch the dogs that set it."

"I would guess so," said Romeo. "I am going to lock the door now and go and see what we can do about eating."

"Tell the cook that I don't care if he has any food prepared, said Axel.

"I will eat toast and coffee and rolls and fruit if nothing else is available."

The door was closed, the lock was latched, and Axel went and sat on the edge of the bed. *Sounds like there was a successful raid on that warehouse,* he thought. *I hope they didn't get it out before most of the dope was cooked.*

Axel only sat there for about ten minutes, and Romeo and his buddy returned and unlocked the door. "Come on," said Romeo. "The cook says he has a lot of things we can eat that were left over from dinner time last night."

When they got down and talked to the cook, he showed them a lot of things they could eat. One good thing was boxes of cereal from the States. Axel made himself a bowl of cereal and topped it with bananas, milk, and sugar. Two bowls of this, and a few of the sweet rolls the cook had, more than filled him up. The two escorts ate heartily from this fair and continued to ask the cook some questions about the raid that had hit the place. The cook said he didn't know the details, only that the whole delivery that had arrived yesterday of the coke was probably burned up. He didn't know the status of the warehouse or the men El had left there.

A few hours passed, and soon, there were men returning from the fire. Finally, along came El, and he waved his men to the large conference room inside. El got up on the wooden stage and began to give the men an assessment of the damage. "There is good news and bad news," he said. "The good news is that the three men who had been in the house were knocked out and not killed. They are recovering. One man inside the warehouse had been knocked out and died in the fire. The good news is that the total packages had not burned, only about half. The packages that were on the outside of the stacking burned, but since the packages were wrapped in metal foil; it formed a sort of protection for the packages that were in the internal portion of the stacks. So, we lost about half of the packages. The other good news comes from the bad news. The house and warehouse are unusable, but I had been considering moving the place of storage to here anyhow. There is not enough protection there. What I will do is have Jose go with me tomorrow afternoon into Nogales and buy a large closed truck that is capable of holding the whole load of packages. On delivery time, the packages will be loaded on this large truck instead of the warehouse, and the truck will be brought back here and parked in a fenced in area. This place is a better protected area. At times, during the day of pickups, we will have one of the men down at the warehouse location. When a pickup source arrives at that location, the word will be passed by cell phone, and we will send one of the smaller pickup trucks down there with the delivery."

"The phone-to-phone connection will allow us to provide our customers with better safety. This happening today might actually work out better for us in the end. I have great confidence in the armament of this compound and the men that are here. Instead of three men watching over things, we will have ten times that amount. If we determine we need more, I will get more. So, perk up, and let's give thanks that three of our comrades are safe and well. If anyone tries this again, they will come up against an army rather than the small number we have been using for the warehouse. Tell the cook to break out the wine and glasses. We will drink to our good fortune." Axel sat at his seat and was flabbergasted at the way El took this knocking and made it look good. Before long, he was drinking wine with the rest of them.

Axel had wanted to find a way of monitoring where El was at all times. He wanted to find which bank he used and the exact day he would be making a trip there. In order to do, this he felt he needed a cell phone that he could take apart and make a monitoring gadget that he could place on El and another phone that he would modify that allowed him to pick up the signal from the bug on El. During his raid on the warehouse, Axel had picked up one of the cell phones from the man he killed in the warehouse and three of the phones from the men in the house. He also picked up one of the nine-millimeter guns that he thought he might need for effect later on for one of his forays. With these cell phones, they would provide the parts he needed to make a transmitter and receiver.(Remember, Axel as a youngster had a hobby of working on electronics and he made the computer that was in his body) Axel took the cell phones apart with a small knife he had that had eight different kinds of instruments on it, such as a Phillips screwdriver, a blade screwdriver, scissors, two knife blades, and some other instruments. With these, he had worked away that evening and made the bug.

Next, he made a receiver that worked quite well; the closer the bug to the receiver, the louder its signal and the further away from the receiver, the quieter it reacted. It wasn't as accurate as the commercial types, but it did give him a good idea of how far away El was. Next, he had to find a way to bug El's clothes. He had noticed the days when he wasn't around that he wore this nice suit. It must be what he wears when he is at the bank. If Axel could get the bug on his suit, he would find a way to find the bank he was in when they went to pick up a truck tomorrow.

His thoughts went beyond the bank and the truck; as he knew his time was up as far as this location was concerned. He also knew that if El was around that he would give a call to Primo if he was missing, and Adam stood a good chance of being eliminated. This brought him to the conclusion that he must take El with him when he left. This served two purposes; if he had El, then there would not be a message to Primo also, it meant he would not have to kill him. He didn't want to kill him, but he didn't have many choices. His duty was to get rid of the top guy and as many of his men as possible or have the information to the agency of who was who and let them do it.

He had grown to respect El, and this made his choice easier. If anyone in the agency wanted to kill him, that was their business but not his. The more he thought of it, he had decided to turn his receiver on and monitor El when he was at the bank. He would then know the bank, and he would make sure he was at the bank at the same time, so he could take El as a prisoner at a time when he was away from the compound and wouldn't be missed for several hours. Axel's guess was that El would go to the bank to check things and maybe make some transactions. After that, he would go with Jose to a truck dealer to buy the truck. After that, Jose probably would take the truck, and El would drive the car back to the compound.

Axel felt he should take El just after Jose left with the truck. That way, Jose would return to the compound, and if anyone asked about El, he probably would say that he was in town and would be back soon. The more he thought about it, the more he liked the idea. Now, he had to find a way to bug El's suit coat. El's bedroom was on the second floor like his room. El normally went to bed about eleven, and Axel was put into his room at ten. He knew which window was El's room window, and he would have an hour or so to jump out of his window, jump up to El's window, and go inside and plant the bug. When Romeo took him to his room at ten, Axel immediately got the very small (about the size of a penny) transmitter and inserted the battery he had taken out of one of the cell phones. It was dark outside, which made the job a lot easier.

Before long, Axel had made his leap to the ground below and a subsequent leap to the window of El's room. All the windows were opened at night on the second floor to allow for some cooling. The suit was found and the transmitter dropped into a small slit that Axel made with his knife so that he could slip the transmitter inside the lining of the coat near the bottom. He cut a few stitches of the thread that was sewed to the lower part of the lining and stuffed the transmitter in it. This way, it was hidden and wouldn't flop around. He then checked with his receiver and got a very strong signal from the transmitter. With that done, he retraced his tracks and was back in his room in twenty minutes.

The next morning at breakfast, Axel saw that El was there with the suit on, and Jose was sitting next to him and eating. When breakfast was done, Axel told Romeo that he wanted to go to his room and rest. He said he wasn't feeling good and needed some rest. As they left, Axel grabbed a sweet roll and a Coke to take to the room. Romeo obliged him and escorted him to his room. He told Romeo that he didn't want to be disturbed until dinner was ready. While in the room, Axel took what he wanted to leave with to go back to Tijuana and packed them in a small bag along with the receiver. He checked the receiver, and there was a signal. It was strong, since El was probably just down at the first-floor breakfast room. He went to the window and reviewed the yard below. He knew that there was the guard over by the gate, but that was slightly out of sight. There was none of the men on that side of the house, and he looked back at the parking area and saw that there was no one in the lot. Of course, there was the parking keeper who was in his shack, but the window faced toward the parking lot and the wall. Axel felt this was a good time to leave, and he jumped, hit ground, rebounded, and was on the wall and over with several swift movements. He then ran like a deer toward the car of El's he had hidden in the woods about a mile down the road. As he ran past the knoll, he noticed only the head of the guard who was watching the road. Axel was soon well past that point. Axel could run at about thirty miles an hour with his energy level up, and he doubted that El and Jose would drive down this road any faster, since it was not the best of roads. Soon, he was at the car's hiding place, and he took the wires he had disconnected of the hot-wire and connected them to start the engine. He backed out a little ways, so he could just see when El and Jose went by on the road, and they wouldn't see him. He sat there and waited.

After a half hour, he became concerned that El hadn't come by yet. He wondered if something had come up back at the compound, and they had found that he had flown the coup. Just as he was getting fidgety, he saw a car coming down the road, and he was delighted to see it was El and Jose driving by with Jose doing the driving. He waited till he felt they were out of sight and backed onto the road and began to drive toward Nogales. He had never been there and hoped he wouldn't have any problems with finding them once they got there. He had a signal from the transmitter, and it was getting louder, which meant he was approaching them. *This car of El's is a good car*, he thought. Soon, he saw a sign that indicated that Nogales was five miles away. *Great*, he thought.

Soon, Axel was entering Nogales and was getting a strong signal. He stopped a man walking along the sidewalk and asked in his Spanish, "Where is the bank?"

The man told him to go to the first stoplight and make a right, and it was two blocks down the street. *Great*, he thought. *I will go down a block and park if I can and wait till El comes out of the bank.* He knew when he parked that El was nearby, since the signal was almost as loud as it was when he picked up the signal back at the house. He looked around and saw that their car was parked on the other side of this one-way street. Now, he would just wait till they came out and hopefully made their way to the place that sells trucks. There probably was only one in this town.

Soon, he saw Jose come out and go to the car. Axel waited for El to be coming out also. He knew he would be coming out, since Jose didn't drive away but waited. About fifteen minutes passed, and there was El coming out and going across the street to the car. Soon, they pulled out, and Axel waited to see which way they would go. They turned at the next corner, and he pulled out and went to that corner and looked as he made his turn. Their car was stopped at a stoplight two blocks away, so he moved very slowly until the light changed and they had moved on. They made a right turn at the intersection, and Axel soon made the same turn.

About two blocks down the street, he could see a big sign, "Automobiles for sale" (in Mexican), and he went by the lot and looked to see where they were. They were talking to a man, and he was walking toward a place in the lot where Axel could see three big trucks and several pickups. Axel went and parked the car, and just before he got out, he decided to call Tori. He waited, and soon she answered. "Hello," came her beautiful voice."

"Tori, Axel here. If things go right today, I will be leaving Mexico sometime later in the day. I will probably have to go to Washington before returning home and wanted you to know."

"That's wonderful," she said. "I miss you and can't wait to see you."

"Same here," Tori. "I have to go now and will talk to you when I have more time. Take care. I love you."

Axel stopped his transmission and got out of the car with his bag. He then hurriedly ran toward where he saw the car that had brought El there. He felt that El would be coming back to this car. As he arrived at the car, he noticed they hadn't locked it, and he opened the door on the side away from where they were and slipped into the backseat. From here, he could have a good vantage point. If El came this way, he would be in business. If Jose came this way, he would have to put him down and then go toward where the three trucks were located. Soon, he saw the salesman, Jose, and El walking toward the man's office. Axel waited and removed the gun from his baggage, and after a few minutes, Jose came out of the office and headed toward the three trucks. Axel continued his vigilance, and after a few minutes, he could see the one big truck being pulled back, and soon, he had made a turn from the parking space and headed back toward where they had entered the lot.

He stopped and looked out the window, and soon, El came out and waved him on. El went back in the office, and Jose pulled the truck out of the lot and was on his way. *Great*, thought Axel. *Soon El will be coming this way, and it will be time to get him to give me an airplane ride or else.* Axel then turned the receiver off, since he didn't want the signal giving him away when El came toward the car.

Axel made a call to the agency and told Kim he would be capturing El Encima and would be on his way back to Tijuana to free Adam. He told him that he should contact the Mexican police and direct them to the compound here at Nogales. "The compound now has the cocaine in the truck or soon will have it in the truck, and they won't have a leader, so it should be a piece of cake. I have to go now," he said. "I will let you know the plane number and flight number of the plane that will fly me to the Tijuana airfield. I want the Mexican police to meet the flight and take El Encima into their custody. I don't want to have to deal with him while I am trying to get Adam. Tell the Mexican police I am an undercover agent, so they won't bother me. Also, tell them that they should not let El Encima make a phone call for at least five hours. I don't want him to call Primo and warn him that I am coming; meanwhile, tell the U.S. police or the drug authorities at San Diego to raid the car rental place where Primo was shipping the drugs and money back and forth past the border police. You know the details about how they do it with the insertion they put under the car where the cars are designed to receive them, and the bottom of the car doesn't look any different from a normal car. Tell the Mexican police to pick up any of these cars that are on the Mexican side of the border. I have to go now."

About fifteen minutes passed, and El and the man came out of the office, and the man shook El's hand, El carried the papers he had received and approached the car. Axel crouched down in the backseat and waited. He heard the car door open, some papers being placed on the front seat, and El entering the car and sitting down. Next, there was the sound of the ignition and the starter, and the car began to move. Axel waited till they had left the lot and had gone about two blocks and then came to a stoplight. Axel took the gun and placed it in the back of El's head and told him to drive to the airport. El was shocked. "How in the hell did you get out of the compound and here?" he asked.

"I will tell you later," said Axel. "Right now, I want you to call your pilot at the airfield and tell him you are coming to take a pleasure flight. I don't want you to say anything except you decided to take a flight today. Tell him it's a beautiful day, and you felt like a flight to relieve some of your pressures. If he tries to talk much, I want you to direct him to have the plane ready, and you don't want to talk about it."

"What if I don't do that?" asked El. "Then, I will shoot you in the back of the head," replied Axel. "I don't want to do that. I like you, but I will shoot you. You have my brother as a prisoner, and I am not in the mood to make conversation. Do you understand?"

"Yes, I understand," said El with a rough, disturbed sound to his voice.

"Pull over at the first place where you see a good place to park and make the phone call, and do it quickly. Keep in mind that I have a pilot's license and will understand when you are straying from the proper words I have told you to use," instructed Axel.

Before long, they parked, and El took out his phone and called the pilot. The conversation was fairly straightforward, and it was obvious that the pilot on the other end knew who was boss and was used to taking short direction from El without questioning his reasons. After the phone was hung up, Axel told El to get out of the car with his hands held in front of him. El got out. "Now," Axel said. "I want you to relieve yourself of the gun you have in your arm holster. Take it out with your thumb and index finger. I don't want to see any other digits of your hand moving or this gun will go off."

El smiled and reached his gun and took it out of the holster with the thumb and index finger. "Lay it on your seat, keeping in mind that I don't want to see any fingers moving. Just drop it on the seat." El followed the instructions. "Now, take off your suit coat, so I can see you better," directed Axel. "Lay the suit coat on the hood of the car." Axel continued, "Now turn slowly around, so I can see your belt." El smiled again and slowly turned. There in the back there was a small gun stuck between his belt and his shirt. "Oh yes," commented Axel. "I didn't think you would only have one on you. Now, with your back to me, reach back with your left hand and do the thumb and index trick once again."

El followed the directions and held the gun with his thumb and index finger and pulled it from his belt line. "Now, just drop it on the ground," directed Axel. The gun was dropped. "Now, turn around, and lift your pant leg on your right leg, so we can look at your leg for a holster," directed Axel. El followed those directions, and there was no gun holster on his right leg. "Now, let's look at the left leg," directed Axel. This time, when the pant leg was raised, it exposed a nice little holster and a small gun. "Probably a twenty five millimeter," commented Axel. "You do come well armed. Maybe that was why the smile, huh, El? Do the thumb and index finger on that little fella, and I want you to make sure you only grab the handle. Keep in mind this gun is pointed right at your chest, and I know how to use it."

El relieved the holster of the gun and dropped it at his feet. "Now, I want you to step back five steps while facing me," stated Axel. With that command, El moved five steps away from the car. Axel then opened the back door and got out. He walked over to the two guns lying on the ground, picked them up, and threw them in the bushes. He reached inside the front door to the seat, picked up the other gun, and threw it in the bushes. Then, Axel got back in the backseat of the car and instructed El to take his position in the driver's seat of the car and close the door. This again was followed as instructed. "Now, let's move this car to the airfield and your pilot and plane without any funny business," instructed Axel.

It took about a half an hour to get to the airfield and El drove the car over to where he normally parked when taking a flight. Axel told El, "I have the gun in my hand, and it is hidden by the bag I have with me, so don't try anything funny or you and the pilot might not see the rest of today. Just tell him you are going to take a flight to Tijuana, and he better have enough gas."

They got out of the car, and the pilot walked over and said, "Hi, El Encima. What got this flight to go?"

"I have to deliver this guy to Tijuana," said El.

"No problem," said the pilot. "Let's go over to the plane."

As they got to the plane, the pilot reached in and pulled out a rifle from his seat and aimed it at Axel. "Okay, what is the charade?" he asked. Axel showed him the gun he had on El Encima and told him to drop the rifle or his boss would get dropped.

"Don't listen to him," shouted El. "Shoot the son of a bitch."

"I am warning you," said Axel. "This can only mean trouble for you and El. Just put the rifle down. Believe me; you do not want to shoot that rifle."

"Shoot him," shouted El.

With that shout, Axel moved away from El and said, "Yes, go ahead, and shoot me if you dare." With that move away from El, the pilot thought there was nothing to stop him from completing this act and fired the gun at Axel. The bullet hit Axel in the chest and flew back past the pilot. The pilot and El stood with their eyes wide open in utter disbelief of what had just happened.

"Shoot again," shouted El; and again, the act was carried out with the same results. The pilot and El were frozen in disbelief.

"Now," said Axel, "let's have that pea shooter buddy, and let's get in the plane and get on to Tijuana." With that comment, Axel reached over and took the rifle from the pilot. Suddenly, El made a move to take Axel. Axel turned and picked him up above his head and said, "Now, I don't want to have to throw you in that airplane, so I am going to put you down and you better get in without any more ideas." With that said, he dropped El to the ground and pushed him toward the other door of the plane. El looked at Axel and could not believe that this young guy could lift his 225 pounds like it was a small sack of flour and toss it like he just did.

"What are you?" he asked.

"Just a twin brother that wants to go and get his brother," shouted Axel. "You guys should have left well enough alone."

Before long, they were taxing down the runway for a takeoff and the flight to Tijuana. When in flight, El looked at Axel and asked "What kind of human being are you?"

"I am a secret weapon of the United States," said Axel, as he looked El directly eye to eye. "I am the one who took your warehouse down and soon your compound. I came here to get my brother, but you changed my course of things and caused yourself some big problems. If you would have left well enough alone, I would have stayed in Tijuana, and your life would have been a lot easier. When you had them fly me out to your part of the cartel, you brought more trouble than you could handle."

"Are you a robot?" asked El.

"No, I am just a normal human being with a few touch ups from the agency that allow me certain capabilities that were provided by the United States of America."

The remainder of the flight was quiet except for the roar of the engines. Axel heard the pilot give the flight and plane number to the controllers at the Tijuana airfield. With that, he gave the agency the silent phone call (El was unaware) to the agency and filled in the information that he said he would be giving them. "We should arrive within a half hour," he said.

As the plane made its control pattern for landing in the Tijuana airfield, Axel reached in his bag and took out a small rope. He took El's hands, put them behind him, and tied the rope tightly around them. As he completed this move, he said, "That's to protect you from trying something stupid. When we land, the Mexican police will be there to take you away. I wouldn't want to see you get hurt. I have learned to respect you as a person, even though I don't respect what you do to society with your drugs. I hope you don't get physically hurt, and you learn to use your obvious talents for doing something positive in the future. I want you to know that I have learned some things from you, things that will be helpful to me in my life. With your brains and obvious respect for human life, you could provide some useful talents for doing good things in this world." With that, Axel tapped El on the shoulder and looked out the front window of the plane as it was coming in for a landing.

As he looked toward the landing, he heard El say, "Thank you. That is one of the nicest things anyone has ever said to me, and meant it."

As they landed and taxied to the berth provided for the plane, it was being followed by two cars with police signs written on the sides of the cars. When the plane reached its berth and came to a halt, a loudspeaker blared out, "Please remain in the plane and open the doors." It repeated this command. The pilot opened his door, and Axel opened the two back doors.

A smartly dressed policeman stood by the door on El's side of the plane and another on Axel's side of the plane. Each had another policeman holding a rifle just behind these two front men. "Slowly get out of the plane," was the command of the officer on El's side of the plane. El got out on that side and Axel on his side. Axel was accompanied around the back of the plane and onto the other side where the obviously lead policeman stood with El.

Axel reached out his hand and said, "I am Axel Tressler of the United Stated Agency."

The officer had a picture that Kim must have sent him, and he looked at it and at Axel and said, "Welcome agent Tressler. It looks like you caught a big fish; maybe a whole school of fish, since other forces are hitting the Nogales compound as we speak. You are free to go. We have provided a car for your use. When you have completed your task here and your report to your people, you should return the car and report to the Tijuana Central Police Station.

Axel turned and looked at El. "Sorry about that, but I was just doing my duty as an American. I would wish you luck, but I am afraid you wouldn't make it good luck." With that, he walked away and toward the car awaiting him.

Axel had been thinking about how he would handle the freeing of Adam. He felt it would require less energy to go in the evening when most of the men were in the house. He would take care of the outside guards first and then enter the rear of the building. He would handle any of the men he encountered as he made his way to the upper floor where they had held Adam. He hoped he was still in that room and in good health. Sooner or later, he would take care of Primo. That was his number one priority after he felt that Adam was safe.

Smashing Primo and freeing Adam

A xel went to a nearby restaurant and had a good meal. He wanted to make sure his nutrition was in good shape. He didn't know how much energy he would need to use this evening. Axel kept going over his plans for this evening to make sure he was doing things in an order to ensure Adam's safety as he went through the rip out of the cartel. He read the paper to see what was happening in the world, and there were some good articles about the top government's actions on cleaning up the payoff recipients in the government's public services, starting with the upper level and the top levels in the police and Mexican army. The more he read, the more he wondered if El Encima would be handled properly with the police he left him with. *El has a lot of money, and I am sure he is trying to buy his way out of his problems today*, he thought. Before he knew it, time had passed, and the sun was going down. He took another drink of Coke, picked up a couple of candy bars, and paid the lady at the register. As he walked out and toward his car, he became anxious to get this over with and get Adam back to his family. It had been months since he had been able to see his wife and kids.

Axel drove through Tijuana and out to the road that turned off toward the cartel house. He drove to a place about a mile from the house and turned off the car lights. He then drove to a position about fifty feet from the turnoff to the house. He didn't expect anyone to see him, but he didn't care if they did. His planned actions were going to be rapid, and they wouldn't have time to do much before he was in the house. He got out and said to himself, "Axelvation two and hood down," and was rapidly on his way up toward the first guard. He rammed the rifle he held against his body and hit him in the neck, and he was gone. Axel rapidly ran to the other guard, and, just as the guard raised his rifle to shoot, he jammed it through his head. Axel ran to the back of the house and dispatched of that guard. He then went to the back door, and it was locked. He grabbed the knob that contained the lock and gave it a rapid pull, and the door was left with a hole where the knob had been, and the other half of the door latch went flying in the air.

He ran into the house, and there were two of the gang talking at the bottom of the stairs. He took their heads and rammed them together and was next running up the stairs toward the door of Adam's room. There was a guard sitting outside the room, and Axel was happy to see that. It meant someone of importance was in there. Axel grabbed the guard head and spun it, and that was that. He didn't even bother with the key to the room as he grabbed the door knob and gave it the same kind of pull as the back door, and away went the knob and latch. Axel entered the room, and Adam sat up in bed and his eyes were big as saucers. "Axel," he cried. "I am so glad to see you."

"Don't talk," shouted Axel. "I have to get you to safety and then clean this place out. Put on your clothes, and hurry."

Adam jumped into his pants, slipped on his shoes, grabbed a shirt, and was ready to go. Axel grabbed him and ran down the hall and down the steps, and as he went down the steps, he shouted to Adam, "Grab the rifle of the guard out the back door as we go by his body." Adam scooped up the rifle as Axel ran by the fallen guard. Down the driveway went Axel till he got to the car. "Take the car, and drive about a mile down the road. Lock the doors, and if anyone tries to stop you, shoot them. I don't think there will be anyone coming, and I will be along in about fifteen minutes."

Just as he turned to run back to the house, Adam shouted, "Axel, if I know Primo, he has already slipped out the side door and made it to his helicopter just on the other side of the woods. You should probably go back there first." Axel stopped and waited till Adam had turned the car around and headed down the road.

"Now, I have to find a big, chubby cartel giant," he said to himself as he ran past the house and into the woods beyond. The woods were only about fifty feet deep at that point before entering a clearing, and the helicopter pad was just beyond. As he got through the woods, he saw the helicopter beginning to rise off the ground. He hurriedly ran toward the rising bird. It was about twenty feet off the ground when he got to it. On the way, he shouted, "Axelvation three, and hood down," and he reached a point just below the ascending machine. He leaped up and grabbed the axle of the landing gear and punched a hole in the bottom of the rising bird. A few more npunches and he was able to pull himself into the copter. As he did, Primo had a gun and fired at his head. The bullet hit Axel in the forehead and ricocheted back toward him and stuck the pilot in the shoulder. He fired twice more, and this time, one bullet ricocheted back and smashed into the instrument panel, and the other bullet struck Primo in the chest. He got an awful look on his face of wonderment and fell to the floor.

It was obvious that the pilot was having a difficult time controlling the copter partly because of his wound and partly because of the damaged control panel. "Just let this machine down. Don't worry about controlling it. I'll take care of you." He grabbed the pilot, went to the hole in the floor, and leaped through it toward the ground. As he was about to hit the ground, he hollered, "up" and made the soft landing he had learned to control. He immediately leaped sideways about fifty feet to avoid the falling copter and covered the pilot with his body. The copter smashed to the ground with a loud crash and burst into flame. Axel left the pilot, leaped toward the pile of metal that made up the copter, smashed the window on the one side, and pulled Primo out. He laid him next to the pilot and listened to his heart. It was still beating, and he called 911 on the internal phone. He gave them directions to where they could find the copter and the two people that were hurt. Just after that, he called the phone number the policeman had given him and told him he where he could find the house of the cartel and told him about the injuries he had reported.

"The one man is the head of the cartel here in the Tijuana area that provided drugs along the Pacific and into the United States. I will head toward your main station and wait for you to clean this up. I will give you all the information I have and how the cartel works their deals."

That being completed, Axel began to run toward the house to clean up any armed guards so that the police wouldn't have to. As he neared the house, he was met with a volley of shots coming from three of the group.

He ripped the automatic off the one while smashing his fist against his body and turned and shot the other two. *That's three that the police won't have to fight*, he thought. He then ran down the road to the car, jumped in beside Adam, and shouted, "That's one cartel that won't be operating for a good while."

With Adam driving, Axel told him to drive to the main police station in Tijuana. "I have to give a complete report to the officer in charge." He then described what had occurred back at Primo's place. "I think the pilot will be okay, but I don't think Primo will make it. That's up to the hospital and fate. The odd thing is that I didn't shoot Primo or cause his possible death. He shot himself, and one of the bullets caused the copter to crash and gave him additional damage. So, his damage was of his own doing. Maybe karma was at work and taking care of things, so I wouldn't have to."

"All I know," said Adam, "is that I kept praying every day that you would be okay, and sooner or later, you would come, and we would be free to return home. The whole time I waited for you in the car I kept going over in my mind whether I was dreaming or if this was for real. That kept going through my mind till I saw you in the rearview mirror running toward the car, and then I was happy. You are a wonder, Axel. No one would have been able to handle this like you just did. A half hour ago, I was in that room and just getting into bed with this terrible feeling I get each night that I lie down in that bed. And then, you burst into the room. I have gone from very depressed to exhilaration in about a half hour. Unbelievable!"

Axel was relieved and happy. "I haven't heard from you or about you in all the days at El Encima's compound. I checked each day with the agency, and all they could tell me was that your dot was still showing on their screens. Of course, it only meant you were there. It didn't tell us whether you were alive or dead. They said they saw the dot, and it looked like it slightly moved, so that encouraged them to think you were not dead. They told me that it might not be a movement, but just a blurring dot. The amount of movement you would make in that house could not be resolved on their system. Evidently, you didn't go golfing or playing tennis?" questioned Axel.

"No, I never went anywhere," replied Adam. "After you left, Primo confined me to the house with my escorts. Which reminds me, what happened to the two escorts we had who went with you to the compound?" asked Adam.

"They are still at the compound," said Axel. "They actually were nice men. They both were quiet and just went along with what El Encima told them to do. I will tell you the whole story while we are waiting in the police office for the top cop."

Adam and Axel checked in the main police station, and the person who had the duty told them that Captain Renoldo had called about Axel and left a message that he would be here in about two hours. He had to clean up the rest of the raid on Primo's compound. They were taken to a nice room to await the captain's return. While waiting, Axel told Adam about everything he could remember since they last saw each other. "That was a terrific job you did," said Adam. "You had to do that and restrain yourself because of me being held here. It's amazing the extraordinary capabilities you have. As much as you were born with and the computer system you developed for in your body, it could only be put to this extraordinary use when Kim had the agency cover your body with the special thin material they developed from spider webs and titanium nanotube material. I look at you now, and there is no way I know that you are clothed with that material. Does it bother you at all?"

"No, it doesn't bother me," Axel replied. "It makes me feel powerful in my mind but not actually on my body. It gives me a sense that I can do anything and not worry about it. You and the agency are the only ones who know about it. Even at the agency, it is probably Kim and a couple others. Tori doesn't know about any of this. I feel odd around her not knowing, since we are so close, and she never seems to indicate there is anything different about me. She gives me more credit for being brave and caring than I deserve, but that is it. I guess one of these days I will have to tell her if we are to remain together. I have been thinking of her the whole time this was going on, and I believe I am going to ask her to marry me."

"That's wonderful," yelled Adam. "I was hoping this would work out for you two. I like her and hoped that you found in her what you were looking for. I know you were always the one that was hard to please."

Axel looked at Adam and said, "You married a winner too."

Adam and Axel sat around the station for about three hours before the captain arrived. "How did you make out?" asked Axel.

"Great," replied the captain. "We took Primo to the hospital, and they said he is in critical condition but should survive. We went to the compound and picked up the remainder of the hoodlums, and they will be coming here in a van within the next half hour. We took El to a special holding place for people like him of high silhouette. We want to make sure he is under 100 percent surveillance. We also took the pilot to the same place."

"I don't know if the pilot is part of the smuggling cartel," commented Axel. "He might not be any more than a pilot that El uses and might not know about the cocaine smuggling. I never saw him do anything like that, but he is a devoted person toward El. He tried to shoot me when he believed I was taking El to someplace where he didn't want to go. He didn't know at the time that I was a U.S. agent."

"We will find out," said the captain.

Axel then asked the captain if he had received word from the U.S. authorities about the rental car method of cocaine and payoff transport.

The captain said he had been contacted by his superintendent to find and hold any of those rental cars. "Your people have already raided the rental car place in San Diego, and they sent a listing of the car rentals in this country. We are in the process of hunting down those cars. The listing sent by your people shows the rental cars destination, so we know where to look. This puts us in pretty good shape on that. Now, I would appreciate it if you fill out a deposition concerning all the things that happened in the Nogales location and the location here. You must sign it as a U.S. agent. When you are done with that, I will check it, and you two will be free to go. We need Adam to fill out a deposition also, since he was held hostage, and this will be considered kidnapping besides the drug charges."

"That's an important point," commented Axel. "They kept me as hostage at the Nogales location, so they also can be charged with kidnapping. I will include that in my deposition report."

The captain took the two of them to an office, and a woman brought in the forms they were to fill out. It took over an hour for the two reports to be filled out, and it was becoming late in the day as the sun had gone down. Adam looked at Axel and said, "It doesn't look like we will be going to Washington today. I forgot to ask the captain if we still have the house in San Diego or if it is under the control of the U.S. police or our agency. I will give the agency a call. Kim will be home now, so I will call him at his house."

"Let me take care of that, Adam," said Axel. "I don't need to leave this room, and if he has any questions I can't answer, I can ask you."

That being said, Axel called Kim and asked about the house and about transportation. Kim told him the house was under agency control, and he would take care of contacting them to allow them to stay there. He told him that he had already told the captain there to provide a car to drive while they were in Mexico or the San Diego region. "I will make a plane reservation for you two out of San Diego on a morning flight. I looked up the schedule there, and there will be a flight out of San Diego to Dallas and then from Dallas to Washington D.C Dulles.International airport,. It leaves at 9:15 AM You can pick up the tickets at the Delta Airlines counter. Drop the car off at the Masters Car Rental. They will know about it, and the captain will know where to pick it up.

"Adam is going to call his wife," said Axel. "She will probably meet us at the airport tomorrow and drive to their home in Arlington. So, you don't need to worry about that transportation. I am sure she will be excited to pick him up. Adam is going to call Laura now, so she will know about the connections."

"Great," shouted Kim over the phone. "That is a great feat you accomplished there. There's no one else that I know of that could have accomplished what you did down there."

"Thank you," said Axel. "I can give you part of the credit," said Axel. "With that skin covering you gave me, I wasn't worried about accomplishing the goal. The covering saved me several times. The last time was when the pilot of the plane shot me with a rifle two times with no effect. That is a marvelous, impervious outfit. It's too bad you can't make this for more people."

A last minute surge

"That's not the reason for not making it for anyone else," Kim said.

"If we spent a hundred million dollars for any other person, it would be a waste. It would only protect them from being shot. With you, your internal computer, your ability to communicate real time undetectable, your ability to raise your strength to levels not accomplishable by anyone else, your ability to jump up to high heights, or jump down unbelievable levels without being hurt, your ability to run at a level of a racehorse, and your ability to swim at levels unattainable by others are all the reasons why you got this impervious suit. This suit of undetectable armor, with those other capabilities, makes you a human dynamo. There is no one else on this earth that has your capabilities. If you think we aren't going to be using your capabilities in the future as a service to this country, you are kidding yourself. I am so excited about your success that I feel like I personally accomplished this. I know I didn't, and you should tell Adam that I am so proud of his part in this scenario. He is going to get at least a week off when he gets here to take his wife somewhere at our expense. The same goes for you and your Tori girlfriend."

With that, Axel was done talking and told Adam of his conversation. "Now go and make a call to your wife," Axel directed. "She is probably in bed worrying about you. I am sure the captain will let you use his private phone. You can let her know when we will be arriving, and she can meet us at the airport."

With that direction, Adam nodded and proceeded toward the captain's office. He got about halfway across the room when the captain burst out of his office and shouted, "The holding building is being assaulted by a cartel gang with heavy armament."

Axel heard this shouting and ran out and toward the captain. "What's happening?" he shouted.

"The holding building is being raided. They are trying to get El Encima out," shouted the captain.

Axel turned and hollered to Adam, "You make your call to your wife and head for San Diego. Make sure you make extra copies of my deposition and your deposition to take back to the agency. I forgot to make a report on my deposition concerning the weapons raid. It was the inputs from us as to where the weapons were being delivered and dispositioned. I'll see you later."

Then, he turned and faced the captain. "Take me with you,'" he shouted. "There is no way they are going to get my prisoner. There is no way El is getting away. I will make sure of it."

"Okay," said the captain. "Here, grab this rifle."

As he handed the rifle toward Axel, Axel said, "I won't need that. Let's go."

Out of the building ran the captain, and about five of his men jumped into two other vehicles and headed toward the holding building. As Axel jumped in the captain's car, he shouted, "How far away is this place?"

"It's only about eight minutes up the street and over to the building," shouted the captain.

Axel's heart was pumping, and he directed himself silently, "Axelvation three and hood down." Before long, they were within shooting range of the building, and it was obvious the police were outmanned by this cartel gang. "They don't want their chief leader to be imprisoned," Axel shouted.

The captain, his five men, and Axel make up a courageous force of six, but it was obvious there was at least twenty of the cartel gang, and some had AK-47 rifles. The captain had told Axel that the holding house had about six men inside, with three of them being active police. Now Axel saw the gang and where they had located themselves. Several were close to entering the front door of the building.

Axel jumped out of the car and leaped toward that front door. The captain hollered, "No, Axel, get under cover. They will kill you," being unaware of Axel's capabilities.

Axel ran toward the building's door, and as he got about ten feet away, the two gang members turned and began shooting. They were poor shots and never hit Axel, and they never got another chance as Axel pounded each across the head like a sledge hammer hitting them, and down they fell, dead. He then turned and ran toward a group of five of the gang that was hiding behind the protection of an automobile. As he got about ten feet from the car, they directed their attention to him and started to point their guns in his direction, but just as they were beginning to shoot, he leaped up and cleared the car, and he was now behind them. He grabbed the rifle of one of them and shot one of the others. He took the rifle and whipped it at high speed through the head of the one whose rifle it used to be. He shot one more of them before grabbing the head of one and spinning it around. He then kicked the last one of them so hard his foot stuck in the man's stomach. Those five being disposed of, he turned his attention to another batch of cartel gang and cried out loud, "You are not taking my prisoner."

He rapidly sped toward that vehicle, and as he did, he could hear someone from the holding building shouting, "The prisoner is getting away."

Axel grabbed the rifle of the first of the gang he reached and turned. El was running in the other direction. Axel took the rifle and threw it like a spear at El's retreating frame. The rifle flew through the air and struck El in the back and penetrated his back. Down he went. Axel turned and continued his onslaught. There before him were four faces with wide open eyes staring at what had just happened. He grabbed another rifle by the end and swung the rifle like a baseball bat and kept swinging it till there was none of the four left standing. All of a sudden, it was quiet.

Axel turned and saw six other men walking with their hands in the air and the captain and his men holding pistols and rifles in their direction as they surrounded them. This was all that was left.

"Now, captain, you have six prisoners instead of one. I hope these six realize what happened to their amigos and what they have now given for their dope ring buddies and their top (El Encima). They have given up their lives for nothing worth a peso."

Axel was still breathing hard from the excitement of the last ten minutes. The captain walked over and said, "I have never seen a display of strength and speed like what I just now witnessed. What are you? I have to believe at least one of the bullets hit you during that foray. The gang was emptying their bullets trying to keep up with you. Are you some kind of athlete that can run and jump like that? I can't believe what I just saw."

Axel pulled the captain aside and said, "I would appreciate it if you didn't tell anyone about this. This is between you and me. I am a special agent of the United States. It's obvious that you saw certain actions and its best that they are kept in confidence. My government would appreciate it. Maybe these cartel gangs will learn to stay away from the law in this country. I know people like you captain are trying, and you will win this war with these cartels. With the financial problems in the world right now, maybe the lack of free funds will reduce the demand for these cocaine snuffers. I hope so. I know the United States needs to work on their responsibilities of reducing the weapons being sold over the black market from the States to these Mexican cartel gangs. They also need to someway get the word to stop the use of cocaine. They end up as the big users of the cocaine that travels from Colombia through the Mexican cartels to the States. Their use provides a large income for these Mexican cartels. On the other side of the coin, the weapons end up killing more Mexican people than Americans. It's probably one of the reasons there are big migrations from Mexico to the States. They feel safer in the States than among the nutty cartel groups and their infighting. Personally, I feel good right now. Maybe, if you drive me real fast, we can still catch Adam before he leaves your country. He might still be at your station, since we weren't gone that long. If we hurry, I can get a ride toward home; I need it."

Adam was just leaving the police station when the captain's vehicle pulled into the station. "Wow, that was fast," shouted Adam. "Must have been a false alarm, huh?"

The captain shouted, "There are a bunch of guys back there that wish this was a false alarm. They found out, thanks to your brother, that it was their last alarm."

Axel jumped out of the captain's vehicle and shouted, "Think I can hitch a ride home?"

"Don't know why not," said Adam. "It takes the same amount of gas and energy to take two as one. Besides, I have got used to you being around."

Axel walked over and shook the hand of the captain. "Thanks for having me along on that journey back there. Maybe one of these days I will bring my girlfriend or wife down this way, and I promise to stop in and see you. By the way, what is your name captain?"

"Emanuel Presco," replied the captain. "I sure would be glad to have you as a guest, and maybe we can go and hunt some more cartel gangs one day; adios."

"Maybe," commented Axel as he turned to get in the car with Adam. "Adios, Captain Presco," he shouted.

Things worked out well with the house in San Diego for the night, and the next day, Adam and Axel boarded their flight and were on their way to Washington, DC. Axel called Tori on her cell phone and told her that both he and Adam were on a flight toward Dallas and then to the Dulles International airport at Washington, DC. She was very excited and asked when she would get to see him. Axel told her he had to report in to the agency with Adam, and if things went right, he would be heading toward her by the day after tomorrow.

"That's so wonderful," cried Tori. Axel could hear her crying on the other end of the phone, and he got a lump in his throat. He had never had a woman, besides his mother, cry over him, and this filled him up with emotion.

"Don't cry sweetie," Axel said. "You are supposed to be happy."

"I am happy." she said. "I am just so happy that I cry without trying to cry. I guess that's what emotion is all about, and right now I am emotional."

Axel told her he would give her a call that evening when he was safely in his room at Adam's house. "I think I mentioned that Laura is going to pick us up at the Washington airport," he added.

Then, Axel leaned back in the plane seat. He was kind of pooped out from all the excitement and lack of sleep the last two nights, and he fell asleep. He was awakened by the landing in Dallas. Both Adam and Axel were interested in the latest news, and they picked up several newspapers to read while waiting for the final leg of their trip. After a couple of hours, they were on the last leg of the trip.

Laura met them at the baggage pickup, and Axel told Adam to go to Laura his loving wife, while he picked up the bags. "Right," shouted Adam, as he ran toward his wife. He grabbed her, and he picked her up off her feet and gave her a big hug and several kisses.

That's wonderful, thought Axel. *I want that to happen to me one of these days when I grab my wife and pick her up off her feet, especially after an experience like Adam has just gone through.*

Soon, they were driving toward Arlington. "I hope you two are hungry," questioned Laura. "I made you homemade soup, and we will have some baked potatoes and a nice roast of beef and gravy."

"That sounds wonderful," said Axel. "We ate pretty well while away, but there is nothing like a homemade meal. That just sounds great."

While they were driving along, Laura told Axel that she had picked up his tickets for the flight out the day after tomorrow. Axel looked at the tickets, and they showed a takeoff at 12:15 PM. "We had better leave the house at nine the day you leave," said Laura, "just to make sure you have two hours at the airport to check through your baggage and pass through security. If we get up at eight, it will give us time for you to eat breakfast. Tomorrow, Adam and you will drive to the agency in Adam's car. I will have supper ready at around six thirty. If you are going to be later than that, Adam will give me a call."

That brought the two of them up to date, and soon, they were savoring the great meal Laura had cooked. After the meal, they continued their discussion about Mexico and the wonders of their adventures. Laura was aware of Adam's being held hostage, since she had been contacted by Kim when Adam was taken and being held in the cartel's site outside of Tijuana. She also was somewhat aware of the agency's work on Axel when he had originally been in the Washington, DC, area months before. Adam had told her of some of the work that had been done on him. However, she wasn't aware of the extraordinary power he had at his disposal as a result of the extra mitochondria and his ability to communicate with it through the special computer he had designed and had installed in his body. Adam had asked Axel if they could discuss this when they were going to have dinner, and Axel agreed to allow Adam to at least make Laura aware of his abilities, since she wanted to know how Axel was so prominent in the rescue of Adam.

With Axel's previous permission, Adam started to talk about their mother and the accident. Laura knew this accident had occurred and that Axel was born several days after Adam, but she didn't know the consequences of this late delivery. Adam began with this fact and then relayed the findings that occurred many years later about the results of that delay in the birth of Axel. Adam began to explain, "Evidently, while Mom was awaiting rescue, she was breathing hard and going through a physical transformation of the baby she still held in her body. This is not a normal occurrence, but she was breathing hard, and there was nothing the two other survivors could do to relieve her of this problem. She hurt and suffered, and the heavy breathing must have been due to the transformation that was occurring with the baby she was carrying. She didn't know that she was going to have twins. Mom also didn't know that there was any difference in Axel compared to me, other than she had to carry him longer and through a lot of pain."

"When Axel was about twelve years old, it became evident that he had a lot of energy, and Mom took him to a specialist to see what would cause this. After three days of tests, they found that Adam had an extraordinary amount of mitochondria in each of his body's cells. You might not know this, but the mitochondria are the energy cells of the body. While Axel was working on his doctor's degree in biology, he spent extra time on studying the mitochondria, and while working on his thesis, he developed a very small computer that could be addressed by talking to it rather than using a keyboard. This resulted in a very small computer chip that worked by using password codes and the voice. He had two objectives; the first was for his doctorate thesis, and it was the development of this computer that could be put in the human body and be used to help perform certain biological communications and hopefully improve on a person's ability to overcome certain physical problems. What he did that wasn't part of his thesis, and no one but the people in this room know about (plus Kim of the agency) was to develop the computer to call up three levels of his mitochondria that provides him three levels of energy, each much higher than a normal human."

"With his ability to call up these energy levels, I talked to Kim at the agency and told him that my brother had this extraordinary capability, and the agency should think about how they might be able to take advantage of it. This excited Kim, and he had been working with the development of an extremely strong material. He talked to his staff, and they decided to have Axel come to Washington, and they would test him for these capabilities. If they indeed existed, and if he indeed could call them up, he would be a perfect candidate to take this expensive material and provide a special skin-level covering that was almost completely impervious. You know that I was the benefactor of the capabilities that Axel possesses."

"With these capabilities, he is a dynamo. He is not only strong, but he is fast, he is a high-speed swimmer, and the odd thing is that he can use the computer and its capability to address the Internet to talk to the Internet without making a sound. He just has to provide a password, and his computer Internet system is activated, and he can think what he wants to say without speaking out loud. He also can use it like a telephone and call anyone just like the Internet capability. The other strange capability he has is to turn them on without anyone knowing, and it picks up the conversation around him and transmits it at 100 percent. If he wants, the conversation we are having could be going to the agency right now, and they could be listening. This is an unbelievable tool for an agent in the field. To top this all off, he can understand and speak ten different languages. Other than these little oddities, my brother is quite normal (and he smiled as he said that) and doesn't use these capabilities unless they are needed in an emergency. He can send or receive a telephone call anywhere, anytime at his convenience. I guess that extra bonus he doesn't need to use for emergencies."

Laura was speechless, hearing of Axel's unreal capabilities. She looked at Axel and said, "Give me a call on my telephone now." Axel looked at Laura and began his call up of their phone, and within seconds, the phone rang. Laura was sitting there in shock. She picked up the phone and said, "Hello."

Axel, without talking out loud, said, "Hello, Laura. Can you tell that I am talking to you?"

Laura looked at Axel and shook her head back and forth. "How about sending me an e-mail? I will turn on my computer," she said. The computer took a minute or so to turn on, and she turned on her Internet. Then, she nodded to Axel. Axel sent a message without talking, and Laura watched the words come on the computer in utter disbelief. "That amazing," she shouted as the message came on the screen.

"Hi there, Laura; we have to make each other a promise. You have to promise you will never tell anyone about these crazy things about me, and I will promise never to use my telephone or Internet in your presence unless you give me your permission. That way, neither one of us can embarrass the other. Do you promise?"

Laura looked at Axel and said, "How can I do anything to hurt or embarrass you after what you have done for Adam, let alone you are my brother in law?"

Axel stood up from his chair and gave Laura a big hug. "I would do anything for you, Adam, and my nephew. Twins either grow up resenting each other or grow up loving each other. In my case, I love my twin."

Adam chimed in with the comment, "I love you, Axel, and I have had a few extra days more than you to love you." With that, he walked over and gave Axel a big hug and said laughingly, "Now don't you hug me because I don't know how hard you will squeeze me. You are dangerous." They all had a laugh about that.

The next day, Axel and Adam spent most of the day at the agency with Kim covering what they had learned about the cartels during their rather short time. Axel commented, "If business would decrease significantly, I think the cartels would kill each other out. If the users in the States would stop buying their crack and cocaine, the market would compress, and what market was left would be fought over by the cartels They have no love for each other, only the love of the money that comes in with very little work from the sales of their dope. They have very little costs."

"The Colombians do all the work growing and preparing the stuff for sale. They have to do a lot of payouts to keep the government from shutting them down. But once the stuff leaves the country, there is a trade route over land, overseas, and in the air. The major route is over land through Central America to the lords in Mexico. From here, the split of what goes to each cartel is determined pure and simple by the level of business each does. The two major arteries are the Gulf cartel and the Pacific cartel. These break off into about five major arteries each. The two we took down were the two from the Pacific cartel that broke off into the Tijuana and Nogales ones. There is a large cartel that is located around Ciudad Juarez, and another one working out of Chihuahua and maybe another out of Conchos that come out of the split for the Pacific cartel."

"It is obvious where the trade goes from there if you look at a map of Mexico and the interface with the States. The good news is that these three major cartels that we didn't hit are probably set up the same as Tijuana and Nogales. They have one guy like Primo or El Encima that probably heads up each and is the brainy person. If you take him down, there is a good chance that the cartel would wilt like I believe Tijuana and Nogales will. However, the wilting will not be long lived. There will be another brainy guy to come along within a year, and after another year, they will be back at the same level of business. But this means a given cartel will be at a low level for two years, and there will be some fighting among them and with some of the other cartels for the business lost by the guy you put out of business."

"Of course, when you think of the Gulf versus the Pacific cartels, there is a place in the center of the border between Mexico and the United States where there is a point of conflict. This is on the border between Mexico and Texas. The big suppliers of Texas from the Pacific cartel are Ciudad Juarez, Chihuahua, and Conchos. On the Gulf side, there are Monterrey and Nuevo Laredo. All five of these each has a top guy heading up their cartel. The three on the Pacific side and the two on the Gulf side have no love for each other, since one can take business that the other wants to supply. If there is some way of promoting this conflict among them, it would help to have them fighting each other rather than fighting with our border patrols. Probably the best way would be to stop the buying of the stuff at the Mexican/Texas border. With less buying, there would be more fighting among the cartels, and this would be solving two problems at once."

Axel said, "Sometimes, I think the best and least expensive way of handling the cocaine issue would be for the United States to buy all the Colombian cocaine and cut off the source to these big cartels. I bet we could buy all the cocaine from Colombia at a cost that is less then we spend in fighting them on land, on the seas, and in the air. I bet we spend over five billion dollars a year fighting this problem, and we could probably buy all the cocaine from Colombia for two billion dollars. Add to that that the Mexican government and local police spend over five billion dollars a year fighting the drug cartels. Colombia would probably be receiving as much as they are receiving now. They would lose fewer lives, they would free up their police for other issues, and they would free up people for other jobs. The country of Mexico would lose fewer lives than they presently lose due to cartel infighting of Mexican against Mexican, cartel losses with the Mexican police, and collateral losses of the common Mexican due to the cartel/police fighting. They lose over six thousand Mexicans a year in this war, and the loss of lives at the border with the United States. All this and the United States and Mexico would save several billion dollars left over. Those are all guesses by me of the amount of money and people involved, but it sure would be easier to control. I wish we had a magic wand."

Both Axel and Adam provided as much information to the agency during their debriefing (who would provide it for the other drug-fighting agencies), as they had more detailed information about the methods used by the cartels as well as their 'Modus operandi. than they ever had before about the cartels, their leaders, and their working patterns. It was hoped that this debriefing would eventually help in the battle with the drug problem. When the day with the agency was complete and their debriefing was over, they returned to the house and a dinner with Laura. Axel went to bed early, since he had to get up early and have Adam drive him to the airport.

Before going to bed, he decided to call Dean Hayworth at the university to tell him he would be back on Monday to begin his classes again. The dean was glad he was returning and hoped he had a successful time off from teaching. "It was very eventful," he told the Dean. "One of these days, I will tell you what I went through on this break from the university. It is a classified secret, so I can't tell you now, but one day, I will."

They talked a little more, and then Axel went to bed. He laid there for a while thinking about the venture he had gone through, and he wished he could tell the dean and Tori and the whole world, but it must remain a secret. He knew that its disclosure would cause him other ventures that he might not want to pursue. *I wonder what will come next*, he thought, and then he fell asleep.

The next morning, they were all up, and soon, Adam and Axel were on their way to the airport. Adam let Axel off at the main entrance and thanked Axel for all he had done for him, the agency, the United States, and Mexico. He didn't stop there and commented that Washington and the agency would probably be calling on him soon again. "You are a walking, running, and fighting battleship, and we cannot find that anywhere else. There are going to be times when your combination of talent will be needed. Maybe it won't be with the agency. Maybe there will come a time when one of the cities is having trouble, and they talk to Kim, and your name comes up. I hope you think about it and give what you can."

"I know you have a woman you love, and you have to lead your own life. You are a doctor of biology, and perhaps, that will be your everyday calling, and perhaps, this technical knowledge you have plus the physical power you have will lead you into fighting problems where this combination of skills is required. I am very proud to be your twin, and there are times when I envy what you have. I have a lot in my life and my family, but there are times when I wish I had the dynamo you have in your frame. God bless you, and I hope things continue to work out well for you. I love you, brother."

Axel gave him a wink and said, "I love you more than anyone in the world, including Tori. We are of the same make, and I hope you continue your successful profession and the love of your family. You take care, and drive home safely; don't go to work today. Go home, and spend some time with your wife and kid. Don't go to work till Monday. They owe you that. In fact, tell them you won't be there for a week after this Monday, and maybe you and your family could fly out to Frisco. We would have a great time, and you and Laura could meet Tori. Take care, but have fun. I'll see you when I see you." With that, they gave each other a hug, and Adam drove away.

Tori's realization

While waiting for the flight, Axel wanted to give Tori a call, but it was not quite nine in the morning, and that meant it was not quite six in the morning on the West Coast. So, he figured he would call her when he boarded the plane or later when he was in Dallas. The plane would leave at ten thirty from Dallas International airport, which was seven thirty on the West Coast. When the time arrived, Axel dialed her on his internal phone, and it rang several times before there was the quiet voice of Tori answering. She was still in bed. Axel told her he was on his way home, and the flight was through Dallas and would arrive in San Francisco at approximately five thirty West Coast time; Tori was beside herself. She was so excited. It had been some time since they had seen each other, and she just wanted to see him as bad as he wanted to see her. When Axel hung up, he thought to himself that Tori was excited about him. He hoped that lasted.

When the plane was approaching the San Francisco International airport, Axel looked out the plane window and thought about all that had happened while he was gone. He wondered if he could stand the rather mellow life he had lived before receiving this transformation to an action person. He enjoyed the excitement of the battle with the terrorist threat in Washington and the more-than-exciting venture in Mexico. He was especially proud of being able to be The Follower and save his brother. He looked below and saw the San Mateo Bridge, and the plane was now close to landing in San Francisco. He thought, *What a beautiful sight*. It was still light out, and he could see the hills on the left, and looking across the aisle to the window on the other side of the plane, he could make out what must be part of Oakland or a town close to it. There was that large pile of salt sitting along that shore from the company that produced commercial salt. Yep, he was home now.

Axel hurried to the baggage pickup and hoped Tori would be either there or just outside in her car waiting for him. As he arrived at the baggage pickup, the bags hadn't arrived yet. He ran outside to see if she was there. No Tori. He kept looking for her car. A few minutes passed, and then he saw her car, and it pulled up to the curb where he was standing. The window came down on his side, and she hollered from the driver's seat. "Do you have your bags?"

"No, they haven't arrived at the baggage turnstile yet," he responded.

"I can't park my car here," yelled Tori. "They don't permit it. I will drive around the airport and be back here in about five minutes. If you aren't there, I will know you don't have your bags yet, and I will keep on circling."

Axel waved her off and threw her a kiss. She threw one back and pulled out. Axel returned to the baggage turnstile and awaited his bags. Finally, everything came together, and he was jumping in the car and giving Tori a long kiss. "I sure missed you and all the things wonderful about you," he said.

She continued driving but said, "I wish I could squeeze you right now, but that would be hard on the driving and maybe hard on that thing between your legs, huh?"

"You have that right," he said.

Tori said, "I am going to take you to my place tonight. Ellen is away for a few days, and I started to cook you something before I left. I can finish when we get there, and you can stay the night. In fact, you can stay over the whole weekend if you want. Is that okay by you?"

"It rings bells in my ears," he remarked while looking at her beautiful face. He thought to himself, *She is not only beautiful in her face; she is beautiful all over. She looks great in those shorts with those fantastic legs and curvy body. God, I wish we were in her bed right now. I can't wait, but I guess I must.*

When they arrived at Tori's apartment, they no sooner opened the door and got inside, and they were making love. It seemed to Axel that this time was even better than the last time. Maybe it was due to being away from each other for so long and thinking about each other every day; whatever it was, it was great. Maybe they learned to take it a little slower and a little easier and made it last longer. The humping was a little slower, and every time it felt like she was going to come, Axel would slow down and kiss her tits. Then, she climaxed but told Axel to keep going because she loved it and could climax again soon.

Axel kept his lovemaking in control, and Tori actually came three times before he came. *What a great feeling*, he thought. And then, he returned to kissing Tori's lips and face again. "I love you, Tori. I love you, Tori, and I want to live my life with you."

"Yes, Axel, I missed you so much, and I never felt this way about anyone else in my life."

Lovemaking lasted the whole weekend. They finished up at Axel apartment on Sunday, and he took her home that night and returned to his apartment to prepare for the next day's appearance at the university. The next day was kind of fuzzy for Axel. It was different to be back at the university and teaching. During the day, he got to see Tori and Ellen between some of his classes and the lab that day. When he went home that night, he was worn out more than the physical events he had gone through for the agency. He called Tori and told her he had to rest. He wanted to go and hit the sack. She said, "I know you have been running around so much and need the rest. I'll see you tomorrow."

Wednesday started out quite normal for Axel. He had taught two earlier classes and ate lunch. He met Tori and Ellen at lunch and bought them their lunches, and they asked how he was making out with his teaching. He responded that it was quite tiring compared to what he had been doing. It was due to using the brain more than the brawn, he said. They continued their discussion, and Ellen got up and said she had to leave. "It was nice seeing you back here at school," she said to Axel. "I hope to see you and Tori together more often."

Axel thanked her for the commented, and off she went. They were done eating, and Tori and Axel continued their small talk. "I have a lab to teach at three o'clock," commented Axel. "When is your next class?"

"I have a physiology class that starts at three thirty," she remarked. "It is down by where your lab is, so I will walk with you to the lab and maybe see you after your lab is over. How long is the lab?"

"It is a two-hour lab, so you will be out of your class about a half hour before me," he answered.

"Where do you want to meet?"

"I will have to read something out of one of my books for a class tomorrow, so I can sit on the bench outside the lab and see you when you come out," she said.

"That's great; maybe we can go to my place, and if you need any help on any of your classes, I can help you. Does that make sense?" asked Axel.

"No," she remarked. "That doesn't make sense. You know if we go to your place that I will not get any of my studying done. Why not go and get a coffee and roll, and then I will head home after that?"

"Yeah, you are right; you won't get any of your school work done if you go to my place. So, let's go to Joe's Pizza place and have a coffee and pizza, and you can head home," said Axel.

She nodded, and they picked up their papers and books and headed toward Axel's lab. "You teach them good. I want our students to be the best biology majors in the country," she commented.

As they approached the lab, suddenly they heard a loud explosion, and one half of the door leading to the lab blew open. Tori and Axel began running to the lab. As they got to the open door and looked inside, there were two students lying on the floor with flames on their bodies and a huge amount of flames along the horizontal direction of the long laboratory work bench, with about fifteen students on the other side of the wall of flames with no way out. Axel immediately gave the signal to his inner self, "Axelvation three, hood down." Then, he threw his body on the first student to douse his flames. As the flames were snuffed out, he leaped and jumped to the next student and threw his body against her to suffocate the flames. She was screaming, but he soon was able to douse her flames.

Meanwhile, he was hollering to a man standing at the door. "Get the medic up here fast, and dial 911." Axel then leaped up, and within seconds, he realized that there was no way to put out the fire with those fifteen or so students trapped on the other side of the flame. He knew he was in high speed with the third level of his energy and began running through the flame and grabbed two students and ran back through the flame and set them down. He turned and ran through the flames again and grabbed two more students and returned them to the safe side. He repeated this action until all of the students were safely near the door leading out of the lab.

Then, he thought, *"How do I put out these flames before they spread or some of the chemicals explode?"* Then, he realized that if he could draw all the oxygen away from the flaming area that the flames would go out. Axel ran to the edge of the flame on the door side of the room and began spinning like a top or tornado. He had once read that the lowest pressure on earth was the center of a tornado. He spun his body so fast it was nothing but a blur. As he spun, the flames began to point toward his body from all over the room's fire. All of a sudden, the flames went out like a switch had been turned. His spinning had created a vacuum that drew all the oxygen from the lab room's air and from any of the chemicals on the long laboratory table. He then stopped and took in a deep breath and told himself, "Cease Axelvation three."

Axel stood there, and he was now facing Tori who was about twenty feet away. Her eyes were wide open, and her body almost in a frozen stance as she looked directly at Axel's eyes. He knew what she was wondering, and he knew he had some explaining to do. There was no way out of this one. As Axel ran toward the door, the students he had carried from the flames all cheered him. Fortunately, they were out in the hall and hadn't witnessed the "tornado" he had generated to put out the fire or he would have more explaining to do.

The next hour was consumed with Axel and Tori watching the medics giving medical injections to the two students that had been burned. This was to reduce the pain from their burns till they could get them to a burn hospital. They also covered their bodies with a material that keeps air from reaching the surface of their skin and keeps the pain down. Axel also spent a good bit of time trying to find out what had happened to cause the explosion and the fire. He knew that the chemicals in these labs could be dangerous, but the first things the students were taught in their first lab period they attended was how the various chemicals worked and the dangers involved. Axel had been at this university for over nine years, and there had never been as much as a small fire. Someone did something wrong. The more he questioned the students that he had carried out from the fire area, the more it looked like one of the two students that were burned had done something because the whole incident had started on that side of the lab. The ambulance had taken the two away, so he would have to talk to them later. Axel kept trying to do things to take up time because he knew from Tori's look that she was sort of shocked from what had gone on and how he had handled the situation.

When Axel and Tori were ready to leave, Axel told her he would follow her on the way to her place. She said, "Good, I want you to tell me the truth about yourself. I am tired of being fooled." Axel replied with a sort of soft comment that he understood where she was coming from.

When they arrived at Tori's apartment, they were happy that Ellen wasn't there, so they could have the privacy they needed. They barely got through the door when Tori turned and shouted in a loud voice, "Okay, tell me what's going on with you; and no trying to avoid the subject. I want the whole truth."

Axel looked at her and said, "How about we cool down and have a drink, and I will go over it for you?" She looked at him and realized she was unsettled and nodded to his suggestion. She got out some bourbon and poured a drink for each of them.

"Do you want something with this?" she asked.

"No, I think this is fine. Before I give you the scoop on me, I want you to know something important. I love you, and I have wanted to ask you to marry me, but the problem you saw part of today complicates everything. I want you to know I didn't tell you for your own protection and because I had made a promise to not tell anyone. This was a promise I gave to the agency." At that point, Axel stopped talking to see if she got that message. He wanted her to realize he loved her and didn't mean to deceive her. He took another swallow of the bourbon.

"Go on," she urged.

"It's a long story and begins with my birth. My mother was pregnant and in a plane wreck. She and two other men survived and made up a sort of camp about a hundred yards from the wreck. She didn't know that she was going to have twins. Well, she almost didn't. Adam was born within an hour after the wreck, but she continued to have something like labor pains. They were severe at times, and she kept gasping for air. The two men were able to take trips to the plane, which hadn't burst into flames, and retrieve some baggage and make bedding out of shirts and pants and other things. This situation existed for over two days without their seeing any planes in the air searching for them."

"They decided at the end of the second day that they had to set the plane on fire to attract searchers that would see the flame during the night. The two men wrapped two rocks with underwear taken out of the wreckage, and they walked to the plane and dunked the clothed rocks in gasoline. They lit the rocks and threw them at the wreckage, and almost immediately, there was a huge flame as they ran back toward their small camp. A few hours later, they had a helicopter come over their camp and dropped a cellular phone using a long rope. They were then able to communicate with the helicopter, and by the next morning, they were rescued. They took Adam and my mother to the hospital where labor was induced further, and I was born. My mother decided to name Adam after the first man on earth, and she named me Axel because she thought of a rear axle to a car, which always follows the front (first) axel."

"I was raised like Adam, and there was no difference noted in our development. However, when I reached puberty, it was noticed that I had a tremendous amount of energy at times. My mother took me to a specialist who was a doctor of physical therapy, and after three days of many tests, he told my mother and me that I had some extraordinary physical differences from normal. I should mention that my dad had died just the year before, so you won't hear anything about my dad in these discussions. Also, as I discuss the human cell and the organelles that surround the nucleus, you will be quite aware of this due to your background in biology, but I am going to explain anyhow, since it is important." Then, Axel explained the rest of his differences and how it gave him extra energy.

"When I was young and my dad was still living, he had a friend, and he would take me to his house, and I would watch my dad and his friend work on electronic circuits. This interested me and became my hobby. When I graduated with my undergraduate degree and had decided to go on and try to gain my Master's and Doctor's degrees, I also decided that I was going to take my hobby and make something of it also. Eventually, I would make circuits that did unique things. Eventually, I decided that a great thing to do would be to build a computer with a phone and Internet capability built in. I worked on that during my first summer. By the first year of my graduate work, I decided to invent a computer that didn't need a keyboard. I wanted a computer that understood my voice commands and eliminated the keyboard. I had reached this goal by the time I had received the equivalent of my Master's degree in biology. I presented this as my Master's thesis, since I felt that this could lead to a technology that could help the human body."

"During my work on my doctorate, I decided that a friend of mine could duplicate the circuits I had developed for a computer in a single integrated chip, and I paid him five thousand dollars to do this. Eventually, I had a computer the size of a dime including a small battery that could do all the things I had envisioned. However, I was not satisfied. I wanted to be able to have this computer installed in my body and be able to communicate with my cells and the mitochondria. I wanted to be able to turn on three levels of the mitochondria and have the three levels of energy that each could provide."

Axel then described how much energy each of these levels gave him. At this point, Axel decided to take a break and have another bourbon drink. Tori was sitting in her chair stunned with what she had learned. "Do you want another drink or anything?" he asked Tori.

"Yes, I believe I need something after hearing what you have told me so far," she said.

With the above background, Axel sat down with his drink and began to explain things again. "After I received my Doctor's degree, I decided to stay at the university and teach. I also felt this was a good place to work on improving what I had achieved with my body and how to control this capability. I didn't know if I would ever need these capabilities, but I wanted to spend the time to perfect what they gave me. I had a password that I could use to activate the computer and to use the Internet and to use the built-in cell phone capability. I finally was able to activate any of the functions without saying them out loud. Adam and my mother were aware of these capabilities. I was glad she was able to see me achieve this."

"Meanwhile, Adam had majored in criminal science and eventually went to an agency in Washington, DC. Named "United States Science Agency (USSA)." He married Laura, and they had their boy after only a year of marriage. This is where my capabilities really came to the forefront. Adam's job in the agency was such that he got involved with working on an antiterrorist group. At one point, he told his boss, a man named, Edward Kim, of my unique capabilities. Sometime after that, the agency had gained a special capability, and they were trying to determine where they could best use this capability. Adam reminded

Kim of my capabilities, and eventually, Kim decided to have me out there, so I could demonstrate my unusual capabilities."

"When he saw what I was able to do, he brought me into his confidence. He described that they had developed a material made up of spider webs and nano tube titanium that was extremely thin and unbelievably strong and had a very high strength when woven into a type of body cover. It was however very expensive, costing about one hundred million dollars to fabricate, and it was not cost effective to put on a normal soldier, so they had put off using it. When they saw my capabilities, they were convinced that if they designed a covering for my body that I could be a secret agent for them, a super spy."

"At the time, I told them I was interested in the capability but not interested in being a spy or special agent. However, they felt that they could invest their time in me and that I would serve as a test sample of the capabilities of this super material. Later, they told me that they felt if I ever got this to work that I would be interested in serving my country. After making a covering for my body, they tested it for its invulnerability and my ability to function with it. It is so light in weight that I don't know I have it on. In addition, it is breathable; allowing me to not feel any difference in my body's normal functions. In order for it to function to its fullest, they designed the head covering to not be on until I wanted it to be on. It is so small when folded that it is like a pimple on the middle of my head, a small pimple covered by hair. When I give a certain command, the head covering releases in less than a thousandth of a second and covers my face and even my eyes. I see through it without noticing it's there. Another command and it is snapped back into its folded condition and unnoticeable."

"They tested the strength, flexibility, and everything they needed to provide them the confidence that it was impenetrable. They shot guns at me; different kinds and at different ranges; with and without the helmet being over my face and head. But they never shot me in the head with the helmet not in place. They had me jump up to high heights. They taught me how to jump down from high heights, which was not as easy it turns out. If I were to jump from a twenty-foot height, it would put a tremendous strain on my legs. To prevent this, when I approach the surface to which I am jumping, I just say to my computer, 'up,' and just as my foot touches the surface, the ATP energy tries to lift me in a jump.

However, the downward force of the landing is offset by the upward force of the command to jump, and they almost cancel each other, and I bounce up about two or three feet. It's like a soft landing."

"While in Maryland, I swam in the Chesapeake Bay, and when my helmet was activated, I could swim under water with my eyes open and see things like there was no water there. I could swim anywhere between twenty and thirty miles an hour depending on which level of energy I had activated. This means I can cover between thirty-five to forty-four feet per second. There isn't anything in the water that I can't pursue unless it is a speed boat. To top this all off, I had provided my computer with a capability of speaking and understanding ten different languages. All I have to do is have my phone or Internet activated, and as a person speaks any of these languages, it is carried to my computer that translates it and sends it back to me within microseconds. So, I can understand and speak any of these ten languages without being detected."

Tori said, "That's terrible. It took me four years to learn Spanish well enough to converse with it intelligently, and you learn it as it is being spoken by someone. That's because you have that computer inside you. So, you really did do something to advance biology with that computer. Maybe someday that can be put in many people, and they can at least use that capability of the body computer."

Axel looked at Tori and said, "Now, you know what my body capabilities are, and I hope you understand why I kept this from you. You probably wouldn't have believed me anyhow."

"Probably not," responded Tori. "I still have a hard time believing all this. What did you go to Washington and then to Mexico to do?"

"That's a long story," replied Axel. "In general, the agency found a way to place me in a suspected terrorist cell to find what they intended. I was used as a spy to work within the terrorist group that was located in Baltimore. The agency had planted a mole in the terrorist cell. The leaders of the cell were trying to contact a man who had experience with biology and could put their plan into effect. The mole convinced them that he knew a young doctor of biology, and he told them he thought the man had something against America. When he showed them my credentials of being a doctor of biology, they had him contact me, and I went to Baltimore and played the part."

"What they had planned was for me to take embryonic stem cells or adult stem cells and propagate them into the millions. After this, I was to find a way to install a deadly virus inside each of the propagated cells. This would give them millions of virus-contaminated cells. First, I was to prove it with virus cells like the ones that cause a common cold and show that it didn't change the biology of the stem cells, and they still remained undifferentiated. After proving this, they had arranged to obtain some of the very few viruses in the world from the flu epidemic that killed so many people in the 1918– 1919 flu epidemic. This was to be installed in the millions of stem cells that I had produced and that were still undifferentiated with the hopes that the cells would remain undifferentiated until they would be injected into birds, and the birds would be contaminated with the virus."

"Then, they would have dropped the birds on large population cities, and this would start a deadly virus equivalent to the one that struck the world in 1918–1919. By my infiltrating this terrorist cell and proving I could do this function of propagating stem cells in the manner in which they were interested, it brought me close to the men who lead this terrorist cell. When the leaders made contact with their source of the virus and he delivered it to the Baltimore site, I was then able to use all the capabilities that the agency and I had built into my system, and I was able to extinguish all the members, or at least the top members, of this terrorist cell. This very dangerous situation was avoided by my actions. I was proud of what I had accomplished."

"The trip to Mexico was to find and free my brother, Adam. The agency he works for had sent him to San Diego to establish a mock cocaine business in the hopes of making connections with the large cocaine market supplied through Mexico. Their main hope was to find the operating base of the Pacific cartel, which is one of the two biggest in Mexico, and put them out of business. Adam did a great job of establishing a big business that eventually brought him in contact with one of the top leaders of the Pacific cartel. In the course of trying to provide the agency with the exact location of the operating base of the Tijuana cartel, he was taken hostage and held at this location about thirty miles from Tijuana."

"The agency felt the best way to get him out of there was to send me as his drug business partner and try to talk them out of their suspicions.

If nothing else, they felt if I could free him in exchange for me being their hostage—that I had the where with all to get out of there alive. While in the Tijuana location, El Primo of that location decided to keep both of us. Later, he was to send me to his leader El Encima (the top) located in Nogales. El Encima was not only the top man in the Nogales operation, he was the top man of the Pacific cartel. I knew that I had to find a way to destroy this location as well as escape while keeping El Encima from contacting El Primo and having harm come to Adam. Eventually, I was able to take El Encima as my prisoner and escape unnoticed, and we flew to Tijuana on his small private plane. El Encima was turned over to the Tijuana police, and I made my way to the location where they held Adam and was able to free him and take a wounded El Primo as prisoner. The Mexican police and army were able to take both the Nogales and Tijuana strongholds and eliminate them. The total operation did great harm to the drug cartels of Mexico. We know this is a short-term victory, but it will take them some time to rebuild this lucrative business back to where it was. I was very proud of what I had done for my country and the country of Mexico."

Of course, Tori listened to this with her mouth wide open. When Axel was done, she just kept looking at him. She didn't have any words to express her feelings. She didn't know what she felt. She looked at this man who she loved and wondered if he was for real. *Is he a machine or a man?* She asked herself. *Should I be proud of him or scared of him? Everything he does, he does for good. There is nothing mean or intimidating about him. He was born different, but has lived indifferently. He is always warm toward me, and I have never seen him do anything but good for people. Is he a saint? Is he someone I want to marry? One thing I know; he is strong and I have always felt safe around him. He is handsome, smart, kind, good, and when he turns off his energy button he is normal."* Extremes kept flowing through her brain, and she found herself in a trance, dumbfounded, and unable to cope with the scope of events that led to this confession by Axel. She looked at Axel and said, "I think I need time to absorb all this. I am going to go home and take a hot shower and lie down and rest. This is like being hit with a big, indefinable, puzzle. Don't call me. I need time." Axel looked at her and could understand her shock and the questions on her mind. He didn't respond as she walked out and got in her car and drove home.

Axel went back to trying to understand what had happened in the lab. He got some feedback about one of the students that had been burned and who was responsible for the accident. He had read an article on one of the Internet Web sites on how to manufacture a bomb with some ordinary products that one could find at a farm feed store. He thought it would be safe to try this during his lab, since there was all the equipment he might need to do this. The Web site had explained how dangerous it was when mishandled and could explode. Evidently, he had done something wrong and mixed it with some of the chemicals they had at the lab. It didn't explode, but it burst into flames. Axel said the lab instructor for that lab was reviewing which chemicals were involved.

Meanwhile, Axel knew he was worthless as far as trying to figure anything out after the affair with Tori. His mind was on her and how he might overcome this issue. He thought, *"How could something that was done to save people from harm cause this kind of problem?"* He knew it was a shock for Tori to find out so many things all at once. Now, he was sorry he hadn't told her some of this months ago, but then he thought it might have actually been worse than when they hadn't found their love between each other. *She probably thinks I am a freak*, he thought. *Maybe I am a freak. No, I can't think that way after my mother went through what she did to have me. I am an accident of birth, but I have used it to help people. My mother will be proud of what I have done and proud of what she has done. I must not forget that. One day I must sit down with her and tell her of these adventures. She has been proud of Adam and me. She has been proud of making it through those first few days before having me. So, no matter what Tori thinks, she has to get over it. I sure am not going to apologize for what I am and what I have accomplished.* With that settled in his mind, Axel went about his work of teaching the one class he had left for the day. The lab he was supposed to have taught ended up teaching Tori something about Axel and maybe the students who learned not to play with fire.

Axel didn't hear from Tori that week. He knew the school year was ending, and she would be graduating. He hadn't even talked to her about what she wanted to do when she was done with her undergraduate work. *How selfish*, he thought. *I should have showed more interest in what she was doing and what she intended to do in the future. I guess I got all tied up in what I was doing and not thinking about others. Now, we have this standoff situation, and I have no idea what she intends to do.* He knew one thing; his insides were going around as they had been for the past few days. Not hearing from Tori was making it hard to sleep and hard to concentrate on his work at the school. He knew he had to give out grades for students that took classes from him, and he knew he had to make sure he wasn't emotional when doing this.

He had to get his emotions squared away, and he felt the best way to do this it to get hold of Tori and find out what she was thinking and how he could resolve some of her feelings. He decided to give her a call on her cell phone. He dialed. "Hello," came that soft voice.

"Hi," said Axel. "Any chance of seeing you and talking some more? I feel bummed, and I need to talk to you."

"Yes, I feel the same," she said.

"Where are you now?" asked Axel.

"I am waiting outside classroom 2202. My class starts in about ten minutes." "How about I meet you outside of 2202 when you are done with the class?" Axel asked.

"Yeah, that would be okay," she said.

"Okay, I will be there; good-bye."

Axel waited outside of 2202, anxious to see her and more anxious to see if he could get over this problem. As the class let out, he saw her coming, and he met her in the hallway. "How about getting something to eat?" he asked.

"I am not all that hungry," she replied, "but I could go for a roll and a cup of coffee."

"Me too," he said.

He felt relieved that they would go and eat anything; just being with her made him feel good already. *She could have said no*, he thought, *but she didn't.* They walked out of the school and down to a small coffee shop about a block from the main school building. As a teacher, he didn't like to be seen eating with one of the undergraduate students. It was sort of frowned on, but he didn't really care at this point in their relationship. He wasn't playing a game; he was serious, especially about Tori. They talked small talk as they walked to the coffee shop, and it sort of relieved the stress.

As they ate their rolls and talked, Axel said, "I know what you heard the other day was a shock to you. You have to believe I wanted to tell you this many months ago but could never find the right time, and there was a good bit of the time when I was away. I was caught between my love for you and the thought that if you knew, it might put you in danger. One way of getting to me would be through you or Adam. The agency told me to keep it a secret because of the danger it could cause you. I have tried to divorce my actions with the agency from this school and you. I never meant it to be a secret forever. As soon as I knew that you shared my love, I had intended to tell you and ask you to marry me. Then, the Mexico thing came up, and I surely didn't want you worrying about me while I was gone. Keep in mind that there were three things that got me this way—my birth, my development of the computer, and the agency."

"Probably the only one I could have shied away from was the agency thing. But then I thought to myself, 'Axel, this is your chance to use your God-given gift to do something good, something good for our country,' and that made my decision for me. What are your feelings about this, Tori?"

Tori pecked away at the piece of roll in front of her and then looked up at Axel and said, "I guess I was just hurt that I had to find out the way I did. Then, I thought that maybe you might always keep things from me. Then, I began to feel sorry for myself as I thought about the past things that have happened to me in my love life. In the end, I had to just walk away from it and settle things in my mind. I know you love me. I know you are caught between your various strengths and your love for me. I knew I was proud of what you have done with your talents. I have wondered if we had a child if it would be normal. But with all of that said, what do I think of our chances to live together for life? I couldn't answer that; could you, Axel?"

"I don't know," said Axel. "I only know a couple of things; I love you, and I want to use this talent I possess to do good. Maybe you could think of me as having two jobs, one as a professor and one as a servant to my country; one as your husband and one as your hero. There is no other woman in the world with these two opportunities from one person. I know it might be hard at times when I might be away, but you are a strong woman. You can rest assured that I will be okay with the armor that the agency has provided me. I also have the opportunity to turn down anything the agency wants me to do. You don't have to worry about having children with my complications. The mitochondria are carried by the woman, not the man. So, you don't have to worry about that problem."

Tori looked at Axel and said, "You are like two people Axel; the one Axel I know and love with all my heart and the other Axel I don't know and I will have to learn to understand him and learn to love him. He is a good person and I feel I will learn to love him like I love the professor Axel. I love you Axel."

Axel looked at Tori and said, "Tori, I think you will learn to like the second Axel when you meet my Twin brother, his wife and kid and then I take you to the Agency and you meet Kim Edward. The Agency will no longer be a mystery to you. You will like all the people you meet back East. The people in the agency are no different than you and I. They are technical people doing a job for this country. You will like and maybe even love them all."

The discussion continued for the better part of an hour until finally Axel said he had a suggestion. Tori listened. "We have had a great life together so far. We have enjoyed each other day after day. What's to say it won't stay that way, even if I have to go away every so often? Why don't we forget marriage for the time being and just continue the way we have. Why not give it a one-year test to see how it works out? We live together for a year in the same house just like we were married and see if we are compatible under those circumstances. That would be a good test. What do you think?"

Tori looked up at Axel and said, "That makes the most sense of all of this. I am willing to do that if we get to make the decisions together. Will you agree to that?"

"We have made the decisions together up until now, haven't we?" asked Axel.

"We didn't make the decision about Baltimore or Mexico together," said Tori.

"Oops," said Axel. "You are right. I agree that even those decisions have to be made together," said Axel. "Living together for a year and sharing all decisions are the only way to go," he confessed. "This includes the decisions relative to the agency. Maybe we will be lucky, and the agency won't need me for anything for the next year."

With that decided, Axel reached over and gave Tori a kiss. Then, he got serious and said, "You graduate next week. What do you intend to do for the next year or longer?"

"Well, I have been offered a job at John Hopkins back in Baltimore in their biology department that looks like a good opportunity. I have also had some interviews here locally with the drug companies and some of the startups that have their products in the medical field. I haven't made a decision yet, but need to fairly soon."

"And who is going to make that decision?" Axel asked.

Tori looked at him and smiled. "You trapped me," she screamed out.

"No, I didn't. You trapped yourself when you said we would make decisions together like we were married." They both laughed, and this was a good laugh, the best one they had had since last week.

"I guess we have to talk about these different opportunities over the next week and come up with a decision together," said Tori.

Axel said, "You know there are many start-up biotech companies here in Silicon Valley. I believe they would be an ideal place for you. Your education would fit into most of these companies. Besides, I would like you to be around here where I am. If you decide to go to John Hopkins, then I will have to get a job at John Hopkins or some place around Baltimore."

The Follower's new assignment

They decided to get another roll and cup of coffee to seal the deal. Just when they sat down to eat their goodies, Axel's phone rang. He took the phone out of his jacket pocket and said, "Hello, this is Axel." Then, Tori could see him listening on the phone, and while he was listening, he looked over at her and smiled. "It is the agency," he said. She heard him discussing something, and she heard the name Kim. Finally, she heard him say, "Send the plane."

He hung up and said, "The agency and the country have an emergency. Turns out an American ship was attacked by pirates outside of Somalia, and the upshot of this is they have the captain and another member of the ship as hostages on a raft in the Indian Ocean. They believe I have the right combination of powers to be able to relieve this situation and save the captain and two Americans held by the pirates. I am sorry that I didn't discuss this with you, but I had to answer them immediately, so they could send a fighter plane to the San Francisco airport to fly me to Ethiopia and eventually to a place in the Indian Ocean where they will drop me in the water not far from the hostages. I was pretty sure you wouldn't have any negative feelings about my going to help relieve this situation. I am sorry this came up just when we were getting somewhere about our future together. I would have asked you but I knew you would be in agreement, especially since they said they know of no other way to get those people free from harm."

Tori looked at him for about ten seconds, and he was wondering what she was going to say. Then, Tori spoke, "All right, my hero, where do I have to drive you?"

With that, Axel felt a shot of relief and gave her a hug and kiss, and they were off toward the San Francisco airport. When they arrived at the San Francisco International airport, Tori drove up to the area where international flights go out. Axel got out of the car and leaned in the driver side window. He said "I love you Tori and will be thinking of you the whole time except when I am freeing those people. After their freedom I will be thinking of you till you are in my arms again." Tori smiled and said, "I will miss my Axel and the other Axel till both of you return. I hope neither one of you gets hurt." With that said, Axel leaned in farther and give her a big kiss as he held her face up to him. "Now give me a big smile I can remember till I get back." She gave him a terrific smile and he gave her another big kiss. With that he was gone until the next time, and there will be many next times.

John Durbin Husher